"HOW MAY I SERVE THEE, MASTER?"

Mufiqua, the son of the great Khan, struggled against the power calling to him. But the voice was stronger than he was, the face always there to greet him no matter which way he turned. Finally he gave in to this ghostly master.

"There is work to be done, Mufiqua," said the satanic voice. "Open the box in front of you."

In a stupored trance, Mufiqua walked slowly into the next room. A small, oval box of aged wood lay there. Inside was a doll, a replica of a Hun commander holding a sword and shield. Next to it was a long silver pin.

With a bowed head, Mufiqua followed the ghostly command of his master's voice inside his mind. Glassy-eyed, he thrust the long pin through the tiny links of mail on the doll's chest.

In another part of the castle, his brother Temugin, commander of all of Khan's armies, screamed with pain and clutched his chest...

GRAHAM DIAMOND
SAMARKAND
DAWN

PLAYBOY
PAPERBACKS

Published simultaneously in the United States and Canada by Playboy Paperbacks, New York, New York. Printed in the United States of America. Library of Congress Catalog Card Number: 80-82850. First edition.

Books are available at quantity discounts for promotional and industrial use. For further information, write to Premium Sales, Playboy Paperbacks, 747 Third Avenue, New York, New York 10017.

ISBN: 0-872-16781-X

First published February 1981.

COME, O WEARIED TRAVELER, SIT BESIDE ME, LISTEN
TO THE TALES I HAVE TO TELL; OF THAT SPLENDORED
CITY OF LONG, LONG AGO, WHERE EAST MEETS WEST IN
THE LAND OF FABLE AND MAGIC.

COME, O WEARIED TRAVELER, HEAR AND BELIEVE OF
THE GOLDEN AGE OF SAMARKAND.

Part One:

THE PLANTING
OF THE SEEDS

1

Hamsin, it was called. Hamsin. The intolerably hot desert wind that swept down without warning: dry, relentless, bringing with it the swirling dust of desert sands. It struck like a hammer blow, sending men and beasts scurrying, hiding, praying, and often wailing. For when it was done, nothing was ever quite as it had been before. As timeless as the barren sandy wastes themselves, and as vicious. Tales of the hamsin were whispered by the superstitious and by sages alike. Hamsin. Carrying upon its breath an omen. Only fools would dare challenge it.

Up and along the desolate, dusty street the solitary figure hurried. His cloak was tightly clasped at his shoulders, held before his shadowed face against the onslaught of wind. A simple dyed scarf covered his nose and mouth, draping the snarl of his lips and the downward stroke of his broad mustache. His eyes were as black as the night, deeply-set, cruel like his father's. Had it not been for the effects of the drug, they would have shown the same animal intelligence, the same malevolent cunning.

Mufiqua tightened the scarf against a sudden gust that whipped venomously down from the white, flat mudbrick roofs. From some unseen alley a mangy dog, scavenging among the garbage, barked in fright. Other than that, the street remained silent. Ghostly silent.

Cursing under his foul breath, Mufiqua squinted hard into the flying dust and hastened on his way. He was slowly coming around again, the drug wearing off. He could feel the bite of wind more strongly now, began to forget the hasty rationale that had dragged him from the palace. It was a foolish thing, this midnight traipse during the windstorm, an action expressly forbidden by his father. Not that the Great Khan of the Huns believed the local superstitions of the hamsin. But mingling in the city might invite trouble. Samarkand was a strange place, as alien to

9

Mufiqua as he was to it. A city of religious fanatics and beggars. Whores and whoremongers. Where a marketplace was as filled with spies, assassins, and traitors as much as it was with merchandise. A broken city. A sad city, bereft of gaiety, forever beneath a pall of gloom and shadows as real as the minarets from which the holy muezzins daily called the people to prayer.

Mufiqua hated Samarkand. It was swagger and adventure that called his thoughts, except for tonight. He would much rather have been somewhere in the field, leading one of his father's conquering armies against the Persians or the Turks. Five years he'd been forced against his will to wallow in this wretched place with no glory to show for it. Ah, but that would change. As surely as his father the Khan grew more demented every day in his unsated desire for revenge, so Mufiqua would soon come into his own. One day Kabul would die—and if he had his choice, it would be soon.

Yet it was not thought of patricide that brought him out of his rooms this evil night. As his mind cleared more rapidly, he remembered only the woman. The beautiful dancer whose veiled face he had never seen, but whose charms and enticing loveliness had left a too-strong imprint upon his sluggish brain. She had swept beside him seductively, hips swaying to the rhythmic beat of the drum and melodious tune of the pipe. Supple-breasted, flesh a desert-tanned copper, like cream stirred to gold. And her eyes, almond orbs, wide, smoldering with tiny fires. Thin gold bracelets had adorned her slim arms, dark hair tussling over soft, bare shoulders and down her back as she twirled, around and around in tiny circles, hands clapping, long legs slightly parted while her belly quivered. Then she was gone. Fled from sight among the teeming crowds before Mufiqua, seventh son of Kabul, could call her and reward her efforts.

He did not know her name, nor from where she came. All he knew was that the woman had obsessed his dreams, night after night appearing before him until he could no longer stand it. He'd sent his lackeys to search the entire city for her, sparing no effort or cost, bribing, threatening, sometimes resorting to punishment to elicit her identity from the close-mouthed fools who bartered in the market-places and frequented the smelly taverns. All without success. Weeks had gone by, restless nights passing without gratification, until he could stand it no longer. He must have her! Must possess her once, else sanity be forever lost.

And then, inexplicably, when hope had vanished, word had come. The dancer had been found. Sharon, she was called; wild daughter of hillmen, a wandering gypsy who danced in whatever street or city she might.

Mufiqua swore he would return with her this very night, bring her back to the walled palace no matter the objections of the Khan or his older brothers. The dancer was his, *must* be his! Nothing could alter that fact.

The name of the cunning slave dealer who had brought Sharon's identity passed his parched lips: Amar. Completely untrustworthy, of course, as were all the treacherous followers of Islam. Nevertheless he was quite useful upon occasion, possessing an uncanny ability to obtain whatever aphrodisiacal delight in flesh that came to Mufiqua's fancy. For almost a full year now this man Amar had been in his employ exclusively, even willing to gather gossip and other information about Kabul's secret lusts, passing it on to Mufiqua for a fair price. Information that one day would bring about the Khan's downfall.

Mufiqua chuckled. One day Amar would be dealt with as well. The fact was that the old man now knew far too much. But seeking out and finding the dancer, Sharon, had certainly prolonged his longevity. The seventh son was grateful.

Disguised as he was in common garb, no prying eyes watched as he turned at the windy alley and made his way to the only doorway beyond the strewn rubble. He stopped, lifted his hand, and knocked upon the aged wood as instructed. Three times quickly, then two more. A sliver of pale-orange light spilled out into the dark alleyway, the heavy oak creaking on its hinges as it slid slightly open. Mufiqua could not see the face of the smaller man barring the entrance, only a pair of steely eyes looking him over carefully, treating him with the same disregard he might reserve for any other commoner.

Haughtily, Mufiqua flung back his cloak with a twist of

the wrist and stood to his full height. The staring eyes blinked when the cowl was thrown from his head; the door opened wide.

"I am Karim," announced the smaller man with a bow, hands drawn to a pyramid, fingertips touching the bridge of his nose in a sign of respect. "Welcome, my lord. I have been expecting you."

Mufiqua stepped inside, where a dimming haze permeated the air. There were lace drapes before him and he pushed them away with assurance, entering a chamber of velvet pillows scattered atop thick, colorful Persian rugs. A brazier burned incense at both corners, wispy smoke rising to the low mudbrick ceiling.

A slavegirl swept her arms before him, waited for the son of the Khan to unclasp his cloak and pass it to her. She bowed again as she withdrew, silent and barefooted, and Mufiqua looked after her with lustful eyes.

"Do you like her, my lord?"

Mufiqua turned. Karim, a squat, broadset fellow with triple chins and a sweaty brow, stood grinning, gold front teeth aglitter in the pale light of the single lamp. A grunt was his only reply. Impatient, for Mufiqua was as impatient as he was surly, the young son of Kabul sneered at the richly-robed merchant. "I did not come to admire slaves," he hissed. "Where is she?"

Karim's full grin only broadened, which greatly annoyed the young prince. "Sharon has touched the hearts of many men," Karim drawled, quickly adding, "but I have never known one to brave a hamsin to see her."

Mufiqua bit off his curse before it left his throat, drew the small leather pouch that dangled from his corded belt. The coins jingled appetizingly. When Karim's eyes darted toward the money, Mufiqua hid a small, satisfied smile. His host's greed was expected but repulsive just the same. These people were all alike, he knew. Pious, sanctimonious, prayer-spouting hyprocrites who would sell both mother and daughter to their greatest enemy—if the price was right. Mufiqua abhorred them all.

To his surprise, the smaller man made no move to grab the pouch. With the same sly, mocking smile he clapped his hands, brought the slavegirl running back into the hazy room.

"Bring our guest something to drink while he waits," Karim snapped. Then facing his guest again: "Wild mountain wine, my lord. Strong and heady. A treat for your taste, when compared to the pale city blends you are no doubt used to drinking."

"I came here not to sample wine, nor to be made drunk," Mufiqua hissed. "Only to see the girl."

"And so you shall my lord. And so you shall." He bowed with a long frown. "But even at this very moment she still prepares for you, to greet and please you properly. Surely you would have it no other way."

While he spoke, the slavegirl returned, standing before him with downcast eyes, holding a silver tray upon which lay a silver chalice and pitcher. Karim himself poured, and Mufiqua watched expressionlessly as the blood-colored brew splashed into the goblet.

"Taste, taste, my lord," urged his host eagerly, gesturing for Mufiqua to rest upon the resplendently tapestried cushions. The son of Kabul took the goblet, and with eyes fully opened and staring warily at the merchant, he drank a long and soothing draught. It *was* a good wine; the merchant had not lied.

He sat after Karim refilled the chalice, choosing a double-backed golden cushion against the wall. Years of dealing with the backward folk of Samarkand had taught him never to leave his back exposed. A plunged knife had too often been the reward of carelessness.

"And now," said Karim, rubbing one hand over the other, "what other delights may I please you with?"

"You may please me with the girl, merchant," Mufiqua rasped. "I want to see the girl. I have waited too long. Can you understand that? I burn for her as no man has ever burned for a woman. Do not play games with me, Karim. Bring her now—or pay the price."

"She is coming, my lord. I promise it." Karim snapped his fingers and the slave refilled the chalice. Mufiqua was momentarily placated, sipping with drooping eyes, face beginning to flush. He began to sweat. It was hot inside this windowless room, unbearably so. He pulled a silk kerchief from his robe, wiped away grime and sweat from his forehead and neck, sucked in a lungful of the hot, incense-laden air. Karim was before him, fat belly quivering with mirth, mirth obviously at the prince's expense.

"I'll make you less than a man, merchant," Mufiqua swore, "if she isn't brought to me now. *Less* than a man— do you follow me?"

Karim started to shake, hands and knees wobbling. Mufiqua locked eyes with him, and although the merchant seemed frightened, a glimmer of defiance remained behind the treacherous eyes. Mufiqua would have struck him then and there, emptied his gut, had it not been for the sudden tinkling of Chinese bells. Both men turned abruptly toward the parting lace curtains, transfixed by the shapely silhouette slipping silently into the room.

Mufiqua shook his head to clear it, instantly forgetting his anger. He half rose from the cushion, eyes squinted tightly. Despite the haze and shadows he recognized her; his heart began to thump wildly, loins aching with desire as she appeared. Yes, it was the dancer, Sharon.

The tanned beauty smiled as her eyes met his, raven-black hair glistening as she unpinned it, letting it fall seductively across her shoulders and over her breasts. Draped in translucent veils of pastel colors, her hips swung slightly as she crossed the chamber and began to dance. A drum was rhythmically beating somewhere. The dancer, aware of her charms and the spell she had cast over the Khan's seventh son, lifted her arms above her head, fingers weaving snakelike patterns while fingerbells softly tapped. Through the mist she came toward him, supple flesh gleaming in the dim light, firm thighs and belly tauntingly brushing past him.

The first veil fell to the floor, exposing rounded shoulders and a long, thin neck. The second tumbled through the air, tossed aside wantonly, bosoms now free to quiver with her dance. Mufiqua opened his mouth slightly, thick tongue darting between his lips. A hand made to grab her, Sharon twirled from his grasp, a small, triumphant laugh emitting from her yet unseen mouth.

Mufiqua stirred. The woman parted her legs, swung her hips in a slow circular motion, arms outstretched and calling to him. Agony and ecstasy were one in the prince's fevered mind. He wanted her, needed her, would pay any price at all to possess her. Yet still she remained out of reach, even when he stretched to touch her. She was teasing him, he knew, taunting him, increasing his hunger until he could stand it no longer. His craving could not be controlled; like a maddened beast he leaped from the cushion, knocking over the chalice, so that the dregs poured darkly over the Persian rug. He lunged for her and grabbed her roughly, pulling her to him, so that her soft flesh pressed against his bulging muscles. His face buried itself in the gentle curve of her neck, lips wetly kissing, a hand running through her hair, harshly stroking it.

The dancer made no move to push him away. Docile and limp she hung in his arms, urging on his passion with guttural noises from deep within her tender throat. Mufiqua yanked her down upon the floor. The dancer's breath quickened with his animal pants and gasps. Side by side they lay, then Mufiqua jerked on top of her, parting her legs with one hand while the other fumbled loose the belt from his peasant robe. For an instant their eyes locked, Mufiqua's wild in his torment and lust, hers glassy and tranquil, but burning with fires that never dimmed.

His lips covered her mouth. The dancer let him fondle her, encouraged his yearning by stroking his brow and cooing in his ear. Mufiqua looked at her and grinned. No word passed between them, no word was necessary. All communication was there in his fiery eyes, his groping hands, his unconscious pelvic thrusts while she clung to him and let him have his pleasure. His robe was all but off and her flimsy veils discarded—when suddenly he stiffened. Mufiqua lifted his face and looked at the girl questioningly. His lips shook as he tried to say something; he felt his head swim, put his hands to his forehead. Something was happening to him, something he could not explain. His body broke out in glistening perspiration; mindlessly he made to grab his fallen robe, draw his dagger. Karim was standing in the shadow of the curtain, gold teeth ablaze with his smile.

"The wine!" gasped Mufiqua. He glanced at the fallen chalice, its sweet but deadly contents soaking into the wool rug. *The wine! The wine! The bastard poisoned the wine!*

He rolled off the girl, ready to kill. She stared without expression at him, darting her dark eyes toward the merchant. Mufiqua made it to his knees with his brain spinning. The room was going around, the world was going around. Karim was laughing; he was sure of it.

I'll slit that pig's throat before I die! Mufiqua cried out without being heard. *I'll have his head displayed on a pike for all to see and . . .*

He gurgled and slumped forward, nose smacking harshly on the bare stone floor beyond the edge of the carpet. He twitched spasmodically three or four times, and then he moved no more.

Sharon jumped to her feet, quickly covering herself with the scattered veils. Karim stood over the limp, drugged body with a large curved knife in his hand. The metal glowed in the lamplight; he made to kneel and run the blade through Mufiqua's gut.

The dancer pulled at his arm, caught his gaze. "No, Karim!" she flared adamantly. "Remember the bargain—he belongs to us!"

The wily merchant spat into the pale face profiled against the floor. "My daughter," he seethed. "This *animal* enslaved my daughter for the palace." Tears flowed openly as his mind flashed back to the terrible day the child was taken. Whisked away to Kabul's brothel by soldiers who only laughed when the girl's mother fell on her knees before them and begged, pleaded that she be allowed to remain. But no, the cruel and sadistic Hun king and his lecherous sons needed a constant supply of new flesh to sate their heathen appetites. His daughter, like so many others, had been dragged from her bed, screaming and wailing, desperately trying to break free. It was a useless and futile gesture. For over a year now his Lina had been gone, for over a year she'd been used and used again by numberless men, savages who had conquered Samarkand more than half a decade before. Lina was a whore. Defiled, turned into a painted harlot to service any man at any time. To Karim she was better off dead. By the holy name of *Allah*, had his precious child been before him now, he would have used the knife on her as well.

"Why do you want him?" croaked the merchant to the strange woman from the hills who had posed as a common street dancer. "What good is a man like this to you? Kill him now! Rid Samarkand of at least one vile son!"

The woman was adamant. "We don't *want* him," she corrected. "We *need* him. My friends have use for Mufiqua."

Ruefully the aging merchant in caravan goods sighed, turned away. He did not know exactly whom this woman was. Nor whom her peculiar friends were, those who had contacted him through Amar the slave dealer. But their enemies were his own, and when he was told that a son of Kabul was the prize, he had had few qualms in assisting them.

The woman put her hand to his shoulder, looked at him kindly, with more than a spark of understanding. "Your plight is no less just than our own," she told him, speaking rapidly for time was running out. "But trust that this man can be invaluable to us all in the future."

Karim's face underlined his astonishment. "You intend to let him survive?" he asked. "After all this? After putting both me and yourselves into such peril?"

"There is no time to explain," Sharon replied curtly, eyes darkening again. "You have done your part better than we hoped. Now leave us, merchant. Come back at first light of dawn."

Karim hunched his widely-set shoulders, walked away in a pronounced stoop. A broken man, a lost man. Careless of the raging wind of the hamsin he opened the door and wandered off into the night.

Sharon waited only a few seconds after he had gone. She knelt beside the stricken prince, drew a small vial from the folds of her veils, opened it and pushed it before Mufiqua's nose. The seventh son's nostrils flared at the sting of the salts. He began to come around, his eyes growing.

From the lace curtains slipped another figure, this one dark and hooded, with intense dark eyes that took in much. He had once been a mullah, a holy man of the palace itself, schooled in the world's secrets and mysteries. Called by many a madman, a lunatic, he alone had foreseen the fall of the once-mighty empire and had vainly tried to make them listen while yet there had been time. Zadek, he was called. Zadek, son of a Kazir, that tribe of wild and fiercely-free hillmen, who had once called Samarkand holy but who now fought against the scourge of Huns more furiously than they had ever fought their predecessors. Zadek, a mystic and a prophet, as cunning as he was insane, whose knowledge and powers had become renowned and revered among the Kazirs as much as Sharon's own.

Sharon bit her lip pensively as she turned to the approaching mullah. "Hurry," she said. "I've brought him back to consciousness, but it won't be long until he falls asleep."

Zadek grunted in response; he bent before the groaning Mufiqua, yanked his head back by the hair, forced the younger man to look deeply into his eyes. With his cowl pushed back, a shock of gray-black hair atop his head and a sharply-pointed goatee of similar hue, the mad holy man seemed more a devil than priest.

"Can you hear me?" said Zadek in a low, soothing monotone.

There was no response; Mufiqua's eyes rolled in their sockets. Sharon peered worriedly at her mentor, the man to whom she owed so much.

The mullah pressed a heavy thumb over Mufiqua's eyelid, forced it open. "Can you hear me?" Zadek repeated. It took long, agonizing seconds until a flicker of life showed in the eyes. The son of Kabul slowly nodded, transfixed and nearly in a hypnotic trance. Sharon shuddered and stepped back. Zadek's sorcery always frightened her, from her earliest days while yet a princess in Samarkand's palace. *Teacher,* she had always called him. *Teacher.* A respectful title that lingered even until this very day.

"I . . . hear . . . you," said a sluggish voice.

The robed priest smiled. "What is your name?"

The younger man had difficulty answering. "I am . . .

the seventh son of the Khan, the great and magnificent Kabul, ruler of half the world. . . . My name is . . ."

"Your name is Mufiqua," Zadek told him. "As you claim, son of Kabul. . . ." He glanced briefly over his shoulder when another figure entered between the parted curtains of lace. She was dark-skinned, with short, clipped hair and large, intelligent eyes. Dressed in similar garb to the mullah, simple and worn. Were it not for the piece of antelope's horn at the end of her knotted-leather necklace, no one would have suspected her true title: *saya* of the Kazir Stronghold, Clan leader in her own right, who could call forth a thousand loyal horsemen at the snap of a finger.

The saya lifted the lamp from its place, brought it closer until the light burned brightly into Mufiqua's eyes. The prince of the Huns winced at the brightness; Zadek's thumbs forced him to stare. "Look at the light," urged the mad mullah gently. "There is nothing to fear. Look at the light."

The saya began to rock the lamp, slowly at first, side to side in the same motion a mother might use to rock her infant's cradle. Mufiqua's eyes had trouble at first in following; Zadek's instruction, though, made it impossible to turn away, and after a very short while he was completely unable to.

"I am Zadek," said the cowled holy man, "and from this day my voice alone shall command you." He waited for the words to sink in. "Do you understand? I alone am your true master, Mufiqua. Never forget that. . . . When my instruction is given, you shall pay any price to carry it out."

Mufiqua nodded, swallowing feeling the burning sensation in his throat. "I . . . I understand . . . *master*."

It was a dark and shudderingly frightful smile that crossed Zadek's mouth; he looked up at the two women and held out his palms in a smooth gesture. "He is prepared," he announced flatly. "What is your will?"

Sharon fidgeted, cast a long fretful glance at the saya. Carolyn masked a small smile of her own. "I am ready," she said. "Instruct him well, holy man. We have much to do, and little time."

2

Le-Dan was a large man, well-trimmed despite his advanced years. He toyed with the apple in his hand, taking his first bite savoringly, relishing the juices as they swilled over his tongue. The hammock in which he rested, slung carefully between two great cypress trees, remained perfectly still, even when he leaned over the side and spat a seed onto the grass.

His companion, equal perhaps in age but certainly not in physical fitness, belched loudly as the last of his grapes were swallowed. He wiped his hands on a soiled napkin, rested his head back against the trunk's bark, squarely facing the man in the hammock. Sunshine, gay late afternoon light, filtered glowingly through the leaves and boughs. It was a most pleasant country setting, peaceful and tranquil, and to see these two men now no one could have ever guessed the reason for their meeting.

Le-Dan drew a breath, let it out in a long blow of his puffed cheeks. At first glance there was nothing striking about him; he seemed stern yet jovial, like an uncle who loves dearly his nieces and nephews but is constantly in need of exercising authority lest they take advantage of his disposition. A strong man of independent thought, but a fair man as well—as many of his troops had reason to be thankful for.

The second man, portly and balding, was far more the ambassador than he ever was the soldier. Outwardly aloof, even disinterested, but inwardly studying and noting his adversary's every move, recording it in a perfect memory. Lucienus never forgot—anything.

He folded a betel nut between his fingers, placed it gingerly in the back of his mouth, resting it beside gum and cheek. The flavor delightfully spread, and Lucienus smiled.

"Well?" said Le-Dan. Hands at his sides, eyes closed beneath white, bushy brows, he listened to the singing of the birds nesting among the branches.

Lucienus smacked his lips. "Well what? What else is there to say about the matter, my dear fellow? You and I have been friends for more years than I suspect either one of us wishes to recall. We've seen kings like this come and go, time and time again."

Le-Dan peered over at his companion. "Not kings like this one, we haven't. Not like this devil. What we've seen over the years have been washerwomen by comparison."

The portly man chuckled. "You always overestimate everything. Your emir was weak—a pushover, if I may be so bold as to speak it openly. Never had a chance, none of you did."

"How could we?" answered Le-Dan with a shrug. "The Khan's forces were overwhelming. You know it's true when I say that not one of my legions fled. To a man we stood our ground and fought: in the valleys, along the plains, why, right into the rivers themselves. Anything, anything at all to halt this maniac and his scourge."

"That's why I was amazed when I received word that you were still alive; you have no idea how wonderful it made me feel. I tell you, right then and there, in the middle of court, I fled the scene and ran to pray. Down on my knees, exactly like those beggar mullahs your land is so famous for. Yes indeed, there were real tears in my eyes. Genuine tears of honest relief and joy."

"You were so positive of my death, then?"

"Hard not to be, good fellow. If memory serves, the Huns conquered both your ill-fitted armies and entire empire in a matter of weeks. Ran amok like a bull let loose in the field. . . ."

"Hmmm. An interesting analogy. I certainly let down all those who put their faith in me—not to mention their lives."

"Be pragmatic, dear fellow. Pragmatic. The devil with your honor, your noble sense of duty."

"Don't forget that I'm a soldier. Always have been, always will be. It's the only decent trade I know. You needn't laugh, Lucienus. Well enough for you to retire and live like a country squire. It's not your land that's been so, so—"

"Raped?"

"Raped. Yes, fitting enough. Those are not your people under the yoke of such incredible tyranny."

"Tyranny, *bah!* Already you sound more like a politician. Listen to me, old friend, tyranny is a word that opposing sides too often hurl upon each other. Why, look about you, man! From the Great Wall of Cathay, to the borders of the Turks, this ripe apple of a world is well carved and apportioned. Sad but true, this beastly Hun does indeed reign across your beloved steppes and homelands. But why press the fight? You are safe at last. Persia offers you a home; it always does to men of such high caliber. Stay here among us. Even as a soldier, if you insist—if you'll take my advice you'd be nothing less than a gentleman. A man of breeding and quality. A scholar, or even a damned poet, if the fancy strikes you. Anything at all; my country will lay it at your feet. We respect you, my childhood friend. We like you."

"You have an ambassador's way about you, all right. What you've said, in too many words, is that the answer to my request is no. Persia will not lift a finger against these Huns, even though you fully know it's in your own self interests."

"Ah, but is it? The last thing my king wants or needs— and I readily agree—is to make an enemy on our northern borders. The Khan may be a barbarian, but experience has well taught me that even among heathens there is a cunning. If he were a fool, how would he have come so far so fast? No, strange as it may sound to you, in some ways I can only admire him."

"Admire a butcher?"

"Admire a man who with nothing, came out of the mountains half a world away and successfully gained himself an empire that spans all the way from China to the Black Sea."

"And Samarkand is his seat of government. My home, Lucienus. I shan't forget."

"Don't go sentimental on me, Le-Dan. It's most disconcerting to see a soldier talk about a place he hardly ever saw—or have you forgotten that your duties took you away from the city for far more of your valuable time than you were there? Chasing shadows, if I can quote your last letter dated, oh, more than five years ago."

"Chasing Kazirs, Lucienus. A tribe of the steppes scattered across the desert and—"

"My dear fellow, I know about as much as I want to! These Kazirs were considered bandits, were they not? Renegades of Samarkand that called your city holy and swore an oath to wrest away the throne from your very leaders."

"They had some legitimate grievances, don't forget. After all, Samarkand truly once did belong to them. My own ancestors banished them. . . ."

"Banished them—and proceeded to spend the next one hundred years trying to rout them and cut them down. Rather like the farmer whose horse has fled in the middle of night and then shuts the door, wouldn't you say? A poor way of dealing with one's enemies, I should think. You should have slain them all in the beginning."

"Perhaps. At least it would have been easier that way. But my people are not savages, Lucienus. We would have been happy to find some accommodation with the Kazirs—it was they who demanded all the pie and not just a slice."

"So an ally became an enemy."

"Kazirs are bound to Samarkand by blood, don't forget. The same as I. Still, I must give credit where it's due. Never have I seen such savage and brave a band of fighters. They really believe in this holy war of theirs, this *jihad*, to regain what was lost. No matter how many of my troops I'd commit to the effort, no matter how many of their villages I'd razed or fields I ordered burned, always they sprang back to life. Like phantoms. I tell you it was uncanny."

"Maybe God was truly on their side."

"Don't think I've never considered the notion. 'Shadows' was a good analogy, Lucienus. You can't defeat a foe that stands before you one moment and vanishes the next."

"Wisely said. If these loose reports we receive from the north hold any validity, these very outlaws of yours now lead the only fight to free Samarkand from its conquerors."

"True enough, and I'll be the first to admit it. Doggedly they continue the struggle against overwhelming odds. I know I couldn't do it. Not without Persia's full support at any rate. Any attack is begging suicide."

"All the more reason to accept an appointment here, good friend. But what you ask, as you know, is not in my own power to grant. However, even if it were, I'd still harbor grave reservations. Granted that these renegade Kazirs have been able to keep their heads intact so far, how much longer, in reality, can they persist? Gnats biting at an elephant, dear fellow. One good swipe of the elephant's trunk and what's left?"

"Oh, I don't know about that, Lucienus. At the beginning I would have said the very same thing. Now, though, I'm not so sure. They're an odd bunch, these Kazirs. When the conflict first began, all sorts of strange rumors floated my way, to the mountains and the rag-tag army I was trying to regroup."

"Oh? What sort of, er, rumors?"

"I know you too well, old friend, to believe you haven't heard them as well. My spies spoke of an ancient prophecy. Mumbo-jumbo that the Kazirs devotedly believe in, but that nevertheless bears some semblance to the truth. For instance, I know for fact that Kabul's eldest son led an entire legion through a place called Grim Forest to lead an assault upon the Kazir stronghold. What happened to them is too incredible to take as true, but this much I do know—only one man, the Khan's son, returned with his life. And he was turned into an infantile idiot. The hillfolk are a superstitious lot, but it can't all be the gossip of fisherwives and holy postulants who babble secretly in Samarkand's bazaars and plazas."

"Were you not my friend and distant cousin, I'd swear you half believe this nonsense. Look here, man; it's said that the Kazir rebels are guided under the influence of a woman—a woman who bears what they call a gift and serves as rallying point for all the Clans. Also that she has received the blessing of this forest's witches and been bestowed the titular leadership of every campaign. Magic, sorcery, and I don't know what else. Even that this woman, the one named Panther of the Steppes, is herself a royal princess of the very nobles whom the Kazirs fought for a hundred years!"

"It does sound far-fetched, I'll admit. But she would not be the first to be guided by the stars."

"No; I daresay this Kabul is guided by his own stars, his own barbaric logic. As was the great Alexander, whose visions changed our own world forever."

"The reign of Alexander is long since passed, Lucienus. Now we find ourselves confronted with another set of visionaries and zealots. As I said, I am a soldier, not a politician, not a soothsayer. If all I sought for the rest of my life was a nice lucrative appointment to your court, I would have come begging for it long ago. What I ask of you, of Persia, is a chance to fight—and die, if necessary—upon my own soil."

"You really mean that?"

"I damn well do. This Panther of the Steppes may be the blackest witch in hell for all I care. She and her cohorts, though, have put a severe cramp in the Hun's march of further conquest. If not for her and her outlaws, even mighty Persia might now be running for the hills like jackals before Kabul's advancing hordes. Never forget that the Khan hates this woman, would do anything to have her in his grasp."

"Gossip says that she plucked out Kabul's eye."

"After he raped her. Yes, I've heard that tale as well. Listen to me, Lucienus; I don't know where the truth lies, only that she is the fragile thread upon which *all* our lives now cling. Whatever else she may be, she's also a woman. Flesh and blood like any other. And were it in my power to be at her side now, this very moment, I would give an eye of my own to do so."

3

Although the first flakes had begun to fall less than an hour before, past midnight Sharon found herself ankle-deep in snow. Swirling snow that nearly blinded her as she trekked up the lonely hill, treading over hardened soil until she negotiated the crest. The wind was blowing more strongly; she tightened her desert-woven cloak about her, folding her hands beneath her sleeves. Black hair glistened wetly where it fell from the pinned kerchief that covered her head. With pressed lips and eyes luminous from the cold, she stepped into ruts and gutted folds, boots leaving a tell-tale trail behind. She was alone, though; certain she'd not been followed. This hillock was sacred ground, and not even her closest confidant would dare to tread upon it for fear of sacrilege. Sharon, alone among them all, was permitted, and only she would be able to find what she was looking for. Had any other passed this way, he would have been greeted only by silence, that and the unseen eyes of the forest that secretly watched without understanding and said nothing.

Without fear of *nightthings*, forbidden and unholy creatures of the black, she reached the gnarled roots of the lumber oak, lifted her gaze and swept it among the snow-laden boughs. Here not a leaf stirred in the wind on this winter's night. Nor the whistle of the breeze passing between the branches, nor even the dim hoot of some distant owl to break the solitude. The white mass around her deepened with breath-taking speed, pushing up against her calves and the tops of her boots. Shivering, she waited, staring now at the single plant whose stalk had wrapped around the thickest branch, leaves closed as if against the temperature, protecting each other. It was sleeping, waiting to be called.

As suddenly as it began, the snow stopped. Sharon pulled away her scarf and smiled. It was time.

Ordinary men would have been frightened out of their wits when, inexplicably, the stalk began to slither snakelike up the bough. The leaves on the stem started to stir, shaking off drops of water like a dog shakes its fur. Beneath the shadows the broadly-veined leaves started to part, one by one, much as a banana peel falls when the fruit is opened. Inside rested a flower. A beautiful and perfect flower, sweetly-scented and with wide petals of bright gold, which in the dark surroundings shone almost like a lamp.

"The deed is done," said Sharon to the plant. "Mufiqua's mind has been altered. When the time is at hand, Zadek shall instruct him."

A long silence prevailed, Sharon patiently waiting. She folded her hands before her, bowed her head.

"Then the bait has been taken."

She nodded somberly, eyes weary, sunken from the tense events of past days and the difficult journey she'd made from the desert here to the farthest recesses of the fabled wood. Her life seemed so far away from her now, so remote and distant she sometimes wondered if it were not another being that possessed her body. A new, separate identity that somehow had robbed both mind and form, reshaped her totally into what stood so humbly before this aged hulk of a tree. A woman, yes, but more than that. Far more, far more. Where had it all begun? Where would it all finish?

In as much time as it took a snowflake to fall from the lowest branch to the ground, her thoughts carried her far and wide. Once upon a time there had been a young girl, naive and foolish, who'd dreamed of lovers and children and happiness; a lost child of Samarkand born into a family of such awesome power it seemed it could never be taken away. But taken away it had been. Abruptly and brutally. That girl had witnessed the fall of her city and home, seen the carnage and mayhem that followed while the Hun legions ran amok across the ancient palace, wheeling death and destruction. How old had she been when her father was cut down like a dog by heathen arrows? How old when, fleeing the grim palace corridors for her life, she'd been caught by Kabul himself and ravished, her will broken, her illusions of life forever shattered? Wildly, in blind fury, she had lashed out with the only weapon she possessed: a golden pin for her hair. A pin that she thrust through the Khan's right eye, blinding him for all time, causing him periodic fits of excruciating pain that even a brute like he could not bear, earning his terrible, sworn vengeance.

With Zadek at her side she'd fled Samarkand, found a suspicious refuge among the free men of the hills called Kazirs, until now, little more than five years later, she found herself a leader among them. More than a leader; the living embodiment of a century-old prophecy that to this day she never fully understood or accepted. *Panther*, the Kazirs had named her. *Panther of the Steppes*, earned by the spilling of Hun blood as she led their horsemen into desert victory after victory. A measure of peace had been won, of course; an uneasy truce in which the steppes, alone of Samarkand's once-extensive empire, remained free of heathen domination. Yet what good was this heart without a soul? Until the city itself was reclaimed, all vestiges of the barbaric conquerors overthrown, there could never truly be peace.

This, then, was the legacy and duty thrust upon that once-fragile, innocent child. A mission and a destiny, forever intertwined with the fate of the freedom-loving hillmen. Her love of those close to her was second only to her love of Samarkand. Zadek, the mad mullah; Roskovitch, the scalp-locked barbarian expatriate from the northern, frigid land called Rus; Hezekiah, aged friend of her father, trusted adviser, a man who once stood beside Samarkand's *emir* as minister. Of the saya, Carolyn, there was little to be said. Ever mistrustful, always careful, the woman entrusted as Keeper of the Stronghold continued to doubt Sharon's leadership and ability. Yet she was also a woman whom the Panther knew she could trust with her life. And then there was Tariq. Tariq, her secret lover, her strength and wisdom. Brother of the saya who guarded the mountain passes and the desert, the man to whom she was faithfully sworn but whose life she could never share. Forced apart by war and by the prophecy itself, stealing clandestine moments for themselves, torn apart all too soon by duty that could not be divided.

These were Sharon's generals, the elite of her guard of hill tribesmen, the only ones she allowed close enough to touch her emotions. All the rest were dead. And even of these few, how many more might perish before freedom was achieved?

A teardrop carelessly fell from her eye and rolled down her cheek. Memories of bitterness came to the fore as she stood alone in the moonless dark, quelling her grief yet again while her body trembled. Of them all, only she knew the terrible events that must first transpire before the ancient prophecy could be fulfilled. It came to her at night, often, amid her tormented dreams, and though never did she speak of it, she knew all too well the reality. Dreams such as these never lied.

"Yes," she responded to the flower of the night before her, "the bait has been taken."

"How soon, little princess? How soon?"

The voice came as a whisper on the wind, real yet unreal. In another time, another place, she would have questioned her sanity for hearing it. Not now, though. Too much had passed, too many ghosts cried out their anguish.

Sharon is dead! she commanded to herself. *Killed the day Kabul's evil seed flowed in my belly. I will not let her live! Only the Panther remains in her place. Only the shell. Only the vision of what must be done!*

"I cannot tell you how soon. But my plans are all but complete. I shall peel the palace like an onion, layer by layer, until we are ready."

"Take care, little princess!" came the voice. *"Know thy enemy. Prepare for his treachery."*

"Treachery will be repaid in kind," she answered coldly.

She felt her flesh crawl, felt as though the eyeless plant was observing her, studying her, weighing her responses upon a carefully-balanced scale. Judging her even now to be certain she had acted precisely to instruction.

"There will be no turning back, little princess. No second chance. Should you fail . . ."

Her eyes flashed hotly. "I will not fail! I must not fail! You have guided me well, friend."

"I have done little, child. I cannot protect you against evil—only warn you of it. The rest is in your hands."

"It was the witches of this forest who bestowed upon me the gift. Now they are gone, and a part of me is one of them. I mourn their passing but rejoice that they left me you. You have been wise and faithful to me, friend. What more can a mortal ask? But you can do no more. Now it is my time. The Dawn of Reclamation is almost here, and I, friend and adviser, am not immortal as you are. To fail now is surely to die, and to bring down with me those I love the best. It cannot be. The Calling must be answered while I am able."

The web of intrigue had been set, the flower knew. Carefully nurtured and painstakingly woven with every thread in place. Yet should one precarious thread be cut, only doom might be expected. If the girl, this Panther of the Steppes, did not fully comprehend the extent of the peril, at least she was harboring no false illusions.

A long, dreary silence followed, the rustling of nearby branches singing with the gusts. *"You will come to me again?"* asked the ethereal voice softly.

Sharon was trying not to cry; she put out her hand to affectionately touch the mysterious plant, then withdrew it abruptly, recalling the witch's warning. Any physical contact would snap like a twig the thin cord, whisking her from this life across the threshold to the inner world, a world she was not yet prepared for. Still, the *nightflower* of the forest, the mystical flower that appeared only to her, had become more than a friend. Was it insane to love a plant?

"Yes, I shall come again," she said at last. "You and I have yet work to do, friend. This task I set out to complete is but the first beginnings of the end."

"You must not disobey the prophecy," it warned.

Sharon shook her head, knowing full well the flower's caution. What was it that Zadek had said? *Hate cannot be denied. . . .*

"The saya has entered the palace," she said, turning thoughts back to pressing matters.

"Safely?"

"As far as can be discerned. Unlike my own, her face is unrecognized. She shall not be questioned."

"Good. Good. And your other spies?"

"Intact. Awaiting only my command." With a new and furious gust, snow began to fall from the branches, whipping angrily about Sharon's silhouetted figure. She stared through it to the glistening petals. "I have vowed," she went on, "that in weeks to come the Khan shall be repaid for his crimes in kind. *An eye for an eye,* the Prophet has said. And when I am done . . ." Her voice trailed off, eyes turned as cold as the frozen waters of the hidden lake. The transformation had been made, once again her heart as hard as the desert stone.

"Be careful, little princess," said the sage voice, *"lest you be consumed by the same burning fires you cast upon your enemies."*

Her laugh was as bitter as it was callous. The mirth of a woman who had long before lost all hope for her own safety or happiness. She peered up at the starless heavens, feeling the weight of her people resting upon her shoulders.

"I am tired, friend. So very tired. I cannot rest; nights are often endless for me. . . ."

The tone became sympathetic. *"Then share your burden, little princess."*

The piercing glare of her eyes made her refusal more than plain.

"Not even with Tariq?"

Sharon pushed down a rising sob as she shook her head. "Especially not him, friend. Our love is too strong. I cannot make the one who means the most to me carry such terrible weight. No; the Prophesy must not be altered. I alone am the One. I alone shall see it through to its conclusion."

"Then go with Allah, little princess. What must be done, must be done. Or so it is said."

"Or so it is said," Sharon repeated, letting the sacred words roll slowly from her tongue.

"Come back when next you need me. I shall be waiting."

Even through the sadness of this parting she managed to smile, but turned her back on the strange flower so it couldn't see the wetness of her eyes. As she stepped away into snowy darkness, the long stem deeply bowed, petals inwardly turning. Then the broad leaves covered all, and the mist of the forest closed over them both.

4

The narrow and dusty street was clouded with shadows thrown by the plethora of mudbrick hovels lining either side. The closer Tariq came to its end, the stronger became the reeking, familiar smells of the plaza and open market-place. Past doors scarred with decades of dirt and wind-swept dust, past the squalor and teeming humanity of barefoot, hungry children, past sightless beggars cross-leggedly lining the way with hands outstretched, the dark-haired Kazir slipped unnoticed. He wore the plain white linen *lungi* of the peasants, feet sandaled, head wrapped in a desert *burnoose,* starkly pale against his sun-bronzed face.

Upon entering the bazaar, he was greeted by the innumerable faces of Samarkand. Traders and merchants, caravaneers from every known land of Asia, all come to this crossroads city of the world to barter their goods. Silks and spices brought all the way from Cathay and camel dung heaped in the gutters pungently vied for attention with the scent of perfumes from the Indian subcontinent. Steel from Damascus, precious stones from Mesopotamia, pottery and leather of quality carried all the way from Tyre and Jerusalem. Glass, linens, and grain from Egypt. Foodstuffs of every description; wines, skins, ostrich feathers from Africa. The scent of herbs mixed with the sweat of thousands, matched only by the din of barter babbled in a score of strange tongues. And the slave market, where dealers in human flesh sold strong men and supple-breasted to the Hun masters. Cobblers set up shop alongside butchers, tapping and stitching leather in the midst of strolling prostitutes and vagabonds. Pickpockets and urchins. Offers and counter offers were loudly bandied while flies and insects crawled the walls and buzzed the canopied stalls. Weavers, medicinal practitioners, masons, and carpenters—the market absorbed them all beneath the outer walls of the palace, within sight of the holy Great Mosque itself, where muezzins along the balconies called the faithful to prayer, letting the ever-present throngs of pilgrims and cripples pass through the sheltered, mosaic arches into the courtyard and sacred gates of the inner temple. All this, while Hun soldiers in vests of mail patrolled the streets and walls, ever watchful and suspicious, ensuring a measure of tranquillity amid the turmoil of Samarkand's masses.

Tariq, safe among these pressing crowds, shunned the offers of both wares and flesh, shuddering involuntarily. Was this place, the vital heart of the holy city he loved, its very pulse, all that was shamefully left? He could have wept at the sight of the fleshpots, the whores and drug-dealers, maimed thieves that preyed freely on the poor. This was not the city he knew, not the sacred site where the holy words of the Prophet Mohammed had eagerly been spread so many years before. It was an evil place now, bereft of charm and beauty, a sulking, smelly cesspool of humanity. A disgrace to its people and the eyes of Allah.

He crossed from a stall of displayed birds in cages; with his gaze cast downward, as a squad of helmeted soldiers passed by laughing and making obscene jokes at the expense of a sightless pauper, he came to the black gate of the formerly lavish mosque. Old men stood in groups, chewing betel nuts, exchanging small gossip beneath a blazing sun. A soldier spat openly nearby upon the tiled floor, a sacrilege that in better times would have brought the wrath of the populace down on him. The old men nervously turned away while the soldier glared in open defiance, taunting the religious to utter a protest.

Tariq was a man of the desert. A Kazir, a chieftain. He was glad his father, Shoaib the Goatherd, tribal elder, had not lived years enough to see all this. It would have broken the old man's heart, destroyed him. But times had severely changed since those days, Tariq knew, and it would take much to bring them back.

Beyond the open courtyard where hundreds of the faithful gathered solemnly, Tariq could see the decorated windows of the sanctuary. Made of fine and hard stucco, carved by master artisans while yet wet, the colored clusters vividly reflected strong afternoon sunlight. He walked toward them slowly, not to enter the sanctuary itself to pray but to seek out the one man who stood casually waiting, hands clasped as if praying, eyes seemingly shut against the glaring brightness.

The Kazir approached him cautiously, his face lifting for the first time, his features sharp and dark, handsomely framed by thin brows and curled black hair. He studied the groupings of worshippers on knees bended and foreheads touching the ground. A man could not be too careful in Samarkand. Not even here. Spies were everywhere, and for a few coppers even many of the devout might set their tongues to wagging.

"Are you a pilgrim as well?" said Tariq lowly, speaking the first phrase of the signal.

They had never met before, and the second man acted prudently. "I am a scholar," he countersigned. He paused, looked over Tariq's garb, noted the firm and muscular flesh hidden by the folds of the dusted lungi. From behind came the atonal dissonance of a prayer-singing postulant.

Tariq observed him well, also, seeing in his face more than wrinkles of age. There was a bitterness and mistrust ill-masked in his tired eyes. He was not a Kazir, but a city man. Educated, if his manner meant anything; proud, as shown by his straight back and posture, mistrustful of all hill tribes even though they shared a common enemy.

"I have come to study," Tariq spoke, continuing the charade. "Fortune has smiled upon us both."

His companion nodded, completing the necessary code. "Then I shall be your teacher." They turned and walked among the arches, out of sight and hearing among the shadows. Worn sandals clattered hollowly on the tile.

Once well away from unwanted eyes, Tariq dropped the masquerade. "Amar the slaver says you are trustworthy," he said, evenly greeting his companion's gaze.

"What is it you want?"

Tariq's voice dropped to a barely-audible whisper. "I have, er, a sister in the palace. Entered only yesterday among the girls taken to serve in Kabul's brothel . . ."

"Her identity shall be protected, you need not fear."

With eyes coolly narrowed, Tariq added, "She needs better employment. A position that will keep her a hairbreadth away from the Khan."

At this the scholar tensed. "You ask much, Kazir. The closer to Kabul the greater the risk—for everybody."

"Yet Kabul's brothel is under your control, isn't it?"

The scholar smiled thinly. "A man must learn to survive in dangerous times, Kazir. Amar supplies the women, I select those for the royal harem. The others are given to men of rank—soldiers, ministers, and their ilk. If your sister is beautiful enough, then perhaps Kabul or any of his eight sons may claim her. If not, she will be taken away. It's not in my hands."

Shrewdly, Tariq said, "Ah, but the overseer to the whores, the palace prostitutes, is *she* not chosen by you?"

The question was a trap, the scholar knew. This Tariq had done his research well. "Yes—but there is only one. A eunuch, not a woman. A former slave, castrated by the Khan, who won his freedom by serving the Huns as skilled torturer in the palace dungeons. I named him overseer because I could trust him with the women. I doubt Kabul would readily let me have him replaced."

Tariq thought for a moment, then posed another question. "And what if this eunuch were removed by force?"

The scholar hesitated before replying, then said, "The next choice would be my own. Perhaps another eunuch—"

"Or the right woman?"

He nodded. "If she were suitable. Her duties would be in constant demand; each night she must select women to share the Khan's bed and those of his sons. Currently there are over one hundred and fifty women in the harem. My overseer must keep them all beautiful and ready."

"Soon, your eunuch will no longer be a burden to any of us," Tariq said flatly. "You need not know the circumstances, only that it be done. When the task is complete, I want you to name my sister as new overseer of the whores. Tell Kabul any tale you like." He pressed his face closer to the other man and said, "then stay far away."

His companion, having lived and survived so long amid such intrigues inside and outside of the palace, smiled smugly. "And what, Kazir, if I should refuse? Call you out this instant to those soldiers patrolling the high walls?"

He was surprised when Tariq showed no fear. The young Kazir glanced over his shoulder casually, whistled softly. From the gathered group of kneeling worshippers one man lifted his head and his frame, an awesome man, a giant with shoulders as broad as a wall. The man skirted a glance to Tariq, for only the briefest moment took his hand from inside the sleeve of his robe. He clasped a short curved knife that glimmered angrily in the sunlight. The scholar winced, the message all too clear. Indeed, spies were everywhere!

"Well?" said Tariq impatiently.

His fretful consort ran a thick tongue over suddenly very dry lips and mouth. "Your sister shall be named overseer. But the demise of Castus is up to you. I have nothing to do with it."

A satisfied smile crossed Tariq's desert features. "I knew I might count on you. Return home and wait; palace guards, I would imagine, shall summon you by morning."

5

Constructed upon the highest ground of the city, an acropolis from which tens of leagues in every direction could be observed from the highest towers and teardrop-shaped spires, stood the ancient and splendid palace of Samarkand. Within its stone walls great rulers had governed its empire since the time of Alexander. Now, though, the pomp and splendor of former days were gone, leaving instead only the shell: drab, gray walls ridden with cracks and fissures, upon whose battlements grimly marched the Khan's inner guard.

Torchlight and candles shone gloomily across the sprawling imperial chambers and halls that had once hosted a courtly retinue from virtually every civilized nation. The desperate solitude now bore silent testimony to the recent years of Kabul's reign; men trod softly through these once-hallowed rooms, fearful and respectful of its new occupants, ruthless men brutally plotting and scheming ruthless conquests. Spreading terror into every land beneath the black banners of the Huns.

The private apartment was dark at this hour, devoid of slaves or servants, quiet except for the heavy and labored breathing of one man and the tinkling of the instruments of the cloaked figure at his side.

Kabul lay postrate upon the worn, velvet divan, his head slightly elevated by a tiny, brocaded pillow. Naked save for the plain sheet draped across his loins, he listened to the pounding of his heart, stared expressionlessly up at the high recessed window, at the starlight. The robed man standing over him drew another needle, long and fine, from his tray. He twirled it for a second in front of his eyes, then twisted the tip against Kabul's flesh, inserting it at the juncture of elbow and arm.

The Great Khan's mouth turned down with the initial sting of pain, spittle from his thick lips flying across his once-fiery beard. Gray had long since replaced the crimson, more rapidly in recent years than ever before. Deeplypouched jowls remained covered by the beard, but above it the skin was etched with deepening lines that crisscrossed his features. His body was massive with strong, powerful arms. Broad shoulders, flat stomach, firm thighs. Almost a perfect specimen for a man his age—except for one item. Below his slanted and bushy silver brows a scarred and bulbous canker festered, a sewn sore where once his right eye had been. It was now a swollen, sightless mass that, were it not for his patch, would have made him hideously ugly to look upon.

Another needle pierced into tracked flesh; Kabul winced and sucked in a lungful of late-winter air. This one hurt—hurt badly, causing white-hot flashes of pain to run up his leg and nudge at his spinal cord. Still, the punishing acupuncture was less severe than his spasms, periods of excruciating agony when the dangling nerve-endings of his lost eye sent him into fits of writhing and screaming. Even the most cleverly-designed torture seemed mild by comparison. This Chinaman who stood before him with a slight smile and inscrutable slanted eyes was the only man Kabul had ever been able to find who might bring relief for his pain. Kabul needed him and his craft more than his sons or his generals, more than his women and chancellors. Were it not for these frequent treatments, the Great Khan would surely have died long before. Not from the symptoms, as terrifying as they were, but by his own hand. For even one such as he could not have borne the punishment of the spasms. Now Kabul existed for one thing and one thing only: revenge. Swift and equal retribution for the devil's minx who had caused the infliction.

"Do you feel better, my lord?" rasped the accented voice.

The Khan glanced sidelong at Sing-Li the Chinese physician. As the tireless acupuncturist padded away beads of sweat from his forehead, Kabul replied, "The spasm is gone. I can think again."

The physican broke into a shadowed grin and bowed low before the Khan, hands hidden in his wide sleeves. "You have honored me in letting me treat you this night, O liege. Summon me again, should discomfort return."

Kabul sat up, hirsute legs dangling over the side of the

divan. This time when he swelled his chest, there was an absence of pain, the overwhelming head pain that had forced him to wake and cry out for the Chinaman's skills at once. He toyed with the eyepatch clutched in his large hand, proceeded to tie it back into place. "You may go" was all he said. Then as an afterthought to the Chinaman's back, "Have Khalkali come in."

No sooner had the oval bronze doors parted than a handful of slaves quietly entered. They lit candles and braziers, laid wine and supper before the Khan. Kabul wrenched a breast from the roasted duck, ate greedily, swilling it down with the strong Indian brew.

Barely a few moments later the door opened wide once more. In swaggered a tall, hairy barbarian, a much younger image of Kabul himself, with long fiery locks, well-developed biceps, a brooding sneer beneath a drooping crimson mustache.

Khalkali swept with a grand and overdone bow. "You sent for me, Father?"

Kabul wiped grease from his mouth with the back of his arm. He studied his fourth son a long while, wondering what further intrigues against him this swaggering *seedling* had plotted with his brothers. Ten sons Kabul had sired. Ten different mothers. And Kabul harbored no false illusions; of the eight remaining, each and every one lusted for further title and power, jockeying among themselves, currying favors among the ministers, pretending devout obedience to their father, while hoping for the Khan's death.

But Kabul bore little ill will on this score, even if they did prove to be an unworthy lot. The Khan needed not reminding that to attain his own position it had taken the murder of three brothers, two uncles, as well as his own father to ascend to the Hun throne. It was no secret; he'd bragged about it often enough, in any case. Yet he was still confident that not a single one of his scions would openly dare oppose him; he was still their better, alone or combined. In fact, the hatreds they nurtured among themselves for each other were a great source of amusement to the aging Khan. Many a time he had nourished such rivalries, turning brother against brother, fully knowing that it only enhanced his own chances of remaining where he was even longer.

Khalkali stood erect, bearskin boots caked with dust, attesting to the recent weeks his personal army had spent raiding the Persian frontier; he had only returned this very evening. The flimsy Persian garrisons had easily fallen to the onslaught; Khalkali's own men had returned with saddlebags laden with spoils, and some five hundred captives, more than half young women to pass to the legions as field whores.

Kabul chewed his supper slowly as the youthful warrior recounted his successes. The booty had been good, he saw; more important, they had learned just how weak these Persian border defenses really were. All the more of considerable significance in light of Hun ambitions to broaden even further their vast empire.

". . . twenty thousand men," Khalkali was saying as Kabul returned his attention. "Three thousand horsemen. Give me as many and I can bring you home the Persian crown—and the head of their *shah,* this king of kings as well!"

The Khan smiled thinly. How ambitious his fourth son had become. Nothing like a few quick successes to bolster esteem. *If I gave you such an army to command, dear Khalkali, how long would it be before you turned your trusted troops against me?*

"I will take your advice under consideration," said the Khan.

His son was seething with temper, eager to march, eager to claim the Persian throne and come back a hero. "But, Father! We have now the finest opportunity yet! The frontier is in disarray; I could make a crossing unscathed. It would take months, *months!* for the *sanshah* to group and deploy his forces. Time gives him the chance to defend against us, shore up his legions!"

Kabul listened raptly, twisting the various emerald and ruby rings on his thick fingers. "I have not the forces to spare," he answered. "Your brother Gamal grows impatient in the west. Or have you forgotten we lay siege to the Turks?"

Khalkali pressed his lips in consternation, glaring at the

naked man on the divan. In a subdued tone he said, "Is it the Turks you consider? Or that woman on the steppes?"

The Great Khan grew crimson; he tightened his hands into fists, half a mind to leap out of his seat and strangle the sneering youth before him. Few ever dared whisper of the woman who had stolen his eye; a loyal aide-de-camp once had, meaning no harm, but the damage had been done. As an approaching spasm rollicked inside his brain, Kabul had in a rage had him arrested, both eyes plucked from their sockets, then his tongue, before mercifully giving him his own sword with which to take his life. Talk of the woman was expressly forbidden, and Khalkali showed a foolish bravado in taunting his father thus.

"Son of a whoring bitch!"

The fourth son held his ground, knowing his father was in his dementia only bringing on another fit. Secretly, Khalkali was laughing. *Let the old fool wallow in agitation! He would not dare harm me—not now, not after my bringing home such bountiful treasure.*

Kabul snapped upright, swung himself off the divan, and planted himself firmly in front of his son. Khalkali was smaller in stature and strength; he could still break his back in a fair fight. Perhaps one day soon he would. But the obligations of office had taught even a barbarian much; his fourth son was yet useful to him, a pawn among the other brothers, a field commander for his plans to once again march against the steppes and the phantom Kazirs who ruled them.

He returned to the divan, picked another piece of roasted meat from the plate. "The woman is not your concern," he told his son, returning to calm complacency. "I shall deal with her—and her outlaws—in my own time and place of choosing. As for your own request, denied for the moment. The sanshah has done nothing to turn his armies against us. True, he has harbored fugitives like that man Le-Dan; but for the moment neither is a threat. When we are ready, Persia shall be taken. Plucked like a grape from the vine." His gaze tightened again as he stared single-eyed at Khalkali. "I shall probably bestow upon you the honor of bringing to me the sanshah's worthless head —at the proper time. But always know that *I* will be the one to determine when. Not you."

Khalkali groaned. "You are making a mistake, Father. I tell you this openly and honestly——"

Kabul waved a haughty hand, said, "You may leave. For the moment the matter is closed."

Khalkali bowed respectfully, turned and strode brazenly from the room.

From a secret door behind a Chinese screen another figure slipped into the chamber: Tupol, ninth son of the Khan. His head snapped to the side in a nervous twitch, continual and growing worse with age. A deformed hand hung from a crooked arm; his limp was slight, his eyes crossed. However, a cunning mind had been encased within that deformed body, a mind Kabul was wise enough to value. And although the youth seemed the most harmless man within the entire Samarkand palace, the Khan feared him more than the others. Tupol was cagey; crafty as was his mother, with a mind far superior to any Kabul had ever known. What his body lacked in physical prowess, his constantly analyzing brain more than compensated for. To the Khan he was of immense value, and came as close to being worthy of honest trust as any of the sons.

"My brother speaks too rashly for his own good," hissed Tupol. He played with a necklace of common beads hanging from his neck. "Shall I follow him, Father?"

Kabul patted the soot-haired youth of a Mongolian mother as he might pet his favorite hound. "No," he said, shaking his head and smiling. "Let Khalkali fume, let him conspire with his cronies and brothers. It matters not. I don't even care if he consults Osklath."

Tupol's laugh sounded like a mountain hyena's. Osklath indeed! The first-born of the Khan, due to his strange experiences in the forest fighting against the Kazirs, was now a thumb-sucking, speechless idiot. Turned into an imbecile who could not even be toilet-trained. Osklath himself had taken the life of the tenth and truly youngest son of the Khan, Frizul, for so-called cowardice, thus ridding Kabul of yet another dangerous pest. Now there were eight left. Tupol, confident for the moment of his own safety, wondered which would be next.

"Then what may I do for you this night, Father?" he asked.

Kabul downed his wine, lay back on the divan. An olive-skinned slave silently took away the tray of food, refilled the pitcher. The Khan hungrily eyed her, feeling a swelling in his loins. "I need nothing tonight, Tupol," he said. "Only a woman. Winter nights give me a chill."

The son chuckled. "Getting old, eh, Father?" he chided. Then more seriously, "Does this slavegirl please you?"

"I think not. Amar has said that he's brought a number of exotic beauties to the palace these past days, has he not?"

"Indeed, Father! Egyptian women, with breasts as luscious as melons! And a black-skinned lovely from Africa like no woman you have ever seen! Perhaps you'd like to sample the yellow-haired one from Rus? Or even—"

The mighty Khan stopped his babbling with a gesture of his hand.

"You'll make of me a glutton yet!" he answered with a boisterous laugh. "Bring the matter to the eunuch, Castus. Tell him my desires, and let him be the one to decide."

6

The overseer was obese. In kindness, even to him, there was no other way to describe him. His arms were like stubby branches of well-tended trees, belly as voluminous as a woman pregnant with a full brood of offspring. Short, squat-nosed, multiple-chinned, and with a round, jovial face, he masked the anger of his condition as a voyeur would, by clandestinely sneaking behind the walls of bedrooms, peeking into carefully-drilled holes, watching pairs of lovers cavort in the still of night. That, and absorbing limitless amounts of potent honeyed wine, were his only vices. For the rest, he was a man of strict character, obeying the Khan's wishes and instructions to the letter, keeping his women in line by the crack of the whip when necessary. But he secretly let a few rendezvous with a lover for a few hours now and again among the labyrinth of formerly grand chambers, when, of course, they showed merit.

This night had been a quiet one for Castus. Kept minimally occupied by a few easy-to-handle requests, he'd spent most of the evening sequestered within the small rooms of his apartment, well fed on his favorite dishes, the cuisine supplied by the best palace cooks. Sucking on his water pipe, dreamily watching the smoke rise in tiny circles to the ceiling, he sipped his favorite mellowed fruit of the grape.

While reclining and belching, he called the single word "enter" after a low rap fell across his door. Annoyed at the interruption, he sat back up, tube of the pipe held in one hand, a brass goblet half-drained in the other.

The woman who stepped lithely inside was small, insecure as she briefly scanned the personal quarters she had visited only once before. Meekly she came closer, head lowered, hands clasped behind. Then she waited.

Castus blew air from his puffy cheeks, irritated. "Speak, girl," he demanded.

A small, rounded, elfin face lifted and met his fogged eyes. Draped in a green robe of quality fabric, her dark hair braided and pinned in circles atop her head, she seemed more child than woman. Her skin was fair, unblemished, except for a tiny mole tucked into the curve of her neck. She wore a set of gilden earrings, inlaid with sapphires that gaily reflected the flame of his lamp. "Your tub, my lord," she mumbled. "Have you forgotten?"

Castus looked at her with favor, remembering he'd always taken a liking to this one. She seemed so lost among the others, so fragile, so out of place for a whore. A hard look, though, had begun to replace the girlish features, a sad acceptance had crept into her eyes. She was resigned to her fate.

Castus blew his nose into a silk handkerchief, pulled a distasteful face. He rose from his cushions. "Yes, yes," he grumbled sleepily.

Modesty caused the whore to turn away as he disrobed, flinging his toga across the back of a well-worn settee that once had belonged to a high palace official. Then, naked save for his sandals, he brushed past the girl, buttocks quivering like mounds of gelatin.

The prostitute quickly picked up the robe, following behind. Castus turned left at the end of the short, dimly lit corridor, walked toward the baths. From beyond the latticed screens and walls he could hear idle chatter and muffled laughter coming from the harem pool.

Ah, but if I were yet a full man, he wheezed wistfully, picturing all that supple flesh swimming carelessly in the pool, lounging with bare breasts in the luxuriant halls set aside for them. A single night of pleasure was all he would have asked. Of course, at its conclusion the Khan would have demanded his head; still, the price, to a man bereft of testicles, would have been worth it.

His personal tub, sunken beneath a floor of marble, had been scented and heated to the exact temperature he enjoyed. He dipped one fat-laden foot in first, glanced behind to make certain the girl was there waiting with robe and towel in hand. She was. Castus slipped into the aquamarine-tinted liquid, put his hands behind his head, and floated like the bloated balloon he was. From the side another woman came, soap in hand. She knelt next to the oversized tub, worked the soap into lather along her scrubbrush.

The overseer tilted his head, looked at her. "I don't know you," he said.

She nodded, faced him squarely. Her hair was sandy, clipped short in the manner of local hill tribes. "I arrived only yesterday, my lord," she told him. "Brought here by Amar. Surely you recall—?"

Castus thought a moment, agreed. She was vaguely familiar; but so many new women were brought to the palace these days for selection, it was most difficult to keep track of them all.

She'd been garbed in the simple robe of a novice, a pretty face, but a trifle too slender. Experience told him out of hand that she would be rejected by both the Khan and his sons, brought within a couple of days to the officers' harem and the pleasure of Kabul's highest ranking and most seasoned veterans.

As the woman worked, Castus let his gaze pour over her. She was slightly older than most of the others. Perhaps she'd already been a whore, and well-versed in the games of the bedroom. Or maybe she was famous for other qualities, such as dancing, bringing her partners to new heights of excitement before satisfying them. Whatever, it was not for him to question Amar's judgment. Only the unusual necklace she wore caused him further reason to ponder. Really a worthless, if intriguing trinket. Braided leather, knotted, with a small, shiny bone at the end. A horn, perhaps.

"Is this good, my lord?" she asked, working her fingers into the flab of his back. Suds trickled down from neck to buttocks; he sat cross-legged in the tub and sighed with contentment. Without question the newcomer was expert with her hands, and again he cursed his fate for his condition.

He turned to the girl still holding his robe and grinned. "Watch this one well and learn, Lina," he said merrily. "By Kabul's gods, I'm a fool to question Amar's eye for women!"

Castus sank lower into the tub, urged by the gentle but firm prodding of the other woman's hands. "Mmmmm," he cooed, immersed in the warm water, toying with the bubbles. His muscles relaxed; the newcomer worked his entire body, knowledgeably, surely, as if she had done this very thing for him countless times before. Suddenly she pushed his face further into the liquid until its level reached his nostrils. He coughed loudly. The woman, pushed harder, submerging almost half his face.

He bobbed to the surface. "No, no," he choked, "I can't breathe."

His fat form struggled to rise; her hands pressed him back, the pressure too strong for him to pull away from. He flailed arms and legs, splashed gallons at a time over the side, but still his head was below the waterline.

The hefty overseer tried to roll over; he clawed wildly to grab her arms, opened his mouth to scream for help. Soapy water gushed into his lungs, and he exhaled it with glistening soap bubbles that formed circles at the surface. As his face turned colors, from ruddy to scarlet to purple, he twitched and bobbed, his enormous belly rising from the water like a huge, bald, quivering mountain. His gurgles were muffled by her hands now over his mouth;

her knee pressed hard into his shoulders, pushed him down. Castus squirmed like an eel, then he squirmed no more.

Carolyn held on a while longer, then abruptly released, drew back, and climbed from the tub. She stared down with hands on hips, robe drenched and soaking, forming pools at her feet. The corpse rose slowly to the surface, the face contorted, mouth limply hanging wide. The saya did nothing to conceal her smile as she said to Lina, "You'd better inform the guards. Our overseer is dead. Drowned, I should think, by his own weight."

7

The ever-shifting ocher and golden sands of the desert, now tinted scarlet by the waning sun's shadows, were a beautiful sight to behold. The two riders paused at the crest of a dune, shared a mutually understood smile, then gently kicked the horses' flanks and led them down. The white Arabian stallions cantered easily over hot, burning sands, heads lifted proudly, long manes flowing in a peaceful breeze. The very smell of desert greeted their nostrils and they whinnied, luxuriating in the feel of slackened reins and loosened bridles. And for the wearied riders came the scent of freedom. The two men knew that at last they were home; home where they could gallop the endless plains of the approaching steppes, home where they were released from the distasteful world of the city and civilization.

Over *wadis* parched and dry, as ancient as the huge looming hills and mountains of rock still hazy to the north, the steeds raced, picking up speed, wild and free once more, urged on by the taste of the familiar soil. Open lands that had no ends and no beginnings, stretching for as far as the eye could see; Kazir land, unravished by humanity, unspoiled and pure, the way God had designed it.

Tariq's heart beat faster inside his chest. While the stallion pranced beneath him, his head swam with a thousand memories, memories of childhood, of times when old Shoaib the Goatherd brought him here to experience the sensation that only a child of the desert can understand and love. This was his desert, he knew. Ancestoral birthplace of his people and all their heritage. Nothing was ever going to take it away.

His companion whooped; drawing sword from the saddle sheath, he lifted the curved blade and swung it in wheels above his head. Tariq looked at the scalp-locked, faithful warrior and grinned. Roskovitch was a barbarian from the cold, northern lands of Rus. An exile, cast out of his motherland long ago, he now eagerly lived and lusted for the Kazir way of life. Tariq had been but a small boy when the barbarian had been found half dead from thirst and sunstroke by agents of Shoaib. Taken to the Stronghold, nursed and brought back to health, the sinewy Russian had repaid his gratitude a hundredfold as loyal warrior and aide to the ailing elder. But to Tariq he was even more; the youth had looked to Roskovitch as a brother, learning from him the skills of battle, the uncanny horsemanship that only the barbarian tribes of Central Asia had mastered so completely. Now that Tariq was a man, a chieftain of the Clans in his own right, who but Roskovitch was more worthy to ride at his side? They had shared much together these past years; in both victory and defeat, joy and tears, the Russian and he spent their lives.

It was well past dusk when they completed the trek from the dunes, crossed into the flatlands and savannas of tall yellow grasses that swayed incessantly in a cool desert wind, and approached the distant wind-scarred high walls of solid granite. To a traveler crossing this way, those walls seemed grim and foreboding indeed. An out-of-place, spiraling slab of rock, fortresslike, set by nature crookedly some leagues before the range of smoky mountains that divided the deserts. Yet to those who knew better, this looming, monstrous mass, as untamed as the steppes themselves, posed a clever disguise. For here, within the granite itself, sheltered from the outside world so totally that an entire legion of Kabul's army might pass it and never give more than a cursory glance, stood the very soul of the Kazir freedom. The fortress Stronghold, unapproachable as it was awesome, awesome as it was spectacular.

The riders appeared insectlike from the great heights above, but unseen eyes, trained well in desert night sight, watched them closely, tracking their every move as they reached dangerous territory.

Tariq and Roskovitch stopped and dismounted some hundred paces before the jagged, blue-hued edifice, which by daylight reflected all the colors of the spectrum. Off to the side two trees grew, one an oak sapling, dwarfed by the other, a gigantic red-trunked ogre of a tree. A trunk as thick as three large men standing shoulder to shoulder, unbent, shot straight up into the sky perhaps fifty meters high, nearly as high as the stone barrier itself. For fully a third of this immense height no branches spread, but where they did, they were bare. Tariq handed the reins of his horse to his friend, cupped both hands around his mouth, and sang out a long note in the cry of a loon. Less than a second later the call was answered, the same shrill bird's call, emitted from up amid the branches of the tree's tallest reaches.

The Arabian stallions neighed and dug nervous hooves into the ground. All around came the growing noise of a low rumble, sounding at first like far thunder but steadily increasing in volume until the earth started to shake. In front of Tariq a section of the granite wall started to move, two smooth slabs pulling apart with a groan. Then suddenly there was a black gap before them, a widening fissure leading deep into the rock, a canyon that would have terrified any who had not seen it before.

Roskovitch tightened his hold of the uneasy horses, and then both men rode through the abyss, unfrightened, glad to be home at last.

Inside, Sharon sat restlessly in her tent, hands nervously playing with the slim copper bracelets adorning her wrists. The tent flaps rustled, the wind outside was starting to rise. Her desert-sense assured her that a storm was brewing not far away. A khamsin sweeping down from the mountains, whipping in furious gusts as it broke out onto the monotonous plains and steppes, picking up impetus as it swirled and fed upon itself.

From outside came the noises of men and women gathering their animals, rushing them to shelter across the tent and mudbrick Kazir city. Guards posted along the chinked crenelations in the high walls would seek havens of their own among the fissured rocks, shielding themselves from the wind's onslaught while ever-vigilantly guarding the approaches to the Stronghold. In former years this place had been home to but a single Clan, the saya's, while the many other tribes lived peacefully along the length and breadth of the steppes and desert, even at the fringes of the forbidden Grim Forest. Kabul's unflinching vow to wipe all Kazirs from the face of the earth had changed all that, though. More and more the Clans had retrenched, leaving fields unplowed, flocks untended, drawing an ever-tighter perimeter into the desert, flooding the Stronghold until the city teemed with life, the last impenetrable citadel outside of his grasp.

The candle flickered and almost died when the tent flap pushed aside. Sharon's almond eyes widened, her breath quickening. *Tariq! At last he's come!*

Alone together, the secret lovers embraced, Sharon burying herself in the strength of his arms, momentarily forgetting everything else. Their lips met in a hungry kiss, holding onto each other as though this might be the last time. But as their mouths parted, Sharon turned her face from another kiss, pulled from another embrace, ever fearful that someone might see. For although the Panther was leader in the struggle against the Huns, and as such had been chosen the One to guide their fate, she was still an outsider. Her blood was not Kazir blood, and thus she was forbidden to the youthful chieftain Tariq. It was the Law, the ancient, strict code that had bonded these hill tribes for so many years. For Tariq to openly declare his love, which he would have readily done many times had Sharon not stopped him, would mean a break between the Clans. There were those, even among the unified Kazirs, who still harbored doubts about her; those who knew that, even though against her will, the evil Khan had spilled his seed into her belly. The witches had cleansed her of the venom long ago; yet to many such, shame could never be truly cleansed. Though these very warriors would ride beside her into battle, give their own lives and the lives of their sons willingly under her cause and banner, still they regarded her as an outsider. Worthy of any king or man in the world—except a Kazir chieftain. Perhaps this belief born of tradition and necessity would change, but now was not the time. Total, undivided unity was needed if there was to be any hope of fulfilling the prophecy and wresting Samarkand back from its heathen conquerors.

"I have worried about you these past days," said Tariq, his face drawn and haggard from his long journey.

"And I about you," panted Sharon. "It was not necessary for you to risk entering the city. Roskovitch could have done the job for us."

He regarded her disapprovingly. "It was as necessary as your own secret journey into the forest. A foolish thing to have done, traveling alone like that in winter. At every hour you risked capture by a Hun patrol. . . ."

She hushed him by brushing her fingers against his lips, led him to sit near the cold stones of the hearth. He unwrapped his desert burnoose, shook his curly hair free of accumulated dust. Gratefully he sipped at the chalice she handed him, realizing now how drained he was, under how much pressure he had been to accomplish his dangerous mission as quickly as possible and return to the Stronghold.

Sharon sat opposite, in the glare of the light, girlish features highlighted when the hanging oil lamp swayed. "Rest, Tariq," she soothed, hands in her lap.

He shook his head and stared into the chalice.

"Is everything well?" Sharon asked.

He peered up lovingly at her, thinking her desert-tanned face to be the most beautiful he'd ever known. To watch her now, bathed in the lamp's soft glow, the candle's glare, she seemed so much less the tough and resilient Panther of the Steppes, so much more the young and frightened woman who had first come here so long ago. In many ways he wished he might magically return to that lost moment, capture her in his arms, and whisk her away, riding far across the desert to lands remote and unscathed by the conflict. Some place where they might have peacefully shared each other's lives, raising children instead of armies. Watching their family grow instead of counting casualties and praying for the dead.

"Everything is well," Tariq said, cutting off the memories. "Nearly all the pieces have been set into place."

Sharon breathed deeply. All the years of planning were coming to a close; soon the vise would begin to shut, irrevocably set into motion, feeding upon itself like a surging tidal wave with nothing able to prevent the chain of coming events from transpiring. Everything had to be perfect, though; there was no room for miscalculation.

For the hundredth time in recent days she reached for the parchment scroll concealed beneath the cushions atop her sleeping mat, opened it before her, and scanned the names scrawled onto the carefully compiled list. Nine names in all: those of the Khan's eight sons, his wall of protection until now impenetrable, and lastly Kabul's own name, the final victory.

Mufiqua, the narcotic addict for whom she had danced, now under Zadek's spell, ready to be called upon when needed.

Khalkali, the brazen and swaggering would-be heir, as hateful of his father as he was of Samarkand.

Gamal, worthy warrior—in command of the western legions marching upon the Turks of Constantinople. A venomous, treacherous soldier who let nothing stand in the way of his glories.

As if reading Sharon's thought, Tariq said, "There is talk in the city of Gamal's imminent return. He fancies himself already to be crown prince. Kabul will be forced to meet him on equal terms—as conquering hero."

"Butcher is a more appropriate word," Sharon corrected.

Then there was Tupol, the misshapen, shrewdly cunning youngest son. He would have to be dealt with more carefully. This one would be Zadek's charge; she only hoped the mad mullah had made his plans as precisely as he believed.

Five more names remained on the list. Krishna, the brooding, brutish and sadistic chancellor of the dungeons, a man whose very name brought shudders among the fearful folk of Samarkand. Temugin, as surly as he was arrogant. A troublemaker intent on gaining the throne over as many of his brothers' corpses as necessary. Then Jamuga. A strange man, a loner with few if any friends. The only one of the brothers about whom Sharon knew little or nothing. Jamuga had long before been relegated to Carolyn. Niko, a lover, a liver of high life, worldly gambler and reckless swordsman who'd slain many a husband of wives he'd lusted.

Last, of course, there was Kabul himself. The Great Khan of the Huns, for whom Sharon kept a special and personal hatred. Her friends could do with the others what they may, but Kabul was hers. She alone would mete out his punishment although none of her compatriots yet knew it.

Eight sons. One father.

A tiny, worn leather pouch rested at her side; she reached for it, poured the contents into her palm. Eight small stones, each a different color, glittered in the light. Tariq watched her with growing fascination as her hand closed lightly and she shook them, tossing them to the rug beneath her feet like a soldier might cast dice. The chipped amber stone rested in the center.

"Gamal," she said with a sardonic smile.

Tariq nodded his head somberly. "Then let it begin."

8

The slaves stood in a row, mutely, heads bent, hands clasped behind their backs, links of heavy chains clanking each time one was prodded forward. Amar, the slaver, grinned as his turbaned auctioneer closed the price on a muscular and well-endowed youth from the coast of Africa. He kept a careful eye while the next in line, a frightened, dark-skinned boy from the great houses of Mesopotamia, had his bonds removed and was prodded roughly onto the narrow platform. There, beneath a gleaming, hot sun, he stood almost naked, ashamedly, while onlookers by the score gawked at him, murmured among each other about his qualities.

The Afgani auctioneer quickly read off a list of the boy's abilities. Soft hands assured potential buyers he'd never toiled either in field or barrack, his breeding had been one of quality; trained first as common servant, then elevated in stature to singer for one of the noblest families in all the Near East.

To Amar's disgruntlement, the opening bids were low. Few in Samarkand had use for a slave whose main occupation was to recite poetry, sing and dance to entertain his masters. And as the bidding continued, the cunning slaver cursed softly for ever having bought the lad from the Egyptian caravaneer. The loss was surely to come from his own pocket.

A carefully-planted shill offered a few coins above the last offer, then slipped back into the crowd, smiling as the ploy brought a quick counteroffer.

The Afgani glanced to Amar, saw the frown and, wiping sweat from his paunchy face, extolled the slave. Surely such a refined slave of education was worth a ransom in Samarkand. His very presence would elevate the status of any household. But the dour and mediocre stares told him the buyers had no eye for such excellence. Strong backs and small brains were all they were interested in.

"For shame!" berated the auctioneer, his desperation growing more plain. He pressed open the slave's mouth with his hand, showed the perfect teeth, made the youth straighten, had him turn around slowly so everyone could note his unblemished flesh. "Never has this boy been brought under the lash! Never has he abused his former masters. Good citizens, reconsider his value!"

The auctioneer was greeted with a ripple of sneering laughter. Amar let his gaze drift to the direction of the sound; his eyes widened with some surprise. Standing in a group at the edge of the throng, within close distance to the platform, were three men he feared and despised. The Khan's sons—Temugin, Tupol, and Niko. What had brought them here to the market today he did not know; perhaps they had come for amusement, or maybe they were here to bid on the women.

Amar shook his head. The cream of the lot was always brought to the palace for first inspection. Then why?

Another disquieting thought toyed around the edges of his mind: What if they *knew?* What if they suspected him, had learned of his secret dealings with the hated Kazirs? Should that be the case, his life was no longer worth a copper.

He eyed the visitors without being obvious. They seemed, to Amar's hidden relief, preoccupied with other matters. The slaver sighed; it was an innocent visit, his belief underscored by the banter between them and his auctioneer, whom they had begun to rile.

Hands on hips, the curly-haired, handsome Niko laughed in the face of the sputtering Afgani. With a wink to his snickering brothers, he said, "Your slave seems as brittle as a twig. You should have grouped him with the women!"

Temugin, tight-eyed and arrogant, boisterously laughed, fingering the deep scar from a Saracen's blade running from cheek to the side of his mouth.

Niko, spurred on by merriment and mischief, bounded the platform, his elegant cloak of Persian wool fanning behind, and began to taunt the frustrated auctioneer by mimicking him mercilessly. He pinched the slave's soft flesh in mock admiration, checked his teeth while tapping an impatient foot. "So you recite poems, eh?"

Eyes downcast, the youth whispered, "Yes, m'lord."

"And you sing as well?"

"Yes, m'lord. Sing—and dance."

Niko chuckled. He turned to the Afgani, saying, "Tell me, auctioneer, does he dance with veils?"

The crowd laughed in appreciation of Niko's renowned wit. The auctioneer countered brazenly, "Women have no objections to his performance."

"So? Then the lad is popular with the ladies, eh?" He pored over the slave's trim form with intent eyes. "I would have thought a boy like this spends his nights more intellectually."

"Buggered by his Arabian sheiks, you mean!" guffawed Temugin. "Ask the Afgani if the slave prefers, er, more masculine company to while away winter nights."

"Dear, misguided Brother," said Niko, peering down from the sawdusted platform toward Temugin. "You hear the auctioneer; this slave is most popular with the ladies."

To which the Afgani quickly said, "But no man, Lord Niko, is as popular with them as yourself."

While Niko turned red, both his brothers roared. "Your reputation has followed you to the markets!" catcalled Temugin, digging his elbow into quiet Tupol's ribs. The rest of the crowd smiled, some openly laughing. Indeed, the dashing son of Kabul was well known for his exploits; it was said not a single woman in Samarkand was safe with him around—not even his father's private wives.

Niko grinned as he addressed the crowd. "I admit that I've always been of an amorous nature," he told them in a friendly manner. "But now, according to this Afgani, it seems I'm in for some competition."

"Poor older brother," called out Tupol, speaking for the first time. "Whatever will you do?"

Again the crowd laughed, enjoying the joke at Niko's expense. With a good-natured pat on the back for the auctioneer, he said, "You have caused me a dilemma, friend. I cannot risk my reputation thus. This city is far too small for two such lovers."

"Afraid of the competition?"

Niko glanced to Temugin, his steely-eyed brother digging daggers into him. "Afraid of what? This boy?"

"Better get rid of him while you have the chance," cautioned Tupol with a smirk. Behind his humor, though, there was deadly intent and warning. Temugin was riding his handsome brother with purpose, openly exposing Niko before the crowd as a woman's man and nothing else. A poor choice to be heir to the Khan.

Niko took the bait. "What would you recommend, little brother?"

Before the deformed youth could respond, Temugin in a single movement drew a curved knife from its sheath, tossed it up to the waiting Niko, who caught it expertly by the hilt. The blade glinted in brilliant light. Fear showed in both the eyes of the slave and the auctioneer.

"Kill him," slurred Temugin. "That is, if you have stomach enough for it."

The Afgani stepped between the wavering Niko and the distraught slave. "He is not yet yours, my lord. We've gone to great expense both to buy and feed the slave. . . ."

"Pay the Afgani," rattled Temugin. "Pay his price and slit the slave's belly."

The crowd hooted, demanded the boy's death. Amar

glanced at the bloodthirsty throng in despair, afraid to interfere with the game Kabul's sons played, biting his lip as Niko handled the knife and wielded it before the boy's frightened eyes.

"Go on," called Temugin, eager to see if his brother was man enough to do the deed. Caution flickered across Niko's face, he looked again to Tupol. The cunning, twitching youth grimly smiled. "Kill him, Niko—or buy him."

Niko lowered his knife.

"Bring the boy back to the palace," went on the clever, manipulative Tupol. "It might be amusing to let him sing his songs and recite his poems for us."

"I will give you a fair price," promised the auctioneer, seizing the initiative now that he saw a wedge between the brothers. "It would be a waste to deprive an intelligent slave of his life. . . ."

The look within Temugin's deep-set eyes was filled with scorn, Niko saw. A scorn that had always been there, and would remain even if the slave was killed. "You are wise, little brother," said Niko at last. He casually tossed the blade back to Temugin, grinned his famous, charming grin for the auctioneer. "Have the slave washed and garbed in some decent clothes. Bring him to the palace tonight, and present your bill."

Amar drew a long breath of relief as the Afgani nodded and bowed before the dandy, Niko. But to what use the dashing son of Kabul intended to put the boy he had no idea. Of one thing he was positive, though: None of the Khan's cagey sons did anything casually or carelessly. Niko had a purpose in bringing this boy to the palace; perhaps crafty Tupol realized it even if Temugin did not.

Niko jumped off the platform spryly, his attention immediately turned to the pretty, veiled women scattered throughout the crowd. As the auctioneer had the next slave unchained and brought for display, the three brothers turned from the market and wove their way across the pavilion.

"You're a fool," grunted Temugin.

Niko looked at his mail-clad warrior brother with disdain. "I spend my money in any fashion that amuses me," he retorted. "Go back to your war games, Temugin.

Practice for the day of Gamal's return. Make sure your blade slits his throat before your own is cut."

Amid the reeking of dung and meat on display in the stalls of the market, Temugin regarded his flamboyant brother with a sneer. "Your tongue wags too much, Niko. A piece of advice: Be careful on how many toes you step. A man in your position can't afford many more enemies."

The gutters were lined with beggars, meatless arms reaching to the air, pleading with passers-by. The three brothers ignored them all, picked a path that would lead to the courtyard of the mosque and the palace gates. Unspeaking, they had almost cleared the busy avenue of merchants, acknowledging the respectful bows of passing soldiers on patrol in the city, when from the shadows another figure hunkered before them, suddenly and abruptly. Temugin by reflex drew his knife halfway out from the sheath. Tupol put a hand to his brother's ready arm, and the three of them stared at the shuffling figure.

The man had once been quite tall, they saw, only now he was bent over with age and disease. His face was tightly drawn, pale as the moon, most unlike the bronzed flesh of the other beggars who sat relentlessly in sunlight. His eyes drooped, his lips quivered as he approached. Dressed in the filthiest of rags, he somehow bore himself apart in stature from the many thousands of his kind.

"Noble lords," croaked the man, his hand extended.

"Begone!" hissed Temugin, in no mood for conversation.

The aged man's matted white hair fell over his eyes, and he stooped as he continued. "The stars," he said clearly. "Let me read them for you; let me tell you each his glorious future . . ."

Temugin was ready to push the loathsome beggar away, hurl him to the gutter. He met the beggar's piercing eyes and something made him hesitate.

"You claim to predict the future?" asked Tupol, himself as stooped as the vagabond.

The old man's hands shook as they gestured into the air. "It is the will of Allah that I have been given the Vision," he croaked. "Know ye that my predictions have never been disputed, not even by the kings whom I once served. . . ."

Niko smiled at the old man's senility, felt for his purse to take out a few small coins. "Here, old sage," he said, "spend these wisely on food and drink."

To the surprise of them all, the bedraggled soothsayer refused the offer. "You are a man of generosity, my lord Niko, but it is not the money of men nor the wealth of kingdoms that I seek."

Niko's thin brows noticeably lifted fixing his stare upon the fortuneteller's haggard, deathly features. "You know my name?" he queried.

The beggar smiled a secretive, all-knowing smile. "I do, my lord," he answered, bending his head to bow, his back grossly stooped. "As well as I recognize your brothers, the lords Tupol and Temugin."

"We need none of your trickery, old dog!" snapped Temugin testily. "All sons of the Khan are recognized faces in this foul city of yours. What do you take us for, eh?"

"Only for what you are, my lords. The favored sons of Kabul."

Temugin's temper flared, he would have struck the soothsayer viciously were it not for Niko's blocking purposely the space between them. "Then what is it you want?" Niko asked, face to face with the stranger.

"Only to spread before you the future. To guide the favored sons to their moment of glory. . . ."

"He chatters like a washerwoman," growled Temugin with impatience. "Look at him! He makes the gutter his bed yet speaks to us of glories!" He spat into the street, turned to leave.

"You are indeed a child of your stars," the soothsayer called out after him. "A true son of Scorpio. Independent, determined, a man of passions—"

Temugin stopped in his tracks, spun around. "How did you know my starsign?" he demanded.

The enigmatic smile returned. He looked long and hard at Tupol, the youngest of the sons, saying, "And you are of the sign of the immortal lion. Born to be a leader of men, a conqueror."

Temugin laughed; his vest of linked mail glimmered. "Him? A leader? A conqueror? Why, have you no eyes in your shrunken head, old man? My brother is but half a man! Deformed at birth, bastard son of a woman whose belly had to be cut open to give him life!"

The soothsayer said nothing. Niko seemed disturbed by his brother's cruel tirade against Tupol but caution advised him not to pick a second fight. Tupol did nothing to dislodge his wry smile as he watched Temugin become livid; what thought passed through his mind neither Niko nor the beggar could tell. Tupol was used to such offense; had been subjected to the laughter and mockery of all his brothers since his earliest memories. Each, though, through the years had been carefully recorded and tucked away into deep, musty recesses. Dormant for the moment, but ever ready to be brought swiftly to the surface of recall when needed. At length Tupol turned to the stargazer and said, "You are right, old man. My sign is of the lion. And my brother here—" he gestured to Niko.

"—is of Aries," said the beggar, finishing the thought. "Impetuous, energetic. . . ."

"You know me perfectly," said Niko with a grin.

Tupol was not amused even if his romantic brother was. "You know us all. How?"

"By the aura that surrounds every mortal man. Each of us has it, few have learned to recognize it. Fewer still understand and make use of it."

Niko shifted uneasily. "And you are here to do what, old man?"

The smile could not be erased, not by Temugin's anger, nor by Tupol's mistrust, nor even by Niko's growing fear of what the stars portended. "I am here to read for you, my lords. To aid you one and all against the others. . . ."

Temugin frowned. "Against whom, fool? What have we —sons of the mighty Kabul, conquerors and masters of half the world—to fear?"

"Keep still!" barked Tupol. "I want to hear him out."

"There is much evil in Samarkand," the soothsayer went on in a hushed, conspiritorial tone. "Army against army. Nation against nation. Father against son." And here he paused dramatically to let his words sink in and take hold. "Even brother against brother."

"We know this already," scoffed the youngest, waving his misshapen arm as if to dismiss the matter.

The stranger nodded sternly, severely; he stood up more erect, his back slightly straightening. "Then you, all you three, shall need one such as I to guide you."

"He's deranged," huffed Temugin. "Suffering from brainstroke. Let's be gone from this place at once."

Niko would have gladly gone with him, and in fact was ready to turn and leave, when Tupol said, "What proof have you that your readings are accurate?"

The beggar sighed, lifted his palms outward and upward in a heaven-bound gesture. "Let my predictions speak for themselves. This very night be warned: Danger crawls the palace like a spider. Be ye on guard against it! Then be safe, all three, at least until the armies of Lord Gamal ride like locusts from the west. . . ."

At this, Temugin's interest became fired. He approached the aged sage, took hold of him by the scruff of his dirty collar. "What say you, old devil? Gamal, my brother, rides home?"

"Three settings of the sun, three times the moon will wax and wane. Then shall he return."

"Preposterous," mumbled Niko, pressing his lips. "Gamal is yet hundreds of leagues away from Samarkand. Only yesterday eve the pigeons flew bearing messages of his victories against the Turks."

"Three days," said the soothsayer, repeating his prediction.

The market teemed with life all around, but Temugin was aware of none of it. His mind thought only of the hated Gamal, returning home to a hero's welcome. What changes would his arrival bring? Kabul might be moved to name the soldier as heir as result of these new gains. And so, the most mistrustful of the three suddenly became the most believing. Over the objections of Niko, he said, "Come with me now, old man. If, in three days' time, Gamal truly returns, I shall find further need of you."

The beggar put folded hands to his forehead, hung his chin on his chest. "I am here to serve you, my lord. Ask of me anything."

"For the moment I want only to know your name."

The smile was toothless. "I am called Hezekiah."

9

Yellow crawled the dawn sky, horizons tinted with shades of brightening violet. At first it sounded like the rumble of faraway thunder, distant and remote, a storm across the mountains perhaps, yet another hamsin. As the thunder increased, the darkening of sky and crack of lightning were expected. None came, for it was no tempest of nature that rollicked across the grassy plain and prairies, but rather a human invasion. First came the horsemen, thousands of them, a never-ending number amid the din of trumpets heralding the arrival home of the Western Armies, the taste of victory sweet in their mouths.

Gamal had returned!

Signal lamps were lit from valley to valley, reaching at last the grim towers of the city, where soldiers manning the parapets cheered and spread the word. Kabul, mustered from a stuporous sleep, threw the whore off the bed and bounded up the narrow steps to the observatory atop the golden spire. There, sweeping below in a vast, panoramic vista they came, black ants racing, cresting the hills, pouring out from among the trees onto the flat, open plain that lay before the walls. It was a sight to behold, and the aging Khan allowed a pleased smile to part his features. Indeed, as his secret agents had informed, contrary to the weeks-old legion reports carried in by messenger-pigeon, Gamal had come back from his wars against the barbarian Turks in full display, a public spectacle and proclamation of Hun power unleashed.

Riders fanned forward a hundred abreast, shrieking the names of their generals and gods. On and on they came, square-faced, dark-skinned men, many with slightly-slanted eyes that spoke of Mongol and Chinese blood flowing in their veins. Some were shirtless and bronzed in sweat, others were clad in linked-mail vests and barbarian furs, still more wore armor breastplates and leather helmets with metal triangular wedges protruding from the top. The ground shook like an earthquake from the tremendous clatter of hooves; before the sun had properly risen and purple shadows still lay over the length of the yellow fields, thousands of Kabul's followers jammed the walls, poured through the seven gates, massed together over balcony and roof to catch a glimpse of the magnificent sight.

Whooping and screaming, waving scimitars and hide-covered wooden shields above their heads, the Armies of the West reached the city. Behind the horsemen, five thousand slaves came marching in chains, the clamor of the legions attesting to the total success of Gamal's campaign. Not since the return of Alexander to his native Macedonia had such a welcome been given a hero. At this moment the Huns would have gladly crowned the victorious conqueror as heir to Kabul, named him a god as well, if he chose. And it was with these very thoughts in mind that the treacherous Gamal returned, riding stiffly upon his spotted white charger, lifting high the dark banner of his father in one hand, sword tightly in the other while he kept a loose grasp on the reins.

From another observatory, well across from the high spire at which the pleased Kabul stood watching, the greeting for Gamal was quiet and contemplative. Seven grim men stared from the crenelated wall, seven brothers temporarily casting aside their petty rivalries and looking on poisonously.

"The seer was right," muttered a tight-lipped Temugin.

At his side Mufiqua's eyes stared, still hazy and blurred from the effects of last night's narcotic trance. Pure opium, Amar had told him, pressing the packet clandestinely into the palm of his hand. Mufiqua had taken it thankfully and asked no further questions. That his habit was becoming more than a vice, in fact an obsession, had not yet filtered inside his fevered brain. But now, in the chill hour of early dawn, he too snapped back to reality, watching carefully when Gamal, flanked by aides and flunkies, came blustering through the arched Central Gate to the applause of the throng.

"He would have done well to have remained among the Turks," Mufiqua bitingly remarked.

Swaggering Khalkali, still smarting over his recent brush with the Khan, sneered. Behind him, the ox-shouldered, brooding chancellor of the dungeons, Krishna, held a coiled whip in his hand, flexing it and beating it gently against his massive thigh. Every bit as ambitious as Khalkali and Temugin, Krishna saw Gamal as the number-one threat to his own succession. He despised the swagger in them all, thinking them, in their own manner, all fools. Each and all lacked torturer's skills—the very skills they would need to remove him from the grasp of power. Krishna had not asked for such grisly work in the dungeons, but his appointment had taught him much about men and about the narrow thread between sanity and insanity, life and death itself. To his brothers Krishna was regarded as no more than a dutiful executioner; certainly not a warrior. Only a mindless, glorified turnkey who lived in the shadows beneath, in the bowels of the palace. Krishna, of course, had other ideas, carefully nurtured over the years.

Tupol's head helplessly twitched as he peered from near the end of the long wall, keeping his silence while his brothers ranted.

Niko observed them all in a casual manner, shuffling a deck of playing cards restlessly in his hands as he leaned with his back against the rough stones of the tower wall. Jamuga, as always the most secretive of the lot, stayed alone, holding his own counsel, aloof from the rest and seemingly uncaring. Son of an Afghani tribeswoman who was forced into the Khan's harem and then thrown away for a field whore when Kabul wearied of her, slit-eyed Jamuga had gained his place among his half brothers by wits alone. The hard desert look remained etched in his features to carry on his mother's legacy, a discomforting reminder both to Kabul and his siblings that only he of them all flowed with blood related to the indigenous peoples of Samarkand. Only Jamuga might somehow be able to rally these superstitious, religious tribes and band them together in his own cause. For this reason he had always stayed apart, realizing how precarious his position among them really was. Few questions would be asked should one morning his lifeless corpse be found with a blade stuck between his ribs. Thus, Jamuga, although also despising the folk of these conquered lands, was the obvious one to claim their support when the time came.

Secretly he hoped for the outlaw Kazirs to unwittingly do some of the painful work for him.

Seven brothers, each more hateful and loathsome than the next. Seven brothers. All now turned with jealous eyes upon the eighth.

10

The dark, winding corridor, twenty meters beneath the floor of the Great Mosque, was bathed in a strange blue-white phosphorescence. Sandals hushed against brittle stone, Sharon, garbed in loose-fitting mullah's robes, hurried alone through the snaking labyrinth, aware of the damp chill that bit harshly into her flesh, the foul reek of some unseen cesspool with its constant *drip drip drip* flowing down the limestone walls.

These were strange cellars, she knew, built countless centuries before while Samarkand was yet a young city. Some claimed the edifice of the mosque was older than the palace itself. Constructed with secret access to and from the city in mind, its architects had created a maze of passages to confuse unwelcome intruders. Sharon, though, knew exactly what to expect. She'd been here before, while yet a child, a princess of the palace, brought by Zadek and taught well the one correct route through the grim puzzle of complicated passages that eventually converged at an almost-forgotten chamber beneath the stately walls of the temple's holy sanctum. And to Sharon's knowledge, apart from the sly, mad mullah and herself only one other in all of Samarkand knew of its existence—the very person she had stolen inside the city to meet with now.

Shadows shifted as a flicker of light soon became apparent. A flinty odor swam to her nostrils, telling of burnt charcoal alight in a brazier within the forbidden Oracular Hall. Her sense of the past came rushing in at her, an uneasy *deja vu* of other times and places. There had been much joy in those lost days as well as the grief; a girl's time for games, for picking flowers, for strolling through the resplendent gardens of the palace, now moribund and weed-infested. She subdued with difficulty these flooding memories, on this her first sojourn back within the confines of Samarkand, and thought instead of the necessity for this concealed visit. No one need remind her of the penalty should the sequestered rendezous be found out— nor of the torment to be suffered if caught.

The chamber greeted her with a welcome flush of brightness. It was oblong and windowless save for tiny, clogged vents that clung to the corners of the ceiling. Supplicants and priests used to gather together in these disquieting rooms long ago, where now there were only ghosts left to wander the grim, lightless corridors, weeping with the windsong of a hamsin for living brethren yet suffering nearby inside the fouled dungeons of Kabul's palace.

More out of habit than fear, Sharon tucked her right hand within her sleeve and gripped the hidden dagger. She stepped through the oval threshold cautiously. Silhouetted beside the crumbling Doric pillar stood a shell of a man, crooked and misshapen, his long, arthritical fingers bent inward, his facial pallor as gray as death itself. A pitiful figure he seemed, broken and scarred matted white hair falling over face and shoulders. A face that would have sent decent women fleeing down the street at first sight. Sharon, though, didn't flinch. For a long moment she paused in her steps across the cracked multicolored tiles, and slowly allowed a smile to work its way over her face.

As if by sorcery the bent man before her straightened, stood fully erect. The twisted fingers unbent, the pained expression vanished, and from beneath soot and grime and filth his eyes shone brightly. He would have bowed humbly had not a wave of her hand commanded he forgo such obligations.

Sharon's eyes scanned the once-opulent hall, seeking signs of perfidy. Then, assured they were truly alone, she came to her companion, placed both hands upon his broad shoulders and grinned. "Well done!" she congratulated. "The disguise is perfect; I'd never have recognized you."

Hezekiah smiled himself. For weeks he had studied the beggars of the markets, the crippled and misshapen, emulating their speech and posture to such a degree that now he actually lived and breathed the role he played. However, the scars along his jowls, back, and chest were real enough; painful reminders of the many months of misery spent inside the Khan's dungeons, daily tortured until his fortuitous escape. To have reached the safety of the steppes and the Kazirs had been a rebirth for the former minister of Samarkand, the Hebrew who'd been until the city's downfall more than right hand to the emir and Sharon's murdered father. Like the Panther, he, too, had vowed to return, promising that those responsible for so much pain and bloodshed would be repaid.

Gloomy phantasms cascaded across the convex ceiling as Sharon moved away from the pillar and toward the sheltered recess and tomblike antechamber. Voice lowered, she said, "You were not severely questioned?"

Shadows crossed the soothsayer's hawkish features; he shook his head, regained his former twisted posture so effectively that to Sharon it seemed he was undergoing a metamorphosis. "Our scouts did their work well. Came the dawn of the third morning and, like an apparition, Gamal's armies appeared. Temugin became white. I saw him flee his chambers, join his brothers along the tower battlements."

"Then he's convinced of your accuracy?"

"Without question. He has shielded me from his siblings, directed that I read the stars exclusively for him."

Sharon's eyes flashed questioningly. "You will be safe?"

"As safe as any man in this dreaded palace. I am under his personal protection, you see. Temugin values me; I must be sure not to lose his trust. . . ."

With Mufiqua effectively but unknowingly under Zadek's hypnotic control, there were now two brothers of the eight whose minds could be bent. Carolyn now supervised the whores, and with it easy access to the Khan. Given these footholds beneath Kabul's very nose, it seemed the plan was progressing perfectly. There were nine twisted minds in all to deal with, to further poison and sow the seeds of ambition and hatred. Sharon felt her heartbeat quicken; poison was a two-edged sword, she knew, lethal to whoever tasted it. She must never let her own personal hatred interfere with what must be slowly and painstakingly done.

Give me strength to fulfill the prophecy! she prayed. *Then do with me what You will. Punish me for my hatred and thirst for revenge—but give me time to do what I must!*

"Sharon are you ill?" The gentle voice and soft touch of Hezekiah's hand upon her shoulder snapped her back from her netherworld.

"I'll be all right," she told him, shrugging off her malady, pretending both to him and herself that the nightmares left no lasting mark. "Are all our preparations set? Has the hour been choosen?"

"The saya has worked out the details perfectly. In honor of Gamal's victories the Khan has scheduled a feast. Ambassadors from every nation shall be in attendance, watching from the stands while his armies display. Games, Kabul calls them. Games—intended to throw fear into every heart. Kings will cringe when their emissaries speak of what they have seen. There will be no tribute any of them shall not pay. The Khan considers them pawns in his grander schemes, and this event shall more than anything before impress upon them the futility of warring against the Huns. Even Persia will be represented."

At the mention of Samarkand's neighbor and former ally, Sharon's face paled. Persian blood mingled with her own, it was no secret, and the very thought of this mighty empire being forced to grovel at Kabul's feet like an obedient dog sent cold shivers crawling down her neck. "Who," she asked, pulling together her composure, "has been deemed to represent the sanshah?"

Hezekiah's eyes clouded and he sighed a heavy sigh. The name was one that Sharon would readily recognize. "Lucienus," he said simply.

The Panther of the Steppes recoiled. *Lucienus!* "My father's uncle?"

The Hebrew nodded darkly. "I am sorry, Sharon, to be the one to inform you, but, alas, Persia seeks not the same fate that befell us."

"But Lucienus is a friend!" she protested, her voice rising with hostility. "He loved my father, loved

Samarkand! Surely he is not being brought here to grovel before the Khan!"

"Your uncle is a clever politician, child. I know not his motives, nor those of the shah he serves. But that he will be the one to represent Persia there is little doubt. His entourage should be arriving before the week's end."

Sharon took this news personally. Memories of her jovial uncle flashed through her mind, of summers at her father's estate, of Lucienus' frequent but brief stays. Of the dolls and shells he would bring her, laughing as he teased her and bounced her on his knee. "The world changes, Hezekiah," she remarked bitterly.

His nod was somber. "Or so it is said."

"Very well, then." She turned from her friend so as to wipe the welling tear in the corner of her eye without his seeing. "We shall have to make certain my uncle has more to report when he goes home than he might have thought."

"The banquet commences on the last day of *Ramadan*."

"And the games?"

"The morning after. Kabul wants these emissaries to witness his strength with bloated bellies and fogged eyes."

Sharon laughed, the echo reverberating across the stone walls of the chamber. "Then we must do our best to be good hosts as well. Send them scurrying home with more gossip than they bargained for."

Part Two:

SOWING THE HARVEST

1

Kabul screamed. Sudden, unexpected pain stabbed through his eye and brain like a thunderbolt, sending him reeling from wall to wall, caroming over the divan, knocking braziers and marble statues, pottery, and plates from the ornate table. The girl on the bed leaped up startled and screeched in horror. Naked she bounded up, running barefoot over the tiles to escape the frothing madman before her.

The great Khan of the Huns pulled at his hair; he ripped off his eyepatch, exposing the hideous sore, and staggered before he fell to his knees. Hairy fists pounded upon the floor, spittle flew from his lips, blood stained his knuckles where he struck them against the floor.

Two spear-holding guards burst into the room, pale and aghast at the sight. "The fits!" cried one, frozen to his place. "The fits are upon him!"

The whore bolted past them both, flailing her arms wailing as she scampered down the dimly-lit corridor, not caring how many gathering courtesans gaped at her.

"Fetch the physician!" barked the senior of the guards. The second man snapped out of his stupor and went charging in the same direction as the girl in search of the Chinese acupuncturist.

Kabul, meanwhile, had risen to his feet, stumbled across his splendid chamber, grabbing at anything in sight. He yanked a richly-woven Indian tapestry from the wall, tore at it with his hands until the fabric began to shred. Gnashing his teeth, raging like a lunatic while tears streamed out of his good eye and down his face, he heaved himself back and forth, back and forth, ranting, raving, pleading, begging for the terrible pain of his affliction to cease.

From across the verandah Khalkali hurried into the room and watched his father with dismay. The Khan had gripped his hands around his own throat and had started to choke himself.

Khalkali stood motionless while the soldier put his weapon down, went to assist the yowling Kabul, although in truth he had never witnessed such a spasm before and did not know what to do.

"Leave him!" commanded Khalkali.

The guard looked up at the son with fearful eyes. "But, my lord! We must do *something!*"

"I said to leave him!" hissed Khalkali. The guard rose and bowed, stepped away.

The Khan was moaning now, rolling over and over atop the scattered rugs, banging his head mindlessly onto the stone tile, his entire body writhing, chest gasping. For just an instant he saw his son through his misery, saw Khalkali stand and not do anything to help. Kabul's hand struck out but whether to beg assistance or to kill his offspring was uncertain. In his anguish Kabul could not see the small smile of satisfaction his son wore.

"What's happened?" It was Tupol who had come into the chamber next, the deformed youth breathing hard from his run up the stairs from his own chambers on the level below.

"What do you think is happening, eh?" sneered Khalkali contemptuously, eyes darting back and forth between the agonized man on the floor and the stupid brother fixed at the entrance. "He's having another fit."

Tupol glared at his older brother. "And you'd just as soon stand and watch him die?" The youngest son glared across the room.

"Don't worry," offered Khalkali, stifling a yawn. "The Chinaman's been sent for; the Khan's pain will soon be eased."

Tupol digested the scene around him, glaring at last to Khalkali and saying, "Perhaps one day fate shall pluck out one of your own eyes, Brother."

A pervasive loathing always filled him whenever he thought of his uncouth older brother. More than any of the others, Khalkali had taunted him throughout his life. Considering himself the greatest warrior among all the sons, brazen Khalkali had made the suffering and anguish of prisoners a specialty, a torturer whose thirst for human suffering rivaled that of beastly Krishna. But at least, in Tupol's opinion, for Krishna there was an excuse: The dungeons were the only life he had known. Khalkali was different; and ever since the day when the Khan appointed Gamal commander of the Western Armies, the stirring hatreds had been fueled to a furious pitch. And no matter what Kabul's sins, he was still the Khan.

While his brother gaped with amusement at their father's misery, Tupol quickly drew a small flat stick from his pocket, a stick he carried for such an emergency. He hovered over the twitching Khan, dodging his kicks and swinging fists, and when Kabul had all but lost consciousness, he bent down and forcibly thrust the stick between his clenched teeth.

The Khan bit down hard, nearly cracking the brittle wood. Khalkali stood expressionlessly, his eyes intent on the younger man. Tupol soothed Kabul's sweaty brow while the wails diminished to choking sobs.

Suddenly there was the clatter of boots outside; Tupol and his brother looked to the door where the strutting guard returned with the shadowed figure of the awaited Chinaman, Sing-Li. Under his arm, protecting it as if it were the most prized of treasures, the Physician from Cathay clutched his box of instruments. His slanted eyes knowingly surveyed the scene, and disregarding both sons, he commanded the guards to lift the groaning Khan and carry him to the divan.

Kabul, in his delirium, fought them, but he was growing weaker, as always happened during the waning moments of a prolonged fit. His arms hung limply at his side, though his hands still balled into menacing fists. The Chinaman expertly unlocked the snaps of his paneled box, raised the first fine needle between thumb and forefinger. The silver shaft glimmered momentarily. Tupol looked on with fascination as the somber Chinaman twirled it along the instep of the Khan's foot, then poked it deep into flesh, so deep that it came out at the other side of his ankle. A bubble of dark blood formed, quickly coagulating. A second needle punctured Kabul's left wrist, a third penetrated the fleshy fat of his breast. At this Kabul screamed, the needle working its way downward. The Chinaman edged the needle in deeper, pulled away. He drew a long breath, stepped back and waited. The Khan slobbered, froth dripping from the corner of his mouth and onto his beard. Then he sighed deeply and slumped.

Khalkali leaned over and stared at the white face. Kabul did not seem to breathe, and his son's heartbeat quickened. "He's dead!" he rasped to no one in particular.

Tupol froze in his place, eyed the inscrutable Chinaman suspiciously, wondering which brother had perhaps been able to buy the physician off.

The Chinaman smiled. "Not dead, my lords," Sing-Li told them in his Eastern tone. "I have slowed his muscular responses. His heartbeat is weak, but will regain its normal beat in a few minutes."

Tupol shuddered; he'd never liked nor understood this strange man brought to Samarkand from the East. He never could read what thoughts lay behind those black eyes, that peculiar, mysterious smile that seemed to mock them all even while his words spoke respect and his instruments worked wonders.

The physician ordered all lights in the chamber extinguished.

"The Khan needs to sleep," said the Chinaman as he withdrew the needles and placed them carefully back into the tray. "The pain is gone, see for yourselves."

Tupol was surprised to see the hulking figure of his father yawn, then roll over peacefully on the divan. This acupuncture seemed more like witchcraft than medicine, making him more uneasy all the time. It was no secret that his father depended on it like a soldier depends on his sword, or the sailor depends on the stars to navigate. Already, and with some justification, every one of the eight brothers had begun to wonder how much influence this Cathay physician wielded. The two were together for far more hours than any of the sons, and even Tupol had begun to question the Chinaman's motives. Still, there was no doubt that this Chinese sorcery had kept Kabul alive and sane. For the moment at least it served each of the sons equally well.

"The banquet is set to start," said Khalkali before the Chinaman turned to leave. "Our father must be ready for it; to greet our guests, sit among them and let them see—"

A nod of comprehension and a small wave of the hand cut him off. "The mighty and glorious Khan shall be ready at the appointed hour," promised the Chinaman.

"You are certain?" asked Tupol.

The physician slid among shadows, his eyes flickering at the grim silhouettes before him. "You may wake the Khan in three hours. For tonight all pain is gone."

The brothers glanced at each other, and by the time they looked back, the Chinaman was already gone, cowl over his head, shuffling down the tiled, ill-lit corridor.

2

The day was hot, intolerably hot for this time of year. The special emissary from the court of Persia, instructed personally by the divine sanshah, took his place in the stands, sitting among a host of foreigners who babbled away in tongues both barbaric and unfamiliar. He impassively waited for the spectacle to begin.

Slaves fanned the guests with ostrich feathers, shaded their heads with feathered umbrellas from the glare of the morning sun. Beyond the uncomfortable stand—which had been constructed hastily for the hundreds of foreign guests —the fields already teemed with life. Thousands of Kabul's Hun followers and other barbarian allies had gathered, some since the night before, to find a good spot to watch the morning's events. They were loud and crude, wearing furs and heavy robes of wool, ill-dressed for such weather and even more ill-mannered.

Lucienus mopped his brow with a silken handkerchief. His mind scampered back to the night before, and the great feast that this unstoppable Hun had held for the dignitaries. The Samarkand palace had changed much since his last visit here, he realized. Gone were the splendor and opulence of the emir's court, replaced by halls of squalor and filth. Oh, of course he knew about Kabul, realized that a barbarian from the steppes of

Central Asia would not have much to offer in the way of Persian fineries. Yet the city he returned to had proven worse—far worse—than his boldest expectations.

Samarkand had become a vulgar shamble, as was the grand palace itself. Gaudy, tasteless, its courtesans as rude and crude as the lowest beggars, lacking as much in table manners as in education. Lucienus had been appalled. While he was forced to eat with his fingers in the Great Hall, those around him were having a wonderful time. They ate like pigs, stuffing themselves until they vomited. They smelled like undried camel dung, drank heady brew until they passed out or were dragged from the hall for fighting. Before the main course was finished, Lucienus had witnessed three fist fights and one murder. One of Kabul's sons, the gross one who tended the dungeons and whose name he couldn't recall, took insult at a clumsy slave and speared him to death in full view of the guests. It was after supper, though, that the real brawling started. Generals of the Khan laughed and jested while paid gladiators maimed and butchered each other. They fought with starving hounds and a bear—a great ugly beast, captured in the hills and dragged to the palace in chains for this special event. Then the female slaves were raped openly, the Khan's sons partaking in the fornication and bestiality. Lucienus himself, as most honored ambassador, had been offered his choice of the Khan's concubines —and it had been a diplomatic coup for him to gracefully refuse without insulting his hosts. A belching, foul Kabul had laughed boisterously when the fun-loving son named Niko had offered the Persian his personal boy slave to take to bed.

But if one memory of the evening prevailed upon Lucienus, it was fear. Stark, unhidden terror. For now he had seen first-hand the horrors of which his friend Le-Dan had spoken. He'd never believed the constant reports flowing into Persia with escaped slaves and caravaneers. Now, though, he knew them to be true. Yet Kabul had also served his own purpose in letting the foreigners witness all this. In effect he was telling them to beware. That his empire, rightly claimed as the vastest in all the world, could crush like a grape any and all nations that dared oppose him. And slaves from every land too

weak to withstand his onslaughts grimly attested to that
fact. To Lucienus, the message was clear: If Persia valued
its freedom and civilized way of life, it must not lift a
hand against the Khan. It must submit to the raids of the
Huns, pay whatever tribute Kabul demanded, or see its
land ravished in the same manner as Samarkand.

Deafening cheers rose with the first blasts of the horns.
Lucienus snapped from his thoughts, stared across the open
fields to where the Hun horsebacked archers had gathered.
The crowd roared with delight at the sight, and around
him the visitors from so many tribes, Afghani and Kurd,
Mongol and Russian, looked on with breathless anticipation.

Glancing to the side, Lucienus saw Kabul lift himself
from his carved, serpent-armed chair to address the
gathering. As he spoke of his empire, its victories and
future conquests, the ambassador was fascinated by those
who stood closest to the Khan, obviously demonstrating
to all the importance with which they were held. At
Kabul's left was the deformed, stooping son called Tupol,
a physical weakling compared to his brothers. On the right
was the man most whispered about in the gossip Lucienus
had picked up these several days in Samarkand, the
Chinaman, claimed to be the Khan's most trusted aide.
Speculation was rife, particularly among the palace servants
and slaves. Why him? wondered Lucienus. What power
was it that he held?

Directly behind the awning beneath which Kabul stood,
sat the other sons, sullen and murderously silent, out of
favor. Their eyes could not hide their jealousy and hate.
The Persian hid a shudder of revulsion as he tried to
analyze them one by one. The world would suffer a
harsh fate, he was sure, should one of them ever wrest
the throne and gain true power. Maniacal, godless
heathens one and all. Wicked and bloodthirsty, from the
beastly Gamal to the whoring Niko, the drug-addicted
Mufiqua and the killers Krishna and Khalkali. The sight
of surly, hot-tempered Temugin made Lucienus crawl with
anxiety, but none disturbed him more than the desert-
featured, slit-eyed Jamuga. Bastards all, in fact as well as
deed. It made his head reel. He respected and honored
Le-Dan for wishing to return and wipe them from the

earth, while also scorning him and thinking him a fool for even contemplating such a course of action.

Yet they must be stopped. Lucienus knew that now; he could no longer pretend to himself otherwise. If nothing else, only to protect his Persia from their hands. Yet even the sanshah cowered at opposing such a brutish horde. Who then? Who could prevent the awful, unthinkable calamity?

He shook his head, wiped his brow again. It seemed hopeless.

The crowds became silent. Kabul lowered his arms abruptly after his speech, and the trumpets blasted once more. Everyone held breath as the faraway horsemen started to ride toward the flat, hooves causing the ground to rumble.

Upon spotted stallions and geldings came the front line of bare-chested warriors, silver and gold amulets dangling from thick chains around their necks. They rode like Lucienus had never seen men ride horses before, away from the swaying grasses toward the flattened tracks where scarecrowlike targets had been scattered. Each target had been fitted with helmet and armor, like a man; each held in its straw arms both a wooden shield and a curved sword.

A lone cornet blew a long, piercing note. The steeds picked up speed, riders whooping. The riders loosed a torrent of arrows that sailed through the air, slamming into the scarecrows' hearts. The throng gasped at the marksmanship, and the impressed Lucienus leaned forward, chin in his hand, staring while the bold archers reloaded upon the galloping horses and hit the straw enemy again and again, felling them.

Pleased, Kabul glanced at his guests in the stand and laughed, clapping his hands loudly while those around him yelled for more. Only the aloof Tupol and the equally disturbing Chinaman showed no emotion.

More war cries, another volley. Then the line of riders fanned off into different directions while another, even more terrible line, came charging from behind sheltering rows of trees along the crests of distant hills. Like a tempest, like a dreaded hamsin, these warriors came dressed in European-style shirts of mail, intertwined

ringlets of metal, double-coiled and virtually impenetrable
to enemy arrows. The scales of their shirts glimmered
in the bright, swords swung in wheels above their scalp-
locked and shaven heads, as they bore down at breath-
taking speed. Awe-struck, Lucienus cringed as these
weapons sliced off the straw heads, sending helmets flying
and tumbling. Then, as the first line completed the field
and a new line appeared from the trees, the first rank
swung expertly around, doubled back, *thunking* their
swords against the wood of the hapless shields. The latest
line of horsemen rained spears through the air, and like
the arrows, almost every one hit a mark. Within moments
the broad field was littered with shafts, a terrible display
of Hun ability and power.

The ambassador leaned back and gasped. No army
on the face of the earth could stop them!

The first line, with a seemingly single motion, dismounted, swords yet in hand; and while pages ran to
gather the scattering horses, they formed a Romanlike
phalanx, shields held high. The deadly rain of spears from
the next line poured down over them. It was only mock
combat, yet no less harrowing than if this were a fight
to the death. Leaping, screaming riders hurled themselves
from their saddles, knives set between their teeth and
glinting, and fell upon the slowly marching line. Soon
there were hundreds, then a thousand, and still from the
trees and hidden folds in the land came more and more.

The crowd was going wild. Kabul beamed, urging them
on. Lucienus turned to see him. The Khan's eyes were
ablaze, proud, hungry for more. From all around the
cheers rose to deafening pitch; Lucienus wanted to cover
his ears, shut his eyes against this madness. For an instant
his eyes met Kabul's, and he was positive that the Khan
was grinning, laughing at him, scorning both him and his
empire.

The trumpets blared yet another time. The din of battle
ceased; warriors sheathed weapons and jumped for their
saddlehorns. Then, surrounded by swirling clouds of
thick dust, they rode away from the open field, leaving
behind the havoc and litter, disappearing like the ghostly
phantoms the Kazirs were renowned to be.

From far, far away a solitary horseman appeared. A

hulking man dressed in a leather corselet and a helmet with noseguard, he was mounted upon one of the finest Arabian horses that Lucienus had ever seen. At sight of him the throng lost control. Had it not been for the line of guards keeping them behind their ropes, they would have trampled thousands to greet him, given their lives merely to touch his sleeve or kiss his muddied leather boots.

Kabul watched, licking his lips with his tongue. "My son," he crooned, arms spread wide as though to enfold him. "Gamal! Gamal!"

The mass of barbarians picked up the cry. "Gamal!" they chanted, louder and louder. "Gamal! *Gamal!*"

Gamal came prancing, his mare's mane flowing exquisitely in the wind. He paraded on display, raising his twin-edged broadsword high into the air, his other hand gently gripping the reins. This was his moment of triumph, and even Kabul himself had become swept up amid the swelling exultations of the crowd. The heir apparent pulled off his helmet, flung it to the ground. In his splendid armor, fiery crimson beard, he seemed the reincarnation of Kabul himself some thirty years before. Hero. Conqueror. Leader of men and nations. Scourge of the Huns.

"Gamal! Gamal!" sang the multitudes with growing urgency.

Shrewdly this bold, cunning son scanned the faces of his brothers, outwardly hailing them in greeting, but inwardly taunting them, demonstrating for once and for all that he and none other would gain the coveted throne when Kabul's days were at an end.

Stoic and grim, save for the false hail of bragging Niko, they sat mute.

Already Gamal was making plans. His agents for months had been in the palace, bending Kabul's mind against his brothers and in his favor, seeing to it that when he arrived, he would be ushered inside the gates by thousands of his faithful followers. He would see to his brothers—relegate them one by one to the farthest-flung outposts of his empire, let them rot in their lonely garrisons, separated, weary, forced to protect his frontiers while Samarkand bowed at his feet. Glorious day! thought Gamal. Nothing could stop him now! He was invincible!

He dug his boot into the mare's flank, urged the horse on. The Arabian steed broke into a trot, then a gallop, kicking up dirt along the worn tracks where the battalions of his finest troops had paraded. He tightened the grip on his ornate sword, taken from the corpse of a Christian Turk, set his eyes upon the last standing scarecrow, making to slice off its head with a single stroke. The heathen throng urged him on, continuing to shout his name. Gamal laughed lustily, picturing the composite faces of his siblings in the straw features of the scarecrow. He sang Kabul's name on his lips, seesawing the reins, simultaneously shifting his weight in the saddle as he crouched and bore down for the kill.

The onlookers oohed and ahhed at his expertise, holding their breath as the razor-honed blade whistled through the air like a lightning strike, cleaving off the target's head, sending it tumbling down the track. The crowd went wild; Gamal sat up straighter, laughed, waved the victory sign. His thoroughbred steed reared back on her hind legs, whinnied with her magnificent mane freely flowing. Against the backdrop of blue sky and gentle grass both rider and horse posed statuelike before the teeming throngs lifting their voices in excitement.

Then suddenly, without explanation, the horse began to snort and kick. Gamal pressed forward, tried to soothe her, wondering if perhaps she'd been stung by a hornet or caught a sharp pebble in her hoof. The Arabian mare shook to break free of its rider, then bolted. Kabul jumped out of his seat, hands clutching at the thin beam railing. The crowd hushed as the horse raced off the track, watching in confusion, unsure whether this was part of the exhibition or not.

Gamal tossed his sword to the ground, took firm control of the reins with both hands, drawing them in. The mare screeched, scattered mounds of dust as she fought against him, legs wildly lashing. The hero son of Kabul was a master of horses, everyone knew; yet somehow he had lost control. The balking beast ran out onto the flat while Gamal leaned forward, giving free play to the horse's hind legs, knowingly creating less wind resistance.

Again the animal reared, and from the pavilion Kabul could see the crazed look in its eyes. Gamal tried to rein in again; something gave, no one seemed certain what. The saddle's cinch snapped, straps broke free and flapped. The crowd gasped as mighty Gamal helplessly slid from the saddle, his hand lurching for the pommel. His bulky frame dipped from sight, the mare staggered with the weight, then bolted again. Gamal's hands and arms flailed in the air, his torso tumbling to the earth. But his foot caught in the stirrup and he was unable to free himself. Women screamed in horror, men jumped up and gaped. The mare lurched ahead; Gamal was thrown back and dragged.

The back of his head hit the hardened soil like a leaden weight, bouncing three times against rock. He was savagely pummeled while the mailed vest tore from his back and his flesh ripped over the gravelly track. There was a growing tumult among the citizens. Their hero was being pulled like a plow, roughly and savagely. The mare was now frothing at the mouth and dashing madly in circles in an uncontrollable rage. Pages came running, vainly trying to stop the insane horse, to run her down or kill her before she killed Gamal. In a frenzy the mare saw them and only picked up more speed.

Gamal was shrieking, his cries piercing the still air horribly. His face was bloodied, his skull cracked open at the top, oozing a colorless humor. Teeth flew from his mouth; his jaw snapped like a walnut. His eyelids were torn from his face and his blood spilled onto the dirt.

Riders were now closing in on the Arabian steed—loyal troops who had served their beloved general faithfully during his long and difficult campaigns. They hurled lariats at the wheezing mare, blocked her advance, circled back and cut her off. Yet still the crazed animal remained free, dragging Gamal as though he were a saddlebag.

"Shoot the beast!" cried outraged and anguished Kabul, running from his shaded place and reaching the edge of the target field. Guests and dignitaries watched lines of expert horsemen scatter the frightened throngs as they headed for the field. Everywhere was pandemonium; the mare still ran feverishly.

Arrows came tearing across the sky; the mare dodged, jumped a hurdle, bared her teeth and snorted demoniacally.

Other horses reared up in fear of her, their riders at a loss
to steady them and press them forward. Closer and closer
she came to the stands, Lucienus and those around him
looking on in abject terror. Gamal was pulled roughly
through muck and grass, his body smashing against
boulders and stumps, his bones cracking. Archers aimed,
shot, hit the demented animal time and time again, shafts
by the score piercing her belly and throat. The mare lifted
from the ground in pain, screaming awful screams, trying
to rear, to bolt. Then in front of the shaded stand her legs
gave way; she fell shudderingly in a heap and gasped her
last breaths.

Amid the surge of pages and aides women and children
ran crying across the field, past the pressing phalanx of
palace guards trying to restore order. From behind the
barriers came the throngs, grouping around the slain
horse and its rider, recoiling at what they saw. Even the
stoutest soldiers among them were sickened and turned
away, pale and ill. Someone rolled Gamal onto his back.
Black, gaping holes were where once his eyes had been.
His features were unrecognizable. Purpled and flattened
flesh was where his nose had jutted. His crushed skull still
bled profusely, and his crimson cavern of a mouth
continued to ooze dark bile. It was hideous, monstrous,
vile. Kabul winced at the sight, frozen in his tracks, his
head spinning with horror. Before his people, before the
invited guests and foreign dignitaries, he'd been shamed,
made a fool of.

Tupol took charge of the situation. He called for a
litter, ordered the crowds dispersed. Strong-stomached
aides came hurrying; they threw a blanket over the limp
corpse, quickly carried him from the scene.

Gamal's brothers gathered, speechless, shocked. The
Khan put his hands to his face and growled like an animal.
When he took them away, his good eye glared malevolently
at his offspring. All the faces remained blank.

"Which of you," he hissed, "has done this thing?" He
was close to ordering all their deaths at once, right here.
"Well? Who?" Spittle flew from the side of his mouth.
Then he sneered, smiled cruelly at them all. "Or were you
in this together, eh? Planning behind my back for this

opportune moment." He spat in their faces. "Scum!"
Steel glinted as his blade rose halfway from its scabbard.

"Sire, no!" It was Tupol who stopped him.

The Khan heaved a sigh, peered murderously at them
one at a time. "You think you've won, don't you? You
think that with Gamal out of the way, your ascension
shall be easy. . . ."

Not a single one of the six sons met his gaze; they
shifted their eyes toward the ground, the bloodstained,
damp ground where their eldest brother had lain in death.
There was no sorrow for Gamal; but had Kabul been as
observant as Tupol, he would have seen the fear. For now
each, although not willing to protest innocence, began to
wonder just who among them had been bold enough to
remove Gamal. All they did know for certain was that the
hour of murder among them had begun—and once unleashed, it could not be stopped.

Kabul let a small smile work at the edges of his mouth,
and with the Chinaman and Tupol flanking him, started
to walk away, following the litter with Gamal's remains.
Tonight the funeral pyre would burn brightly over
Samarkand. Tomorrow the intrigues would begin anew.

Lucienus, still in a daze from the occurrence, wandered
listlessly from his honored place among the stands, unable
to give comfort to any of the wailing women being led
away from the pavilion. From the corner of his vision he
caught sight of Kabul, the Khan seeming now far older
and more wearied than he had an hour before. All around,
equally disturbed and perplexed, the other invited guests
milled listlessly. Like him, they had come to witness the
spectacle of this glorious occasion—and like him they had
seen far more of a spectacle than they ever dreamed.

So, he muttered to himself as he surveyed the scene,
*it seems there are more cracks in this Hun empire than we
realized.* But which of the Khan's sons had felt powerful
enough to so openly destroy his brother, he was at a loss
to guess. Perhaps, as Kabul charged, they had done it
together. Or maybe not. Far off the sides of the pavilion
he caught sight of a few desert-garbed figures moving
away from the crowd. Two men, one woman. The woman
had glanced his way, Lucienus was positive. Their eyes

had briefly met as she turned to her companions and fled among the throng.

Strange, mused the ambassador from Persia, running a finger gently at the side of his jowls. *Could it be that Gamal's death was not the doing of his brothers at all?*

3

Temugin sat with his head bowed, his hands nervously tapping together between his folded legs. The room was brightly lit, charcoal gaily burning in every brazier, candles gleaming pale-yellow flames atop the table and mantle. The curtains were drawn tightly, the windows shuttered and double bolted. A trusted sentry stood solitary duty outside the spacious apartment, immobile as a statue, one white-knuckled, hirsute hand firmly clutched about the hilt of his sword.

The son of Kabul fidgeted, and although the evening was chilly, Temugin was sweating. He refilled his chalice, cursing beneath his breath. *Trust no one. No one.* That had been the advice of the aged seer, Hezekiah, the man who had so correctly predicted Gamal's return—as well as the imminent danger. Temugin was now taking that advice. After today, after what he had witnessed, he could rely only upon himself. Upon his own wits. And rightly so, for even Kabul had realized that once the murders began, there was no stopping them.

The crusted, mangled old man had proven his weight in gold, as able in his predictions as he was demented. Was it not Hezekiah who had accurately forecast Gamal's return to Samarkand? And had he not also warned Temugin of the personal danger lurking? Hezekiah was a treasure to him now, guarded and carefully kept away from the treacheries of the palace for Temugin's private use.

Trust no one. . . . Trust no one. . . .

Wise advice. Trust no one at all, Temugin had decided. Except for the grizzled soothsayer himself, of course. His need for the old man was greater than ever: to read his stars, keep him safe, help him secure the throne against his siblings. When at last the empire was his, the old fool would be greatly rewarded for his deeds. There would be hell in Samarkand. Yes, living hell upon the earth—once Temugin was named King of the Huns.

In an opposite wing of the palace, in chambers set above the famous hanging gardens, Mufiqua sat with his water pipe, sucking opium, dreaming of days to come, day of grandeur and majesty. The drug-inspired visions opened new worlds for him, new vistas. He saw himself as ruler of the whole world, the stunning, elusive dancing girl, Sharon beside him. He could see her, almost touch her, smell her perfume, hear her laugh and the jangling of her bracelets as she twirled. The memory of what had happened that night in Karim's house had been blurred by Zadek. Mufiqua now only recalled the softness of her flesh, the sensual taunting of her swaying. All the rest was forgotten.

Mufiqua lay back, head propped on silk pillows. His misted eyes followed the dancing flame of the brazier, and once again he saw Sharon, vividly hearing her calling to him, beckoning him to join her forever in a world of purple clouds and glittering stars. Somewhere, somewhere it existed. Not just in his brain, but in reality. Mufiqua smiled in his semiconscious state. The opium Amar had brought him this day had been far superior to any he had ever sampled before. It sent him soaring like a falcon across the sky, into the sun itself. He was a winged angel; no, more than that—he was a god. Nothing could harm him; he was invulnerable, protected by his stars and his birthright.

He thought of Gamal, now a heap of ashes. He could still make out the rising smoke from the ebbing flames of the pyre as his eyes focused past the verandah and across the city. He chuckled to himself. *Gamal was a fool. They're all fools, all of them. Let them play their games, let them maim and kill each other. All the better for me. I am invincible! Mufiqua, the god!* Let any who denied this fact dare to tell him openly. He would choke the life out of them, yes, even that ox, Krishna. With the opium for support, even the dreaded chancellor of the dungeons would be no match. Mufiqua would have him spread-eagle before all his brothers, watch him squirm and beg while a hundred boys buggered him. Enjoy his pain and anguish as the executioner's stake impaled him—slowly. It was going to be a glorious reign when Mufiqua became Khan. Everything he'd ever lusted would at last be his. Yes, even the girl, the mysterious dancing girl, whose smell and feel had never left him. He and she would spend their nights together in this very chamber overlooking the gardens, supplied endlessly by thoughtful Amar, lost in their dreams and visions and fantasies. Let someone else lead the armies to victory. Yes, there would be others to do such dirty work during the glorious reign of Mufiqua. Whom would he keep alive? Who would lead his hordes against Persia and the Turks? He giggled when he thought of Niko. Niko, of course! Let the lover of life and ten thousand women win his battles for him! Or better yet, Tupol! His laughter became a demented howl; he pictured the deformed, limping youth being fitted for battle armor and helped onto his horse. He broke into hysterics at the very notion of Tupol holding a sword and charging wildly among the endless legions of the dung-eating sanshah.

Mufiqua pulled the pipe from his mouth, burped, watched the hazy blue-tinted smoke rise to the stone ceiling. There were images in the mist as well, vague images of terrible battles won under his name, new glories and empires, slaves by the hundreds of thousands, an endless multitude to grovel at his feet, die for him, fornicate with their own mothers for him. It was going to be good, his reign. It was going to be wonderful. History would never forget . . . never forget . . . never forget . . .

He fell over in a stupor, the hazy smoke wisping from the window. He could not hear the sudden and raucous laughter that seeped inside his rooms from the apartments opposite the courtyard.

Niko stretched back luxuriously across the feathered mattress, agreeably allowing the whore to wipe clean his gleaming, naked body with a handcloth dampened with honeyed wine. The ebony-skinned girl giggled girlishly; Niko roared, his flaccid penis beginning to swell again only minutes after his climax. At the foot of the bed a second whore widened her eyes at the sight.

Niko glared at her straight-faced for a moment, then laughed so hard he had to hold his sides. The prostitutes shared his mirth, reaching out and tickling him, probing their fingers up and along his sensitive parts. Niko sat up, held the arms of the black-skinned whore, stared with growing lust at the other. The girl, although well trained in pleasing and pleasure, was unable to stop her flush. Niko noted her firm exposed breasts, like ripe melons, nipples dark and hard. Her tousled hair fell loosely across soft shoulders, rustling slightly with every breath. "Come here," commanded Niko, voice thick and husky. The girl smiled a knowing smile, crawled onto the bed as her companion blew out the candle. And there, in the dark, the high-living son of Kabul took his pleasure, urgency heightened to fevered pitch as the flesh of both surrounded him, kissing, making love to him slowly.

The low and lonely wail of a horn broke through the night. "What was that?" rasped the dark-skinned beauty.

The second and younger whore lifted her face from Niko's belly and stared to the window. A strong breeze was pushing aside the flimsy curtains, and as they swayed, she glimpsed the black night sky, moonless and starless, a dull-orange glow spreading across the horizon.

The horn sounded again, this time even more dismal and forlorn. Niko stared at the funeral pyre, for the first time thinking of the day's events, which had culminated so abruptly and strangely. "It's nothing," he whispered in the still, running his fingers through the hair on his chest and feeling the sticky sweat. "Just the dying flames of my brother's funeral."

"And the trumpet?" questioned the ebony woman, naked save for the necklace and bracelets made of seashells she wore.

Niko listened hard, perplexed. In truth he did not know what the trumpet signified. Sloughing it off, he said, "My father must have ordered his cornet to sound the demise of the pyre," he told them, guessing. The shrill sound had unnerved him, and he gruffly pushed both women aside, stepped through the shadows and filled to the brim his golden goblet. Studded jade and turquoise stones encrusted at the base glittered in the pale-orange glow. Niko walked boldly to the verandah, slid open the door and stepped out into the night. The lights of the city burned around him, a thousand lightless windows suddenly grew bright both across the solemn palace and below in the quiet, dusty streets of the old quarters of Samarkand. Niko grew uneasy.

A hand on his shoulder made him jump; he turned to see the melon-breasted girl hanging onto him, concern in her eyes. "Please, my lord," she stammered, "come back inside."

He nodded, tossing the chalice to the tiles, sliding the door shut, and then the curtains as well. He got back on the bed and grinned, slapping the ebony whore on the rump with an open hand. "Never mind those fools," he said, arms opened wide to enfold them both. "Whatever it is, it's unimportant."

One of the women lowered her gaze. "The city mourns, my lord. The Lord Gamal was a great man, they say. A true hero of the Huns and all peoples who serve them." Unspoken was the phrase: And he was your brother.

Niko scratched his belly, rolled over on his back, sighing while the women massaged his flesh, worked their fingers in and out of the knotted muscles. It was strange, he mused, that while he gained so much pleasure among females, his other brothers would at this very moment be worry-filled and sullen, peeking nervously to see what lurked behind shadows, afraid of unfamiliar footsteps. Jamuga would brood, Krishna would take out his frustrations on some poor hapless soul festering in the labyrinth of dungeons.

Halfwits, Niko thought. Spending their time in gloom when there were the soft arms of women to hold them, sweet wetness to cleanse themselves in. *Let them, then. Let them wallow in their miseries, plot their plots and scheme their schemes. Let them while away their time in futile and stupid dreams, dreams that are never going to come true.*

Then Niko turned over again, reached for the ebony-skinned lovely and moaned softly as his body blended with hers.

There was a constant *drip drip* flowing from the cold, damp walls. Khalkali felt a shiver and tightened his flowing cape around him. He walked unarmed down the steps, returning the salute of the officer on duty at the low-ceilinged black gate, then stood aside while the man fumbled with his keys, unlocked the lock, and swung the iron wide for the lord to pass. A single lantern hung from davits, swaying gently, casting shadows along the length of the corridor. The putrid smell of old urine and feces swept unwelcomely into Khalkali's nostrils. He hated these dungeons. Loathed them about as much as he loathed the chancellor who governed over them. Still, this little sojourn was not for pleasure.

Ever downward the tunnel spiraled, deeper into the palace bowels. Wondering how even a man such as Krishna could stand it down here, he reached the end, turned left and started another march along yet another endless corridor. There were all manner of insects crawling and darting among the recesses of the slimy stone walls. Roaches, spiders, tiny lizards, mice, an occasional rat. It was dark, dank and nauseous. This place wasn't meant for pigs, he assured himself. No wonder brother Krishna was the way he was. Too much time down here would make any man a raving lunatic. Krishna, if what Khalkali saw of him was to be believed, did not have far to go to reach that status. One day they'd lock him up and toss away the key, just as they had done five years before when their eldest brother, Osklath, had returned home a babbling idiot from his mysterious confrontation with the Kazirs.

It seemed like hours before he reached the subterranean quarters of the dungeon's chancellor. Two grim and filthy guards snapped to attention, and Khalkali passed them without a second glance. He lowered his head, stepped across the arched threshold of the keeper's quarters, straining his eyes in the gloomy light. Krishna sat leaning back in an oversize chair of rotting wood, his enormous legs and unbooted feet on an oaken table. In this light and setting, the chancellor seemed more bear than man, more demon than human being. Grossly large, his muscles bulged in sinewy arms, his chest swelled to bursting in his soiled tunic. Krishna regarded his visitor from a pair of sunken, keen eyes. Icy eyes, the eyes of a man who has seen much suffering and pain, all gladly inflicted.

Khalkali chewed at his lower lip, glanced around the squalid room. It was little larger than one of the keeper's cells, he noted. Certainly almost as filthy and as smelly. Krishna was not forced to spend his days and nights down here like this; indeed, there was a fair, spacious apartment always ready for him above. But the chancellor *preferred* it here.

Krishna belched; he wiped his hand across his bearded mouth, gestured without speaking for his brother to sit. A scarred, lice-infested chair rested opposite the table. Khalkali looked at it and shook his head. "I'll stand," he said.

Krishna shrugged. "As you like. You can stick your head in the cesspools, too, if it pleases you."

Khalkali's brows arched disdainfully. "I did not come to fight," he said.

"Oh? Then what? What brings you here to my domain?" He smiled thinly. "It *is* my domain down here, you know. I could do with you anything I like. Torture you, kill you, feed you to any number of maniacs. You'd never be missed, you know. My guards swear allegiance only to me. They do what I tell them—quickly and silently." He swung his feet off the table and turned to face Khalkali evenly. "Nothing can touch me down here, Brother. Not the Khan, not even you. Now speak your business and be off. I find you repulsive."

The fourth son of Kabul swallowed both anger and pride. There was no love lost between the two, never had been. Still, Khalkali had been bright enough to realize that Krishna was not the number-one enemy; he only hoped that the chancellor would realize the same about him. It was important to them both

Khalkali cleared his throat, said, "With Gamal's assassination—"

Krishna roared with mirth, his booming voice echoing.

Some of the insane prisoners picked up the laugh and started to howl themselves, although they had no idea why. Khalkali grimaced.

"You think it was assassination, eh, Brother? You think that our mindless, spineless Gamal could have so easily been tricked? You're a bigger moron than our father."

Fuming, Khalkali managed to control his voice. "It was no mere accident, no quirk of fate, if that's what you're thinking." He leaned his arms over the table, hands flat against the wood, his face too close to Krishna's for comfort. "I tell you without question that Gamal was murdered."

"Prove it."

"The straps, dear brother. The saddle straps were cut—by a knife."

"And the horse?" Krishna chuckled at the thought of the fine Arabian mare of which Gamal had been so fond, enjoying the irony of his beloved horse's killing him.

"I believe that the mare had been drugged," went on Khalkali. "Some slow-acting agent. I don't know how it was accomplished—but I intend to find out. Oh, Gamal's murder was clever all right. Very clever indeed; a masterful stroke. Clean—no blood showing on anyone's hands. In fact, I think we should compliment whoever devised the plan."

Krishna wiped his neck with a louse-ridden kerchief, puffed his pockmarked cheeks and blew out a stream of dank air. "You may be right," he conceded. "But what of it, eh? What care I for what goes on in the palace, eh? Like I said, for all I care, you can all stew each other."

"We probably will," replied Khalkali, demonstrating dark humor.

"Then get to the point, man. Why are you here now? What do you want of me?"

Bathed in red shadows, Khalkali's eyes scanned the room, focused on the slovenly sentry standing duty outside.

"You needn't fret," derided Krishna dryly. "Down here there is little to hide; my men were given their posts because even the Khan considered them the dregs of our army. Cutthroats and murderers all!" He paused, peering intently at the uncomfortable Khalkali. "Should make you feel right at home, no? In any case, nothing they hear shall pass from these dungeons. I assure you."

Khalkali shifted his weight, suddenly feeling itchy all over. Lice and ticks, vermin of every nature, were probably eating through his garments and boots, working their way into his flesh and burrowing beneath his body hair. He'd have to take a good, hot bath when he returned to his apartment, he knew. Spend at least an hour scrubbing to wipe away the stink.

"I am positive of only two things," he told Krishna, playing his hand carefully.

"Yes? What's that?"

"That I was not behind the murder of our brother—and neither were you."

Krishna laughed delightedly, banging his fist on the table. "Well said, dear Brother! Tell me, though, what makes you so certain that I am not the one, eh? How do you know that my own spies didn't get at poor Gamal's horse, feed it the poison, slice into the saddle straps just enough, so that they'd tear at the right moment?"

With a laugh of his own, his eyes grimly dancing, Khalkali said, "Gamal's death was too simple, too quick. Had your hand been in it, the poor bugger'd still be suffering, no doubt right here, while your hot knife carved his flesh off."

"You have little imagination, Brother," answered Krishna spryly, beginning to enjoy the banter with his rival. He half-rose from his seat. "Had *I* been the one . . ." His smile was secretive. "Well, never mind. There are better, more productive ways to deal with an enemy. He wouldn't even scream. . . ."

Khalkali looked away with a shudder, not for a minute doubting that a devious death was in Krishna's mind.

"Still," went on the chancellor thoughtfully, "how am I to be certain it wasn't you, eh?"

"Merely from the fact that I am here."

Krishna resumed his place, again putting his feet on the table, pushing away a buzzing fly with his big toe. "Perhaps, Brother. But even if I admit as much, so what? The point, man! Come to the point! Why *are* you here? What do you want?"

"An alliance." It was simply but dramatically spoken. Krishna looked at his brother cautiously, doubtfully, yet reading a frank and honest openness in the killer's eyes. Without question Khalkali would slaughter him the moment opportunity presented itself; he would do no less in return. That much, though, was accepted among all the brothers. No, he rationalized, Khalkali was here because he was worried—frightened.

"What sort of an alliance?" he asked.

"We each need to guard each other's flank. We are not fools, Brother; we need what each has to offer. I shall offer you all the protection that I can, while you shall do the same for me."

Krishna frowned. "And our brothers?"

"To hell with our brothers!" barked Khalkali. "Don't you see? They may already be conspiring among themselves, seeking allies, breaking former agreements. I'll be open with you, Krishna; I have no idea whatsoever who was behind Gamal's assassination—but I'll say this: I wouldn't turn my back for a single second on any of them!"

"Including myself, no doubt."

At that, Khalkali reached inside the folds of his garments and whipped out a small, poison-tipped dagger. Krishna's eyes opened wider as his brother slammed the blade into the table, steel wobbling with the blow. Then he turned, facing the doorway, leaving the blade only inches from his brother's grasp. "Go on," he hissed. "Kill me now if you want, Brother. Do it! You'll never have another chance, I promise you that." He waited, heart pounding.

Krishna scooped up the dagger, toyed with it, admiring the craftsmanship, the exquisite handiwork of Damascus. For a time he actually did contemplate ramming the poisoned steel through his brother's shoulder blades. Then, on a whim, he shanked it against the wall. The blade clattered, and fell to the floor. Krishna spat in its direction.

Khalkali turned slowly back, framed by encroaching shadows. "Then we have a bargain?"

Krishna nodded. "An arrangement, Brother. An arrangement against the others . . ."

"And our father as well."

Krishna stopped picking his teeth. "You think the Khan may have been behind Gamal's death?"

"Perhaps; I exclude nothing. Remember, it was Gamal whom the crowds adored, not he. Gamal that they hailed as a savior. Surely Kabul hated his eldest bastard as much as he does the rest?"

The chancellor of the dungeons growled low under his foul breath. For all its stink, the world below the palace smelled purer than the world above it. All of Samarkand, the palace no exception, swarmed with traitors and spies —agents of the Khan set to inform on the brothers; agents of the brothers set against each other and the Khan; spies serving Persia; spies serving the Turks; holy men sworn to the allegiance of the Kazirs. An interlocking web of intrigue and double dealing. No, give him the dungeons. Throw him among the wretched, abused, crazed prisoners shackled to the dung-smeared walls. At least *they* were men of honor.

Khalkali held out his hand. Krishna studied him, then took the hand in a solid grasp. Khalkali would serve his purpose well for now, he knew. Be his eyes and ears above ground. Later, when matters had calmed, when the courses of action were clearer, he would wrest back that poisoned dagger from his brother—and Khalkali would rue this moment as he burned in eternal hell alongside the rest.

4

Carolyn, the saya, studied the handful of novices brought this morning to her quarters by Amar's slaver. There were five young women, ranging in age from fifteen to eighteen. Each was beautiful, each had unblemished, perfect skin, stirred by the sun to a soft gold. It was her duty as overseer of the whores to instruct them, take charge of their training. It would be several weeks before even the best of the lot were put on display before Kabul and his sons. As virgins, the women were considered jewels among the rest. From what she had learned in her month in this exalted appointment, often several of the brothers would be at each other's throats to claim first rights over the best.

"That one needs some weight," Carolyn sternly husked to the effeminate eunuch at her side, a man she'd chosen to be her first-ranking aide because of his obvious dull wits.

The eunuch bowed, approached the frightened girl. He took her arm, pinching the flesh, frowning broadly. The girl shrank from his touch. "Careful, idiot!" barked Carolyn. "Do you want to bruise her? Damage Amar's reputation when he brings her before the Khan?"

Browbeaten, the eunuch stepped back. Carolyn marched before the girls, touching the hair of one, fixing the shoulder fastening of another's tunic. At the end of the line she paused, gazing into the eyes of the last novice. Brilliant sunlight poured into the spacious hall from the balconies, beaming among the leaves of hanging plants, settling gently across the girl's soft features. Carolyn indicated for the novice to hold out her hand; it was delicate and smooth, the fingers long and graceful, the fingernails well manicured. Coal-black hair was neatly pinned above her head, although a few locks fell in front of her wide-set, luminous eyes. It was plain that the girl was frightened, yet throughout this ordeal she managed to keep her poise, holding her head high but not arrogantly so, her shoulders set straight. Her young, firm breasts pushed outward against the thin fabric of her loose-fitting dress.

"Where are you from?" questioned the saya.

"The hills, my lady. A poor tribe, my lady. . . ."

"A slave?"

"No, my lady. Free. Sold by my parents to feed my brothers, my lady. . . ."

Carolyn felt a pang of sorrow for her, knowing full well the dire conditions imposed upon the gentle hillfolk by Kabul's tax collectors. She was not the first to be thrown out into the world like this, nor would she be the last. "What is your name?" she asked.

"Jasmine, my lady."

This could be the one I've been looking for, thought Carolyn, careful not to let any of the passing servants note her unusual interest. "Tell me, Jasmine, do you know why you're here?"

The girl tensed; Carolyn could tell that she was fighting back the need to cry. "Yes, my lady. To serve the court, my lady."

"Obey commands and you will find this to be a rewarding life," Carolyn told her.

The girl sniffed. "I know, my lady. I am told that I am honored to be among those chosen to serve."

"But it was not your will?" Many others would sell themselves gladly to have this opportunity, to be taken away from a life of backbreaking drudgery. At best, a girl born of the hills would become an old woman by the age of thirty, bent from years in the fields, wrinkled and withered.

"No, my lady," whispered Jasmine with both respect for the overseer and regret for her lost life. "It was not my will. But when the slavers came to my village, I was singled out by a man called Karim . . ." Carolyn flinched. *Karim!* There was no longer a question but that Jasmine was sent to her for a special purpose. "Go on," said Carolyn.

"My parents had no choice but to sell me, my lady. You see, times have been hard on us. I have five small brothers, and three sisters." The girl sighed; it was obviously painful for her to talk about it.

Carolyn stepped away, hands on her hips, and addressed them in the same manner that Castus, her predecessor, might have. "All of you here today should fall to your knees and bless your stars for your good fortune. Only one slavegirl in twenty is selected for the palace concubines. And of that twenty perhaps a third remain. You here are to be taught; schooled well in the pleasures of the night; trained to give ultimate pleasure to the Khan and members of his royal household. We take no harlots off the street here. Your studies will be severe—sometimes even painful for you. But in return you are offered a life of every luxury our blessed Khan can bestow. You shall be treated as princesses, kept away from the prying eyes of common men, given as a vessel of pleasure to delight and fulfill the fancies of Samarkand's noblest rulers." Carolyn stopped, started to pace back and forth. "You are not whores! Erase that word from your minds! You are, once accepted into service with the hundred and fifty others, no less than concubines of our generous leader, the fearless Kabul. Do you understand?"

The virgins nodded, bowing their heads.

Carolyn smiled. "Good." Then, almost parenthetically, she added, "You are at all times forbidden to leave these quarters. Let me stress the point." And here she purposely kept her gaze on Jasmine. "Any girl caught trying either to escape the palace or enter another chamber without my personal permission, shall be whipped mercilessly. And a scarred back means withdrawal of all privileges. Then, novices, you will be turned over to the barracks—to serve as field whores for our commanders and their troops. Let me assure you all that within a year of such work your supple bodies will have dried like prunes, useless to any man."

The young women shuddered; Jasmine glanced away from the overseer toward the foolish, effeminate eunuch. A small bullwhip coiled from the strap of his belt, and he seemed not at all to mind using it if the overseer so ordered.

Carolyn watched the novices with satisfaction. The girls were frightened of the eunuch—as they should be—and she knew there would be no trouble with this batch.

She let the somber mood linger a moment or two longer, then abruptly said, "Are there any questions?"

In unison, they replied as taught, "No, Mistress."

Carolyn smiled. "Very well, then. You shall all be taken to your new quarters and given—"

Raucous laughter turned every head. From the end of the hall, where several drooping cypress trees intruded across the opened verandah, a swarthy figure pushed aside the armed guards that stood in his way and boldly strode inside the forbidden quarter. In a quandary, the sentries reached for their weapons, wary of stopping him.

Mufiqua carelessly padded around the sunken fountain and worked his way closer to the gathering.

The novices ashamedly fastened their veils and shielded their eyes. From the nearby heated pools and Chinese screens came the sheltered giggles of several other concubines, whose attention had been caught by the intrusion. The eunuch's face grew stern; he glanced to the overseer, waiting to see what she would command. Son of Kabul or no, this place was expressly forbidden to any man except during hours especially set aside. The Khan had set the rule himself—no one could blame either him or the overseer for dealing with this atrocity severely.

Carolyn stepped in front of the women, blocking Mufiqua's way. The drugged, impudent son glared at her through fogged eyes, lifted his arm as if to strike. A few gasps rose from the novices. The overseer, though, held her ground firmly, her figure framed by streams of sunlight pouring down from the ceiling-high narrow windows. Although Mufiqua was about to slap her viciously, Carolyn made no move either to protect herself or to reach for the gem-encrusted curved knife strapped to her maroon leather belt. Instead, she faced him squarely, her eyes ablaze in the manner of every angered Kazir woman. Mufiqua's hand lifted higher, slowed, then trembled. He took a single step backward, nearly knocking into a huge clay flowerpot in his stupor, and Carolyn inwardly smiled. She'd won this little match of wits.

With a polite but reserved lowering of the head, turning her palms forward before him, she said calmly, "Your presence is unwelcome, my lord Mufiqua. Surely you meant no disrespect to your father, but I must ask you to leave and return at the appointed hour. The Khan would be most displeased if—"

"The Khan, *the Khan!*" Mufiqua sputtered, beginning to totter. He was seeing double now, two enraged overseers before him, and twice as many novices as there had been only seconds before. "What care I for the stupid rules my father imposes!"

The eunuch became livid at the outburst; he would have gladly strangled the slobbering son had it been in his authority. The girls became frightened, would have fled had not Carolyn warned them to stay put. Then to Mufiqua: "Perhaps you would allow me to find you a place to rest. By evening I shall present to you the loveliest woman in my charge." She reached out to take hold of his arm, partly to steady his balance, partly to gently urge him away before further damage was done. Mufiqua pulled away roughly, pushing her with force. Carolyn fell back. Mufiqua broke into hysterical laughter at the sight.

Blood was pounding inside his head, his dreams of purple clouds and heavenly visions stirred in front of his twitching face. "Whore!" he barked. "Do you know who I am? How dare you touch my person? *Slut!*"

Carolyn held down her seething anger, forced to remind herself this was neither the Steppes nor the Stronghold. Here she had a role to play, and she must not let her own grievances take command, not now, not while she was so close. . . . "Forgive me, Lord Mufiqua. . . . Noble son of the mighty Khan, glorious—"

A distant rumble of thunder exploded, a thunderstorm rapidly falling over the city. Mufiqua raptly turned toward the verandah to peer at the darkening sky. He chuckled to himself, raised out his arms and called loudly, "I hear you, O Father. Send me your wrath against this *woman* who knows not who I am!"

Carolyn shared a quick glance with Jasmine. Mufiqua's mind was clearly unbalanced, but until this moment no one had considered him totally deranged.

The son of Kabul faced the overseer again. "Do you hear? Do you hear how you've disturbed my father? Bitch of a whoring goat!"

Lightning struck, the horizon swirling with threatening grays and blacks. The guards, eunuch, and novices stared frozen and wide-eyed at the ranting lord. Even the concubines hidden behind the screens hushed.

"Your . . . father, my lord?" said Carolyn.

Mufiqua laughed. "Now do you know who I am, eh? *Now* do you know?"

Swallowing, feeling her mouth turn suddenly dry, Carolyn replied, "You have become a god."

The ground shook with closer, violent claps of thunder; overhead, closed in a swell of dismal, churning clouds.

Mufiqua held out an arm, pointed directly at Jasmine. "That one!" he rasped. "Bring her to my rooms!"

The girl was aghast; with pleading, frightened eyes she implored the overseer to have mercy, not to heed his command.

"But, my lord," said Carolyn, deftly blocking his view of her, "she is untrained! A novice. Surely you would prefer a woman of more experience, one who can fulfill your every thirst, even the thirst of a living god. . . ."

Mufiqua's eyes narrowed; he stared at Jasmine, seeing through the veil not the terrified country girl but rather the woman of his dreams, the street dancer, the female enchantress who'd escaped him for the last time. *Sharon.*

Rain fell, a swift and crushing torrential rain most uncommon in Samarkand at this time of year. Carolyn looked back to the scared novice, then again to the imposing figure of Mufiqua planted before her. *You swaggering bastard,* she thought. *So now you're a deity, eh? Your mind is so twisted and warped by your lusts and pleasures that all reality is lost. Laugh now, swine. While you still can!*

She bowed deeply. "Your command shall be obeyed." Straightening, she snapped her finger at the confused eunuch, disregarding Jasmine's sobbing pleas. She said, "Have the novice bathed and suitably clothed. Lord Mufiqua must be honored this night."

The eunuch's jaw hung like a monkey's. "But, Mistress!" he stammered. "She is not—the girl must first undergo—the Khan himself would never—"

"Stop sniveling like a hag! Obey my orders, eunuch—or suffer more than the loss of your manhood!"

Mufiqua roared at the sight of the recoiling eunuch, wishing he could have been there when his balls had been removed.

"No!" cried out Jasmine. The girl made to run, was quickly stopped by the guards, brutally thrown into the waiting arms of the eunuch. "I'd rather die!" she screamed, glaring at Carolyn, this woman who somehow she'd thought had been a friend. "I'll never sleep with that pig! Never; do you hear! *Never!*"

Carolyn's open hand smacked hard; Jasmine's face darkened with the blow. The eunuch pinned her arms, allowing her to kick out freely, and pulled her away while the other novices looked on in total horror and disgust.

"Remove the bitch at once!" yelled Carolyn, her voice resounding above Jasmine's continued protests. The overseer's eyes remained cold as ice as she followed the trembling figure, her face as impassive as her gaze. Inside, though, she was bleeding. But control meant everything in a situation like this. Everyone would be observing her behavior—the concubines, the eunuch, the guards, whatever other prying eyes might be watching. Spies were everywhere, everywhere.

She turned back toward the drugged brute, a thin smile showing for him. *I'll play your game, bastard. Do your filthy bidding. But you've made a costly error. Thrown this poor frightened child into my arms far faster than I could have managed myself. For that, bastard, I am grateful.*

"The girl shall be brought to you at nightfall," she said evenly.

Mufiqua was no longer seeing double; his head had started to pound, the sure sign that the drug was wearing off. He must quickly return to his rooms, he knew, smoke once more. Tomorrow get hold of the pig Amar and have another package of the elixir brought at once. Oh, the price would probably be raised, as it always was when he needed the opium urgently; still, it was worth the cost, well worth the cost. What is money to a god?

"Nightfall," Mufiqua repeated. He strode from the hall with a victorious grin etched in his sunken features, unaware that the solemn, loyal guards of the Khan considered him lower than a leper.

5

Soon it would be dawn. Not yet, but soon. Sharon had this thought as she sat hunched in the shadows of the sloping dune. She sifted her fingers through the grains, knowing that within a few hours the sun would make them burn like tiny fires. Night, day, night, day. Seasons come and seasons pass. Years, decades, centuries, millennia. Cities, nations, empires.

A looming silhouette, robed, stood fleetingly across from her in the starlight, then disappeared. *Zadek,* Sharon thought. *Faithful Zadek. See how he trails me, watches over me, even when I have told him to keep away.* By all rights she should be furious. What Kazir, mullah or no, would dare to disobey the Panther's instructions? Who but

Zadek would have secretly left the safety of the Stronghold and, alone, followed across the desert to here, at the very edge of the free lands, to be on hand at a time like this. Didn't the mad mullah know the dangers? Didn't he understand the importance of this morning?

Sharon smiled to herself. Of course he did; who more than Zadek realized what this very morning was about to happen, how one of the very last threads would be irrevocably set into place? Was it not the mad defrocked priest himself who had read for her the Glowing Stones of Babylon, foretelling the misty future? Were it not for the strange persistence of the mullah, none of them might be here now. None of them might be able to prevent the final culmination of Kabul's designs to conquer all of the world.

A chill bit through her desert robe; she tightened her scarf over her face, leaving only her angry eyes exposed. It took no prophet, no soothsayer to know and understand the Khan's vicious plans. Thirty years before, he and his tribe had swept out of the unknown plains of Central Asia, bent on conquest. Now he ruled a thousand leagues and more in every direction. An empire rivaling that of the mighty Alexander, of which Samarkand was the heart. Already his numberless regions had struck west, marching endlessly through the cold lands of Rus, sweeping past the Black Sea until they had forayed upon the very steps of the Christian holy city of Constantinople. With the Turks on the defensive, little could stop him from moving across the Bosporus into Europe proper, where crumbling Rome waited to be humbled. Such was the might of the Huns that simultaneously a similar attack was planned for the south, for the empire of Persia. Meanwhile his emissaries cunningly curried the favor of the Indian *rajas*, lulling them with false promises and offers of new wealth —even while clandestine forces surged through the passes of Khyber, waiting for the order to strike and take the entire subcontinent of India. And, when all this was accomplished, there was more—more than any conqueror had dared before: Cathay itself. China—all of it. Hun spies already fermented disorder, turning province against province in Kabul's evil scheme to take the Forbidden City. From Rome to Peking—this was the terrible aim of the

Huns, and it caused Sharon untold grief to realize that not one nation, not one empire, including that of the revered sanshah, was able to prevent it. No, only she, only she and her small army of fanatical Kazirs stood in the Khan's way. A pesky fly determined to topple the elephant forever.

A few gray threads worked their way up from the eastern horizon, signaling the first comings of the new day. Her gaze swept past the dunes, out and over, the scrub-weeded plain. Shadows were growing longer. Shadows of the advance patrol combing the Steppes in search of the elusive Kazir desert forces. She could hear the snorting and whinnying of tired horses. Hun patrols were few and far between these past years, each side willing to do little more than bait the other while their forces gained strength, biding time until the final conflict. Sharon, though, had special purpose for being here now, today, along this windblown dune. Below the mountains of sand nestled the remains of a tiny village. Until the conquest it had been a thriving community of hillmen. Herders, farmers, drawn to this place by its well and oasis. A peaceful village, quiet and serene, where for untold centuries caravans rested on their journeys west to Bagdad, east to the Afghani frontier. Now, as she peered among the rutted remains, there was no sign of life, only abandoned sheds and roofless mudbrick houses. No breakfast smoke rose from the hearths. There were no chickens, no dogs. Nothing. Only the eerie sounds of wind pushing past the poisoned well, rattling aging doors and shutters. A human skeleton clung to shredded cloth, immobile in the dusty street ever since the morning Khalkali's army has swept through, butchering the men and most of the children, gathering up the crying women and dragging them back to Samarkand to be distributed as whores among the hordes.

A tear came to Sharon's eye; she wiped it away, sniffed, and regained her frozen impassivity. The Hun patrol, perhaps fifty strong, was coming closer. Orange streaks had started to pierce the sky, and the Huns shielded their eyes from the brightness. The officer in command sent out three riders some hundred meters ahead, then signaled his men forward. Sharon grudgingly admired the skill of the riders, and knew them to be the finest horsemen in the world—save for the Kazirs themselves, whose prowess had long before earned them the name of "Phantoms."

The Panther of the Steppes positioned herself lower, better concealed, and waited breathlessly. Her eyes were worry-filled; she shifted slightly, digging her boots. *They must not suspect!* she hissed to herself. *They must enter the village in force, as always. . . .*

Some of the Huns were laughing, exchanging crude jokes among themselves. The outriders were already at the well, shields gleaming in new light, craning their necks and grimly peering this way and that. Satisfied all was quiet and deserted, they whistled to call the main force of the patrol forward. Spurred horses neighed, moved in a steady line past the first of the abandoned houses along the sloping outskirts. Down into the dry wadi they moved, then up and out along the weeded track.

A cold smile parted the desert Panther's lips; she thought, *Yes, this is the right thing. Kabul can only be stopped if every single piece is in place. . . .*

The captain of the patrol, a rugged commander with a thick neck, scratched at the edges of his great, drooping mustache and glumly swept his gaze beyond the well and along the curving street. For three years and more he'd been in control of this sector of desert, hating every moment, dreading these weekly forays ordered by his immediate commander, who himself had received instructions from Lord Khalkali. The war against the Kazirs was perhaps the most brutal and hopeless of all the Khan's campaigns. The one-eyed devil pursued these desert tribesmen out of sheer hate and frustration rather than necessity. Had the captain his choice, he would have marched with Gamal. Yes, now there was war, the kind every Hun dreams of. Cities of wealth to be plundered, real armies to be fought—not fleeting ghosts. His comrades had returned to Samarkand with saddlebags bursting with booty—not to mention the slaves, the dark-skinned Turk and Arabian women they had stolen. Gamal had been a hero, Khalkali merely a brooding fool, relegated to governing this slice of useless desert, with scrubweed for plunder—and a silent Kazir knife in your back if you weren't careful enough.

The soldier leaned over in his saddle and spat. All this would soon change, though, he was confident. For secretly, he and several other of Khalkali's top commanders had already shifted allegiance, sworn to fight under Lord Jamuga's banner, once the old Khan died. In Jamuga they saw the Huns' only hope of new leadership—that and the lord's personal promises that if they supported him, they would be rewarded beyond their wildest imaginations. The captain already fancied himself a general, leader of thousands, conqueror of the Indian frontier states, riding back to Samarkand one day in triumph similar to Gamal's. A right hand to the new Khan, Jamuga, over the spineless corpse of Khalkali and his other dung-brained brothers.

He tersely barked for the outriders to move ahead once more, paying scant attention while they disappeared into the maw of the winding, shadowed narrow single street. *A man can't be too careful in the desert,* the captain assured himself, taking firmer hold of his sword. He'd been fighting Kazirs too long for that, seen them appear literally out of the sand, attack, kill savagely, then vanish. Like the wind. Like the onslaught of a sudden hamsin. No, a man can't be too careful.

He held up his hand, halted his weary forces. Impatiently he waited for the outriders to return. Long moments passed with only the sound of the wind.

"I don't like it," someone grumbled from behind. The captain shot the man an icy glance, then spat again. The deserted village did indeed seem sinister in the pale glow of dawn. This squalid hump of huddled mudbrick stood precariously close to the border of free Kazir territory, and as such needed constant attention. If the desert was the hammer, then places like this surely were the anvil.

With a low grunt he lowered his arm and signaled his force to move on without the return of the outriders. Pushing forward uneasily, his head snapped around at a sharp sound. The knife was already out of its scabbard when he saw the wind-pushed door, slanting on twisted hinges, banging gently against the outer wall of brick. *Getting too jumpy,* he told himself. *Soon you'll be believing in nightthings the old hillwomen rattle about.*

They passed the broad, broken-corraled building knowing it to be the smith's. The empty stalls stared gloomily back from within the shadows. For barely an instant something else, dark and malevolent, seemed to move within the darkness. A fleeting form . . .

The captain tugged lightly at his horse's reins, nudged the black gelding closer to the smithy's doorless threshold. Something inside *had* moved, he was sure of that; but whether it was a frightened jackrabbit or a well-concealed man in the rafters above the stalls, he couldn't tell.

Pairs of double horses followed him, the main force lingering a few paces behind, arrows being drawn from quivers. This village was a perfect place for a surprise attack, the captain knew. A veritable trap, what with his men clustered along the narrow street, unable to spring loose and fight freely with the mudbrick structures so closely hugging either side. And where were the outriders, anyway?

The captain drew his sword. Halfway out of his saddle he heard the battle cry, the shrill, familiar Kazir cry of attack.

Simultaneously the doors of the houses banged open, desert-garbed, faceless Kazir fighters pouring through. Archers moved across the roofs, firing down a deadly barrage. A dozen horses reared, screamed. Some of his men slumped, arrows through their necks, hurled to the ground. Huns wheeled their steeds around, weapons drawn, swung low and mightily in wide arcs, slashing through the advancing ranks of the rushing desert men.

Ahead, from the curving track through which the outriders had disappeared, came a thundering company of mounted Kazirs, all robed in desert-white, unarmored, and unafraid of the fierce, mail-breasted Huns. In the rays of the new-born sun the battle was joined, wind howling amid the war cries, steel clashing against steel, dulled *thuds* of men being thrown from their saddles and trampled by frightened, rearing horses.

The captain felt an arrow glance off his helmet; he regained his saddle and managed to swing his mount enough around to get into the center of the fray. His men had been attacked on three sides by clearly superior numbers; the only way clear was the route by which they had come, back toward the dunes. The captain swore foully as an arrow ripped through his sleeve and tore into the flesh of his bicep. Blood streamed down his arm; he careened forward, thrust his blade and speared a rushing attacker. The Kazir tumbled; the captain trampled him to death. "Retreat! Retreat!" he shouted, clearing a path through the melee.

Fully half his force lay dead across the avenue, back to the square and the poisoned well. The Kazirs still had the distinct advantage no matter how well his own men were fighting, and it was then he realized they were hanging back, not closing off the single remaining route of escape, but rather purposely herding what was left of the patrol toward it. *The fools,* thought the captain. *They have us! Why aren't they pressing the advantage? What are they waiting for?*

Still, this was a fortune he wasn't about to question, not with two hundred Phantoms at his back. He hunched in the saddle, broke his way free by hacking a few more running Kazirs, and with a handful of his best men beside him, broke onto the square. Riding like a demon, he made his way away from the well. A group of fresh Kazirs on horseback charged down bravely from the dunes. With the sun in his eyes the captain could not tell their number; he swung his own horse again, retreated to the relative safety of the field. A few stragglers were bolting horseless from the village. The Kazirs cut them down like rag dolls, swooping in low, lopping off heads, blood spraying like a summer shower. The captain urged his horse on, listening to the terrible screams of the dying. Nearby he saw one of his best men hurled as his horse crumpled from a barrage of Kazir snubbed arrows. Another Hun, a brute of a Mongol, stopped the advance of a Kazir, fought brutally with others who streamed from the dunes. The captain took quick assessment of the situation. Of his force of fifty men, at best there were a dozen who had made it out of the village. Of those, except for several pinned down by advancing riders from the dunes, the rest seemed free of the enemy. Strange, he mused; he'd been fighting these desert men for years, and this was the first time ever the Kazirs had not tried to gain their victory to the last man. A tenet of a Kazir warrior was to slaughter the enemy, leave not a single survivor to tell the tale; yet these Kazirs now seemed in no hurry to give chase.

"Behind you!" someone shouted.

The captain grunted as his sword met the thrusting blade of a shaven-headed Kazir, a sinewy, scalp-locked horseman who looked like no Kazir he'd ever seen before. The man snorted, blazing fire in his eyes as he pressed closer to the Hun, slashing, cutting. The captain hacked away, more concerned with breaking free than killing his foe. As their horses straddled one another. the Kazir inexplicably hurled himself from the saddle, lunged for the captain, whose sword came down sharply, gashing the desert man. The Kazir slumped, sheltered himself from the onrushing hooves of other Hun riders.

"Don't kill him!" yelled the commander hoarsely. "Take him alive! We need him alive!"

The fight in the village was done; as could have been predicted, the Kazirs were rapidly taking to the dunes on horse and by foot, vanishing, blending among the shifting sands so perfectly it seemed as though they had never been there. The village itself, though, spoiled any illusion that this fight had been imaginary. Slain Huns lay scattered everywhere. As for the Kazir slain and wounded, they had all been quickly dragged away, leaving only the corpses of Huns to give testimony to what had happened.

The captain sucked in air to quell the punishing pain of his wound; he broke the shaft of the arrow embedded in his arm, then surveyed the silent scene around him. The Kazirs were gone, all right. He knew their tactics well enough to know they would not be back. The village was again deserted.

A Hun sprang from his saddle, examined the wounded Kazir. The captain leaned hard from his saddle, peering darkly down. "Is he dead?"

"No, sir. He'll live." And with a glint in his eye the soldier pulled his dagger and made to slit the Kazir's throat.

"No, you fool!" barked the captain. "I want him tended to—now! As quickly as you can!"

The inexperienced younger man was perplexed. "But, sir—"

Wincing with pain, the captain raised an exasperated hand into the air. "This man is worth his weight in gold! Don't you see, any of you? We've caught ourselves a

Kazir! Alive! Only once have we done so before—and then we had to torture him until he died—and still didn't get any information out of him."

"What makes you think this one will be any different, eh? Buzzards, they are. Desert vermin."

The captain blew a long breath into the sky. "What? And tell the Lord Khalkali that we had a Kazir fighter in our hands and let him go?" Inwardly he thought, *This man is a prize among prizes. He fights for the Kazirs but he's not one of them. I've seen his kind before, when I served the Khan in Rus. Khalkali will be well pleased with my fortune today. So will my Lord Jamuga when I recount what's happened. We have to make this Kazir well, turn him over to Krishna. Who knows what secrets he's got locked in that shaven head of his? A Russian who fights for the Kazirs! They'll make a general of me for this little coup—if these idiots can keep him alive until we get back to Samarkand.*

"Careful," he called as they bandaged the Kazir's wound and slung him onto a riderless horse. "He's lost too much blood as is and I'll bleed each of you a double amount if he doesn't live to reach the dungeons of Samarkand!"

Then off they rode, twelve survivors of fifty. They trotted slowly, backs to the fully-risen sun, completely unaware of the solitary figure who rose trembling from the dunes and observed them.

"Go with Allah," Sharon whispered. Her robe flapped in the wind as she climbed the sanded crest, tears flowing. "Go with Allah, Roskovitch. You played your part too well. I only pray you are as strong as we think; Krishna's tortures have broken the most powerful men alive."

6

It was in the grimmest hours of the night, that black time in which men hold their breath, stir in their sleep, listen to the strange sounds carried upon the breath of the wind. The hags and washerwomen of the city spoke of nightthings, dark demons of the netherworld, ghouls and ghosts come to prey upon the living. In daylight hours men scoffed at these superstitions, these foolish tales of the feeble, yet on a night such as this, with the stillness broken by the dreaded whistling of an approaching hamsin, only a fool did not shudder or wonder what terrible event portended.

The assassin's face was smeared with soil to conceal his features; his abba was black, blending perfectly with the falling shadows of the walls and towering edifices. Almost invisible to wakened eyes, he pulled the cowl over his head and slipped noiselessly along the side of the long, low outer wall of the palace keep. Silently he waited among the hedges, observing the battlement of the great wall soaring beyond the courtyard and hanging garden, where the changing of the guard was now taking place. Dour, helmeted sentries saluted one another glumly, one group taking positions in the lighted tower and crenelated wall, the other group wearied from their tour and making their way down toward the inner keep.

The assassin smiled mirthlessly; from inside his robe he drew a thin length of hemp with a small grappling hook that was wrapped in cloth to dull its sound. He stepped into the open, tossed the rope high, listened with satisfaction when the hook firmly caught the embrasure of the stone ledge. Hand over hand he pulled himself up, muscles taunt, until he reached the top, some ten meters above the garden. His eyes shifted quickly, ever mindful of the guards on duty until dawn. From the highest tower a grim bell tolled twelve times. Midnight. Deftly the assassin hauled up his rope, wound the cord tightly, and placed it carefully in a crevice between the large stones. Save for the lusterless, muddy-yellow flame of the torch pulsing in rising wind, there were few lights to be seen within the many windows of the multiwinged palace. For a second time the assassin smiled, hurrying on his way, out of sight, bounding the steps onto a lower level, then opening an unlocked iron door and creeping inside the passage. It had taken him a very long time to study his route, time the changing of the guard, and determine how long he had. His work had been well-rewarded, though, and now he was ready for the second stage, the moment he had waited for, the time when he would get revenge against those who had dishonored him. This night would live in memory, he told himself. Whether he escaped or not after the deed was immaterial; he'd forfeited his right to life long ago. Death would be sweet—if he succeeded.

The corridor was narrow and long, unlit except for the glow of a brazier in a distant chamber. The assassin strode briskly but quietly until he came out from the passage and upon the threshold of an enormous vestibule. There were many doorways leading to and from this hall and he knew he'd have to be careful in selecting the proper one—the one leading to the Khan's private rooms on the highest level of the tower.

There was a guard on duty in the hall, of course; he'd expected and been prepared for it. The man had taken off his helmet, stood stifling a yawn as he patrolled back and forth, back and forth, up and down the series of bolted doorways. The assassin was grinning fully now, watching the heathen Hun rub sleep from his eyes, stretch tired muscles. When his back was turned, the man in shadows pulled a small curved dagger from the folds of his sleeve, let it slip into his hand. The edge of the blade was smeared with a colorless substance, an alchemist's invisible poison guaranteed to kill within seconds.

The assassin surveyed the chamber one last time, then like a leopard he sprang, catching the hapless Hun unaware. The knife's point cut through the small of his back. The sentry froze, the poison racing through his bloodstream. He slumped silently to the floor, flesh turned a sickly, bluish pall, eyes bulging, mouth hanging limp, lips soundlessly quivering. By the time he dragged the Hun away, the corpse was stiff.

Beads of sweat broke out across the assassin's forehead. He didn't pause to mop his brow as he raced for the correct door, slid open the bolt and slipped inside. So far everything had been perfect. A few unhampered minutes more were all he needed. Enough time to reach Kabul as he slept.

Ephemeral flickers of light danced at the height of a winding set of stone steps. The assassin wiped his sweaty brow, took the steps two at a time. At the landing a vestibule greeted him, his nostrils affronted by the sweetly pungent smell of incense. No guards. Once more fortune rode with him. Another door, wooden, heavily reinforced, was before him. Unbolted. He eased it open, peered cautiously through the slit, gawked in amazement at the plush chamber, the greeting room of Kabul's most private apartment. He could hear murmurings from another room; a woman's voice, followed by the guttural tone of a man's, then a few broken giggles as the woman laughed.

The Khan is with a whore, mused the assassin. *So much the better. I've poison enough for two.*

A quick silent prayer followed; he burst loudly inside the apartment, wild eyed, and leaped for the entrance to the bedroom. The room was black as night. The assassin lifted his dagger high, came screaming, crazed. The woman in the bed bolted upright, naked. She put her hands to her face and wailed.

"Death to the heathen!" shrieked the assassin.

Kabul jerked up, rolled deftly to the side as the dagger ripped the feathered mattress. The assassin made to lunge again. The woman was howling, scrambling from the bed. The dagger slashed out. She moaned, rolled her eyes and slumped, blood pulsing from her lacerated belly. One-eyed Kabul grabbed the closest object, a brass candlestick, and heaved it. The assassin took the blow and fell backward. Kabul leaped, grabbed his sword, wheeled it high. Before he could strike, three soldiers burst into the bedroom, tackled the assassin, and knocked him to the floor, beating him mercilessly.

"My lord, are you all right?" stammered a guard.

Kabul glanced to his consort, whose cold hands clung to the blood-splattered quilt, then to the moaning intruder who lay pinioned between gleaming scimitars. Kabul rubbed his hairy, naked chest and stared down at the assassin's poisoned dagger.

Tupol, sleep clouding his vision, hobbled into the chamber. He looked to the dead girl and gasped.

"It was that close!" boomed Kabul, snapping a finger at his youngest son. "*That* close! How did this dog get inside?" He was livid with rage at the almost-successful attempt on his life.

The soldiers shied their eyes from his wrath. "He must have scaled the wall during the change of guard, Sire," one stammered. "He killed the sentry on duty in the hall, and he—"

Kabul roughly pushed the soldier aside, in no mood to listen to excuses. "Who," he said seethingly to Tupol, "is behind this?"

The deformed son shook his head. "I don't know, Father. Let me have this man to question."

Kabul hovered over the beaten assassin, kicked him, then stared through his single, hateful eye. "You'll rue this little ploy," he vowed.

Wild with the knowledge and terror of what was in store, the assassin made a sudden attempt to lunge for his knife, cut himself quickly and let the poison do its work. Tupol kicked the blade away as the closest guard stomped the assassin's outstretched arm. The assassin yelped with pain. Tupol knelt beside him, put his hands around his throat, and started to squeeze. "Who paid you, swine? Whose money bought your knife, eh?"

The assassin choked for air. He struggled to fill his lungs, speak. Tupol released his grip and waited. "Not . . . not for money," rasped the assassin. "For . . . for honor . . ."

"Honor?" Tupol glanced up at the menacing bulk of his naked father. Kabul stared at him long and hard, then snapped a finger and commanded the guards to wipe the mud from the assassin's face.

"I know this man!" gasped the deformed son. "I recognize him!"

"What?" barked the Khan. "Are you sure?"

Tupol weakly nodded. "Positive, my lord. No question. He is a dealer for Amar. In fact, one of his daughters serves us here in the palace. . . ."

"You turned my Lina into a whore!" cried out Karim, shaking as he lay on the floor. "You'll die for it, butcher of Asia! Perhaps not by my hand, but by the sacred name of the Prophet, you'll die!"

Karim screamed like an animal as the soldier's boot slammed harshly between his spread legs.

"What's the fool talking about?" demanded the Khan.

Tupol shrugged, looked away as tears of pain poured down Karim's sunken cheeks. "He's mad, lord."

Kabul shook his finger. "No, no," he said quietly. "There's more here. How would a common trader like this have been able to learn so much about the palace? Enough to slip inside at will? Eh, my clever, twisted son? Who gave him aid? Or encouragement?"

"I did it alone!" blurted the suffering Karim.

Another kick to his genitals brought another shriek, this one louder and more horrible than the last. He rolled at the Khan's feet, slobbering, sobbing, shoulders heaving, gasping for air.

"Triple the guard at every station!" commanded the Khan to those around him. Then to Tupol, "Find Krishna, have him take personal charge of this man's interrogation. And warn him to be careful! He must exact the greatest amount of pain with the least amount of damage. I want this Karim to survive for a long, long time."

Tupol sneered at the frightened, groveling man. "As you command, Sire. But I believe the poor beggar did act alone."

The Great Khan of the Huns folded his arms, shook his head slowly, stringy hair falling over his patch. "Too many coincidences for that, my son. Too many." He rubbed at his bearded chin. "A dealer of Amar's, eh? No doubt a contact of my addicted Mufiqua's as well, eh?" He kicked Karim again, laughing when the pitiful man moaned. "Who else, slaving-son-of-a-whore? What other contacts, eh? What other agents inside my palace? The Persians? Afghanis?" He paused and sucked in a lungful of hot air, temper beginning to boil. Hissing through clenched teeth he added, "Or is it the Kazirs that you serve?"

Karim stiffened, eyes wider and more frightened than before. "No one!" he whimpered. "Alone! I acted alone! By Allah, I swear it's the truth!"

"And by your Allah you'll have a good deal more to snivel about," reminded Kabul, thinking of Krishna's methods. He turned away, ordering the remaining guards to drag the prisoner out. He didn't know which of the Hun's dark gods he would thank for this tide of events, so he thanked them all. Because of the stupid, vengeful act of an outraged father he would, for the first time, glean an understanding of the network of spies serving those opposed to him. Coupled with the Kazir warrior captured in the desert, Kabul realized that for the first time his hope had a very real possibility of coming true. Karim and the Kazir were going to lead him directly to the woman, the bitch who stole his eye, and for whose capture he would pay any price at all.

7

The odor made Carolyn want to retch; the foul smell tickled her nostrils, a slimy, vile stink that permeated the air. Doors creaked open for her as she passed, the concubine trailing meekly a pace behind. Burly dungeon guards bowed respectfully before the overseer of the whores. Carolyn had rarely been down to these bowels of the palace, these putrid corridors reeking of death, disease and torture. It took all the courage she could muster to make her way through them.

It was rare for Krishna to request the company of a woman, Carolyn had noted. Often she had wondered about his perversions, asking herself what would make a man, even an animal like him, prefer to dwell in the underworld. The chancellor of the dungeons was a strange man; in many ways the most peculiar of all Kabul's remaining sons, so it was with some surprise that this morning she had received his request. Carefully she had selected her choice for him, knowing his taste ran more to the dark-skinned beauties of Arabia and India than the yellow and brown-haired women of Rus that Khalkali and Jamuga seemed to prefer. That was why she had chosen Nania, a child of the jungles, seductive but defiant. A woman whose background serving the Rajas made her more compatible to the lustful Krishna than the delicate, sugared girls of Persia or Damascus.

There was also another reason for Carolyn's sojourn into the underworld. Late in the night word had come to her from a trusted palace guard that an assassin had made an attempt on the life of the Khan. She was dumbfounded to hear it had been Karim; the aging trader must have taken leave of his wits, she was sure. Why else would he have placed so much in jeopardy for such selfish motives? Didn't he realize what he had done? The attempt had most certainly *not* been part of the Panther's scheme to regain Samarkand. It was a foolhardy, insane act. Because of him all plans were in peril. Carolyn had immediately sent word to the Stronghold, risking her own safety in order to warn Tariq and Sharon of the grave turn of events.

Damn his eyes! she thought. *Karim may have ruined everything. Everything—at a time when we're so close.*

The fool would be made to talk—that was a certainty; and Carolyn found herself thankful that Karim had little to tell. In truth he knew nothing about Kazir plans, except for the time he had lured Mufiqua to his home. But even that was too much. Once he talked, Amar was certain of arrest, thus provoking even more arrests as the Khan would try to isolate the enemy agents within the Samarkand palace. One by one they would find themselves in mortal danger, from the lowest slave or servant right up to Hezekiah, posing as the soothsayer, and, should matters really get out of control, to the saya herself. Were it within her power, she would have murdered Karim right here and now, even if it meant compromising her own position. Silence the dealer forever. But all this was not in her power, nor even in her authority as leader of the Stronghold. Today she hoped to get a fleeting glimpse of Karim, mark his cell, number his guards, then wait for opportunity. Hence, the carrier pigeons that had flown tonight bore an urgent and dire message: the Night of Atonement must be moved up, carried out quickly no matter what the risk. Waiting was too precarious—for, should Karim crack, the palace and the city would be placed under marshal law, with such security that everything would be lost.

The dungeon guards led them down the final corridor to Krishna's private quarters, the same stench-ridden chamber that Khalkali had visited and where he had made his pact. Yes, Carolyn knew about that as well, she thought with some satisfaction. A few hours alone with a palace harlot had set to wagging the tongue of a sentry. And then there had been Lina. Ah, how much Carolyn had come to count upon that girl's quick-thinking brain. Lina had many qualities, many uses. Alone in Khalkali's bed she'd made the savage more drunk than he was accustomed to, and after climaxing their love-making, it had been easy to coax the swaggering son of Kabul into boasting about the new agreement. Carolyn had listened to Lina recount the news but had neither been troubled nor perturbed by it. On the contrary. If anything, she'd been pleased. Let the brothers divide among themselves, let them turn against each other. In the end this would serve the Kazir purpose. Thus, it had been a clever calculation for her to have another of the prostitutes, one of Niko's favorites, sweetly whisper of it in his ear, hoping it would pass eventually to Tupol, and maybe Jamuga as well. It was also her hope that these three might then form a new alliance of their own, isolating both the drug-addicted Mufiqua and the brooding, mistrustful Temugin, who, since Gamal's untimely death, had yet to venture forth out of his rooms.

Now, though, all these careful plans would have to undergo drastic change. Karim had stupidly seen to that. *Damn his eyes!* And for the moment at least not even Lina could be told, for even she might turn against Carolyn, if it could help her father.

Hulking shadows crisscrossed the lime walls as Krishna stood as she entered his quarters. His frame seemed awesome to the saya, a veritable Goliath, and she shuddered at the unpleasant thought of anyone having to willingly bed with him as the concubine with her was about to do.

Carolyn bowed, said, "Lord Krishna, I have brought the woman for your pleasure."

Krishna wiped a greasy hand over his mouth, let his eyes pour up and down the figure of the dark-skinned concubine. "You have selected well, overseer. Go. Call back for this one at dawn."

The whore did her best not to appear frightened by this monster of a man. At Krishna's command a slave came into the room and gave the prostitute a silk gown. The girl took it in her slim hands, stood frozen. "Put it on," growled the chancellor. He indicated a black abyss of an adjoining chamber. The whore drew a deep breath, tried to smile at the beast, then glanced forlornly to the overseer as she disappeared behind the soiled curtain.

"I said you can go," Krishna said dryly.

Carolyn wanted to stall for time, find some way to make him tell her the whereabouts of the assassin. It wasn't necessary. A wailing scream made her flesh crawl as though a huge spider were on her. Krishna saw her discomfort and laughed loudly. "No reason to shiver, Overseer," he told her. "It's only the new arrival." Another scream, worse than the last; perspiration beaded Carolyn's palms.

"Who . . . who is he, my lord?" she managed to ask.

Krishna scratched at his groin, ran a finger across his throat in imitation of a knife. "The would-be murderer of the Khan," he answered. "Carried with him a poison-edged blade. Poor bugger; he'd have been smarter to use it on himself." And as if to add weight to his words, Karim screamed a third time, his wail such a horrid shriek that Krishna himself winced.

Poor devil, thought Carolyn. *Death at my hand would be a blessing.* Then to the chancellor, she said, "I hope you plan on making him suffer for his deed."

With a mirthless chuckle, Krishna looked deeply into her eyes and said, "A very long time, Overseer. He might even outlive you and me. Right now we're only toying with him. Sticking hot coals and the like under his feet. Plucking out the hairs on his legs one at a time. . . ."

Carolyn was sickened but she forced a smile, the same sadistic kind of smile that Krishna wore. The cruel chancellor regarded her for a long moment, then said, "Would you like to see my handiwork? But perhaps it's not for a woman's eyes. Not for the eyes of one as lovely as you."

The saya swallowed, met his gaze. "I would consider it an honor, my lord."

Krishna laughed. He looked to the sentry, mindful of the girl waiting for him. "Take the overseer for a look," he commanded. "Not too long, mind you. Just enough so she can see how we repay treachery against the Khan."

The soldier, as much a sadist as his master, bowed stiffly and grinned. "This way, mistress."

The heavy door shut, Krishna dousing the oil lamp and returning to his whore. Grim, maniacal laughter split the air as the guard took the lead and gestured for Carolyn to follow. They marched gloomily down the passage, unmindful of the reeking pools at their feet. Soon there were cells on either side, thick barred prisons, iron-gated, with walls of solid granite. By the flickering flames of torches set randomly along the corridor walls, she was able to catch glimpses of the occupants within. It was ghastly; the most shameful and terrible thing she had ever seen: men and women, some missing limbs, others blinded, garbed in rags, bodies festering with sores. Buckets of slop sat in muck inside the cells, filled with slimy water, thick with roaches and vermin. Some of the prisoners stared as she passed, others sat meekly, stooped and bowed, gazing mindlessly into distant space. Still others called out after her; some laughed; some taunted; some mistook her for a new arrival. All, though, even those toothlessly grinning, watched with the same pleading on their skeletal faces. Their frames were like sticks, bellies bloated from starvation, hair fallen from their heads, hands twisted and mangled from torture.

Dear Allah, why do you let them survive? Better they be dead! All of them.

Realizing her plight, the guard looked over his shoulder at her and said, "There's worse than this, mistress. Far worse. These are the good ones, the ones who've behaved, you might say."

Worse? Worse than this? It wasn't possible! Or was it?

Her companion abruptly stopped. A barred door groaned open and three grim torturers walked out into the passage. They stared at Carolyn, one mumbled to the guard beside her, " 'Ad enough for today, 'e's 'ad. 'Morrow we be back." Then they turned and left, making sure the door was relocked. Not that the poor bastard inside could have fled in any case. Carolyn grasped at the bars and stuck her face between the slats. There, crumbled on muck and vomit, was Karim, or what was left of him. A small charcoal fire dimly burned in a brazier. Karim's bare feet were swollen, pus-filled lumps grossly bulging over his toes and ankles, halfway up his calves. He was semiconscious, on the border of delirium. Her eyes stared blankly at him, and his own caught the look of horror. For just an instant there seemed recognition. Then it was gone; Karim moaned, rolled over, blacked out.

"All right now, mistress," said the guard. "You've had your look. Better we go."

Carolyn numbly nodded. She paid no attention to the prisoners this time as they walked the long way out, but as they came to the final hallway, the one that led directly in front of Krishna's quarters, she nearly fainted at what she saw. Another new prisoner was being hauled into the dungeons, a man wounded and bandaged but who even so walked with an arrogant defiance. The saya gasped at sight of him, while he, meanwhile, pretended not to have seen her.

It was Roskovitch.

8

Naked but for a soiled covering around his loins, Karim the trader lifted his head and peered about agonizingly at his cell. His hair and beard were matted, caked with congealed blood. His lower lip ballooned out more than twice its normal size, purpled, festered with pus-laden blisters. With great effort he dipped a cupped hand into the dregs of the water bucket placed beside him, forced a splash of the slimy liquid into his mouth and groaned. The straw at his feet was infested with roaches. The trader forced himself up, his back against the jagged, damp wall. Insects were crawling between his toes, over his legs. Karim did not have the strength to flick them off. A large welt rising from his cheekbone had almost shut his left eye; the eye watered incessantly, spewing pus and a thick, colorless humor.

The once-gentle trader shuddered at the memory of his last interrogation. When had it been? An hour ago—or yesterday? How long had he been down here like this? Time had no meaning down within the bowels of the Khan's evil dungeons. Was it daylight, or was it night?

Did a hot sun blaze outside or did stars weave a tapestry across the sky? Karim had no way of knowing. Here, it was always black and bleak, silent and forlorn, his solitude broken on occasion by some hideous scream echoing from another unknown cell where another unknown human being shared his grim fate.

Karim had told them nothing. Not even when the towering chancellor himself had supervised the torture. Oh, they'd been clever, these bestial Huns, giving him food and false promises of medical attention, while riddling his flesh with burning coals and white-hot needles. Snickering, they allowed him to slip into blissful unconsciousness, then revived him and began the questioning again.

"How did you gain entry inside the palace? Who are your contacts within the walls?"

Karim had looked dismally into the shadowed faces and remained silent, his ultimate defiance.

"Which masters do you serve?" asked a soft-spoken voice, purposely honeyed to veil the venom behind it. Again Karim had not responded. Then he was stretched out, legs spread-eagle, hands bound behind his head with dampened leather cord that tightened the more he squirmed. A flaming, blue-hot poker had hissed and nudged his belly. His body hairs curled and smoldered, smoke rising from the singed flesh. When they had branded him, the stench of burning meat stank. He remembered his cry, how his mouth had twisted, a mournful sob wrenched helplessly from his gut. A bucket of latrine water had brought him around. The voices were persistent. *"Who are your contacts? Who was your accomplice? Name the traitor, gain your freedom . . ."*

Karim had cried before them, insisting he'd acted alone, out of honor. His inquisitors had sneered, rolled him over, forced him to his knees and lashed him with knotted bullwhips, laughing as he howled.

Then the dreaded bull of a chancellor took charge personally. Karim had felt the wine pushed down his throat, drank it thankfully at first. Krishna had someone hold his head and stuffed the neck of the goatskin container into his mouth. Karim was choking, coughing, until a mixture of vomit and wine fountained from his stomach while his head reeled. His inquisitors were laughing, kicking him as he twisted and cavorted across the floor, heaving his guts onto the straw only to have his face forced in it by the sadistic chancellor. Then he passed out.

The brazier was burning again, the iron poker was being readied. Karim crawled to the corner, mucus dripping from his nose, pus oozing from his cankers. The straw was wet with his own urine, smelly from when he had soiled it and himself during his sleep.

The inquisitors were huddled together, whispering among themselves. Karim, dazed and semiconscious banged his head against the stone wall in hopes of crushing his skull and taking his life. Quick, expert hands pulled him safely back to the center of the cell before much damage had been done. When the tip of the poker changed hues, glowed eerily like a nightthing's devil torch, the inquisition began again. The same questions, always the same questions.

Pins were stuck beneath his fingernails, the brand brushed lightly against the soles of his feet.

"For the love of the Phophet, kill me!" he implored as the chains rattled in their hands. Krishna held up a shadowed hand and stopped his men. Then he knelt down beside the prisoner, gazed deeply into his eyes, a gentle hand upon Karim's bruised shoulder. "Spare yourself further pain," he spoke softly, kindly. "You'll never leave this cell alive, Karim. Why prolong your agony?" To the trader's surprise, he drew a dagger from within the folds of his sleeve. The curved blade glimmered in the light of the glowing coals, and Karim stared at it and gasped. It was his own dagger—the same poison-smeared blade with which he'd attempted to assassinate the Khan.

Krishna saw his expression and smiled thinly. "One prick of this against your flesh and you'll die peacefully. Eternal oblivion. Isn't that what you'd like, eh, trader?"

Karim swallowed painfully and nodded. "Please," he sniveled. "Cut me. Cut me now. . . ." He tried to reach for the dagger, Krishna quickly held it out of reach. "No, no, my friend. Not yet. First you must pay a price."

"What . . . price?"

"A few answers to simple questions, nothing more."

Tears mingled with blood in Karim's swollen eyes. "But I've told you," he rasped thickly, "I acted alone. . . ."

The chancellor shook his head, heaving a sigh. His men had started to rattle their chains again, the smoldering poker ready. He began to twitch, drawing away; Krishna's powerful hands kept him in check. "You have a choice, trader. Think it over now. The chains—or the dagger. More torture, or peaceful sleep in the cradling arms of your God. . . ."

"I had nó accomplice; why won't you believe that?"

Krishna eased the blade back inside his sleeve, into its sheath.

"You will find me a man of limitless patience," Krishna told him. "I am in no hurry; believe me." He leaned forward with a malevolent grin. "Before I am done everything will be told—gladly."

"I know nothing," groaned Karim. "Nothing."

"The palace is filled with agents of our enemies, trader. We are not fools, and this information is no secret to either you or I, eh? All I need from you are the names of the others. Even a single name might suffice. . . ."

Karim whimpered. It would have been the easiest thing to give in, tell the dreaded torturer all. Even to fabricate a tale, devise his own set of conspirators to please the chancellor.

"Come now, trader. One name, then. What difference can it make to you now? There are so many who would see the Khan dead, no?" He leaned in again, his breath heavy upon Karim's face. "Tell me. Which master do you serve? Which traitor?"

No answer came, and the cruel chancellor's face turned to stone. "Perhaps," he offered, "this deed was the bidding of one of my brothers?"

Karim looked at him, unspeaking.

The grim torturers closed in around the hapless prisoner, and this time Krishna made no move to stop them.

"One man could never have come so close, acting alone," said Krishna. "And soon, I assure you, you will beg to admit the truth."

All Karim remembered was recoiling in horror as the pain began again. Then, mercifully, he'd blacked out, not waking until now.

That had been the last interrogation. As he sat up, huddled in the corner like a rat, the realization of the stupidity of his act made him weep. He lifted his gaze to the ceiling, bemoaning his plight. There, in the depths of terror, he prayed to Allah that some hand might yet come and rid him of life.

9

The air had become fetid, the earth at her sandaled feet muddied, from the vicious thunderstorms that had passed during the small hours of the night. The winding streets of the outer city, within sight of the awesome black-iron gate and the camped caravan barely beyond the high gray walls, were like anthills teeming with life. The stalls were filled with fresh supplies of goods, and the traders of the market babbled loudly in half a dozen tongues to the many desert-robed visitors come to barter.

Sharon was dressed in the plain sand-toned robe of a pilgrim on a journey to the holy city of Mecca. With her veil tightly clasped and covering most of her face, her cowl pulled above her head against the glare of the hot sun, she stepped slowly across the byways, slipping unnoticed among the milling crowds, unsuspected by the watchful sentries manning the walls at the fringes of the market.

The enormous bulk of the palace hung solemnly in the distance, its reinforced battlements interlocked with a series of towers and bastions upon which grim soldiers eternally marched. The Huns were everywhere, all garbed in similar fashion. According to rank, each wore either a horned or plumed leather helmet; sheathed killing-daggers tied at the sides of their buckled belts; curving, scabbarded swords dangling from their hips.

Sharon's eyes darted up and down the bazaar; she brushed away dragonflies, searched carefully among the thick rows of stalls. Across the way, where a camel marched slowly to the whip of his rider, she saw the beggar. The blind man was as thin as a rail; he sightlessly pleaded to passers-by.

Crossing the byway, she shied her gaze once more; three soldiers had brusquely dragged a suspect from a sandalmaker's musty shop. The crowds paid scant attention while the stern guards viciously shoved the hapless citizen down an alley. Such arrests were common in Samarkand, all the more so since the still-mysterious death of noble Gamal. It was no secret that Lord Jamuga had taken control of governing the city proper, and he abused the masses more than even Kabul himself.

The beggar's head tilted her way; Sharon paused. "Alms, for the love of God," muttered the sightless petitioner. Sharon drew a copper and placed it in his palm. "The Prophet's blessings upon you," he said, stooping and humbling himself. "May the children of your children—"

"I seek not fortune but glory in its place," Sharon told him in a quick, low voice, speaking the hidden greeting of the Brotherhood.

At this, the beggar stopped dead, cocked his head, narrowed his hazed eyes and stared at her so piercingly that Sharon wondered if he truly were sightless.

"How may I return your favor?" he asked cautiously.

Quietly, she said, "I am told you are Adnan; I come to you to find the apothecary."

"You ask much," he answered.

Her reply was swift and proper, "In return for much that I have to give. Now quick, old man. Where do I find him? My matter is urgent."

The beggar backstepped, the disguised pilgrim following casually so as not to attract attention. "Down there," mumbled Adnan. "Follow the street until you reach the empty shop." Then before she could say another word, he was gone, hobbling away, hands outstretched and seeking another benefactor.

Sharon walked cautiously. Near the corner of the street she stopped. In front of her stood a hovel, bleak, doorless, and foreboding. Warily, certain she was not secretly observed, she stepped inside. The shop was dark, empty save for a counter near the back and a few shelves laden with dark vials. A centimeter of settled dust scattered across the floor, a dim odor hinted of stale medicines. In the recesses of the shadows she waited, aware that here, mere steps from the busy marketplace, the outside world seemed to eerily stop. Like time suspended, as though she had stepped across the threshold of the netherworld the witches had long ago told her of.

"Yes?" came a sudden whisper of a voice, and she turned to see a man standing behind the counter, a pot-bellied, round-faced, bearded man.

She cleared her throat. "I have come to see the apothecary," she announced.

Her host stared a long while, then said, "I am the apothecary. Who sent you?"

"The Brotherhood."

He eyed her skeptically. Sharon let down her veil, stood defiantly as he studied her features. "You are not a Kazir," he said at last.

She shook her head. Then, wary of saying too much, she replied, "I am their trusted emissary."

The apothecary smiled; he heightened the flame of his oil lamp, watched her carefully as shadows danced back from the light. "I know who you are," he told her. "I know exactly who you are."

Sharon's facial muscles tightened. *How? How could he possibly know?*

Enigmatically, as if reading these secret thoughts, the apothecary said, "No harm will come to you in my shop, Panther. Take your hand from your knife."

He'd seen that, too! But how could he possibly—? She withdrew her hand from the hidden blade, stood with her arms clasped together. "You know much, apothecary. Such knowledge can cause you grave peril."

He smiled at her mysteriously. "What do you want?"

"The same as you," she answered swiftly, mincing no words. "To rid Samarkand forever of this Khan and his hordes."

"The Kazirs are my enemies," he said.

"As once they were mine as well. But we have much in common, you and I. Our feud should have died long ago, the day Kabul took this empire by force.

He admired her courage, her defiance of him even though she stood within his grasp; yet despite this, she spoke on behalf of his foe, the savage and free tribes of the steppes and deserts who for a century and more had fought to win Samarkand back from his own people. Her people also—once. "There are those who would call you a traitor," he said. "There are those who would say you have betrayed both your home and land; that you have become no better than those whom you would destroy."

"The world is filled with fools, apothecary. While we stand divided, you and I, the sons of Kabul plot further conquest. To enslave us all. Is not the scourge of the Huns a worse plague than any Kazir has ever been?"

He mulled over her words slowly. Yes, he knew she was right. The Huns were indeed a plague, the Kazirs the only ones standing in Kabul's path of complete conquest.

"What do you want of me?" he asked at length.

"My agents say you have spoken with the Persian, Lucienus. He, in turn, knows where Le-Dan can be reached—"

"The Persian ambassador has returned to the court of the sanshah, Panther. Carrying with him the offers of the Khan for alliance."

Sharon ground her teeth, glared at the apothecary. "Persia will never align with the barbarian," she seethed.

"Oh? How can you be sure?"

"Because Persian blood flows as much in my veins as it does in yours! Because even the Kazirs share the same root of the same tree. Because good will never bow before evil."

Outwardly the strange apothecary was emotionless; inwardly he felt inspired by her fervent belief. "I have no say over such matters, Panther. If you thought otherwise, you have come here on a fool's errand. Return to your steppes while you can. Tempt not God's protection of you, lest you find yourself in Kabul's dungeons."

He was toying with her now, she knew. Precisely because of Kabul's dungeons she had come here today, risked her very life to speak with the one man she was certain could help. The news that Carolyn had sent of Karim's attempt and capture had sunk her optimism like a leaden weight. Everything was now in peril; time was ever short, minutes and seconds taking on powerful meaning. There was no way she could get at Karim; the saya would have to do it herself. But Sharon also knew that Carolyn's own timetable had been badly damaged. The awaited Night of Atonement must be pushed forward—dangerously forward. Her appearance before the apothecary told just how desperately she needed help.

"I shall be responsible for Kabul's dungeons," she said at last. "Yes, and for all the palace as well."

His smile returned. "Then why are you here? Go then, fulfill your Kazir prophesy."

"Not merely the Kazir's prophesy," she reminded. "But the will of Allah. God himself has set forth the tasks before us; He alone has ordained what must be."

"Then again I must ask, Why are you here?"

Should she trust him, she wondered. Take her chances? Speaking of what was to come with an outsider was risky. There were those in the Stronghold who would have cut out her tongue before letting a single hint of what was to be be openly spoken. Yet what else could she do? It was no longer in her hands.

"Get word to Le-Dan," she said coldly, deciding to take the risk. "Offer him our support and help against the armies along the frontier."

The apothecary's brows rose. "You would expect General Le-Dan to commit his entire force against the barbarians on such a promise? You cannot be serious, Panther. Aye, it is true that Le-Dan plans for the day he may march against this butcher—but only when he knows the time to be right, only when he is certain of Persia's full support."

"There is no time for that!" cried Sharon with flashing eyes, pounding an open hand on the counter. "If Le-Dan truly loves Samarkand—as he claims—then in God's name force him to act!"

Uneasily, the apothecary said, "I will be frank with you, Panther. My own ears inside the palace have told me of what's happened. This trader, this Karim, can ruin everything. You see, even Le-Dan has his agents within those terrible walls. And because of the attempt upon the Khan's life, and because of the unsolved manner of Lord Gamal's peculiar death, our agents have urged us to temper our plans with extreme caution. You see, unlike you, we have no prophesy to fulfill."

"You are a fool, apothecary!" she snapped. She leaned over the counter, eye to eye with him. "You must urge General Le-Dan to muster his forces at once! Sweep across the frontier, then march upon the very walls of this city we both love."

As shadows crawled along his hawkish features, the apothecary kept a steady gaze. "I do not trust what you tell me, Panther. Nor do I trust these Kazirs you lead against Kabul. Your desert Phantoms. Should Le-Dan agree to your offer and march, how do we know that you don't plan some treachery against him, eh? How easy for your Kazirs to watch over the battle, allow each side to deplete the resources of the other, then, at the opportune moment, strike at us both, claim yourselves as masters of Samarkand over my general's corpse!"

"That is a lie!" she flared, shaking as she glared at him, his mistrust plain to see. "Neither I nor my forces would ever go back on a word freely given."

His smile deepened. "Prove it."

It was now or never, she was sure. She must tell this man as much as she dared, hoping against hope he would believe her.

"There is a night coming, apothecary," she began, speaking in a voice that was barely a whisper. "A night like no other in all the histories of all the world. The fulfillment of the Kazir prophesy, the Night of Atonement. The final and absolute judgment when this Khan and all his sons shall pay for their crimes. I swear this to you, apothecary, fully knowing my own fate. And when the dawn of the darkness comes, the halls of the palace shall cry out with the ghosts of the slain."

Her companion involuntarily shuddered as she told him these things; he could feel the short hairs curling on the nape of his neck, feel the power of her voice eat into his soul. Aye, these were strange folk, these desert Kazirs. Experience opposing them assured him that once a promise was made, it was no empty boast. If this Night of Atonement was to come, then it was to come soon—much sooner than he had ever dreamed.

Darkly, he said, "When, Panther? When will you strike?"

Mysteriously, Sharon answered, "With the coming of the Wind. The Devil's Wind . . ."

She spoke of things rarely mentioned during hours of sunlight, ancient, mystical beliefs from the depths of the Grim Forest where men of sense never set foot. "Do you speak of a hamsin?"

She lifted her hand, balled it into a tiny fist and wielded it before his startled eyes. "A hamsin like none before, apothecary. Fire to fire, ash to ash, as the witches foretold. The Night of Atonement, apothecary. Let the people of Samarkand bolt their shutters and cower in their beds. For when it comes . . ." Her words trailed off.

Mesmerized, he repeated the name of the Devil's Wind.

"Yes," she instructed him. "That will be the signal. Let General Le-Dan prepare for it and wait. Until then he need not engage the Huns in battle, only gather his armies and be ready to take the city."

Then she stepped away, a mere apparition herself in the dimmed light.

"Do we have a bargain, you and I?" she asked.

He looked at her long and hard, at last nodding, half out of honest desire to aid her cause, half out of sheer fear of the Devil's Wind she predicted. "You can trust me to relay the message at once," he said. "But understand that I can only advise Le-Dan, not order him. The final decision will be his and his alone."

Her smile posed an unfathomable riddle. "That is all I ask of you, apothecary," she said, slipping back toward the waning light of the street. "Send your carrier pigeons immediately, and wait for the appointed hour. For Samarkand—nay, the world—shall never be the same."

10

The dream was the same as always, as vivid and real as the very day it happened, never changing, never changing. The chamber was dark now, as it had been then, the slumped body of the slain emir at his feet, the dagger ripped through the Samarkand ruler's chest. His face was twisted, eyes wide and frozen, stiff hands uselessly clutched at the blade. Congealed blood ran a grisly track along both sides of his open mouth.

The girl was standing above the corpse in horror. He'd hit her when she fought off his advances, torn her *khafti* and gaped with lust at the sight of her young, supple breasts. She'd vowed to kill him if he touched her, and the scene amused him greatly. This Samarkand bitch, this spoiled girl of royalty, warning him, Kabul, king and master of the Huns, not to come nearer. He would tame her, all right. Make her whimper at his feet, grovel like a dog and beg for more by the time he was done.

The girl was thrown to the floor, squirming, sobbing as his hands probed her tender flesh. Then he was inside her, swimming deliriously, his thrusts quickening with his heartbeat. It was then, at the final moment of ecstasy, that she struck, wielding the sharp golden hairpin like a dagger, piercing it through his eye and pulling away while he screamed.

The Khan awoke precisely at that moment, as he always did. He gasped for air, hand covering his useless eye, and could almost feel again the unbelievable pain. With labored breath he peered around the dark chamber. The pitcher of wine still sat upon the tray, the silver chalice knocked over, contents spilled over the bearskin rug. Curtains rustled slightly, and he could feel a dampness in the squalid air, sense the coming rainstorm that approached the city on a strong mountain wind.

Kabul sat up; the whore was soundly sleeping at his side, wrapped snugly in the linen sheet, fair hair spilling over the pillows. It was hours before dawn, he realized, and, not wishing to wake her, he gently reached down and swept up the fallen chalice, refilled it with wine. He noticed that his hand was slightly trembling as it always did after the nightmare. He fondled the goblet, stared down into the depths of the crimson brew, thinking bitterly of his stolen eye. And before him, in these silent hours of night he had come to dread, he could see her face as clearly as he could see the distant tower lights through the curtains. That face, yes, that lovely, haunting face, laughing at him now, taunting him, softly vowing her own revenge even as he vowed his.

"We understand each other well, eh?" he mumbled, staring at the wine. "Neither of us can rest until our vendetta is complete." The face glowered back at him, eyes burning like coals. Kabul regarded the vision for a time and smiled. "We live only for each other, don't we bitch? Our lives are forever joined by the same evil thread. You in your way, I in mine. My advisers call me mad for feeding upon our mutual hatred. Yet you and I understand why. Neither of us can be complete until the other is dead. Neither of us can rest nor sleep. I fill your dreams even as you fill mine, eh? Yes, we alone know what drives us; we alone would tear the very world asunder for only a moment's chance at the other's throat. Plot and scheme against me, you nameless whore of the desert. I welcome it; I welcome your coming and the chance to see you once more. No demon in hell can stop that appointed meeting, bitch. Come to me, swiftly. I have waited too long. . . ."

The face in the wine listened until he was done, then slowly began to fade until it disappeared. Kabul lifted the chalice, turned it in his hand, then drank as though the brew were her blood. A satisfied grin parted his lips; he lay back contentedly. *Vendetta,* he thought. *Only this keeps me alive. Gladly would I bargain with any devil, sell my soul and condemn it to a thousand unspeakable hells, if only you would be delivered into my hands.*

The wind had started to swirl harder outside, pushing aside the curtains and flooding into the room. The whore grew chilly in her dreams and tightened the sheet around her. Kabul rested naked, sweating, keeping his smile as the voice of the wind whispered, *Soon, Kabul, it will be soon.*

Part Three:

THE BITTER FRUIT

1

"Recite me a song; I am in a poetic mood."

The singer bowed before the bronzed figure of his master, sweeping his arms grandly as Niko relaxed across the piled Persian carpet, his chin in his palm. Across from him the flesh of the three nearly-naked concubines glistened. They'd taken baths of milk, perfumed and coiffed themselves for hours, preparing for this night's coming pleasures with the most handsome of the Khan's sons and his well-appointed slave and constant companion. Niko had never been as selfish as his brothers, freely offering the singer his choice of women each night, including Niko's own favorites. It was said among the palace prostitutes that the slave was a lover second to none, save for Niko himself, of course. During these past months the romantic son of Kabul had come to enjoy the singer's rivalry as much as his company, turning an ordinary night's companionship into an orgy of love-making.

The strapping young slave, dressed in fine Indian silks, began his song in a gay, almost feminine tone. He sang of the waters of the Nile, evoking grand images of Egypt and all her past glories.

Niko's eyelids drooped heavily as he sipped from his ornate goblet. Harsh rain beat against the windows of his apartment. The whores sat aroused, enthralled by the song. The fun-loving son of Kabul let his eyes wander from one curvaceous hip to the next, aware of the pleasures that were to come this night, focusing upon the hard, brown nipples of the bare-breasted women, their soft bosoms.

Everyone was having a good time, the room filling with laughter and gaiety while several silent slaves gracefully slipped between the merrymakers, anticipating their every desire. Niko's hand lashed out and loudly smacked the well-endowed buttocks of the closest whore. The girl turned with both reddened face and behind, stared at him

137

and giggled. Wine was flowing, she spilled her own accidently while parodying the singer, and Niko roared with glee as the singer, himself slightly tipsy, tripped her, grinning as she fell face-first to the plush carpet.

"To life, Lord Niko!" another of the whores called, raising her chalice. The liquid spilled over her chin as she eagerly swallowed.

Plates filled with exotic dainties cluttered the floor, the food half-eaten. Niko rolled over, rested his head at the foot of one of the velvet divans. Beneath his loose tunic the hard, masculine lines of his strong figure emerged. "I have a surprise for you all," he announced, holding up a hand, gaining their complete attention.

"A surprise?" mimicked the Abyssinian girl, black skin in stark contrast to the cream-colored rug she sat upon. She looked at her master eagerly, as did the others. "What sort of surprise, my lord?"

Niko grinned, turned from face to face, at last fixing his gaze on the singer. "It has come to my attention," he said, "that my companion here has been taking too many liberties with the concubines . . ."

A number of good-humored catcalls came from the women.

"No, now listen to me, all of you," said Niko, unabashed. "The overseer herself—whatever is her name?—has personally conveyed to me an expression of displeasure."

The Abyssinian turned over and squealed. "My lord, such is impossible! Your slave has brought us nothing but pleasure!"

Her companions laughed and agreed, the singer bowed, nearly toppling over into the arms of a passive attendant.

Niko wavered as he managed to stand, and confronted his faithful companion directly. "This overseer says you are to be punished." The singer's face began to pale. Niko laughed hoarsely. "Let me see now," he mumbled, scratching his head. "What sort of punishment can there be for a man whose loins forever burn?"

"Make him take us all on," blurted the yellow-haired whore from the north. "Yes," chimed the third, the beauty called Lina. "One hundred and fifty women, each to be satisfied upon peril of his head."

The lordly son of the Khan roared. "I fear such punishment would kill the poor fellow," he remonstrated. "Surely no man, whatever his crime, deserves such a fate!"

"To die in paradise is no punishment at all," observed the clever singer.

"Then you accept the challenge?"

The younger man shrugged, smiled. "If it is my lord Niko's will, then so be it."

The women went wild with laughter and applause, leaving Niko to feel he'd been bested. "Just a moment," he said, calming them down. "In truth, my friends, I had another punishment in mind."

"Oh?" questioned the black-skinned girl. "Surely not to rob him of his manhood?"

Niko pulled open the singer's robes, stared at his limp member. Even in its flaccid state it was huge, like a horse. "To make of him a eunuch would break too many hearts," he sighed sorrowfully as the whores stared in admiring wonder. "Still, I can't have myself being continually on the losing end every night, now can I?" He reached for another goblet. "So," he went on, "I have decided on the only alternative."

The singer regarded his master with puzzlement, the whores waited in eager anticipation.

"I have decided to free him—free him and marry him off."

"*No!*" said Lina. "It would be shame to rob us of his values—"

"My mind is firm," rejoined Niko to the disappointment of them all. "Now all that remains is to find him a wife." He winked. "A proper wife who would keep him in his place."

"I know!" said the girl from the north, a mischievous twinkle in her eye. "Marry him off to Mistress Tania!"

Everyone broke into raucous laughter. "Yes, to Tania! That bitch has taken five thousand men in her time," chortled the Abyssinian. "A whore of whores! Why, men have died in her arms! They say her tricks of ecstasy can kill the strongest!"

"Aye, and even the most knowledgeable in the bedroom," added Lina.

Niko turned to the distraught singer. "What say you, man? Shall you wed the biggest slut in all of Samarkand?"

He hung his head, burped loudly without covering his mouth. "My lord would make of me a martyr," he said quietly.

"And if Mistress Carolyn is unhappy," remarked the yellow-haired lovely with a sneer, "then marry him off to her!"

The women giggled and Niko shared their mirth. "Yes, that would solve two problems together, wouldn't it?" This new overseer was too fastidious for his tastes, too abiding of Kabul's strict rules. At least the eunuch Castus, her predecessor, poor obese fellow, had allowed the rules to be bent now and again.

Niko yawned. "I shall have to think over this matter," he said decisively. "Select a mate most carefully. After all, we don't want our singer to be unhappy, do we?"

"He can warm my bed any time he likes," said the Abyssinian with a devilish grin. She looked to the quiet slave, adding, "But don't let our overseer catch you—otherwise you *will* be robbed of your jewels."

More laughter, more jeers. Niko, heady from the wine, turned back to the singer. "Which of these beauties will you have this night, eh? Take your choice, for I fear that the morrow might see you wed."

There was genuine surprise in the slave's dark eyes. It was most unlike his master to allow him first selection. Indeed, it was an honor. He mulled over the matter for a few moments, then said, "I'll take her." He pointed to the Abyssinian while the others groaned. "And her as well." The yellow-haired whore clapped her hands and squealed with delight. Niko grimaced. "You'll have them both?"

The singer's grin was silly and happy. "If this night is to be my last in freedom, lord, and if truly you meant to give me my choice. . . ."

Niko rolled his eyes toward the ceiling. "Very well," he said with a long sigh. "Take them." The girls bounded to their feet, happily followed on the singer's heels, bowing, backstepping into the far chamber. Niko peered down at the purring Lina whose seductive pose hinted at the

pleasures she had in store. The son of Kabul stuck out
his hand. "Come on," he mumbled. "Make me feel this
night like my foolish brother Mufiqua. Let your touch
enhance me until I, too, believe I'm a god."

The rain had stopped. Lina lay back with a feline smile,
looking over at the dreaming Niko. The chamber was
black, not the slightest thread of light to be seen from
the windows nor the vestibule. Niko's hand closed around
her breast possessively; he smiled contentedly in his
slumber, spent, unable to rouse himself and go another
round. Lina was pleased. She'd done her best for him,
she knew, tantalized and titillated him until he practically
begged release from the painful pleasure. Even then she
had refused, subtly working her tongue and hands over his
body, lingering teasingly, heightening his urge, then
abruptly halting her efforts while his drenched body
writhed with sublime torment. The famous lover had been
a toy for her this night. Like a child he had fondled her,
probed the deepest recesses of her being, and Lina had let
him, let him lose himself completely in amorous desire.
It had been at her will and her will alone that he had
climaxed, exploding with furious passion and hunger.
Now sated, he rested as a boy would: drained, gratified
for the moment. But the night was far from over, Lina
knew, and Niko was a man renowned for his sexual
appetite. Had it not been for the vast amounts of wine
he'd consumed, he could have easily gone straight until
dawn with his love-making.

Her lord and master stirred, smacking his lips with
unconscious delight. Lina dropped her hand between his
legs and gently placed her fingertips along his manhood.
The stiffening was slight but unmistakably there. Soon
he would be ready again. Should she rouse him now? she
asked herself. Or perhaps wait just a little bit longer, let
him sink even deeper into his dreams? There was no rush,
she decided; let him enjoy his rest. So far the night had
gone perfectly, why raise a chance of something going
amiss?

It occured to her then, as she rested beside him with
her eyes opened wide and staring up at the shadowed

ceiling, that of all the sons of Kabul, Niko was certainly
the gentlest. Temugin and Mufiqua had hurt her in bed,
bruised her, and her single experience with the brute
Krishna was one that even now made her shudder. His
sadistic appetite had on several occasions cost other, less
knowledgeable concubines, their very lives. Strangest of
all, though, had been Khalkali, insisting that she whip
him and bind him before his urges could be satisfied.
Then there had been Jamuga; that one had taken her to
his bed and she'd been shocked and disgusted to find two
small boys already there. Her only task had been to watch
as he'd made love to the boys, watch and later wipe them
all dry with towels.

She felt a tinge of sadness for Niko as she bided time,
waited until he was ready. But the overseer's orders had
been explicit. She was to spend these hours with Niko.

She lowered her head against his chest, ran her tongue
over his nipples. His eyes half-opened and he started to
come to life. Her hand massaged his manhood, caressed
him softly, touching lightly all the parts of his maleness,
while her lips lowered onto his belly. Niko began to
quiver; his breathing became hard and he stroked her hair,
exulting in the glorious feeling of being so gently awakened
by the touch of her flesh.

"Ahhh," he sighed, his muscles beginning to stiffen. Then
as her tongue lowered again, he sucked in air and hissed
it out between clenched teeth. His back arched upward,
he tried to bring her up toward him, so that his darting
tongue could meet hers, but Lina only lowered her head
further. A low, deep, animal groan emitted from his
throat; her mouth opened wide and she took him teasingly.
Niko pressed forward his hips, ground them slowly. She
was kissing him all over now, doing what she had done
before, focusing his full attention onto his passion, letting
him moan and hiss and loll his tongue while her lips
sweetly heightened his craving.

Passively he waited for her to increase the pressure,
shifting helplessly upon the sweat-drenched sheet, wincing
at the bite of her teeth, the gentle, hungered bites. His
manhood throbbed wildly with need of her, his panting
becoming labored and urgent. Still she held him at bay,
knowingly let him suffer the delicious agonies of desire.

It was too much! Too much for him—for any man—to bear! He was a slave within her power now, unable to command or control, needing to at last be set free of this honeyed misery.

His moans became growls; his hands closed tightly over her head, pushing her, forcing her to confront him, to release him at last from his longing. Again he sucked in air; his lungs were bursting with his need, shoulders shaking. The time was growing close, he knew, wanting it to last an eternity yet pleading for the thunderous climax.

"Lina, Lina!" he gasped, head reeling. "Lina, *Lina!*"

The razor was as fine as a thread, so miniscule she'd been able to conceal it beneath a fingernail. Now she held it carefully between thumb and forefinger. Her teeth bit hard into flesh, the razor swept across his testicles. Niko screamed a ghastly scream.

He kicked her off him savagely, stared at her twisted face, the streams of blood—*his blood*—dripping from her mouth.

"What have you done?" he wailed, wrenching his hands. The whore lashed out again with the razor, slashing his belly. The son of Kabul drew back a fist and smashed it into her face. Bone cracked as she toppled back, tumbled onto the floor. Niko jumped from the bed, kicked, sent her flying. Lina reeled to the wall as Niko glanced down at himself. Dark blood was spilling over his legs; the sperm-sack had been ravaged, his balls spilled from his body, raw flesh where his proud manhood had been. At that terrible moment, seeing what had been done and knowing that it never could be righted, Niko lost his mind. Crazed, frothing, screaming, his eyes bulging, he came at her. Lina bounded up like a leopard. "Death to all Huns!" she croaked, her mouth utterly misshapen, her broken jaw hanging from her distorted face. She came at him with the tiny razor again, lashing, striking savagely. Niko howled and crouched, hands at once to his forehead where a razor cut opened across his scalp. His fists went up, he missed, jabbed viciously with an elbow, pinning her against the wall. There his hands tore at her hair, yanking clumps as she retched with pain and spit out blood.

She was sliding to the floor; Niko held her up. The

whore wailed and kneed him sharply. The son of Kabul hollered with pain, dancing away with his loins on fire and his head splitting. Lina was at his back, trying to jab with her weapon. As Niko spun, a wild, unaimed arm struck her in the face. The prostitute tottered backward, struggled to regain her feet. Her eye was bleeding; her nose was crushed. She nearly collapsed against the bed, coughing, spitting a puce-colored liquid. Niko grabbed her from the back. His strong hands caught her by the throat and squeezed. Lina turned blue, fought like a wildcat, jabbing him, pulling at his ears. Her master was growing weaker; as he groaned, she righted herself and clawed at his face, tearing at his eyes, ripping at his already-scarred flesh. Together, grappling and wrestling, they fell across the bed.

Suddenly the singer and the other whores burst into the dark chamber. Faces frozen at the grisly sight, they looked on in abject terror. The two antagonists no longer seemed human. Naked, bloodied, mangled and twisted, they tried to kill each other. The bed sheets were awash in crimson; blood splattered over curtains and tapestries.

The Abyssinian shrieked, fled in panic, her companion on her heels, wailing and screeching. The singer wanted to do something, to help his master, to kill the insane woman and spare Niko's life. His feet were leaden, though; he could not budge, could not even scream. Helplessly he watched.

Like a vampire Lina sunk her fingernails into Niko's flesh. Niko yelped, slammed her face sideways against the iron bed post. Lina's skull cracked, half her face caving in. In victory the subhuman noble lord roared, dragging her back toward him, choking her. The whore gurgled, dazedly staring into his face. His command of reality was all but gone. She gyrated beneath him, forced loose his grip. Niko pounded her abdomen, blood and spittle flying wildly from his mouth. She thrashed spasmodically, head tilted to one side, neck broken. Again and again he struck, beating her to a pulp, wailing and crying, mourning his robbed manhood. Then, as he straddled her, pervertedly spreading wide her legs as if to make love to her, he slumped. He heaved and gasped one last time, then moved no more. When the palace soldiers finally reached his isolated apartment, they found both corpses intertwined and inseparable. Without waiting for the Khan's instruction, the entire wing of the palace was sealed.

2

Carolyn had been sitting at the edge of the heated pool, her golden body wrapped only in an oversized towel, hair neatly pinned in coils atop her head. She glanced over her shoulder and peered through billowing steam at the first cries and footsteps.

An overweight palace guard came racing in search of her, dumbly fanning at the clouds of vapor.

"What is it, fool?" she asked curtly. "Don't pant there like a dog. What's happened?"

"The whore, Mistress," he stammered. "The concubine, Lina—"

Carolyn's brows furrowed with rising temper. "Speak, dolt! What about her? What about Lina?"

Face white as a ghost's, he said, "She's murdered my lord Niko. Killed him as they slept!"

The overseer was incredulous. "What? On your feet, man! Tell me again, more slowly, accurately. Are you drunk?"

"No, Mistress." He rose and said, "It's true, I swear." And he reconstructed the murder as best he could, repeating what the stunned singer had recounted.

Before she could respond, more soldiers came racing from the verandah, closing off the portico, sending away the concubines milling about. Some of the whores began to shriek, others sobbed, still others ran to their private chambers and bolted the doors. The Khan had already been informed of the deed, and his wrath was great. Who could say how many heads would roll for the outrage?

The overseer dismissed the sweaty soldier and walked calmly from the baths. Guards bowed their heads stiffly, some eyeing her with fear, knowing her duty would be to punish all those connected with the assassination, rid the harem of any and all who bore the slightest friendship for the whore known as Lina.

As she crossed the vast hall, making a straight line between the doric columns and toward the arch, she saw a hasty Temugin, flanked by his stargazer, running to his father's personal quarters. Kabul, it seemed, had sent for all his sons immediately.

"A terrible event," Carolyn said, bowing before the gruff lord. "Please relay to the Khan my rage and assure him that I shall take these bitches well in hand."

"A little late for that," replied Temugin, openly showing his distaste for these concubines. He blessed his stars for the man at his side, doubly convinced now that his strategy of sequestering himself in his rooms had been the right thing to do. He knew the others had laughed. Called him a coward to his back. But he would have the last laugh. Oh, yes! He would still be alive when all of them were dead.

"Out of my way," said Temugin to the woman garbed only in the towel and adorned in her ever-present necklace of antelope horn.

Carolyn quickly stepped aside, cast a quick glance toward the soothsayer. For merely an instant their eyes met, and in that point of time each saw the pleased look of the other. Yesterday there were seven sons. Now there were only six.

In the dark gloom the saya nudged at the shoulder of the man sprawled over the straw. She was dressed in an abba, cowl grimly pulled over her head. When Karim first stirred, he cringed, believing his visitor to be another torturer.

"I know nothing," croaked the trader, lifting a swollen hand to protect his bruised face against the expected blow. "Nothing . . ."

Carolyn shook her head sadly, pained by what she saw. Karim was covered with sores from head to foot, smothered in festering cankers. Grim effects of the flaming iron prods and needles. She put a gentle hand to his brow, lowered her cowl.

"You're not one of Krishna's men!" exclaimed the prisoner weakly.

"No, friend, I'm not."

His bloodshot, sunken eyes widened. "Then who—?"

"One who would not harm you, old man." She leaned closer. "But listen: There is not much time. I run a dangerous risk being here. Krishna is away from the dungeons, and I bribed one of the guards with a whore. . . ."

"What . . . what do you want?"

"To take you away from your misery."

It was a flat, emotionless statement, one that made Karim wince in disbelief. "Then you are not an enemy?" he asked.

She shook her head. "No, trader. I am a friend. Your only friend."

His eyes stared in dawning comprehension. "A Kazir! You're a Kazir!"

"*Shhh!*" A finger went to her lips and she glanced around the cell with growing unease. "You did a stupid thing, Karim. You should have known not to try it."

The old man, who had aged a decade in the dungeons, whimpered. "I meant only to regain my honor," he sobbed. "I swear; I was out of my mind with grief for my daughter. . . ."

"Rest easy, trader. No more harm can come to Lina. I promise you."

He drew back slightly, knowing what she would say before she said it. "She's dead? My child is dead?"

Carolyn nodded gravely. "Last night. But she died without disgrace. Knowing of your capture, she sought only to make her own mark in our struggle. She volunteered, accomplishing her mission without regret—and died a noble death. A Kazir's death."

Karim reached for her abba, crumpled the fabric with his hand. "There was no pain? She died swiftly?"

"Instantly," lied the saya, unwilling and unable to tell the truth.

"Allah be praised!" He looked sharply to Carolyn. "I am at peace," he said. "It no longer matters how much the Huns might hurt me."

She smiled down at him, thinking how truly brave he

must be to have suffered all this in a worthless effort. "I told you before, trader, they will hurt you no more."

"You mean you've come to plan my escape?"

"Only the escape of your soul, Karim. More than that even I cannot do." She forced him to look at her evenly. "I have come to kill you."

His head sank back, and he nodded. "Even for that I am grateful," he admitted. He sighed, glanced around at his hated cell, looking forward to the peaceful oblivion. "I am ready."

Carolyn bowed her head. There were no tears and no sorrow. She drew the knife from its scabbard, held it over his pain-wracked body, and plunged the blade with all her strength into his heart. Karim moaned, then slumped. His lips parted in a smile the moment his last exhale deflated his lungs forever. The saya stood up, wiped the knife clean, stole to the iron bars. And there she fumbled for the borrowed key, locking the chamber and hurrying down the corridor.

One more soul had gone to heaven. There were still many left to be sent to hell.

3

In the poor light of an early dusk, Zadek's profile made him appear no less than the image of satan himself. His wispy triangular beard pointed sharply beneath a jutting chin, crooked nose seemingly hideously deformed against the backdrop of shadows. He entered the tent somberly, without greeting those waiting for him.

Tariq shifted uneasily in the presence of the mad mullah. He kept his gaze evenly ahead, bowing his head as the holy man took his place and closed the circle. When finally he dared gaze at the mullah's dour features, his face was as impassive as the faces of the dead. One of the nearby clansmen made a gesture to speak, but Sharon quickly hushed him to silence. The atmosphere of the Calling was not to be broken.

Slowly, slowly, Zadek withdrew the small, aged leather pouch and untied the cord. Those closest to him leaned forward with rising speculation when he turned the pouch upside down and let its contents tumble into his open hand. The mad mullah sat cross-legged, oblivious to those around him, and closed his vast hand. Within his grasp rested the Glowing Stones of Babylon, a handful of tiny and seemingly worthless stones, useless to all save the few men in the world who'd understood their power.

Zadek shut his eyes, mumbled a few unintelligible words in a strange and archaic tongue. Tariq watched in wonder as, abruptly, the former priest of Islam shook his hand and hurtled the stones to the floor like a set of dice. The Glowing Stones of Babylon formed a perfect half-moon before him; Zadek began to sway back and forth, soundlessly mouthing the secret chant. He seemed to be in deep pain, this man who had seen more of the world and its mysterious doings than any other. His craggy face broke out in a cold sweat, his nostrils beginning to flare while he wheezed. Suddenly, miraculously, the small rocks started to glow, each with its own color—crimson, golden-yellow, azure, and indigo.

The stones began to quiver, to dance and cavort along the edge of the rug at the mullah's feet. With widened eyes those inside the tent looked on, unable to tear their gazes away from the incredible sight.

Zadek was staring now, as a blindman stares, into the empty reaches of nothingness—yet the mad mullah did indeed see something. Something denied the rest, a vision across whose threshold only a chosen few had ever trespassed, and then only rarely, for such voyages were dangerous to those who undertook them—even to one such as Zadek.

For a seemingly endless time, in which the world itself appeared to stop and hold its breath, the mullah continued to sway. The stones intensified their glow, and suddenly burst into blaze, each a tiny bauble of flaming fire, deep penetrating fire that all but blinded those who watched.

"I . . . I am in contact," rasped Zadek, hissing his words through clenched teeth.

Sharon's soft whisper broke through the silence. "Do you see him?" she asked.

Zadek nodded strongly, bobbing forward over the fiery baubles. He spread his large, callused hands above the flames. "He lies in his cell, stilled, unspeaking—"

Tariq felt a pang of fear. "Speak, monk! Is he dead? Is Roskovitch dead?"

The mad mullah slowly shook his head. "He is not . . . dead. He lives, and waits. . . ."

"Has he been tortured?" asked Sharon worriedly.

"He is strong, this barbarian from Rus. He accepts their pains and spits in their eyes."

Yes, Sharon thought, knowing that would be exactly like him. Suffering any torture the Huns might impose, all the while readying himself for the moment of freedom. Sharon loathed herself for forcing this imprisonment upon him, this much-needed assistance from within the very bowels of Kabul's dungeons. Roskovitch was her most worthy warrior, unwavering in his loyalty. The barbarian was as valuable to her as half a legion would be to a soldier like Le-Dan, a rallying force for all the Kazirs. His absence in coming days would be sorely noted. Yet who else could she have so readily trusted? Who else to use to put into place the final pieces of her plan?

"Move on, Zadek!" she hissed to the straining mullah, bringing him out of his trance. "Move on!"

He complied deafly, leaving the scalp-locked barbarian; then back to the Calling of the stones Zadek returned, back to the depths of this netherworld. Blood drained from his ashen face as he shifted his enormous concentration.

Tense minutes later he spoke again. "I see him now . . ." he croaked, speaking each word slowly and dramatically. "The mist is lifting. . . ."

Sharon fidgeted, sharing a quick and fretful glance with the troubled Tariq. "Can you make contact?" she pressed.

The insane man of the cloth hesitated. "He remains far, far away from my beckoning, Panther. Lost within the realm of his drugged slumber, his dreams of perverted conquests."

"You cannot lose him, Zadek!" she warned. "Summon him again—back from these visions. Regain your control, priest!"

The mullah's broad shoulders sagged with the weight of the burden she had imposed. It would not be easy, not with Mufiqua's mind so deranged, not with the effects of the opium so deeply entrenched in his vitals.

Zadek put his fingertips to his temples, feeling his head reel with the pain of his mind transference, and steadily regained his power. Then he smiled.

Mufiqua tossed about, tightening his hands at the perspiration-drenched sheet. He clawed and moaned, fought off the terrible intrusion that hammered away at his fevered brain. Again there was the face, that nameless face he did not recognize but knew he had seen before . . . somewhere . . .

Mufiqua, Mufiqua . . .

He heard his name called, his being forcefully summoned. The son of Kabul tossed and turned restlessly, but the voice was stronger than he was, the face always there to greet him no matter which way he turned.

"Who . . . who are you?" he panted in his delirium.

I have come, Mufiqua. Have you not been expecting me? Have you not known that I would always be close?

Mufiqua sightlessly gazed into the darkness. The voice *was* familiar, he knew. He'd heard it before as surely as he'd been haunted by the face. But where? When? Whose face?

"What do you . . . want . . . ?"

Your obedience, Mufiqua. You cannot escape. You cannot hide no matter how far you may run, how distant your dreams may take you upon your drugged voyages. . . . Do you not know me, Mufiqua? Do you not hear and recognize the voice of your master?

"Master? Master . . ." The word rolled weakly off his tongue. And then it came to him, the flooding memory of the night he had stolen into the dim quarters of the city to seek out the dancer, the woman who haunted his thoughts every night, the woman whom he'd vowed to possess.

"Yes . . . I remember now. . . . I remember. . . ."

The satanic face smiled. *Good, Mufiqua. I knew you would. Now I have come as I promised. There is work to be done, Mufiqua. Much work to be done. I am counting on you. Hear my instruction—and obey.*

The contact was complete. Zadek had managed to pull the addicted son of the Khan onto the same brain pattern as his own. Mufiqua's will belonged to him, and him alone. Whatever the command, it would be done.

"How . . . how may I serve thee, Master?"

The words came quickly. *In front of your door, Mufiqua, there is a box, a small box that I have sent to you. Go now and find it.*

In a stupored trance, Mufiqua lifted himself off the bed and walked zombielike across the blackened chamber. His bare feet made no sound, his naked body numb to the bite of the chill wind. Mufiqua crossed into the adjoining chamber and, with glazed eyes, came to the oval door and opened it slowly. Aging wood creaked. At his feet rested the box, just as his master said. He knelt down and picked it up gently, and returned to his room.

"What . . . shall . . . I do with it, Master?" he asked, holding the package out in the palms of his hands.

Zadek's voice was growing clearer, possessing his mind completely. *Open it. Take out the doll and place it carefully upon the mantel.*

The son of Kabul did as instructed. He lifted the lid, discarded it, then he stared at the contents. The doll was tiny, easily fitting into the palm of one hand. It was a soldier, a Hun commander in exact replica down to its perfectly-sewn breeches and minuscule vest of armor. A needle-length sword dangled from a bronze-colored scabbard, the left hand of the doll holding a perfect rounded Hun shield. Atop its head it wore a horned helmet complete with noseguard and eyeslits. Everything was perfect to the slightest detail, so lifelike that Mufiqua shuddered. Then, as the voice instructed, he placed the doll atop the stone mantel and stood back, waiting.

There is a pin inside the box, Mufiqua. A silver pin. Find it. His hand groveled in the dark; he winced as the sharp point jabbed at his index finger. Carefully he lifted it, twirling it before his eyes, reminded of the needles the Chinaman used for Kabul's acupuncture treatments, only smaller, down to scale with the doll. He mumbled, "What next, Master?"

Take the pin, Mufiqua, bring it closer to the doll. Hold it with care and push it deeply inside the doll's chest.

Mufiqua hesitated, but the strong will of the voice forced him to do its bidding. The son of Kabul lifted his hand, glassy eyes staring uncomprehendingly at the figurine, and plunged the needle through the tiny links of mail.

"Noooooo!" wailed Temugin, clutching at his chest as pain wracked him. The would-be commander of all the Khan's armies rolled off his bed and onto the floor, gasping and moaning. The pain intensified, pounding, ravaging his chest. Like the weight of a wall pressing down over him, the crushing agony seemed to last forever. He flailed about the floor, sputtering and squealing, groveling to his knees. "Stop!" he shrieked. *"Stoooopppp!"*

"My lord, what's the matter?" The soothsayer burst into the room, face alight with concern. He hovered above the tormented man with widened, incredulous eyes.

Temugin stuck out his arm, knocking over a candlestick, forcefully grabbing his trusted seer by his sleeve. Hezekiah deftly knelt beside him. "What has happened to you, my lord?"

"Pains . . . My chest—"

The soothsayer furrowed his brows darkly. "Perhaps I should fetch the Chinaman? He understands the workings of our bodies; his knowledge—"

At the very mention of the Oriental the stricken Temugin became terrified. He gritted his teeth, gnashed them together, and finally forced his words out. "Don't trust him," he croaked. "Can't trust anyone, anyone. . . ."

"But, my lord!" protested the bent, hunched seer. "You are ill. Who can say what manner of fits have overtaken you? You need expert attention at once. It is not good to lock yourself in thusly. Perhaps last night's drink was spoiled. Or the food you ate—"

"Poisoned!" growled Temugin, spitting the thought. "They've . . . poisoned me!"

"Who, lord? It cannot be! I myself have tasted each of your meals before they were brought. Again, lord, I beg that you let me send for the Chinaman."

Temugin shook his head violently, sucking his air in pain-ridden gasps. "Bring no one, soothsayer! They mean to kill me." His grip tightened. "Do you hear? I will see no one! Treat me yourself!"

"But, lord, my knowledge is of the stars. I know nothing of medicines."

The battering in his chest worsened, and Temugin was overcome by nausea. His head swam, and he was knocked back as he vainly struggled to stand. "Help me . . . onto my bed—"

Hezekiah slipped his arms around Temugin's shivering body, picked him up and carefully rested him, propping his head against the pillows. "They want me dead!" he rattled. "They will not rest until I am in my grave." Then he wailed loudly, crossing his hands over his chest, kicking out his feet into the air. Suddenly the pain was gone, vanished as quickly and inexplicably as it had come. Temugin's breath labored, then calmed. His hands sank at his side.

"My lord?" questioned the seer.

"It . . . it's gone," said Temugin. "The affliction has left me."

"Are you sure, lord?"

He took a series of long, deep breaths, turned back to the only man worthy of trust. "This was an attempt on my life, stargazer," he said. "As surely as you predicted the return and demise of Gamal, so has this been another plot."

"I saw it not in the stars, my lord."

Temugin reddened. "Then your reading was wrong! Don't you see? My brothers know the threat I pose to them," he told Hezekiah, his face drenched in sweat. "They have plotted this together! Ah, what a fool I've been! I should have known they'd find some insidious way to be rid of me."

The seer bowed his head respectfully. "Yes, my lord. You are wiser than I in unfolding this dire attempt on your life. You alone see clearly the truth even as my own vision has been clouded."

With the compliment Temugin smiled expansively. "But I am too clever for these foolish plots, eh stargazer?" He coiled a fist. "From now on I will eat nothing cooked within my father's kitchens." He leaned forward, regarding his companion evenly, put a hand to his shoulder.

"Tomorrow, stargazer, you will personally supervise a patrol into the countryside. Ravish for me a village, find a slave worthy of your bidding, and make him a personal vassal, entrusted to my own kitchen. Set guards at the door and let no man—not even my father—enter, upon peril of death." His eyes began to glower as he spoke. "They'll never be able to poison me again, will they stargazer?" He chuckled quietly.

Hezekiah shared his mirth. "No, my lord. Lord Temugin is too clever. Far too clever. Let them sulk and continue their folly. I shall return to my readings, and report to you every dawn what I have discovered."

Temugin lay back, exulted. This time he would be ready for them, he knew. Be ready for anything they might conspire. And he once more thanked all the dark gods of the Huns for the fortune that had brought this soothsayer to his employ.

4

Morning was close. Sharon stirred contentedly, luxuriating in the glow of her being, the tender touch of the sleeping man beside her, the man she had loved for so long. It had been difficult for them to steal away this single night, to capture once again their love in the warmth of each other's arms. Difficult and dangerous. For, as they both knew all too well, the love between her and Tariq was forbidden. Forbidden by Kazir law as much as it was made impossible by the prophesy. But Sharon would not regret these stolen hours, come what may. Nor would Tariq. Least of all Tariq. They had ridden from the safety of the Stronghold in the dead of night, disguised and unrecognized by the loyal desert men who stood lonely vigil. Rode across the steppes, among the shifting dunes until they were well out of sight, alone in their own private world, cherishing these few moments amid the raging fires of their love. Now the night was done, they would be missed, the Kazir fortress a flurry of anxious concern for their safety. Dawn had come all too soon.

Nestling her head in the crook of his arm, she gazed forlornly at the coming of morning, the glorious desert sky and the endless red sands. She should be crying now, she knew. Should be flowing with sorrowful tears, for when they parted today, it could well be for the last time. Tariq had to go his way to do what must be done, she to go her own. The Law was the Law, unyielding and relentless, denying their devotion to each other coldly, promising only fulfillment of their lives in the acceptance of the Prophesy.

Of all who knew her, only Zadek suspected the love she and Tariq shared. His warning had been veiled but clear: The One who leads, the One who commands, can never be whole. She must forever remain apart, denied what other women take for granted. Without home, husband, or family. Only the Prophesy mattered. Sharon was not afraid of the death that awaited her; her only grief came at the thought of losing Tariq. Yet she never spoke to him of these matters, never once gave him cause to question what lay at the end of the road. The saya knew, though. Ah, yes, Carolyn knew. The Panther of the Steppes was a tool, of God and nothing more. When Samarkand was freed and returned to its rightful heirs, her tasks would be complete, her reason for living ended. The dawn after the Night of Atonement would never be greeted by her eyes. *Karma.* Fate. A fate that could not be altered or denied.

But at least Tariq doesn't know! Praise Allah for that!

He stirred with the wind; she kissed him lightly. His eyes opened and he smiled down at her, running his fingers through her tousled hair.

"I love you, Sharon," he whispered.

"And I love you, Tariq," she replied. "But it's late. We have to get back."

He wiped dust from his eyes, staring with a child's wonder at the beauty of the desert, his eternal home. His father, Shoaib the Goatherd, had been buried near here not so many years ago, and Tariq wished no more for himself. No tomb, no marker. Only the sands and the sunrise would greet him every morning for as long as the world existed. Yes, and Sharon would rest beside him, the two of them together, eternally.

"What are you thinking?" she asked.

He grinned, sitting up and stretching his muscles. "About us. About how much we have to look forward to, once we've finished."

He did not see the shadow that crossed her brow. She tossed back her hair, straightened her robe. A small bone comb was retrieved from the saddlebag beside their blanket and she ran it through her hair. Tariq observed her with love in his eyes, frowning when she made ready to get up. He glanced at the tethered horses standing calmly in the dune's shadow, then pulled her sharply to him. Sharon laughingly pushed him away, stopping when his mouth covered hers. The kiss was long and lingering, as satisfying as the night itself had been.

"We mustn't linger," she warned. "We'll be missed. You wouldn't want the Kazir elders to hear we spent this night together, would you?"

He frowned. "I don't very much care what they think," he said, letting anger show.

Sharon touched his face with her fingertips. "No, Tariq. We cannot be bitter. We must not be bitter. Didn't we promise that to ourselves when we began? We knew it would be hard. . . ."

"Yes, but then it was different." He looked away from her, sighing. It all seemed so much simpler then, this secret love. So easy to hide, to disguise. Now it was different. Their work was almost done, yet in many ways only starting. There were too many demands pulling them further and further apart, denying them even these occasional clandestine hours. But Tariq was a Kazir, a chieftain, the only son of Shoaib, the man who'd unified the desert tribes. His duty could not be denied, nor could Sharon's, though sometimes he hated both the Law and his people for it.

"Be not unhappy, my love," she begged. "This night was wonderful; I shall never forget. A perfect moment in all eternity."

He kissed her again, tenderly, with all his heart and

desire. And she willingly returned that kiss, subduing the tears that ached to pour from her eyes. If only things had been different, if only . . . She stopped her musings, shook her head. Life was filled with far too many "if only's."

"When will you leave?" she asked him.

He shrugged. "Zadek says the sooner the better. The inquiry into Niko's death, plus the unexplained manner in which Karim was found dead, have caused a great many questions. Kabul shall soon no longer blame his sons for these recent events. The saya's messages urge us to move with haste."

The hand of God was at work, the Kazirs could no longer bide their time. *If only Le-Dan's support could be counted on!*

"And you?" said Tariq, facing her squarely.

"I await only the news of the next action taken," she said. "Then I shall return to the forest—for the last time." Her composure began to crumble as Tariq's eyes fixed on her, and she fell into his strong arms, weeping. "It's no good, my love," she cried. "We cannot pretend to each other any longer."

Tariq nodded grimly, pressing her face against him. "Our love will not be denied," he vowed softly, looking toward the sun. "When the deeds are done, we shall have our lives together."

Sharon pulled away abruptly, tears spilling. "No," she said, shaking her head, hair flying loosely before her eyes. She sniffed and turned away from him. "Never! It's the Law—"

"The Law was made by men and it can be broken! I don't care, Sharon. We've waited, dreamed too long. . . ."

"I must go alone," she answered miserably. "Please understand. You have your duty, I have mine."

"I'll never understand!" he flared. "You're mine! No man, no Law, can ever change that! I'll be at your side always, until we are one."

His words were killing her. How much she wanted him to be with her now, to share with her what must be! Yet how could she even contemplate such a rash thing, knowing the outcome would still be the same—doom for them both. No, it was better as it was. She would face the future bravely, keep her lover, her gentle lover, well sheltered from the things she was forced to do. It was the only way to save him. The only way.

"You mustn't say that," she pleaded, hands to her mouth and shaking. "You must never even think it! If you love me, Tariq, then believe what I tell you, and never ask me again."

"But why, my darling, why? Why is it forbidden?"

"The Law," she replied, to which he shook his head. There was more here, he realized. Far more, unspoken all this time, although both of them were as aware of it as they were aware of sunrise following the night. More than the strict Kazir code, the harsh code to which the tribe was sworn.

Softly, he said, "It's the Prophesy, isn't it?"

"Ask me no more questions," she said weakly. "Do not probe, Tariq. Let me go to my fate. Karma can never be altered."

That much was true. What was written in the stars had been ordained eons ago. Nothing in the world could change it. "Perhaps," he added quietly, "the Prophesy is flawed. Misinterpreted . . ."

She shook her head ruefully, so full of love for him, yet so burdened by his unrealistic dreams. Sweet Tariq, who sought to change the course of destiny. When she drew the courage to look at him again, she repeated all that he already knew. *"There will be a time when a new leader shall rise among the Kazirs,"* she quoted from the hallowed Book of Wisdom. *"A new leader born of those known as Outcasts. One to whom the desert tribes will rally and die for, one for whom destiny cannot be changed."* She watched his anguish sadly. "I am that One, Tariq. It was Zadek who brought me to you and declared as much, the witches themselves confirming it." She shuddered. "But I was unclean. Forever shamed. Nothing can be done to alter that fact."

"To me you have never been shamed," he said, and she smiled up at him, wanting so very much to believe it.

She reached out and touched his cheek with the lightness of a feather blown by the wind. "I love you, Tariq. Never forget that!"

His eyes locked with hers. "You make it sound as though we'll never see each other again."

Her smile was without joy as she answered, "For certain we shall, my love, for certain we shall. But not until you and I have accomplished what we must. Not until we greet each other beneath the walls of Samarkand."

5

"More wine!" demanded the blustery Khalkali.

As the servant soundlessly poured, the whore Jasmine, scars of her battered face covered by clever use of makeup and eye shadow, humbly bowed and helped him off with his boots.

Khalkali growled as he downed the strong brew, wiping his mouth with the soiled sleeve of his tunic. He belched loudly, picking at a greasy leg of lamb. He grunted as each boot was tugged off and placed at the side of his cushioned seat. Jasmine blocked out the stink of his sweaty, unbathed body, meekly resumed her place at his side, legs folded underneath her, eyes cast down toward the floor, silently awaiting his pleasure.

It had been several weeks since that night she'd been taken by force. The drugged Mufiqua had, as his first act of love-making, beat her mercilessly before making her submit. Most of the scars had healed well enough; the overseer had seen to that. But the scars of her mind would never heal. At night she relived that awful experience, screaming in her fitful sleep, waking in terror as the animal Mufiqua came at her endlessly in his opium-induced stupor. The overseer had called for her sharply at dawn, standing aghast at the sight of Mufiqua's debased ideas of pleasure. Carolyn had bowed with due respect to the glassy-eyed son of Kabul, then gently urged Jasmine up, sheltering her bruised body, and led her away. With great pains Mistress Carolyn had cared for her and brought her back to the world of reality. And for this kindness Jasmine had vowed to be her vassal for life, to do whatever was asked without question. She hated Mufiqua, loathed them all. It had been something of a shock to realize that the overseer herself shared many of these feelings. Not that Mistress Carolyn had openly said anything. Indeed the opposite was true; when Jasmine had spilled her young girl's heart out to her, the overseer had remained silent and impassive. Yet there was something in her eyes, some deep-seeded anger that Jasmine did not understand, assuring her that she was not alone in her hatred. And whatever the reason, for that Jasmine was glad.

Khalkali almost choked on a tiny splinter of bone, coughed it up and cursed crudely. He wiped his hands clean on Jasmine's silklike hair, then patted his belly, satisfied at the meal. A glimmer of carnal lust flickered in his reptilian eyes as he regarded the whore anew.

"Why did the overseer send me you?" he asked.

Jasmine forced a smile, inwardly disgusted. "I know not, lord," she replied sweetly. "Mistress Carolyn said that you required company for the night, and I had the honor to be chosen."

He laughed deeply. "Honor, is it? Eh?" He tilted her face closer toward him, examining her skin in the bright light of the brazier. The purple bruises became apparent. "Perhaps, compared to my brother Mufiqua, my company *is* an honor, eh?" Then he laughed again. "Still," he mumbled, noting her ample breasts, her peasant features, "I can see that this overseer is a woman with a good eye for flesh. Yes, yes. How are you called, eh?"

"Jasmine, my lord."

"Jasmine, eh? A pretty name." He yanked her by the hair, forcing her head back. "Afraid of me, whore?" he questioned.

She shook her head. "No, my lord. Honored to serve you, to give you the pleasures of the night."

"But you'd have preferred another, no?" He peered at her more closely, darkly. "You'd have kissed Niko's feet, hmmm? Moaned with ecstasy had it been his hands all over you instead of mine?"

"No, my lord. I am yours alone—for tonight."

His grin expanded. "And tomorrow another's?"

He let go of her hair and she bowed her head. "Such is my work, my lord. A concubine's duty to her masters."

"Bah." He spat. "Soon there won't be many others to choose from, eh?"

"I don't know what you mean, my lord."

"No?" He sighed, instructing her to stand behind and massage him. Soft but firm strokes put him at ease. "Well, perhaps you don't. Perhaps you don't." He held out his goblet, Jasmine snapped her finger and the attending slave came running, filling it to the brim. He slurped as he drank, clamored for more. Jasmine dismissed the slave and poured the drink herself. For an instant Khalkali's eyes met hers. Then he drank.

"You seem most tired this evening, my lord," she told him, resuming the massage. Her hands expertly worked the tense muscles of his shoulders and back, and the lord groaned with appreciation. "What did you say your name was, whore?"

"Jasmine, my lord."

"Ah, yes. Jasmine."

"Would you like me to bathe you, my lord? Wash your body clean of its dirt before you prepare for sleep?"

"I dislike bathing," he said with a grimace.

"Then would you enjoy my annointing your body with oils? Rare oils from the East, said to wash away a man's weariness." Her hands dug in harder, working up and down, side to side.

"Later, perhaps." He held out the empty goblet. She poured happily, willing to do his bidding. Once it was finished, he slumped forward, content at this moment to do nothing more than to let her fingers continue probing and pleasing him. It had been a long and difficult day. Niko's duties, such as they were, had been passed onto him, thus giving him twice the area of the city to be responsible for. His dear departed brother had left his work in a terrible state, and it had fallen upon Khalkali to right it.

Jasmine was standing before him, smiling. "More wine, my lord?"

Khalkali snapped from his somber thoughts and nodded. "Yes," he rasped, toying with the goblet with both hands before he slaked his thirst. The taste of desert and dust was still strong in his mouth, and try as he might he could not get rid of it. *How I loathe this place,* he mused. *This Samarkand. When I am Khan, I shall leave it*

*forever, build a new city, a glorious city, far, far away
from here. Khalkalistan, I shall name it. Yes, a monument
to me that will survive the ages. Samarkand I shall burn,
burn to the ground and leave not a trace of its existence.*

In his melancholia, the swaggering son of Kabul allowed
the whore to lead him from his chair, lie him down
comfortably on the divan. He sighed as her hands quickly
went back to work.

Has Krishna any news for me? he wondered. *Or does my
brutish brother go back on our bargain, plotting against
me like the others? No, he would not dare. Not now, not
yet. He has need of me, does Krishna. More than I have
for him. Who else can he count on above the ground?*

Jasmine placed the goblet back in his hand, filled it
once more. Khalkali stared into the brew, eagerly drank.
He'd been drinking too much these past days, he knew.
Allowing himself too many luxuries. He must learn to
keep his mind clear, his wits sharp. Yes, that had been
Niko's downfall. Carelessness. Khalkali was positive he
would never make the same error.

He rolled onto his back, his forehead gleaming with
perspiration. The wine was making him uncomfortably
warm, but the fire in his veins was an elixir, his only
antidote to the boredom of his daily routine. The Khan
had done this to him, allowed him to wallow like this
while Gamal had conquered. Those Western Armies
should have been his own to command. Yes, it should
have been he returning as the hero. He, Khalkali, fiercest
son of Kabul. One day he would have his father's other
eye for this, he vowed. Never again would he take second
place behind any man. Any man.

He finished his cup, the whore was quick to refill it.
His eyes lingered on her shape, her small waist, rounded
hips. Her breasts taunted him, sensuous mouth slightly
parted and teasing. "More wine?" she whispered. He
grunted in response, feeling his desire for her begin to
rise. Yes, the overseer had chosen well this night, even if
the whore did bear blemishes.

"What . . . what did you say your name was?" he asked,
speech slightly slurred.

Again the smile, the dancing eyes. "Jasmine, my lord."

He drank some more, started to refuse as she took the pitcher to refill his goblet, then changed his mind, let her pour.

Oh, the wine was good. Tasty and strong. Perfect. Sluggishly he downed the last of it, enjoying even the dregs, feeling his bladder swell. He would have lifted himself to empty it had not the whore started her massage again. Her hands were strong now, stronger than before, grabbing at his flesh, digging into it, heightening the painful sensations.

"More wine, my lord?"

He shook his head. "No," he answered with a gaping yawn, rolling over onto his back. "Not . . . now . . ."

Jasmine, though, did not seem to hear. Dutifully she called for a fresh pitcher, placed it carefully on the silver tray, and poured until the brew met the brim of the cup. Khalkali took it, sipped.

"Is the new brew not to your liking, my lord?" she asked with a frown.

"Fine, fine, whore."

"Then why are you not drinking, my lord?"

He belched as he started to answer. "Because . . . because I've had . . . enough. Too much . . . No more. . . ."

With one hand cradling his head, Jasmine helped him put the goblet to his lips, lifted it and poured the contents into his mouth. Khalkali coughed, spat much of it out, tried to push her away. But the girl was persistent and he didn't have the strength now to stop her. More wine poured down his throat, spilling out of his mouth, staining the sheet darkly.

"Stop!" he sputtered. He rose onto one elbow, felt his head become light, start to swim. The room was going around, her face before him like a swinging lantern, smiling, teasing. The wine continued to flow, he gurgled, then retched. Jasmine lithely stepped back while he heaved his guts over the floor and himself. She brought a towel, wiped his face and the sides of his mouth, stroking his brow. Khalkali followed her eyes, saw as they darted across the room toward the curtains. He tried to sit up, she pushed him back down. Then his mouth was open again. Had he opened it—or had her fingers pried it wide? He didn't know, didn't care. More wine pushed down his throat.

Suddenly the whore was not alone. Someone was standing beside her, bearing the same smile, the same peculiar glint in her eyes. His vision was blurred as he tried to make out who it was. A woman. Another woman. A whore? No. Who? He recognized her slowly, the hair, the stance, the necklace hanging from her throat, dangling over her breasts. It was the overseer. Carolyn.

"More wine, my lord?" said Jasmine seductively.

He shook his head wildly, threw himself off the side of the bed. The overseer groaned as she struggled to pick him up, toss him back onto the mattress. Khalkali pressed his lips together tightly, refusing to drink. The overseer's strong hands were pinning his head down against the pillows. He struggled to free himself, kicked out blindly, flayed his arms. The women shared a glance and grinned at each other. Then his mouth was open once more, Mistress Carolyn's hands yanking his jaw lower, gripping him by his teeth. He quivered as the whore took the oversized pitcher and began to pour. Like a river the wine flooded into his mouth—spilling over him, forced down into his belly, clogging his windpipe, making him cough. Phlegm spat up, fell across his chin. Carolyn wiped it away. The whore poured and poured. Khalkali gagged, choked, tried to wrest himself free. He'd been paralyzed by the brew, he realized. Rendered as helpless as a suckling babe, while the two women stuck a tube into his mouth, pushed it all the way down, and let the wine siphon from the pitcher.

He was whining, gurgling, coughing and vomiting. Spewing up everything. But the wine didn't stop. More of it, more, and yet more. An endless flow. "Kill . . . you!" he slurred, eyes wide but hazed over. The women laughed at him, raising his anger. He balled his hands into fists ready to strike at them both, smash their faces. He was drained, though; devoid of any strength, no more than putty in their hands.

They're killing me! he wailed soundlessly. *Murdering me!*

The wine flowed, increased in volume. The bed was soaked with it, pools forming over the floor, dripping from the mattress like a spring rain. Spittle and vomit flew from between his lips. His teeth clenched on the tube, nearly breaking it. The wine splashed in waves through his mouth, pulsing down his throat, coming out of his nose. It overflowed his tongue, splattered in pools into his belly.

The overseer pushed his head to the side, nose flat against the wet sheet, sticking the tube back inside his numbed mouth. He made a terrific effort to pull away, break free from their control. The hands were all over him now, pushing him firmly into position, pinning him, so that he could do no more than wag his fingers.

"More wine, my lord?"

Puke gushed like a stream, the smell of the wine foul in his nostrils. There was a rag being placed over his mouth, held firmly by one of them, but which he couldn't tell. It plugged the flow of air into his lungs, forced the vomit back down his throat. Khalkali wanted to scream; his head was growing heavier and heavier, lungs bursting, flesh changing to a dark, sickly color. He opened his eyes with great effort, caught the merest glimpse of the overseer as she pressed her face in closer to his, tightly pushed the rag between his swollen lips. He heaved his guts, felt once more the bile being blocked inside his chest.

"More wine, my lord?"

If only I could scream!

"More wine, my lord? *More wine, my lord?*"

Kabul was hungry. His stomach churned as he waited for the food to be brought. He lounged for a few more moments in his bed, then took his patch and carefully placed it into position over his stolen eye. Outside the morning shone gloriously, a bright, warm sun set into a rich and cloudless blue sky. He could see a few birds in flight, distantly soaring over the highest towers, hear the caged parrots in the gardens squawking with delight at the birth of this new day.

The Khan always broke his fast early, a few minutes after rising. It was a habit begun many, many years before, when he was nothing more than a lowly chieftain along the steppes of Central Asia. In those times he would wake in his tent, smile with satisfaction as the smell of the cooking fires wafted to his nostrils. Then, attended by his servants, he would fill his belly, drink his fill of wildberry wine, and prepare for the long tasks of the day ahead. Those had been good times, he mused. Youthful years, when his dreams of conquest and empire had barely begun to be realized. So much had changed since then. So many battles fought, so many enemies slaughtered and enslaved. Yet still he enjoyed waking on a morning like this, and, as in those times long gone, eagerly awaited the arrival of his morning meal. Until he was finished, all other matters would wait. It was the single luxury that even now he never denied himself.

The knock on the chamber door was brisk, the brass knob turning quickly, and two faithful bowed low as they stood at the threshold. "Good morning, Sire," they said in unison, as they did every day.

Kabul scratched complacently at his hirsute belly, bade them inside. Each carried a tray, one bearing only a chalice and wine urn, the other groaning beneath the weight of the covered casserole. The Khan breathed in deeply, the aroma most pleasant. His cooks were the best, he knew, more worthy than most of his sons and generals. He beckoned his servants in anticipation of the food, sat up while each tray was carefully placed at his small eating table. With more bows and smiles they withdrew, leaving him alone to his meal, the way he enjoyed it.

He slipped out of his night garment, strode naked to the table, pulled the curtains wider. Sunlight streamed inside majestically. He poured the wine himself, sipped, and enjoyed the panoramic view of the city from his verandah. A pungent odor trickled from the lidded casserole; Kabul drooped his eyelid, tried to identify its contents. A stew, he was sure. Mutton? Swine? Goat? It made little difference when he was as hungry as he was now.

Savoring the aroma, he gingerly lifted the cover from the steaming plate and stared. For a long while he looked at it; then instead of eating he leaned back and sighed.

The casserole was filled with vegetables; stewed tomatoes, beets, carrots, sprinkled with parsley and pepper, chunks of garnished potatoes. The gravy was thick and deep, small circles of fat swimming at the surface. And sandwiched between them all rested a head—a human head, face up, ear-deep in the gravy. Khalkali's head.

Without a sound, Kabul lifted the ornate cover and placed it back over the casserole. Only then did he get up from the table and summon his guards.

6

"The old man's really gone crazy this time," said Tupol.

His brawny older brother peered up and regarded him lengthily. "What do I care?"

Tupol's bad leg caused him to hobble across the antechamber of the apartment. Jamuga was sitting cross-legged over the rug, watching the wisps of smoke rise and disappear from a stick of heavily scented incense.

"I should think it's of concern to all of us, no?" said the cunning youngest son, fighting a losing battle to keep his face from twitching.

The Mongol-blooded son shrugged carelessly. "Khalkali was an ass," he muttered, not looking his brother's way, not asking for this unexpected visit, wishing that Tupol would quickly crawl back into the recesses and shadows from which he came. He looked up at his scrawny companion, this deformed dimwit. Then he corrected himself. Tupol's body may be lacking, but his brain certainly wasn't. No doubt that crafty Tupol would manage to survive right to the bitter end. Jamuga felt sorry that he'd have to kill him—but then, there could only be one Khan at a time, couldn't there?

"From now on the kitchens are going to be watched by trusted guards every single second," Tupol went on, oblivious to Jamuga's disregard. "The old man's furious—

he wants to know just how these—these murderers—were able to switch the casserole unseen, and have it delivered to him for breakfast."

Warily, Jamuga said, "Why are you telling me all this? I told you—what happened to Khalkali was bound to come sooner or later. The next Khan, he fancied himself. Ha! He'd have done better as a street clown during festivals."

Tupol shook his head sadly from side to side. "Listen," he said, "our father blames us for these murders—don't you understand that?"

"Our father," replied Jamuga dryly, "is the biggest ass of all." Tupol reddened, and Jamuga went on. "Oh, don't worry. You can sneak back and report to him everything I've said. It doesn't bother me in the least. The old man knows better than to toy with me."

The crippled brother was seething, although his face remained an impassive mask. "You take a great deal for granted, don't you?"

Jamuga rose, veins popping from his neck. "Play no games with me, puppy!" he warned, shaking a finger in Tupol's direction. "I know you too well, remember? You can't fool me."

"I don't know what you're talking about."

"No?" Jamuga laughed. "And what about that secret room of yours, hmmm? The one you keep locked and guarded? The one with your *pets?*"

Tupol was flustered. "My spiders are my own business," he hissed. "I came here today in good faith, Brother. If you spurn me, you have only yourself to blame."

"Good faith? What a miserable excuse for a man you are, Tupol! Go on, crawl out of here on your belly. Do you think I don't know the venom you've been whispering in the Khan's ear, eh? Do you think that Gamal didn't know? Or Niko? Or even swaggering Khalkali? Go on, you little bugger, run!"

Tupol smiled viciously; he folded his arms, planted his open legs firmly in front of his raving brother. "And I know you, too, dear Jamuga. Who's fooling whom, eh? Who's been bribing our top commanders to swear allegiance to you all this time? Poor, ignorant Khalkali.

Why, I'd wager he had no idea—not an inkling—that his own men were ready to turn on him at a snap of your finger! Niko's guard as well!" His smile deepened as a shadow crossed his brows. "But Gamal was on to you, wasn't he? Gamal knew your tricks and schemes, eh? Too well for your own good, eh?"

Jamuga swallowed hard, disbelieving his ears. "Are you —dare you accuse me of his death?"

"Accuse you?" Tupol's eyes widened with mock innocence. "Would I say such a terrible thing, *Brother*." He sneered. "We all know that you're a man of honor! We all know you have only our father's interests at heart."

"At least I'm not a gutter rat like you," Jamuga flared. "You're the lowest thing I ever met. Goading Mufiqua, taunting Temugin, spilling lie after lie to the Khan, so that he hates us all."

"You're growing angry, dear Brother. Calm yourself. Save your energies for the true test of who's a man and who's not."

The threat was poorly veiled, Jamuga saw—purposely so. "I won't tell you again, Tupol. Get out of here—now."

The crippled son of Kabul grinned cruelly, bowed, hobbled his way to the door. Jamuga flung a chalice; it hit the wall, crimson wine splattering. Then he turned back around and angrily sat beside the incense burner.

The hand slipped the small tray inside the glass cage. Immediately the tarantula stopped its spinning, crawled quickly down along the thin thread of its silk, and arched over the plate of dead flies. Tupol chuckled as the insects were devoured, watching the grisly scene with enormous pleasure. When the tarantula was finished, he closed the cover over the top of the cage, went to feed the next. All three poisonous spiders relished their meal. He'd been nourishing his pets for months now, taking care of them as though they were his bastard sons. And in a way, they were. For each had been brought to the palace to serve a special purpose, a very special purpose. He was their father, and when the timing was right, they would surely serve him better than any son.

"First of all," Krishna announced, his massive chest swollen with pride, "we broke his thumbs—but carefully, so that the bones would heal properly, a common precaution in case we need to repeat the procedure. Then"—and here he beamed like a mischievous child—"we racked him. Gently, mind you. Making sure he survived, for I know how important he could be."

Kabul growled, curling his lip. His good eye stared down at the limp figure of a man shackled by his wrists to the granite wall. The prisoner remained conscious, defiantly so, even in the face of the chancellor's finest handiwork.

Krishna continued to speak, explaining how carefully he'd nurtured Roskovitch each time he faltered. The Khan, though, seemed disinterested. He nodded now and again, brushing a thick hand at the side of his beard, then walked slowly from the cell and out into the dim corridor. Several aides swept low in grand bows of respect. Kabul ignored them. How this place sickened him, the stench staler than an old grave. How anyone could live in such a place completely befuddled him.

His boots grated against stone as he marched along the winding labyrinth. He worked his way back toward the outer sanctum, where the ventilation wasn't quite as bad, paying no heed to the sobs and moans and insane laughter that rang from the cells. Krishna's footsteps scuttled behind.

You follow me like a mangy dog, Krishna. Grovel at my feet. But I know well enough there'd be a secret blade in your hand if you thought the time was right.

". . . wouldn't you agree, Father?"

Kabul turned, Krishna's eyes brightly shining into his own.

"Agree? Eh?"

The chancellor frowned. "About the information this

171

Kazir pig provided. About the coming assault against our armies on the steppes."

The Khan continued up the narrow steps, back out into the light. At the landing he paused, regarding his son anew.

"What makes you think he wasn't lying?"

"I have my ways, O Khan." Krishna's grin was expansive.

"I don't doubt it." He thought upon those foul cells once more and shook his head. Indeed his treacherous son governed his underworld domain with a skilled hand. That much credit he deserved.

"So you believe everything the prisoner spilled?"

"Men screaming in pain find it difficult to lie," came the wry observation. "I told you, first we broke his thumbs—"

Kabul lifted his hand imperiously. "Yes, yes. You told me. And now you're convinced that this man, this Kazir—"

"A Russian, Father. Roskovitch, he claims he is called."

"Yes, then this Roskovitch, this barbarian, has spoken to you, under torture, of what he claims to be a full-scale thrust against us?"

"Precisely, O Khan. It was most fortuitous that he came into our hands at this time."

The Khan, skeptical, folded his arms. Cool fresh air rushed from the vents and he relished it, the smell of Krishna and his underworld still in his nostrils. "How do we know that this Russian knows of what he speaks, eh Chancellor? A tortured man will say many things to cease his pain, even if only for a few moments. How can you be positive he didn't concoct this whole story, eh?"

"Because, my liege, I double- and triple-checked his every statement. I ordered scouts out into the interior, to the doorstep of the desert itself, and yes, Kazirs *were* seen moving south at night, just as the prisoner said they would."

"South to attack our strongest positions? We've fifteen thousand men and more stationed along the steppes. Would even the Phantoms be so bold as to try and eradicate such a force? No, Krishna, I cannot believe it."

"The Panther is a dangerous woman, Father," Krishna

said quickly, delighting at the sight of his father wincing at her mention. "She employs strange and bold tactics. Desert tactics. Forget not that she's kept us off balance before with her treacherous tricks." His mouth turned expressively down at the corners, and he added, "And has managed to do so for more than five years."

Krishna's reminder was tinged with glee, Kabul noted. The glee of a son too-long relegated to a lightless world while his siblings ran free under the sun.

"I shall keep your point in mind, Chancellor. Yes, well in mind."

"Then do not forget this barbarian predicts the attack in less than a week's time. Is it not in our interest to guard against it?"

"What is your recommendation?"

"To lay in waiting, Sire. To fortify our garrisons with every legion you can spare. . . ."

"Our armies are too scattered," said the Khan thoughtfully. "Do you expect me to recall our forces from Persia? Or from the Afghani frontier? You're a poor general, Chancellor. You ask me to stamp out a brushfire while an entire forest goes up in flames. No, we'll send word to our Steppes commanders, have them readied just in case. Apart from that, I'll not deploy a single legion."

"Not even to catch the woman?"

Kabul's heart skipped a beat; his palms began to sweat, and he ran his tongue across his lips. Oh, if only he could get his hands on her!

"The Russian swears the Panther herself shall lead the attack. Consider, my lord: Within a week's time she could be in your grasp. . . ."

Long and hard the mighty Khan thought, his hatred of the woman overriding all other considerations. Then he shook his head. "We could never recall our Persian armies home in time. It would take a month to muster them back to Samarkand. Impossible. Show me another way."

Krishna smiled. "The city garrison, my liege. Free them. Place them under my command and I'll bring her back to you in chains—unharmed."

"The city garrison? Are you completely at leave of your

senses, Krishna? Leave Samarkand defenseless while we muster for an attack that may never come? Don't talk like a fool."

Gesturing with his hands, Krishna said, "Listen to me; we need not leave the city without defense, only deplete our guard enough to ensure swift victory. Think of it, Sire! The Panther in your hands!"

His father stepped back, looked long and hard at his son. "And what's in this for you, eh? What schemes work the back of your mind?"

"None, O Khan. Only that I may serve you."

"As commander of my home army?"

"Yes, Sire."

"What manner of baboon do you take me for? Do I look like I want to commit suicide?" Krishna paled and Kabul chuckled beneath his breath. "If I turn my most potent force over to you, I see them coming back with daggers out for me."

"But, Lord!" sputtered Krishna. "Do you think I'd turn them against you? That I desire your death, or covet your exalted office?"

Kabul sighed and placed a hand upon Krishna's shoulder, ignoring the look of injury his son wore. "You serve me well in my cellars," he said plainly. "Never try and overstep your bounds. I would not enjoy having to kill you."

The blood was draining from Krishna's face; he kept his gaze locked with his father's. "Then you will not heed my warning? You disregard this danger?"

"I did not say that," Kabul answered complacently. "Yes, it would be like *her* to plan something like this. Perhaps this Russian speaks the truth, perhaps he doesn't. Either way, it is my concern—not yours. And I shall be the one to handle it!"

The chancellor of the dungeon inwardly seethed, while outwardly he nodded and bowed respectfully. "You may return to your duties," added the Khan.

"What of the prisoner? Has he served his purpose? Shall I put him to death?"

Kabul mulled for a time, then shook his head. "I think not, Chancellor. Let him live—for now. I plan to test his information. Should he prove truthful, then you may do with him as you like. But if he's lied . . ."

"Yes?"

"Then maybe he did so for other reasons . . ."

The foul son seemed perplexed. The Khan laughed, a sparkle in his single eye. "Ah, Krishna, you truly are a fool, aren't you? Never mind. You did your job, the rest remains my own." With that, he left Krishna standing there at the foot of the stairwell, venom in his eyes, mouth twitching with hatred, determined not to let this episode conclude against him.

8

Mufiqua lifted himself off the bed in a trance, unaware of the force that guided his every move. He stepped among shadows grim and dancing, crossed from his bedroom and reached the mantel of his fireplace. There, commanded and unable to do otherwise, he picked up the doll.

Stick the pin deeply, came the voice. *In the small of the doll's back. This time, do not remove it. Leave it in place, then place the doll out of sight. Then you may return to your dreams. Sweet dreams this night, Mufiqua. Dreams in which the dancer shall come to you . . .*

"I understand," Mufiqua mumbled in a monotone. He did as ordered, implanting the fine needle in the doll's spine. The inanimate figurine seemed to twitch in his hand as the pin bore through its waxen flesh. Mufiqua blindly returned it into the shadows. He bore an unexplainable smile of satisfaction, the face of the girl shimmering before his eyes. He crept back into bed, and pulled the quilt tightly around him.

"Eeeeeeeee!"

The scream pierced the night. Hezekiah broke foggily out of his slumber and hurried into the adjoining chamber.

Temugin shot upright like a thunderbolt, hand groping behind.

"What is it, my lord?" cried the soothsayer.

"The pain!" wailed Temugin, shrieking. "I can't stand the pain!"

Hezekiah peered at the writhing man, aglow with cold sweat. The sight of it churned his stomach when Temugin, out of control, charged from his bed and beat his fists against the wall. He careened from one end of the opulent chamber to the other, staggering, knocking over vases and braziers. "Do something for me!" he wailed. His hands grabbed empty air. "*Do something for me!*"

The soothsayer's lips quivered. "I am helpless," he stuttered. "Helpless against this evil!"

Temugin's face was twisting like melting wax; he staggered backward, then reeled, stumbling to the floor. "They —they've poisoned me again!"

"No, my lord! It's not possible! Everything you commanded has been done. No food enters or leaves your personal kitchen without five slaves having tasted it first! And then I myself—"

Temugin was thrashing wildly. "Then how, stargazer?" he hissed. "Answer me that! How did they—" He jerked savagely, clutched the seam of his companion's robe.

"Make it stop!" screeched Temugin. "I'll do anything— pay any price, only make it stop!"

Hezekiah drew back in horror. *Shall I murder Temugin now? It would be so easy to slip a poison pellet in his mouth. . . . But no; the Panther has said the time is not yet come. I must obey her fully, nothing must go wrong.* And he watched the writhing lord with a shudder, wishing for the time when he could rid himself of this disguise and walk freely through Samarkand.

Tossing and turning in his sleep, Mufiqua's hands tried to reach her and touch her. But as always the figure of the woman, the dancer Sharon, remained elusive. He could clearly see her before him, twisting, turning, cavorting like a wild gypsy in her seductive dance, hips swaying, breasts heaving, the tinkle of fingerbells enchanting while she drew closer—so close!—yet out of his grasp. He could feel the terrible burning in his loins, the overwhelming desire that quickened his heartbeat. *Why does she taunt me so?* he wondered. *What is it she demands of me before I may possess her? I am a god! How dare she refuse me? How dare she!*

The smile upon her honeyed lips remained a mystery to him. Her eyes, those forever black shimmering pools of loveliness, glowed with the knowledge of his rising excitement. Round and round she danced, arms above her head, hands clapping in time with the drums, hair flying in front of her face, golden skin moist with perspiration. How he longed to have her! The voice had promised her this night, had it not? Why was he still to be denied? He had done what was asked, each night obeyed totally and stuck the pin into the doll. Where was his reward? Surely the Master had not lied? Surely his promise to him would be fulfilled?

His head was swimming deliriously from the effects of opium. "You gave me your word, Master," he spoke out in his dream world, his world of altered realities. "Have I not been faithful?"

You have done everything, came the voice, cold as the grave.

"Then why, Master? See how she teases me—how she taunts me with her laugh and the promise in her eyes. Give her to me, Master! Bring me to the place of purpled clouds and sweet dreams."

Aye, Mufiqua. You have been more than faithful. Thus I swear to fulfill my obligation. Behold, the new world to which only a god may enter!

Mufiqua's eyes opened wide. He was sitting up on his bed, awake, drenched in sweat. But around his bed was something strange. He had been whisked away from his room, he saw, brought mysteriously into that other world. Everywhere, rising, a thin mist lifted, a violet haze, richly hued. He stared, frightened of the unknown that awaited. He could hear his Master's voice, soft-spoken assurances that he, Mufiqua, had at last been given his due.

"The Land of Gods," he mumbled, getting off the bed, stepping into the fog. He held his arms out and pushed into swirling mist. It gave way. Then he took another step, this time gazing wonderously into a glorious landscape, the like of which no mortal man had ever seen. There were mountains in the distance, colossal peaks of such enormity that his breath was swept away. The sky was ablaze in crimson, a dawn perhaps, but such a dawn that his eyes had never dreamed to behold. And billowing clouds scudded closer, the heavenly purpled clouds of which he'd dreamed for so long. Numbed, he watched.

A sweet scent of perfume wafted to him, and at once he knew to whom it belonged, to the only one it could ever belong. Mufiqua turned slowly. There she was, before him, bowing at his feet. *The dancer! Sharon!*

She raised her gaze and looked at him, unclasping her veil so he could see her face. She was beautiful, more beautiful than he remembered. Not just a woman, no, but a goddess herself—his prize, his reward from his Master for his faithful service.

"Yes, my lord," the girl whispered, her dark eyes smiling. "I have come to you."

He hesitated to touch her, afraid this was only another dream.

"Have no fear, Lord," she soothed, reading his thoughts. "You have passed from the earthly world to this place where you shall reign forever." She paused, shyly lowering her gaze. "And I shall be at your side as your consort."

The idea thrilled him, and he bellowed with laughter. "You see, Father," he shouted down to the unfathomable mists that settled beneath his feet. "I *am* a god! Immortal!"

"Yes," said Sharon. "Immortal."

Soft bells rang as she stood, offering her hand to him. Mufiqua took it, felt her warmth flowing. This world excited him, and willingly he let the woman lead him, brushing aside the haze with her hand, taking him to the threshold of the sky itself.

"Our Master is benevolent to those who have trusted him," said Sharon, silken hair tumbling over her breasts. "Together we shall face eternity, Lord. You and I, unhampered by the petty dreams of mere mortals."

It sounded wonderful; Mufiqua nodded, the mist flushed over his body like an elixir, a potent drink of the gods. But then he frowned.

"Has something displeased you, my lord?" asked the girl.

"My . . . my father's kingdom," he muttered. "I was destined to be Khan, to rule the world. . . ."

Her smile pleased him as much as the feel of her flesh. "And so you shall, Lord, and so you shall. The entire world, nay, the universe itself, rests at your feet. For but the asking, Lord Mufiqua. You may rule what you will; the Master has ordained it. Tell me your wish, so that I might fulfill it."

He regarded her strangely. "You can do . . . *anything?*"

"Anything, my lord. You need only ask."

He grinned demoniacally. "Then take me to my father. Bring me before him this instant so he may see the son he scorned. So he may cringe at my feet and beg forgiveness—before I remove his head. Can you do that for me, dancer?"

She bowed, hands in a pyramid to her forehead. "Yes. You have only to put on the amber cloak and step with me into the clouds." Then, magically, she was holding out for him the garment, the finest cloak he'd ever seen, threaded with gold, with clasps of silver. He stood rigidly as she placed it over his shoulders and fastened it carefully. All at once Mufiqua felt his stature rise. This was a cloak of the gods, he knew, embroidered for him upon the looms of heaven, awaiting his arrival. Oh, the Master had been good to him, he now realized, and he thought himself a fool for having ever doubted. Yes, he would step gladly with her into the purpled clouds, return to the ugly world of men, and claim once and for all his rightly place. His brothers would kneel before him, kiss his feet, eat the bitter herbs of regret.

He sucked in a lungful of the heavenly air, swelling his chest. "I am ready for our journey," he told her.

Sharon gestured grandly. Before them two clouds formed together a magic carpet in the sky ready to whisk them down to the mortal world. There was so much to be done, Mufiqua knew, so many wrongs to be righted. It would take time, but then, a god need not hurry. Perhaps he would spend a century as master of the Hun Empire, Sharon at his side. When he tired of it, he would return here, bathe again in the elixir, resume his heavenly role.

The woman closed her hand more tightly around his own, and side by side they left the mists swirling behind, walked boldly into the blazing crimson sky, stepping at last upon the fabled purpled clouds that he'd always known were waiting.

Kabul sat resting on a rock, his feet in the cool waters of the pool. Around him the hanging plants of the rock garden blew gently in the early morning breezes, while the new morning sky beautifully lit the city, causing the palace towers to dazzlingly reflect the golden sunlight. He luxuriated in the surroundings of this homage to nature, casting his gaze first to the small, multilevel waterfall that poured majestically beside the arched rustic bridge, then over at the stunted trees with their swaying branches. He was at peace with himself at such a time, delighting in the fragrance of the roses, the apricot-tinted variety of wild flowers that sat in peaceful rows at either side of the walkway. The setting was enough to lull even the barbarian heart of a Hun, and he mused how foolish this would have all seemed to him only a few short years ago. Age, though, had tempered him, enhanced his perception of beauty in the world, and he thought that he would be most happy when he died to be rested in a place such as this.

Birds were singing in their gilded cages, early-risers like he, twittering away at the perfection of the dawn. Sing-Li, the Chinaman, had been responsible for the building of this place, and Kabul never regretted giving him permission even while his sons had scorned and mocked him for it. Yes, there was much to learn from ancient Cathay, and when at last his armies overran Peking, perhaps he would leave Samarkand for good, and set up his capital city there. After, of course, he had finished for once and for all with those desert Kazirs.

He sighed contentedly, and by chance, while shading his eye from the glare of the rising sun, focused his attention at the pinnacle of the highest tower of the palace. Its gray stone tinted blue in the light, high against the sky, some fifty meters directly in front of him. Kabul would have turned away, gone back to his musings, had it not been for the curious sight that suddenly appeared.

There was someone out on the verandah of the tower, someone who walked with his arms spread open wide, holding the edges of a brightly-colored cloak. The Khan watched most curiously, scratching at his head as the figure stepped perilously closer to the low balcony wall, commenced to step over it.

His eye opened wide and he rose from his comfortable rock. The figure, whoever it was, seemed to be attempting to walk into the sky!

There was no scream, no sound at all. The cloak flapped like wings as the man sailed from the wall, for barely an instant carried by the gusts, then plummeted down.

Mufiqua! Kabul's mouth hung wide, hands shaking in horror. His addicted son sailed in a quickening downward spiral, then hit the ground at the edge of the garden with a terrible thud, his body splattered like an egg, blood spraying wildly like a fountain, staining the branches and the bird cages, sending the chirping birds into a frenzied terror.

Servants screamed and fled; guards in the towers stared down with lurid incredulity. Kabul felt his belly churn; he turned, leaned against the trunk of a stunted tree, and heaved out his guts.

9

Sharon felt cold again; although it was late summer, and the hottest days of the year had arrived, a deep chill encompassed her like a frigid blanket.

With a deep breath and a prayer on her lips, she stepped away from the shrubs, glancing momentarily at the arced moon above the treetops, and began her last climb to the mound. She threw back her cowl, worked her way along the trodden path, the path she had come to know so well, the path she knew she would never walk again. The clearing stood before her, the tallest tree seeming more bent and withered than it had been the last time. Twigs snapped harshly beneath her boots. A sparrow lifted from its nest, flew quickly away; a hare picked up its ears, darted its eyes in her direction, then speedily ran for its burrow.

The stalk started to slither around the nearest bough, the veined leaves of the flower stirring and beginning to part. With labored breath she stepped in front of the tree, hands at her sides, and began the ritual of waiting.

As always, one by one the leaves fell away, leaving exposed the inner flower, the magical nightflower that shone through the glum shadows like a lamp. Real, yet not, like a whisper on the lips of the wind the flower lifted its stem and said, *"You have come at last, little princess. I have been waiting."*

"We have both been waiting, friend. Now the time has come, the time of truth for which you and I have prepared. And I have come back, as I said I would, to tell you of these things, and to ask for your blessing."

The flower quivered, a gesture that told Sharon of its own pain at this meeting. *"You have no need to ask for that which I have always bestowed. We have seen much together, you and I, little princess, have we not? Faced cruelties and perils, suffered for justice and the cause as none should suffer."*

Her shoulders sagged with the weight of her burdens, her only relief coming from the knowledge that soon it would all be done. Finished and complete, destiny fulfilled. The Prophesy fulfilled.

"All has been done," she went on colorlessly. "All has been prepared. Four sons are slain, four remain."

"Four?" There was concern in his tone.

"Karma, friend. We can no longer wait. Karim put all our plans in jeopardy; we acted as fast as we could, and now make the final move."

A long time passed before he replied, a time in which the sky darkened as a rolling cloud covered the moon, then brightened again when the cloud had passed. *"When, little princess?"*

Solemnly, Sharon replied, "At the coming of dawn the first wind shall blow."

The strange plant nodded knowingly. Sharon had the Gift, the knowledge to call but a single time upon the hamsin. And when it was passed into her hands, she vowed with her life and the lives of all she loved that her duty would be done. Unwavering and unyielding, answering the Call of the Kazirs in one swift blow. Meeting her fate without regret or fear, so that at last the desert peoples might once more take their rightful place in history.

"My time is done, little princess. You have no further need of me."

She suppressed a gasp, unwilling to face this final parting, not after so long, after so much had passed between them.

"You knew this, little princess. Knew from the first day of our meeting that this time, this very hour, would one day be at hand. Would that I could stay and guide you further, but alas, that was not meant to be." A single dew drop formed near the flower's petals, and Sharon knew that her friend, so emotionless before, had begun to cry. Tears formed in her own eyes and she tried to push them away, knowing also that far too many tears had been shed in her life.

"Are you afraid?" the flower asked gently.

She pushed a tendril of hair away from her eyes, shook her head. "There is no fear, friend. No pain. Only numbness. For like you, I, too, am prepared for what is to be."

"And your lover—Tariq?"

She couldn't face him. Turning her gaze to the grasses hidden in the shadows, she said, "He understands, shares my belief."

"Now you are not being truthful, little princess. You cannot hide from me the love you carry; it shines like an aura around you, around both of you."

Sharon stifled a sob, miserably wishing she could avoid the flower's all-knowing, all-understanding gaze. "What is to be, will be, friend. Deny not that to me. The Prophesy ordained my coming and passing long before my birth."

With a heavy sigh, her companion nodded, saying, *"Or so it is said."* It was a direct quote from the sacred writings.

"Yes. Or so it is said. The Word of the Book tells no lies, friend. I am resigned."

"Then I cry for you, little princess. Aye, and for Tariq also. You shall never know the fruits of the love that binds you, the right of ever mortal woman and man."

"Please," she whispered, swallowing to get rid of the

rising lump in her throat, "don't speak any more of it. I am only human, friend, belonging not to the netherwold. So frail are we humans, so filled with angers and jealousies and hatreds—"

At this the flower's petals lifted gaily in something of a smile. *"And was it not your own heart that had turned to rock for all these times, little princess? Had not your own hatreds overwhelmed you and turned you from your former self into another."*

Sharon had to smile at her companion's insight and wisdom. Yes, she'd been guilty of all this and more. The lust for vengeance had blackened her soul every bit as much as it had the Khan's.

"Have you changed?" came the expected question.

She thought for some time, examining her feelings, her mortal emotions, recalling her former life and her years as the Panther. At her last visit to the forbidden Grim Forest, she'd felt so confident about what had to be done, so certain that once her thirst had been quenched and the Khan slain at her feet, that nothing else mattered. That *had* changed, she saw now, not knowing when or where or how or even why. But it *had* changed.

"I am still the same," she replied at length, choosing her words carefully. "But yes, friend, I shall not cover my feelings here with you. Things are not the same for me as before. Oh, do not misunderstand—I want Kabul dead, I want my people and my city free—"

"But also you want life? To live freely as a woman, to love and to cherish?"

"Your words hurt me, friend. Yes—I won't deny it. Not any longer, not on this, our farewell. But don't you see? Reminding me of this only makes it worse!" She bit her lip to stop it from quivering, shook her head to stem the flood of tears.

"Cry, little princess," said the flower. *"Cry out your heart, here, now. Become a woman again, if only for a short time."*

With trembling legs she knelt beside the tree, put her arms around the trunk and bent her head against the flower's leaves. There she sobbed, her whole body wracked and fevered, cried her heart out like the small child she used to be, weeping now not for what had been and was lost, but for the future that she knew could never be.

"I don't want to die!" she cried, sniffing, her eyes wet and luminous. "I don't want to stay buried in hatred, in war, in revenge." She tilted her head, stared up at the moon, the glorious moon, weeping unashamedly, shudderingly, the poisons in her system buried for so long now rising to the surface and pouring out. "Why me, friend? Why is it my life that has to be tossed away, thrown to the wind?"

Her companion had no reply for her, but she knew the answer, knew that it was the fate that awaited and could never be undone. When Samarkand was freed, the Panther, the One chosen, would be no more. It had to be that way, could never be altered.

Her thoughts turned to Tariq, to all those she had come to love, and the weight of it was too much for her. She crumpled at the gnarled roots of the tree, her face buried into its fallen leaves, her fists beating angrily at the earth. Too late she had come to realize the evil of the poisons that had rooted inside her, far too late. Wasted time, wasted years passed before her eyes. She should have listened to Tariq when there had still been time, shared some of her burdens, as the flower had asked of her. But no; she'd been too stubborn, too proud.

"Cry, little princess, cry. Spill your heart. And when you stand again Allah, in his wisdom, will have listened."

"How I wish—how I pray that this can be so! But the Prophesy, friend; it cannot be denied! It cannot be denied! And I alone am its prisoner."

"Never lose faith in God," remonstrated the plant. *"Never, for only in His arms shall there be peace and joy."*

Sharon listened; she sat up, dried her eyes and looked at him, nodding slowly. Yes, that was true. If nothing else made any sense to her, at least that much did. "I won't lose that faith," she promised. "Not even . . . not even at the end."

"Then go, little princess; you back to your world, and me to mine. In this life we shall not meet again—but who can say about another?"

Sharon stood, brushed off the leaves, bent low, and blew

the flower a kiss. "Farewell, friend. Farewell, brother. Indeed, in another time and another place surely we *shall* meet again."

The dew drop fell from the petals; the flower bent its stalk and with a heavy heart folded its earthly petals for the last time. And as it returned to its own time and world, it whispered upon the wind, *"Fate is fate. Never run from it."*

"I shan't, friend. And I'll never forget you. Now I go and do my part, even as the Prophesy foretells. For now I see the truth. Thank you. Let what will be, be—or so it is said."

10

At the beginning the morning had been bright, fair; then, across the sky, above the distant mountains and steppes, a dulling haze started to form, a dark-mustard shade that fanned out malevolently across the horizon. The air above the city of Samarkand stilled, grew hot and stale, sultry. Citizens peered from their windows, from their hovels, from their farms and fields; putting down their tools and plows, leaving soil untended, water buckets undrawn from the wells, while they gazed at the sky in awe. It was a hamsin brewing, the old hags of the villages said, making the sign of the horn with their hands to ward off the impending evil, scurrying from riverbanks and markets and gardens and pastures, hurrying back to their tents and houses as quickly as possible. Children were called in from the streets, mothers suckled anxious infants to keep them from crying. Herders tending sheep along the fertile hills of the countryside shouted to their dogs, hurried the sheep from their grazing, brought them swiftly away from the open. Fields of wheat almost ripe for harvest swayed strongly in the steadily increasing wind, while particles of red dust blew in from the desert, settling haphazardly over the streets and alleys and roofs in a gentle rain of sand, portending what was to come. All at once the open bazaars were deserted, merchants and vendors closing their shops, tightly bolting their shutters. The beggars and pickpockets fled the streets in search of shelter; they jammed the taverns, mingling at roadside inns with pilgrims and travelers, wearied caravaneers and petty bandits. Camels snorted, mules refused to budge. Horses whinnied in fear, some bolting from their posts. The soldiers of the Khan who lined the city walls peered out in dismay at the approaching storm. And the warning bells rang loudly. Off the streets! Into your homes! The hamsin is coming! Fatigue etched into their faces, the grim palace guards tightened cloaks around themselves, fixing kerchiefs over their face, waiting, waiting for the desert wind to arrive. It was a bad one brewing, they saw. As evil as any they'd ever seen in Samarkand.

By this time the horizon had been obliterated, the dust swirling gloomily over the distant range of the fearful forest, ever pressing closer, relentlessly smashing asunder any and all who foolishly stood in its way. The banners and flags fluttered with increasing frenzy, here and there a flag pole snapping, hurtling off the walls and down below to the barren byways. Occasionally some brave soul could be seen making his way along the avenues in search of some unknown destination. Stray mongrels barked, ran in packs amid garbage and debris. The wind pushed on, driving even them to find safety. Doors creaked, shutters banged, the sand became thicker, clogging lungs, watering eyes, causing the righteous to kneel and pray and the heathens to grudgingly sit up and take notice. A hamsin had been known to last for days on end—and this one had barely begun.

Before noon all of the city sat behind locked doors, waiting silently with bated breath, wondering about the moment when the wind ceased and the dust settled and they ventured outside to see the havoc and destruction. In Samarkand there were few things, both natural and unnatural, more feared than this, the hamsin, the dreaded storm of wind and sand that appeared so suddenly out of nowhere. The superstitious among them were quick to whisper of other storms, some long since passed out of memory, and of the grim happenings that had transpired during those fretful hours, while the gullible listened, clinging to every word, thankful that they had not been there, and wishing now they were a thousand leagues away and more. For each time a hamsin struck, things were never quite the same when it was done. Something, whether for good or evil, had irrevocably been altered, and not a single soul now among the multitudes of citizens did not ask just what might be different this time. The upheaval was no less than an earthquake—and frequently more devastating.

So it was that no men saw the secret and silent figures who slipped across the dunes in large numbers and made their way through the approaching storm across the steppes, drawing ever closer to the fertile plains and the distant high walls of the city. Zealous patriots, knowing no fear of the hamsin, nor concern for their own lives. Phantoms they had been called, and Phantoms they truly were. Knives sheathed beneath their flowing desert robes, burnooses covering their heads, scarves across their faces, they stealthily moved, ready to be in place for the final battle, the impending Night of Atonement that could no longer be stopped.

The arachnid walked along the edge of the wall, its shadow grotesquely elongated by the dancing dim flame of the bracketed single torch in the corridor. Against the opposite wall its shadow loomed monstrously, a demoniac behemoth, an atrocity free from hell. Its eight legs moved in perfect harmony, the first and third on one side together with the second and fourth on the other. From behind the Oriental screen at the far end of the ill-lit hall Tupol observed his pet's movements with growing delight and anticipation. It gave him untold satisfaction to see the tarantula like this, making him realize that all his pains and efforts in training had not been wasted. Yes, it had been worth it; the spider was doing exactly as it had been taught, recognizing which door to stop at, and where it must crawl to reach the other side.

Dimness showed between the wooden entrance and the stone floor. Before it made its move, the spider paused, flexed open and shut its mouth. Above the mouth, slightly below its pinprick eyes, two hairy chelae jutted, each curved like bone, each ending in a hard, pointed claw—its fangs.

Openings in the tips of the chelae connected with the tiny poison glands, and when the spider stabbed with them, the venom would pour from their sacs and into the open wound of its prey, first paralyzing, then killing.

As if at hidden command the spider lowered its head and spread its legs, quickly scurrying under the door, over the tiles and into the unseen chamber. Tupol lifted himself from behind the screen, stood to his full height and chortled as he rubbed his good hand over the deformed one. It would not be very long now, he knew. A few more minutes at best—no more. Then would come the scream, the horrid scream when his brother realized what had been done. And never again would Tupol be forced to endure his scorn. Besides, Jamuga knew about the existence of his pets, and that was more than careful Tupol could tolerate. Amid the rash of murders would come another, equally unexplainable.

Jamuga lay awake upon the mat, blankets on the floor, hands behind his head, his short stabbing sword close at hand. Save for the glow of a solitary stick of burning incense in the brazier beside his elbow, the chamber was totally devoid of light. The Mongol son of Kabul liked it this way, enjoyed the darkness, believing that his perfect night sight was far superior to that of other men, thus affording him a ready advantage against some daring would-be assassin.

It was too hot for sleep, the tiles of the floor cool, giving him a measure of relief from the intolerable heat. Outside, the wind had started to blow viciously; he could hear the patter of sand against his tightly-secured shutters. The worst of the storm was yet to come, he knew, perhaps days away. Once, while on patrol in the desert, he and his men had been stranded for nearly a week, shunted to their tents while nature ran amok outside. It had been a frightening experience for him, and when the hamsin had run its course, he had left his shelter and peered about in shock to find the entire landscape shifted, new and huge dunes where before there had been none, smoothed valleys and snaking wadis where a week ago had lain mountains of sand that even a camel could not have crossed. Jamuga had learned to respect the wind, thinking anyone who held other opinions to be fools. Like his brothers. Like the gutless Mufiqua who had once dared nature's wrath in search of a woman. A mere woman! Well; what else was to be expected from such a dreg—and to think of it!—that he and the addict shared the same blood. But at least Jamuga was pleased that he no longer would have to deal with the troublesome fool. Karma.

The tarantula crossed the room in shadows, long legs shifting one over the other, creeping ever closer to the tranquil figure. Jamuga stifled a yawn, shut his eyes. Yes, things were going well enough; uncommonly well. Whoever was responsible for these ghastly assassinations had certainly done his job well. Jamuga could only admire the finesse, the poetic justice of each slaying. Which brother, though? For a time he'd truly suspected Niko, wondering if his gaiety had not been a sham, and that secretly he'd been the one to orchestrate Gamal's demise. Then, when the lover had been so cleverly done in, he'd wondered about Khalkali. Of course that suspicion, too, had been tossed to the wayside. Rub out Mufiqua as well.

Who? Who could it be?

He shifted on his side, unaware as the large spider crawled at the corner of the blanket at his feet. It walked a hairbreadth from his thigh, stopped at the pale flesh of Jamuga's fleshy buttocks. There it waited, patiently, as it had been taught. Jamuga rubbed at his arms, distastefully listened to the howl of the wind. Perhaps he should have ordered the overseer to bring him a woman tonight, to keep him occupied, to help him while away these long hours. He shook his head. No, a woman would drain him, he knew. Fog his mind with lust and desire. Far better to be alone, to think, to map out the future and the strategy needed to wrest the throne.

Tupol, he thought. *Yes, I'll have to be careful of that one. Tricky devil. Lecherous. A far greater threat than both Krishna and cowardly Temugin combined.*

The spider was moving again, on the tile but following exactly the curve of his prey's back. Jamuga put a hand behind his neck and scratched an itch. The tarantula stopped, venom overflowing its sacs.

What about the Khan? Could it be—Is it possible that our father is the one? The assassin? Could the bad blood between us all have so warped his mind that he'd want all his sons dead? No, that didn't seem to make much sense. Kabul was *Khan.* A single command to his loyal aides and the executioner's ax would come down upon them all—openly, without the need for these games. *But what if my father enjoys it this way?*

Jamuga sighed deeply. He would have given anything to know the truth. *Anything.* It would make his life so much easier. *Never mind. Half the army is secretly loyal to me, anyway. And half the Palace Guard as well! I'm safe. The safest of all. Let my slimy brothers fret and wallow in their fear. What have I to be afraid of? Should some assassin ever gain entry to my quarters, fifty of my most trustworthy troops would be all over him in seconds. Then we'd find out the truth, eh? By all the gods of hell, then we'd know who's responsible.*

He tossed about over the mat, restless, sleepless. He did not see the spider scurry back as he turned. The noise of the hamsin was beginning to eat at his nerves. If only it would stop!

The hackles rose on his neck as he uncomfortably tried to piece together the puzzle. Then flat on his belly he lay, chin resting over his crossed arms. The spider pushed forward with one leg, made its way unfelt onto the linen of Jamuga's tunic. There it paused again, but only briefly. It quickened its pace and bore down swiftly for the victim's neck.

Perhaps Krishna knows more than he's saying, eh? Perhaps he plots all of this from his reeking dungeons. Perhaps—

The chelae lowered, the fangs bore into flesh. Jamuga felt the sting, slapped at his neck, expecting to crush an unseen wasp. The spider darted back as he turned, crawling, running down his tunic. Jamuga's eyes caught sight of the disgusting arachnid and he screamed, hands yanking at his hair. He bolted up from the mat, stomped with bare feet, trying to kill it. The spider zigged and zagged, dashed inside grim shadows. By the dim light of the glowing incense stick Jamuga followed. His left foot pounded against the stone of the floor, then his right. The tarantula skipped between his legs, hurried for the safety of the damp cracks in the wall. Jamuga lunged; with his body crouched he swept his hand low, hit the spider and sent it flying back toward the center of the room. And there he came down hard, his callused heel crushing the life out of it. Panting, lathered in sweat, he looked down at the squashed *thing* and breathed laboriously with relief. From adjoining corridors he heard the rushing bootsteps of his aides. *That was close,* he mumbled to himself. *Too close. . . .* And he thought of Temugin, rage burning in his slanted, reptilian eyes. Suddenly he froze. *Gods of hell! I'm bit! The spider bit me!* Already his neck and half of his face had become numb. The guards broke into the room and he confronted them with unmasked terror etched into his Mongol features. "Spider!" he shouted, mouth losing its ability to move, tongue rapidly swelling and unable to form vowels.

"Mercy of heaven!" gasped a sentry, looking first to the crushed tarantula, and then to his stricken lord.

Jamuga took a single step, found his legs had become lead weights. *Paralyzed!* he screamed to himself. *I'm paralyzed!*

The spider's rare and potent venom was already racing through his bloodstream, attacking his brain. Jamuga was dizzy; he stumbled, tried to stop from falling. He saw the floor come rushing up at him, felt his face smash against the stone. He stuck out his arm, fingers desperately trying to point in the direction of Tupol's rooms. The guards looked at each other with anguish and incomprehension.

"What is it, lord? What are you trying to tell us?"

Jamuga tried to speak—oh, how he tried!—but the words would not, could not come. *Tupol! So it had been Tupol after all!* If only he could say it, warn the others, tell the Khan about his favorite son's pets, soon to be unleashed against them all. His eyes were clouding, forms of his men growing blurred. They were lifting him, and limply he hung in their arms. *I must warn the Khan!* Jamuga was screaming at them with his eyes. But they did not hear, they did not see, they did not know. His lungs refused to take in air; Jamuga's face turned a sickly blue, and by the time his aides had carried him to the threshold of his door, his glassy eyes stared up at them grotesquely. He was dead.

* * *

"It was not our doing!" insisted Carolyn.

Hezekiah peered at her questioningly. It was dangerous for them to meet like this, even in this private chamber beneath the concubine's quarters. Still, perilous or no, the saya had sent for him with urgency, an urgency that startled the seer, and made him wonder what dire happening had transpired. Had the Night of Atonement been put off? Had the Panther's plot been found out? Was it possible that Sharon was dead? Or that the Kazir Stronghold had been captured in some unexpected lightning strike? All these dire possibilities gnawed at Hezekiah when the whore, stealing through the palace in the dead of night, had come bearing the saya's message.

"There is more afoot here than we realized," the wearied minister said with a heavy voice. He peered grimly about the chamber, aware of the tiny ducts running from the low ceiling—ducts to which prying ears might be placed.

Carolyn agreed uneasily. She understood his concern, lowered her tone to a whisper. "I don't like it—it bodes ill for us all."

"Are you positive of all this?" asked Hezekiah with an air of incredulity. "Perhaps the Panther's plans were changed and she could not get word to us in time. . . ."

The saya blew out a long breath, restlessly paced before him. "Impossible. Jamuga was to be my charge, to be dealt with by me and none other. No, this act was committed by someone removed from the Brotherhood."

This was indeed souring news, Hezekiah saw. That there was another assassin loose within the palace did not bother him—but that this murder came at such a time, when already the Devil's Wind had begun to blow and the hour for the awaited Night of Atonement lay so close, disturbed him greatly. "How—how did the son die?"

With a shudder she tried to conceal, Carolyn said simply, "By a spider. A tropical tarantula, as deadly a creature as ever crawled the world. The poison was virtually instantaneous—"

Both their head dramatically lifted in the direction of the ducts. There'd been a noise, a sudden, quick, unexpected muffled sound. Someone was listening.

The Hebrew put a finger to his lips, continued to talk, speaking gibberish in a barely audible voice as he stepped slowly to the narrow enclosed stairwell. He pushed open the arched door a crack, peeked to the top of the landing, where the exposed pipes crisscrossed the walls. There was a kneeling figure, slight and frail in the shadows, huddled close to the pipes, ear to the open duct. Hezekiah slipped his hidden knife from beneath his robes, pulled the door wide. Light spilled onto the steps. The figure jumped up, ready to flee.

"One move and you're dead!" snapped the aging Hebrew, knife held high, ready to be flung. He'd been a marksman in his time, Carolyn knew, and his sure and steady hands, arthritic though they might be, were still deadly at close range.

The figure straightened, stood shivering. A dark cowl covered all features. Hezekiah strained to see. "Come down here," he commanded. "Slowly—one step at a time. Keep your hands raised; one bad move and I'll kill you without a thought."

The eavesdropper nodded, complied and walked carefully down the narrow steps, nearly stumbling several times.

"Remove your hood," said the soothsayer, and gasped when he saw that it was a woman.

"Jasmine!" cried Carolyn.

Hezekiah turned soberly to the saya. "You know her?"

"Of course I know her! She's one of my girls. She's—"

"A whore?" His eyes were narrowed and suspicious; angry.

Jasmine bowed low before the overseer, tears in her eyes. "Forgive me, Mistress. Please, I beg you."

"What were you doing here?"

The girl was beside herself with fear. "I . . . I," she sputtered, seeking words. "I meant no harm, no harm . . ."

"We must get rid of her," Hezekiah muttered glumly.

Jasmine turned white, her eyes wild with the expectation of death, her shapely form shaking with fear. "No—please! I heard nothing, nothing!"

"She's lying," Hezekiah told the saya flatly. He glared at the palace prostitute, sending her into uncontrollable fits.

"Get hold of yourself!" snapped Carolyn, slapping her harshly across the face. Jasmine picked up her head, pushed a shock of long, damp hair away from her tearing eyes. The seer's curved knife glittered in the dull light, wielded warningly before her face. She swallowed hard, sucked in air, then shifted her gaze toward the overseer.

"How came you here?" Carolyn questioned.

"By accident, Mistress. The eunuch said you were not in your quarters, that you'd gone to inspect the wine cellar for the Khan's coming banquet, and—"

"She's lying," hissed Hezekiah. "The passage to the wine cellar turns well before this landing."

"I became lost!" cried the whore, searching Carolyn's stoic face for sympathy. "You must believe me! I heard voices carried from the steps and, thinking it unusual at such an hour, paused to hear what was going on. These are wicked days in the palace, Mistress; I thought only to hear what I could and immediately report it back to you."

Carolyn fondled her antelope's horn, studied the girl intently. Could any of this be true? she wondered. Was it possible. . . . ?

"I do not trust her," said Hezekiah, a quick eye to the stairwell in search of other prying eyes. "Let's be rid of her."

"She's been a faithful servant to me, Minister," reminded the saya. "Remember: It was Jasmine who lulled Khalkali into his stupor; without her I could never have finished him off, not alone."

"Of course you can trust me, Mistress!" blurted the terrified girl. "Have I ever let you down before? Tell me! Have I once, just once, not been everything you've asked of me?"

That much was true, Carolyn knew. Still, the whore's excuses were a bit too lame. The overseer sighed, turned her back to the seer. "Get the truth out of her, Hezekiah. Quickly. We don't have much time."

In the bat of an eyelash the Hebrew had slashed his blade through the air, cut off a curling lock from Jasmine's flowing hair. The lock tumbled like a feather to the ground. The tip of the blade pressed softly against her jugular. One cut and she was dead.

"The truth," he rasped. "The truth."

Her lips were quivering, lipstick smeared, mascara smeared across her lashes. "I . . . I told you. . . . Please. . . ." The blade dug deeper, almost at the point of drawing blood. Jasmine flinched, held her breath. *"The truth!"* repeated Hezekiah, growing weary.

The whore stared glumly at the fallen lock nestled at the toe of her shoe. Yes, this man would kill her, she knew. Slay her without the slightest hesitation for his cause. The overseer would do no less. Jasmine knew she was trapped.

"Please," she begged. "I'll never tell—never say a word of what I overheard. Let me go, please let me go!" The knife's tip was cold against her slim throat, working down toward her breasts, leaving a thin line of blood. At her cleavage the blade stopped. Hezekiah's eyes were smoldering. "What were you doing here?" he asked.

The words blurted out. "I was commanded to follow the overseer! Day and night—to follow her every movement and never release her from my sight!"

Carolyn spun around in shock; she shared a stunned glance with her companion, froze in her place. "What?"

"Forgive me, Mistress," pleaded the girl, breaking down, hands to her face and sobbing wildly. "I had no choice! No choice!"

Shaking her by the shoulders, Carolyn said, "Whose orders, whore; whom do you serve?"

"Don't you understand? I didn't do it for myself! But my family was threatened—he said he'd kill them all, if I didn't become his agent!"

"Who?" demanded Carolyn. "Whose agent?"

"Amar the slaver!"

Hezekiah felt his skin crawl; he'd never trusted the devious peddler of flesh, always had cautioned the Panther in her dealings with him. Now, it seemed they had all been duped.

"For what purpose?" said Carolyn. "Why did Amar want you to spy on me?"

"I don't know, Mistress; I don't know!" She broke down again, and Hezekiah twisted her arm up against her back, forcing it until the bone nearly snapped. Jasmine squealed with pain. "Amar—Amar was under orders," she cried out. "His own life was in peril!"

"By who? Speak!"

"By the one man who plots to wrest the throne and the empire from the Khan!"

"Which man, whore! His name!"

Her head sank and she sobbed again. "Sing-Li! Sing-Li, the Chinaman!"

Carolyn's face dropped; astounded she looked at the distraught stargazer. "Sing-Li? It's not possible. Krishna, yes. Tupol, yes. Any of the sons. . . . But the Chinaman? Kabul's private physician?"

Jasmine laughed a crooked laugh, her face contorted. "You are both as blind as Kabul! Can't you see? While the eight sons plotted against each other, while the Kazirs provoked the murders, Sing-Li has been secretly scheming to take all power!"

"Never!" barked the saya. "Kabul would not be so stupid. . . ."

"No?" the laugh returned. "Tell me, who is it that the Khan turns to in his time of suffering, eh? Who, above all others, including the treacherous Tupol, has gained Kabul's ear and become his confidant? Without Sing-Li's sorcery Kabul would be dead! I tell you the Chinaman knows too well what he's doing. Kabul is in his power— he needs him—trusts him—counts on him to prolong his life. Without the needles the Khan would suffer unspeakable agony. Sing-Li's design is to warp Kabul's mind, keep him totally under his control—and wait for the right moment to seize the city. The others are nothing; the Chinaman laughs at their deaths, laughs because the Kazirs are doing his tasks for him! They pave the way for his succession."

"Merciful Allah," mumbled Carolyn. "We've been blind! All this time, we've been blind!"

An evil glint shone in Jasmine's eyes. "My instructions were simple. Get close to you by any means. Learn what you were up to, allow the deaths of the sons to continue, meanwhile reporting every word to my true master."

Suddenly Carolyn felt cold; sickeningly cold. "Then . . . then the Chinaman knows . . . about the coming struggle . . . ?"

"He knows everything," Jasmine said defiantly. "Amar has given him his soul as well as my own. We are both his puppets. . . ."

Hezekiah dropped his knife hand to his side, stared fretfully at the gloating whore. "What are we to do, saya?" he asked.

She shook her head. "I—I don't know. Warn the Panther. Yes, and Tariq as well."

"Too late for that. Tariq's already somewhere in the city; aye, on his way to the palace. As for the Panther," he shuddered, "by now she's committed all our forces, summoned the Devil's Wind."

Carolyn bit her lip, cursed herself for being such a fool. "Then we'll have to act alone, you and I."

"But what can we do? Surely this Chinaman—"

"*Roskovitch!*" said the saya, snapping her finger. "We've got to get him out of the dungeons—fast. Then we'll spread word throughout the city—"

"Amidst the hamsin? And even if we could, how do we get Roskovitch out? We'd have to get past Krishna."

The saya tensed at the very mention of the brutish chancellor. Of all the sons it was he that she personally dreaded the most. But now there was no longer any choice. There was no time at all; even being here now could cost them everything.

"I'll get to the dungeons," she said briskly, feeling for her secret dagger. "And I'll find a way to break Roskovitch out."

"How? The chancellor will kill you."

"I'll have to risk it. You go back to your rooms. Wake Temugin. He trusts you. Warn him of the plot, then take his guards with you and have the Chinaman placed under arrest."

"It's too late for that," chortled Jasmine. "Sing-Li is by now on his way to the Khan—informing Kabul of the Kazir treachery. By noon you'll all be caught—and slaughtered. You've failed, Kazir saya! You've failed!"

"Not yet!" snapped Carolyn. "Not while the hamsin blows! Not while the Devil's Wind stirs and sweeps down over Samarkand!" And there was such a conviction in her eyes and voice that Jasmine grew white.

"Go!" commanded the saya to the Hebrew.

He nodded, turned, then glanced behind. "But what about her? What about this whore?"

Carolyn smiled thinly. "Leave her to me."

11

"Hurry!" snapped Carolyn.

The line of distraught concubines hurried along the dank stairwell, sandals padding over the stones steps, as they wound their way lower through the secret passage and toward the murky entrance toward the subterranean labyrinth.

Jasmine fumbled with the set of keys the overseer had given her. At the foot of the grim, arched door she stopped, seeking the right key to fit the lock. The saya gruffly pushed her while a trusted whore held high a small, smoking torch. The beclouded flame flaring, Jasmine found the right key and fitted it into the lock. It clicked dully.

"You'll never get away with this," uttered the traitor. "Krishna's guards will stop you before—" Carolyn spun her roughly out of the way and signaled for the women to cross inside the passage. "You'll do exactly as I say, Jasmine," she reprimanded. "*Exactly*." Her dagger was tight in her hand, drawn and ready. Jasmine nodded, backing off.

Carolyn was the last to cross the threshold, and all at once the awful, sickening smell of the dungeons filled her nostrils. The other whores huddled together in a small group, frightened, worried.

Carolyn stood before them, her face masked in darkness. "You know what you have to do," she hissed, and one by one sent them running off in different directions, each to seek out and find the patrols of the chancellor's guards, and to keep them occupied with their wiles for just enough time for the overseer to break the prisoner free.

"What about me?" said Jasmine, her dark eyes watching the others disappear into the shadows.

The Kazir saya smiled thinly. "You stay with me."

Then off they ran also, turning left at the corner of the cavern, working toward yet another downward passage where grim torchlight spilled across a foul pool. Unspeaking, both women held their breath and splashed through the ankle-deep, reeking liquid. From afar came the mumbled tones of dungeon guards. Carolyn stopped in her tracks, panted. A moment later she heard laughter, the subtle squeals of her whores as they playfully kept the men from their duty with vague and teasing promises.

Buy me the time I need! Carolyn's thoughts cried. *You must buy me the time I need!*

Then off again she scurried, the hem of her khafti wet and stained. Jasmine stayed right behind, heart thumping, face distraught with anguish. She knew what the Kazir was up to, knew that even together there was little chance of turning loose the barbarian Roskovitch. But even if they did, even if the other girls managed to keep the tunnels clear long enough for the prisoner to be whisked from his cell, how were they to get away? Surely Krishna would be close, expecting such a bold move against him to come sooner or later. The saya was begging for her death—and going to drag her along with her. If she could have killed the overseer, she would have done so right then and there.

Carolyn paused again. A sharp draft was slashing from the vents above, a cruel chill entering the passage as it broadened and led onto the first tier of cells. Moans and whimpers came whispering on the air, the cries of the dying and maimed and tortured wailing in their tombs. It was an awful sound, horrible. The treacherous whore turned to run; Carolyn caught her by the arm, spun her, slapped her harshly.

"We must leave this place!" Jasmine begged. "Now— while we can!"

The overseer pushed her against the wall, face so close that Jasmine could feel the heat of her breath. "Another move like that and I'll leave you here forever—understand? Now, which way? Which way to Roskovitch?"

Jasmine swallowed, aware of the pressing steel of the knife against her belly. "Sing-Li says there's another stairwell, down to the lowest level, where the chancellor's quarters—"

"Show me!" She shoved the whore back into the tunnel, breath fast and clouded from the cold. Jasmine weakly nodded, led her along the passage until it ended abruptly at a broad, jagged wall of limestone—with no escape.

The knife came up again. "You lied to me, whore!"

"No, no!" moaned Jasmine. "Look." And she knelt to the ground, wiping away layers of thick dust with her hands, exposing a circular metal slab, a sewer cover, placed carefully into the ancient stone. Jasmine struggled to lift it, groaning as the saya lent a hand. On their knees they worked to get a good hold of the roughened edges. Slowly the heavy iron loosened; they pried it from its fitting, sweated to lift and push it aside into the shadows. And there, gaping for breath, they shuddered and peered down into the well, a gaping black hole, seemingly bottomless.

"How do we get to the bottom?" asked the saya.

Jasmine drew a deep breath, met the overseer's eyes. "There are handholds set into the wall. Here." She arched herself over just enough to grab one of the hooked bars of metal hammered firmly into the cold stone. "Sing-Li's used this way before, Mistress. When he's spied on Krishna. The well takes us to the wall of his quarters; from there we can climb down the pipes and break free. There won't be many guards on duty at this hour. And if the keys you made fit properly . . ."

Carolyn grimaced at the ordeal that lay ahead. They would have to negotiate their way down in total blackness, soundlessly, knowing that the slightest disturbance would arouse the cagey chancellor. Freeing the Russian was fraught with peril.

"You first, whore."

Jasmine let out a long breath, slipped over the side, and hand over hand began the descent into the pit. Carolyn watched her for a few moments, then she stashed her dagger carefully in her belt, swung around and gripped the first handhold. The smell made her head swim; in the darkness her eyes caught sight of tiny hideous winged insects crawling up and down along the chinks within the curved stone. Only the thought of her duty kept her going.

"My lord Temugin! Awake, my lord!"

The surly warrior roused from his slumber quickly, his hand automatically reaching for the scabbarded blade beneath his pillow. His eyes cleared and focused upon the face of Hezekiah. The stargazer was panting, sweat pouring from his forehead, his mouth crookedly twisted with obvious anxiety.

"What—what is it?"

Hezekiah recoiled as the blade glinted from its sheath. "Forgive me for waking you in this manner, my lord," Hezekiah begged, bowing deeply and humbly. "But I have matters—pressing and urgent matters—for your ears that cannot wait."

The vile son of Kabul sat up, legs crossed, peered questioningly at his trusted seer. "The pain," he deduced, "you've found the one responsible for my pain?"

"Aye, my lord. But that and more." And here he moved in closer, his hulking form bent across his lord's upturned features. "I—I have discovered the plot in its totality. The murderer, my lord. The man who has robbed your brothers of their lives."

Temugin's eyes stared blankly; then they began to glow, dancing with the taste of the news. "Who?" he asked in a hushed tone. "Which one? Tupol? Krishna? Speak!"

Hezekiah sighed, said, "Neither, lord. The man is—Sing-Li."

With shock and disbelief, Temugin pulled the seer closer. "What say you? The Chinaman? Are you insane, stargazer? The *Chinaman?*"

"I swear by the stars, lord! The plot has been exposed to me this very night! There is no question of it: The Chinaman seeks to twist the Khan to his purpose. Is it not true that already he holds the power of life and death over your father through his needles and sorcery?"

"Yes—but—but Sing-Li has no power, no forces in waiting to carry his banner. How could he? How could he ever. . . ?"

"With Kabul's sons out of the way his path becomes simple, don't you see? The Khan shall have no one else to turn to; already Sing-Li has built himself a place within the palace that can never be shaken. Think, my lord. Kabul needs not Krishna to survive, nor Tupol, nor even yourself. Ah, but the Chinaman, yes. Without his magic Kabul will die!"

Temugin shook his head incredulously, his mouth hanging stupidly open. Yes, the pieces of the puzzle were fitting into place now! Thank the dark gods for this stargazer!

"There are those secretly in the Chinaman's employ," the seer went on quickly, "ruthless souls who care not for the glory of the Huns, but only for their own selfish ambitions. Due to the courage and foresight of the overseer we have uncovered plots within the palace concubines themselves! Yes, my lord! Believe me; Sing-Li's treachery is widespread!" He glanced gloomily around the darkened chamber. "The walls have ears, my lord. We must not tarry. . . ."

The son of Kabul scratched his head in perplexity. "Then we must stop him! Warn my father, tell him—"

"Oh, how very wise you are, Lord Temugin!" Hezekiah bowed with respect and adoration. "Yes! We must warn the Khan. But we must tread carefully! For your father loves and needs this man, and will not lightly take your word against Sing-Li's."

Temugin beat an angry fist into his palm. "You're right. The Khan will never believe such a story, not without evidence. He'll accuse me of trying to turn his mind against the one man who eases his pain." He put his fist to his head. "What are we to do, Stargazer? Speak to me! Advise me!"

The little smile of triumph that worked the edges of Hezekiah's wrinkled mouth went unnoticed. He pretended to be lost deep in thought; then he looked to the anguished lord and said, "There is one chance, and only one chance. We must find this Chinaman and prevent him from reaching your father's ear."

"What? *Now?* In the dead of night?" Temugin was aghast at the suggestion.

The seer sighed with impatience, rattled by the slovenly, slow-witted, would-be sovereign. "Yes, lord—now. Immediately. This very hour. Rouse your personal bodyguard, my lord, then march with them to the Forbidden Wing, the unholy chambers in which Sing-Li sequesters himself and plots his evil. Then hold him prisoner and make him talk. Make him admit everything!"

Temugin thought for a moment, weighing the scales. Kabul would be displeased at this little venture. Outraged that he, Temugin, had taken such bold action without authority. Yet does not a commander command? A leader lead? Should not a future Khan of all the Huns take drastic action in the name of the empire?

He jumped up boldly from his resting place, quickly threw on his tunic and corselet, fastened securely his knife onto his leather belt. "Yes, Stargazer," he hissed, face growing dark with his rage. "Sing-Li must be stopped! We'll go at once!"

Hezekiah backstepped and bowed in reverence. "Your will is my law, my lord," he said, thinking, *What is the hour? Has dawn come? Are all our forces in place throughout the city?*

Temugin swilled a cup of strong brew, hurled the vessel against the wall. "Guards! Guards!" he barked as he swaggered through his rooms. "Run when I shout for you, you scrawny dogs! Follow me! The palace is under siege!"

The wind was howling, the windows pounded with millions of grains of flying sand. The room was below ground level, its single window high atop the stone wall, twin narrow slits barely below the intricate mosaic. Tariq crossed among the shadows, stood tall on his toes and with outstretched arms reached the sill and pulled himself up. The hamsin was blowing mercilessly, smashing against the sand-blasted walls of the Great Mosque's compound, swirling clouds of biting dust that made glimpsing the sky all but impossible. Still, there were rays of brightness flicking across the heavens, and a dim pall in the west that grew more violent and frightening each minute.

The Devil's Wind stirs, he said to himself, mouthing the words in awe. He dropped back to the floor, cast an eye to the hourglass. The last of the sand had all but trickled down.

By noon all movement inside the city walls would cease, he knew. Kabul's strongly-armed legions along the walls would be rendered helpless against the onslaught, and his own men would freely slip through the streets and take their positions. By evening the first sign of the awaited Devil's Wind would become apparent; the hamsin would deceptively still, the air calm. And then, only then, beneath the total black of a moonless and starless night, it would blow. Down from the mountains, over the Grim Forest, picking up speed across the steppes. Its fury would only be fueled as it reached the plains, and by the time it struck the sacred walls of Samarkand. . . .

Tariq shuddered. He would not think about it now. No. Now was a time for his own concerns. The lamp would be lit from the minaret in the blackness. Then he would leave this chamber, leave and strike quickly at the outer defenses of the palace. Nothing could go wrong. Nothing must go wrong!

He thought of his sister, Carolyn, where she might be at this moment, hoping that all went as well inside the hated palace as it went without. And what of Roskovitch? Had the faithful barbarian been freed yet? How much had he been made to endure during his time within the dungeons? If anything foul had happened to the scalp-locked Russian, Tariq would have revenge.

A pulse throbbed wildly in his throat, and he shook his head, pulling away from the grim thoughts. No, everything was as it should be. If it wasn't, he'd have been warned. And Roskovitch had done his job well enough. For days Kazir scouts had been reporting troop movements from the city. The Khan had bitten at the Russian's false tale. Depleted his forces inside Samarkand at the last possible moment, trying to hide the movement of his legions under the cloak of night. But nothing escaped Kazir eyes. Nothing. And now Kabul would sit upon his throne defenseless.

Tonight. This very night. The Night of Atonement.

What the Kazirs had planned and sacrificed for all these years. *Revenge is mine, cried the Lord*. Tariq smiled a sinful smile.

And Sharon? Where was she at this moment? While his own forces shifted across the alleys like ghosts, even amid the lash of the hamsin, where was his lover?

Tonight, my beloved. Tonight we shall meet. Tomorrow it shall be done. The fighting over, the Prophesy fulfilled.

Yes, this night even the Panther would come home. For good or for evil, Samarkand's destiny could not be altered.

Part Four:

THE NIGHT OF ATONEMENT

1

Roskovitch gasped as he heard the lock turn and the bolt slide away from his dungeon door. Gloomy light spilled inside and he shaded his eyes with his hand. Two silhouettes stole into the cell.

"*Saya!*" he exclaimed, recognizing Carolyn instantly.

The Kazir overseer stared down at him, wincing at the squalor and filth of the place, then quickly drew to the wounded man's side and knelt beside him.

"Saya, how did you—Has the time come?"

She quieted the puzzled barbarian, pulled her knife from its sheath. Then with a single swoop she slit through the leather bonds at his feet and behind his back. "There's no time to explain," she told him in whispers while Jasmine nervously guarded the entrance. "Can you walk?"

The Russian sucked in a lungful of the dingy air and nodded. He rubbed at his raw wrists, stood slowly and gained his feet. "I can walk," he replied, adding, "and do anything else asked of me."

Carolyn's face was masked by darkness as she smiled. "Good. We're going to need you—and quickly."

It felt good to the burly scalp-locked barbarian to once more be in control of his body and mind. These weeks in Krishna's foul cesspools had left him much time for contemplation, time in which he'd vowed to confront the brutish chancellor man to man. Now it seemed that wish would come true.

"We've got to be away from here now, Mistress!" blurted Jasmine uneasily, her dark eyes scanning the dim corridors.

Roskovitch wiped spittle and blood from his swollen lips, pushed down the ache in his side. "I'm ready."

Carolyn sighed, thankful for the speed and ease in which they had found him, made to go. Then, almost as an afterthought, she spun back around and reached her hand deeply inside her dress. A Kazir knife, sheathed in leather, pulled from the cleavage between her breasts. The Russian grinned from ear to ear at sight of his favorite knife, the one he'd always carried. His hand snapped it out of the air as Carolyn tossed it. He caught the blade by the hilt, stroked it lovingly along the side of his scarred face. The steel haft glinted. "Lead on," he said, feeling his strength return.

"Listen," said the saya with concern as they made for the iron-braced door. "Our plans have had to be altered. There's been another plot underfoot inside the palace, one we didn't count on." He peered at her darkly, and she went on, "The signal will have to be given immediately— even though the Devil's Wind has not begun to blow."

Roskovitch tensed, gleaning an understanding for the first time of the saya's distress.

"Our task is to buy the Panther time, barbarian. Do you understand?"

He nodded. "How much?"

"From dawn till dusk."

His face soured and he drew a long breath, letting it hiss slowly from between clenched teeth. Twelve hours! The plan had been so perfectly timed, timed down to the last second, and he wondered, not daring to ask, what had gone wrong.

"Hurry!" squealed Jasmine.

The saya sneaked to the door, peered glumly down the passage. There were footsteps drawing closed. Heavy footsteps. *Please, Allah, let the soldiers not pass this way!*

All three crouched behind the massive iron of the cell's outer wall, holding breath and waiting. The trample of boots increased followed by a laugh, a roaring demoniac laugh. Carolyn's eyes met the Russian's in panic.

Krishna!

The huge chancellor planted his feet wide apart at the end of the corridor, massive fists on his hips, a perpetual scowl etched across his pockmarked, cruel features. And there he stood, not moving, not budging a muscle, the sound of his coarse breath breaking the total silence.

He knows! the saya cried to herself in despair. *He knows and he's waiting for us!*

Roskovitch gathered his courage and drew the dagger, letting the sheath fall soundlessly to the scattered straw on the floor. The belly laugh ricocheted off the thick walls, echoing again and again until it seemed that an entire army stood taunting them and not just a single man. But then the chancellor was indeed more than one man. A giant, a behemoth, with shoulders as broad as a horse, arms as thick as tree trunks, sinewy biceps straining to break from the constraints of his tunic. Larger than life, the sadistic son of Kabul swelled his chest and dared them to take a single step forward. His powerful hands closed on the hilt of his sword, a weapon so heavy and cumbersome that average men couldn't even lift it. He spat in disdain, smashed a beetle that crept from a crevice in the wall. "Well?" he boomed with scorn. "What are you waiting for, eh? The escape is clear, I promise you. The only thing that stands in the way of your freedom is—me!" Then he roared again.

Roskovitch leaped from the cell, shrieking a Rus war cry. The edge of his knife slashed upward at Krishna's face. The chancellor deflected the blow with an open hand, as a man swipes at a gnat, then howled. With his left hand he seized the barbarian, callused fingers wrenching at the soiled shirt, and jerked Roskovitch up into the air as if he were a rag doll. The Rus's arms flailed helplessly, and stars flashed before his eyes as he was thrown, his head slamming hard against the pale limestone of the closest wall. Then Krishna loosed his fearsome blade from its scabbard, swung it mightily above his head and brought it down angrily with both hands, a blow meant to slice the barbarian in two. Roskovitch rolled; the blade clamored against the rock, sparks shooting in every direction.

Roskovitch got to his knees, cut wildly through the air, hoping to draw the bigger man off for just enough time so he could regain his feet. Krishna's head snapped to the side, his frame immobile. With one hand he scooped the Russian up again, flung him a second time down the passage. Roskovitch hit the stone, his arms outstretched. Krishna came pounding forward. It was then that Carolyn jumped from behind the door. Her own knife lashed with frenzy across the chancellor's face. Blood pulsed from the wound, spilling down his cheek, into his beard, dripping over his mail. Krishna straightened and blustered like an animal. His fist struck out, slammed against the door, threw Carolyn back. The saya felt the fabric of her garment tear as Krishna's hand lurched for her. She spun, chopped with the knife, burying the tip of the blade three times into the joints of the chancellor's fingers. Enraged, Krishna howled, stamped his feet so viciously that the floor seemed to shake, and pushed the woman back inside the cell, nearly tearing the door from its braces as he charged inside after her.

Jasmine kicked high. Her foot caught the chancellor squarely in the groin, and as he winced, turned to face this new threat, she deftly threw herself to the floor, crawled between his enormous legs, then swung her knife hand high, catching him in the small of the back. The son of Kabul lifted his arms as he turned, stared down at the stumbling whore. His shoulders hunched and he swung his arms like a bear, catching her by her flimsy dress, hauling her to her feet, then heaving her all the way across the cell, where she came crashing down on the straw mat.

The scalp-locked barbarian came surging inside, began to circle the chancellor. A glint of pleasure rose in Krishna's eyes as he realized he'd have the chance to kill all three at the same time.

Roskovitch studied his prey intently, not dropping his guard for an instant. Seconds later Carolyn was stalking him also, prowling in a wide circle, barely out of the reach of his elephantine arms. In a daze, Jasmine slowly managed to pick herself up. Some of her ribs had been broken by the brute, yet somehow she found the strength to hobble back to the confrontation and circle the chancellor in the same way her companions were doing. It was like trying to cage a mountain bear, she knew, a wild, crazed, frothing, mountain bear who sought to kill them.

Roskovitch feigned a lunge; as Krishna spun to fend the thrust, Carolyn struck again. She felt the blade sink into the fat and muscles of his gargantuan thigh. Krishna howled, bolted upright. The saya pulled back, the knife tight in her hand. Blood smeared over her fingers, down her arm. Krishna jumped in wild frustration. His elbow smacked against Carolyn's shoulder, and the saya staggered backward, feeling as though a wall had toppled over her.

Jasmine swept in low, the chancellor pivoted, grabbed for her. The whore arched backward, biting her lips to keep from screaming. Krishna took hold of her arm, wrenched her around savagely, the bone snapping loudly. The whore wailed, tumbled to the floor but Krishna would not let go. With a victorious cry he pulled her up, drew her close and started to squeeze one hand around her throat while his sword arm continued to keep the other attackers at bay.

Jasmine was squealing, turning purple. Roskovitch lowered his head and surged forward with all his might, the crown of his skull cracking into the chancellor's side. Krishna hardly flinched. Jasmine's arms swung wildly, scratched at his face, his eyeballs, her fingernails digging into the soft flesh. Krishna yelped, tossed her aside, put a hand to his stinging eyes. In that split second Carolyn advanced and struck, her knife cutting upward against his back, working deeper. The chancellor of the dungeons hollered, blood spluttering from his lips. He danced about the room, dropping his sword, feeling for the embedded blade. Roskovitch dived in closer, plunged his weapon straight through the thin link mail of Krishna's vest, catching him between two awesome ribs. Staggering, Krishna's eyes rolled in their sockets. He stared hatefully at the cunning barbarian, then, hissing his breath, crumpled to the floor.

Carolyn darted to Jasmine's side. The girl was unconscious, eyes open but seeing nothing. Her body had taken a terrible toll, she realized. An incredible toll at the hands of this monster. It was unbelievable that she was alive at all.

"I think he's dead," panted Roskovitch, glaring at the stilled form.

The saya shuddered. "And not a moment too soon. I don't know how much longer I'd have been able to carry the fight."

"Nor I," admitted the Russian grudgingly. He turned from the giant, focused his attention on the girl, ignoring the pain in his broken hand. "What now?" he asked.

Carolyn wiped her hands free of Krishna's blood, stared down fretfully at the whore. "We'll have to leave her, barbarian," she said.

"But she'll die!"

"I know—but what else can we do? Jasmine, through her own treachery, brought this upon herself. In any case, we're needed above. I don't know for how long Hezekiah can keep up the ruse alone. He's—"

They turned at an animal growl. Krishna was on his feet, pounding his chest and roaring with demoniac mirth.

"By the Prophet's holy beard!" gasped Roskovitch.

The Hun warrior scooped up his weighty sword and began to brandish it above his head. Carolyn leaped to one side, Roskovitch to the other. The weapon sang demoniacally, hitting against stone, humming through the air.

"Back!" shouted the scalp-locked barbarian. "Get back!"

The saya's head missed being lifted off her shoulders by the swishing blade by a hairbreadth. Her heart pounding, she felt a growing numbness in her side as Krishna let loose an open hand and sent her careening back into the cell.

The son of Kabul was breathing heavily, monstrously, coming after her one step at a time, oblivious to the knife jabs that Roskovitch planted against his mail. The giant reeked of sweat and blood and anger and the awful bile that was spilling from his mouth. Roskovitch was sure that even were he to cut off each of the chancellor's appendages, somehow the brute would still continue the battle.

Carolyn scuttled to her feet, jumped sideways, slashed with her blade. The pain in her side intensified and she cried out, but as she did, her knife found its mark. The blade sliced off the tip of Krishna's bulbous nose. The chancellor reeled, tasted the blood as it poured like wine over his mouth. His face twisted; he came after his prey with renewed fury. The saya slipped on urine-damp straw, fell before his feet. Krishna bowled over, accidently tripped. Roskovitch dived at the writhing form, dug his dagger through mail and flesh. The blade broke when it touched bone, implanted in Krishna's collar. The raving, frothing Hun whirled around on the floor, grabbed the barbarian by the neck and yanked him closer. He struggled to be free of the death grip, feeling life ebbing out of him as the huge fingers pressed relentlessly around his throat. Jasmine was moaning, Carolyn shrieking as she stabbed at the chancellor over and over. Suddenly the hands were weakening; Roskovitch gasped, blessedly feeling air swell his bursting lungs. Krishna's tongue was lolling from his mouth, a deep, unearthly growl rising from somewhere inside.

At last the scalp-locked barbarian was able to break himself free. As he staggered to his knees, still panting, hands wrapped around his middle, Carolyn plunged her blade one last time through Krishna's gut. She hovered over him for a moment, withdrew the dagger, and put her ear close to his mouth. Through his pain Roskovitch lifted his head and looked at her.

The saya sighed a long sigh. "He's stopped breathing" was all she said.

Roskovitch shut his eyes in thankful prayer, staggered toward the orange light of the corridor. The cell was a shambles, blood splattered everywhere, the straw tossed hither and yon, the iron-braced door resting grotesquely off its hinges. He'd never known or even seen a man like Krishna before, he knew. Never even dreamed that one could possibly exist. It had been sheer fortune and fortune alone that had allowed him and the saya to bring Krishna down. It should have taken ten men. Twenty!

"Come on, barbarian," said Carolyn, a gentle hand on his bruised shoulder. "Let's get out of here."

Roskovitch nodded weakly, and together they stepped from the gloomy cell. Their feet marched slowly along the passage, and it was in the shadow of the torch hanging from its brace in the wall that they paused. Carolyn, feeling a new set of goosebumps run down her back, slowly turned. Her face turned white. Roskovitch did not even have to ask. He turned, careful not to aggravate his bruises, stared darkly back toward the cell.

Krishna, body wracked, bleeding, stood malevolently at the entrance, his sword once more in his hand. Taking slow, deliberate breaths, he was moving forward again, this time rocking from side to side as he made his way along the passage.

Roskovitch put his broken hand to his temple, shook his head. "We'll never kill him," he said. "Never."

The saya disregarded his pessimism and drew her knife boldly. Krishna seemed more to crawl through the shadows than walk, his vest of mail dripping with crimson, his shirt torn open at the throat. He was limping from the gaping wound in his thigh, staggering from the blinding pain in his belly and ribs, his face distorted and almost noseless, mouth quivering as a mixture of blood and spittle ran down his chin and beard. But his hulking frame moved on defiantly, frighteningly, unyieldingly. Like a ghoul or a zombie or a nightthing come forever to haunt its enemies.

Krishna deftly blocked Carolyn's courageous thrust. He gurgled as the woman was thrown to the floor by the sheer force of his body. Then his demented eyes focused on the barbarian, and through the pulp of his face Roskovitch was sure he saw him smile. Yes, it was him that the chancellor was after. Only him. The woman didn't matter, his own life didn't matter. Until the scalp-locked barbarian was dead, he would not die either.

Roskovitch remembered he was weaponless, his finest blade still sticking up out of Krishna's collar, where it had lodged. Without taking his eyes from the satanic Hun, he fought off the pain in his hand and grabbed firm hold of the torch. The flame was ebbing, the oil-soaked rags barely clinging to the wood. But it was thick—and Roskovitch had a club. A club against a man who wouldn't die.

He dared the Hun to take another step closer. Krishna showed no fear. He slid his left foot forward, clumsily advanced. The club hissed through the air, its knobby, flamed end crashing against the chancellor's face. Instantly it turned color, whiskers singed by the fire, flesh and bone flattened by the power of the blow. Krishna groaned, kept moving. Roskovitch, not believing what he saw, for such a blow would surely kill the stoutest of men, winced. He backpedaled, slid from side to side as best he could in the narrow passage, trying not to afford the chancellor a solid swing of his sword. Undaunted, Krishna came on.

Seconds dragged like hours. It looked as though Krishna would collapse at any time under his own weight, but somehow he never did. Roskovitch led him on, dodging, moving constantly, never becoming a steady target. But soon he would be at the end of the corridor, he knew, close to the chancellor's quarters, where guards would be within calling. If the devil was to fall, it must be soon.

Krishna came on; Roskovitch sucked in a deep breath, feigned a thrust, jumped to the side as the heavy blade swung at him, then came up with his club, slamming it under the chancellor's chin, cracking his jaw. The flames caught the beard, and all at once Krishna ignited into a human torch, his hair, his beard sputtering with bright-yellow fire, burning his flesh, his ears, his chest and arms and hirsute legs. The chancellor screamed with unearthly fervor. And like the human torch that he was, he ran back down the passage, the fire only fanning, crying, cursing, engulfed horribly. He fell into a heap of smoldering meat, roasted alive, still twitching while Carolyn lifted herself and stared at him with wide, terrified eyes.

It was a ghastly sight, this human roast, like a squealing pig on a skillet, like a live pheasant in an oven, ungutted and stinking. The saya retched and fled, falling at last into Roskovitch's waiting arms. Together they took one last, brief look, knowing the dreaded chancellor would be dead when the screaming stopped. They rounded the corner of the passage and raced for the secret tunnel Jasmine had shown, willing to pay any price for not ever having to return to the dungeons.

2

The Khan sat unceremoniously, elbows on his desk, head resting in his hands. He shut his good eye and seethed silently, the two trusted generals before him uneasily shifting, casting fretful glances at each other.

At length, while the first threads of daylight pushed through the bamboo curtains and the hamsin yowled, he peered up at them both, face haggard and drawn. "Why wasn't I warned of this sooner?" he asked weakly.

The armored, plumed-helmeted generals were taken aback by his lack of forceful command. They'd expected him to greet this news with shouts and threats, maybe a beheading. Instead he sat there like an old man, tired and strained. But the anger was there all right, in his eye, his single eye, and he regarded them murderously while they stumbled for answers.

"Our carrier pigeons were hampered by the foul weather," one claimed righteously. "You know these desert lands, Sire, understand the problems of communication—"

Kabul silenced him by banging a fist onto the wood. "Communication?"

They bowed in unison. "Yes, O Mighty One, glorious savior of the world. This hamsin, you see—"

"Hamsin, hamsin! I'm sick of the word, understand? Sick of your excuses as well! Tell me, for how long has the wind blown, eh? A day? A day and a half?" They nodded and he seemed to calm. "So. And how long ago was this message from the south dated?"

The older of the generals swallowed with apprehension. "Twenty days, Sire."

"Twenty days! *Twenty days!* And you stand here now and tell me this? That an army—Le-Dan's army—has crossed the frontier onto our lands? Nearly three weeks after it occurred?"

Both soldiers were shaking. They'd known their khan for too many years to recall, fought with him side by side, ate where he ate, slept where he slept, dreamed his dreams. And they understood perfectly well what he would do to them for this.

"We suspect that the pigeons were intercepted, Sire. Held somewhere across the steppes, then released only yesterday."

Kabul sulked; he downed a swallow of wine from a goblet, frowned at the taste, and spilled it all onto the floor, the way he would make their blood spill for this.

"Can I trust no one? No one at all? Gods below! I'm served by idiots! When the pigeons were late in arriving, didn't you wonder? Didn't it give you cause to speculate, and perhaps see the necessity of flying off a column into Persia?"

"We, we thought it best not to provoke the sanshah so openly, Sire."

"You thought not to provoke the Persians," mimicked the Khan. "So instead you did nothing. Not even get word to me."

"Not true, lord!" whined the younger general, bowing humbly before his liege. "We did send word—several times. But it took some time for us to realize that the messages were being intercepted."

Kabul threw up his hands in exasperation. What dolts they were! Didn't they sense from the beginning that something was afoot? How was it that he, with only one eye, was able to see things so much clearer than those still with two?

He felt a dull throbbing come into his head and he knew that a spasm would come quickly, if he did not regain his self-control. In the manner that Sing-Li had instructed, he took a series of deep breaths, letting them out slowly, flexing his hands into fists and then releasing. It had something to do with the flow of his blood, the Chinaman had said. Allowed more blood to rush to his brain, prevent the attack. *Ah, what would I do without Sing-Li?*

His generals waited nervously as he completed his exercises. At length he sighed, turned to them once more, his face its normal coloring. "Assess for me where we stand today," he said dryly.

The older soldier complied. "As you know, Sire, we rode ourselves from the edge of the desert through the windstorm to bring this news. There is no longer any doubt. The renegade soldier, Le-Dan, had left his sanctuary in Persia and boldly made an open threat to us. Even now he marches his forces on Samarkand."

"That close?"

They nodded somberly, grains of desert sand falling from their beards.

"And what do you, my trusted southern generals, propose doing about it?"

"Smash him at once, Sire. Call out your local troops—"

Kabul laughed loudly, bitterly, but with real mirth. "I see," he told them. "Fight a battle immediately, amid the worst sandstorm in memory. And do it even though I've already depleted half my forces to meet a Kazir threat along the steppes."

"A Kazir threat, my lord? Surely you haven't left Samarkand defenseless to chase these hill Phantoms?"

The Khan waved an imperious hand. These two would never understand. Never. There was no point in trying to explain. Oh, the world was growing more complex daily. The Turks pressing him in the West, the stubborn Hindus and Afghanis to the East. Now this, a new danger from Persia. A weaker sovereign would have crumbled long ago, yes, long ago.

"You are fools," he said. "Grown too old and too fat for your positions." They shifted uncomfortably, surprised when Kabul leaned back and yawned, looked toward the windows, where the howling wind mercilessly beat. "I've conquered Le-Dan before," he said quietly, recalling the battle almost six years before, when his legions had trampled Samarkand's empire underfoot. "He's a pest and nothing more. Let him come with his army. The Huns will be ready."

"But, lord!" protested the younger general. "He comes with the might of the sanshah behind him!"

Kabul reached into the fruit bowl, took a handful of dark grapes and crushed them, the juices trickling between his large fingers. "*That* will be the fate of the sanshah," he announced. "He'll rue the day he let Le-Dan beguile him. Now to other matters. If I gave you both leave to ready yourselves against Le-Dan, how long—"

"I *must* see the Khan!" boomed a voice.

The sudden commotion taking place outside the resplendent room of state cut Kabul from his thoughts. He peered obliquely beyond the tall Doric columns to the closed twin oval doors. Outside would be his sentries, under instruction to admit no one while he met with his southern commanders. "Our liege is not to be disturbed!" he heard a sentry shout hoarsely, and that was followed by a spate of obsenities and another demand to be let inside.

Kabul rose from his place, angered at the outburst, growing red as the doors suddenly burst open and his crippled son Tupol came hobbling inside, straining to fight off the guards hanging onto him. "Father!" he cried. "Father! I must speak with you at once!"

The Khan snapped a finger, the guards bowed and stepped back. Tupol fell to his knees, shaking. The generals moved unnoticed into the shadows of the columns, watched as Tupol began to shriek his words incoherently.

"Get hold of yourself!" snapped Kabul. "On your feet! What's the matter? What's happened, eh?"

"The end, Father! It's the end!" A bead of sweat fell from Tupol's nose, and the youngest son took hold of his deformed hand to keep it from quivering.

"Well? Speak!"

"Insurrection, Father! Against you! Krishna is dead!"

"What?" Kabul turned ashen, peered dramatically down at his sniveling offspring. "What are you talking about, fool! Stop sniveling and tell me!"

With his hands now to his anguished face, Tupol cried, "It's true! My brother has been burned alive by assassins! And Temugin has lost his mind! He's taken his private guard and broken into the Forbidden Wing—"

"The Chinaman's quarters?"

"Yes, Sire. There's an awful tumult, Father. Screaming, fighting. Temugin's men have slain Sing-Li's personal entourage, and the Chinaman's been made his prisoner! He's going to kill him, Father! Kill him!"

The Khan staggered back, his hand yanking at his hair. Was the whole world insane? Sing-Li to be killed? By Temugin? *Temugin?* What in the name of all the dark gods was going on? "Who gave such an order?" He bellowed so loudly that everyone in earshot cringed. "By what right has Temugin done this?"

"I know not, Sire," whimpered Tupol. "Only that Temugin has vowed to slay the murderer of all my brothers."

Kabul was stunned. "Has Temugin given his mind to opium? He accuses *Sing-Li* of the murders?"

"Yes, Father! All of them! And he's going to proclaim himself as heir to your throne, rightful heir, Father—the office that you have sworn to me!"

"To you?" Kabul's eye blinked uncontrollably, he glared at his son with total incomprehension. "Are you mad? Are you all mad?" He spun with the pain, the shooting spasms that rocked his head. The seizure was close, and this time he wouldn't be able to stop it; he wouldn't even be able to call the Chinaman for his needles!

"You're all against me!" raved Kabul, rocking on his heels, reaching out to the carved arm of his chair for support. "All of you! It's a plot, a plot! Guards! Arrest them all!"

The soldiers glanced at one another fretfully, then to the tottering Khan, who had begun to froth at the mouth. The southern commanders shared a quick look, then bolted for the door.

"Stop them!" shrieked Tupol.

At the command of the youngest son the daggers went flying; both generals stumbled and fell, rolling over the tiled marble floor, the blades in their backs.

Kabul dropped to his knees, groaned and put both hands to his head. "The pain!" he roared. "Stop the pain! Call the Chinaman at once!"

Tupol hovered over his father's swaying form, not knowing what to do. He could kill the pitiful Khan right now, he knew, proclaim himself as ruler here and now. Then he'd be free to deal with Temugin and his cunning stargazer, yes, deal with them without the use of his pets. But what of Sing-Li? How much power did the Chinaman truly have over Samarkand? And what about the armies? Could he ensure their loyalty once they'd heard of his patricide?

Kabul stretched out his arm pleadingly. "Do something, Tupol! *Do something!*"

Licking his lips, the clever youth stepped back out of reach. "Yes, Father; I shall. But only if you'll proclaim me heir at once! Before these guards, so that they'll bind you to your word!"

"My lord Tupol!" gasped the first sentry. "We can't do that! The Khan—the Khan's not in his right mind!"

"Shut up!" Tupol turned on them all. "I'll make you commanders!" he promised treacherously. "All of you! Generals! Yes, even generals! Just swear that my father had his wits about him!"

They looked at one another greedily, each knowing that such an offer would never come again.

"Well?" demanded Tupol, his face hard and cruel.

They nodded and bowed. "Hail Tupol! Hail, the heir to the throne!"

The deformed son smiled with wicked satisfaction, glared down again to his stricken, sobbing father. "Well, old man?" he demanded. "Shall you pay the price for Sing-Li?"

Kabul managed to lift his head and look toward his child. "I'll—I'll kill you for . . . this. . . ."

Tupol laughed. "You'll kill no one, you old gutter rat! How long I've been at your feet, in your shadow, groveling. Watched while you hailed Gamal, primed Krishna, made false promises to Khalkali and Jamuga." He spat at the twisted form of his father and even the soldiers in league with Tupol gasped. "Now say it! Say I'm your heir, for now and forever! Say it, you swine; *say it!*"

"Yes!" cried Kabul, rolling on the floor, out of his head with terrible torment. "Yes, I swear it! You are my heir! You *are* my heir! Only help me!"

Tupol grinned and folded his arms. "You heard it one and all?" he asked of the soldiers. And one by one they dourly nodded. They had heard. Lord Tupol was to be the next Khan.

"Good. Rest here, Father," he said to the moaning man on the floor. Then briskly to the guards, "Find every man you can! We're going to take the Forbidden Wing by force—and kill my brother Temugin if he raises a finger against me."

3

Holding out his hand, Temugin displayed the duplicate of the Khan's seal ring, peering sharply at the silent figure. Sing-Li sat stoic and solemn, his Oriental eyes gazing straight ahead at the son of Kabul but seemingly seeing nothing. All around, the Forbidden Wing had been turned into a shambles, result of the brief but bitter fight that had taken place as Temugin and his troops had smashed through the doors of the private quarter, putting to the sword all those in protection of the Chinaman, sealing off the chambers one by one and claiming this bit of territory in his own name. Now, the fighting done, Sing-Li defeated and a prisoner, the wing of the palace seemed curiously deserted, empty save for Temugin and his men, who stood grimly at the entrances, their eyes and armor reflecting the braziers.

"Admit your treachery!" boomed Temugin, angrily waving his ringed finger at the seated physician. "Sign this document now—and spare yourself my father's torture." Hezekiah unraveled the hastily-scribbled parchment upon which the names of each dead son and the manner of his murder had been thoroughly documented—a confession meant to rid the Huns once and for all of the devious criminal.

The Chinaman tilted his head and glared at Hezekiah as the seer began to read. His tone was low and serious, and Sing-Li listened intently, an inscrutable smile on features. The sound of the pounding wind outside contrasted harshly with the grave silence within, and although it was full daylight by now, the sky remained a bleak and forlorn gray.

"Well, Chinaman?" demanded Temugin when the list was read. "What have you to say to that? Shall you admit to our Khan what you have done?"

There was no reply, and Temugin flushed with anger. The Chinaman was goading him, he knew. Provoking him.

"It's no use, my lord," said a soldier stationed behind the screen. "He'll never freely sign. Let me have him, Lord Temugin. Let's see if my blade can wag his tongue a bit."

Temugin paced over the Oriental carpet stained with the blood of Sing-Li's trusted bodyguard. He scanned the chamber, not noticing the broken jade and porcelain artifacts scattered across the floor, thinking now only how to force the Chinaman's admission of guilt, so that Kabul would not doubt the confession.

"What say you, stargazer? Do we turn him over to my guard?"

Hezekiah interceded between the flaring son of the Khan and his immobile prisoner. "He must sign without coercion, my lord. Otherwise the Khan will never—"

"My lord Temugin!"

Other soldiers came racing inside the room.

"Well? What is it?"

"The courtyard, lord!" rasped one, pulling aside the bamboo curtains and exposing the view below. Temugin turned and stared. A melee has started, he realized; a scrambling cohort of the Khan's own personal guard had forced their way into the Forbidden Wing and were surrounding and battling with his own smaller force. "What—? What's the meaning of this?" he shouted.

The soldier fell prostrate, bloodied weapon in hand. "The Khan has called for your immediate surrender, my lord."

Temugin's eyes bulged, a blue vein protruded down his forehead and wildly pulsed. "My *surrender?*"

The mayhem was spreading, from the courtyard and gardens, up along the winding stairs, and spilling into the corridors. Shouting, screaming, the clash of steel on steel as Tupol directed the bloody assault against the unprepared and inferior guard of his older brother. One, two, three at a time Temugin's men went down beneath the onslaught of swinging swords. Blood spilled like wine as the wounded and dying shrieked.

Temugin roared like a wounded jungle cat; he spun from the window and the view of the carnage, called for those few soldiers within earshot to make a stand in these quarters. Kabul's forces burst onto the landing, Tupol in the vanguard. "Brother!" screamed Temugin, and with blind rage he pulled his sword from its scabbard, ran insanely down the hall.

"Kill him!" cried Tupol, sputtering. "Kill them all!"

Hezekiah's face grew taunt with the rising din. Sing-Li, seeing his chance at hand, leaped up from his seat, knocked the stargazer off his feet. As Hezekiah staggered, Sing-Li boldly hurled himself through the bamboo curtains and the panes of glass, rolling onto the verandah. The power of the punishing hamsin rocked inside the chamber. Hezekiah covered his eyes and tried to follow, but the wind pushed him back with demoniac force, and by the time he fought his way to the window, he saw the slippery form of Sing-Li, head covered by his cowl, scramble toward the low wall of the hanging garden and lift himself over.

"The Chinaman's escaping!" Hezekiah yelled, flying sand clogging his vision momentarily. And by the time he had regained it, Sing-Li had vanished, vanished secretly somewhere within the confines of the palace compound.

The fight outside the room echoed through Hezekiah's numbed brain. He turned to see a bloodied Temugin retreating from the corridor, breaking across the threshold. "They're going to kill me, stargazer!" he whimpered. "Do something, do something!"

"There is nothing I can do," panted Hezekiah, wincing as another of Temugin's loyalists fell.

"The Chinaman!" wailed Temugin. "Get him! He's my only protection!"

Dumbly, Hezekiah pointed to the window, where the wind was wildly smashing against the broken glass. "Sing-Li's gone, lord. . . ."

"Gone? *Gone?* What do you mean?"

Tupol broke into the windy chamber just as Temugin reached the bamboo curtains. The crippled son stumbled over the writhing body of his brother's last soldier, his face now warped with the taste of the power in his grasp. His eyes were filled with scorn as he saw Temugin cower behind the seer. "You are under arrest, Brother!" he said, spitting out the words. His garments were smeared with blood; in his good hand he brandished a twin-edged hatchet awash in crimson. Until this moment he'd never before realized how much he enjoyed killing.

"Arrest, Brother?" said Temugin. "For what?"

"For crimes against the new Khan."

Temugin narrowed his brooding eyes. "The *new* Khan, Brother?"

Tupol laughed demoniacally. "Me, brother! *Me!* Now to your knees! Bow before me, grovel like the hound you are—and plead for your life!"

The older son of Kabul regarded his crippled brother incredulously. All his dreams, all the promises made to him by Hezekiah, at that moment shattered before him like the illusions they had been. "Can you not do something, stargazer?" he whined.

Tupol laughed even more as Hezekiah shook his head. "Bow, you pig of a whoring mother! Bow!"

At that instant Temugin lost all control. With an animal scream he lifted his sword with both hands, swung it high above his head, and came charging across the room. He lunged for Tupol, bringing down the fearsome blade in an arc, hoping to cleave his head off his shoulders with a single blow. Tupol crouched, spun, let loose his hatchet. The stocky weapon cartwheeled through the air and caught Temugin with such force that the older brother was heaved off his feet as the hatchet sank with a *thud* into his chest. Temugin reeled wildly backward, gurgling throatily, slamming against the far wall, crumbling before the bamboo curtains.

"My brothers are all dead!" chortled Tupol. "All dead! I am the Khan!"

Hezekiah, amid the insanity of the gloating cripple and the cheers of his supporters, buried his face in his hands and plunged himself out onto the verandah, fighting for his very life against the might of the raging hamsin.

"After him!" he heard Tupol shout dimly. "The star-gazer must not get away!"

4

The Hun captain, magnificent in his glittering armor and plumed helmet, squinted his eyes from the tower battlement and swept his gaze across the gloom of the day. It was difficult to see much with the swirling wind and clouds of sand everywhere, but as he focused along the maze of tiny, distant streets, there was no doubt about the figures slipping from house to house, gathering in groups along the fringes of the deserted marketplace, gathering, constantly gathering.

He was a dour and mirthless man, friendless and brutish. But a fine soldier, a very fine soldier. And his wise eyes knew at once that these movements throughout the city forewarned trouble. For why else, amid the ravishes of the hamsin, would men be moving toward the walls of the Great Mosque and the palace compound.

His men on duty in the towers paid scant attention to these happenings, content to while away their time with grumblings and poor jokes, wishing that the brutal windstorm would run its course quickly. Never in their most fanciful dreams would they have thought that an attack could come at such a time.

The captain shouted to his aide for the warning to be given. But through the din of wind his words did not carry. The second-in-command along the wall shook his head, gestured to the captain that he could not hear the instruction. The Hun commander gritted his teeth, angrily cursing this befouled weather, ran across the parapet and up the stone steps that led to the high tower. Then he cupped his hands around his whiskered mouth and shouted again. "The signal! Give the signal! The city is under attack!"

From atop the domed roof of the lower mosque a robed figure appeared, crossbow in hand. His aim was perfect even in the wind, and the snubbed arrow careened high through the air, unseen amid the dust, and caught the Hun captain in the back of the neck. His second-in-command looked on wide-eyed, unhearing as his commander screamed, pirouetted off the steps and fell from the wall. In death he gave the warning that in life had not been heard.

All at once the cries were everywhere. Out of the alleys and byways and clustered streets they came, hundreds upon hundreds at a time, weaving knowledgeably through the labyrinth of hovels and onto the boulevard, finally reaching the somber walls of the sacred temple itself. Knives glittered in the subdued, eerie light, and at the gates they grappled with unsuspecting guards, silently cutting their throats, flinging the iron gates open wide, then bursting through in hordes, scattering this way and that. The assault had begun.

Bells clanged across the walls. Hun troops, startled and barely awake, rushed from their barracks to take up positions. "Kazirs!" shouted the officers of the watch to the troops. "The Kazirs are loose in the city!"

The roar of wind continued, this time fanning the fires that had been purposely set. Women and old men ran from their homes, screaming and wailing as billowing clouds of black smoke rose above the searing flames. Samarkand was afire!

"Insurrection, my lord!" said the general, bowing low and grandly before Tupol. "It's taken hold everywhere, from one section of the city to the next. The peasants are out in the streets, howling while these Kazirs overpower our positions."

Tupol growled angrily, hobbled to the balcony of the room of state. In the corner lay the Khan, moaning and writhing, oblivious.

"What are we to do, Sire?" said another general. "It won't be long before they reach the palace or—"

"Shut up and let me think!" barked Tupol. The soldiers lowered their heads. In his rage the crippled son of Kabul flung a brazier to the marbled floor, walked briskly toward the tightly shut windows. Kabul was sniveling, holding his hands to his wounded eye and groaning.

"Will you be silent?" Tupol kicked his father roughly in the ribs and stepped over the writhing body. Kabul kept on whimpering, rolling over the tiles. "I must think!" said Tupol, fingertips gently massaging his temples. "I need time. . . ."

"There is no time, Sire," someone said.

Tupol looked around to identify the voice.

"The Kazirs are pressing every advantage," the soldier went on boldly, knowing that he was tempting his liege's wrath. "Reports are coming in constantly. First they've taken the Old City. Then marched on to the tier of the Open Market. We had a hundred men stationed at that post, Sire, and it fell within minutes. The Great Mosque is under siege, the fires spreading quickly with this damned wind—"

"I don't want to hear any more about the wind!" flared Tupol. "And if there's insurrection, it's your job to stop it! Stamp it out before it takes hold!"

The soldiers bowed again, backstepped as Tupol paced before them. "Yes, Sire, but how are we to fight these Phantoms in a storm? I tell you these Kazirs are uncanny! They fear nothing, *nothing!*"

Tupol grabbed the general by his collar and flung him halfway across the opulent hall. "Coward! Consider yourself removed from your command." Then to the other startled soldiers: "If any more among you wish to relinquish your own command, say so now—or stop whining and put an end to the rebellion!"

"Yes, Sire," they mumbled, and to a man they bowed and hurried from the room of state, out to where their solemn aides stood waiting for new orders. Dry lightning cracked, lit up the sky. Tupol stared and scowled. *Fools,* he told himself. *Frightened by a handful of outlaws. By wind, by their own shadows. All shall pay for their cowardice. Pay with their heads!*

Kabul lifted himself to his knees, rocking with the intense pain smashing through his head. "Sing-Li," he muttered weakly. "You—you promised to fetch me the Chinaman—*ooof!*"

The kick of Tupol's boot to his groin doubled the Khan over.

"You promised! You promised!"

"I told you to shut up, old man! How am I supposed to think, eh? To find a way to stave off this disaster and save your rotting empire from crumbling, eh?"

"But you gave me your word! *I* am still Khan, not you!" Tears were streaming out of his single eye and he rolled with the blows searing his brain. "Sing-Li," he sniveled. "Bring me Sing-Li!"

"I told you already!" Tupol boomed, shuddering as another and more violent strike of lightning catapulted across the dark heavens. "The Chinaman is gone! The Oriental coward! Fled the moment he could, before my forces could recapture him from Temugin!"

"And where is my son Temugin? What have you done to him?"

Tupol laughed, regarding his father with unabashed scorn, this glorious Khan, this leader of millions, this scourge of the earth now reduced to a useless invalid. He spat in his face, and Kabul crawled away on his belly, moaning. The pain, although it had begun hours before, was not lessening the way it always did. If anything, it was becoming worse, aggravated by the realization that this time there would be no Sing-Li, no Chinaman with his black box of needles, magical needles, that somehow cured his affliction.

A shattering downdraft of wind hurled against the portico, swept inside the room through the cracks in the glass doors. Tupol roused from his spiteful thoughts against his father and stared forlornly out. It was afternoon already, he knew. The fires were ablaze, as they had been throughout the morning, out of control. Now the entire sky seemed little more than a reflection of the leaping yellow flames. He could not see the many battles that were rampaging among the snaking streets, nor hear the shrill cries of battle, but he knew all too well that the Phantoms, the ruthless Kazirs, would yet be converging across the length and breadth of the city, slowly whittling away at his own strongholds. A quick skirmish here, followed somewhere else by a massed frontal attack, cleverly encroaching upon the palace gates while the dreaded wind hampered his plans for counteroffense.

Damn this hamsin! Damn this whole city! Once the rebellion is crushed, I'll burn all of Samarkand to the ground and let the vultures feed off the ashes!

And then suddenly, inexplicably, that wish seemed to become an instant reality. All became still and silent, the grim and smoldering city standing naked in its solitude. Tupol winced, listened to the sound of his own harsh breathing, his heart thumping within his chest. Even the ailing Khan noticed the sudden change in the air and heeded it, picking up his pained head and staring at the limpid sky.

"It—it's stopped," whispered Tupol in amazement. "The storm has stopped!"

Then he hobbled to the bamboo curtains, pushed them roughly aside, slid open the tall doors of glass and stepped eagerly onto the stone of the portico. His view afforded a grand panorama of the city, and it was with shock that he realized all fighting had ceased. His men stood dumbfounded in their positions along the high walls and battlements. The enemy forces disappeared behind their own barricades and emplacements. The cessation of wind had caught them all off balance, left them gaping in awe at the return of silence. The fires still burned, from one end of Samarkand to the next; but Tupol smiled, knowing that they, without the furor of the hamsin, could be put out readily enough. That is, should he decide he wanted them put out.

"Now," he exclaimed, lifting his twisted, deformed hand to the sky and bending the crooked fingers in a parody of a fist, "now all is mine!" He swore loyalty to the foul gods of the Huns, his belief in them renewed, understanding that without the wind against him the battle had surely turned in his favor. The Kazirs would be isolated, trapped within the walls between the fires and his forces, doomed to a quick, savage death. This was the stroke of luck he had needed and it could not have come at a better time.

"The hamsin is ended!" he rejoiced, his demoniac laughter returning. "Now Samarkand is truly mine! Nothing can stop me now!" And for the moment the grim clouds that had begun to mass beyond the dark forest went unnoticed.

Carolyn leaned forward and bit her lip pensively. She climbed up to the last step, slid out of the shadows and peered through the slit between the stones. Beside her the scalp-locked barbarian stood motionless. There was not a sound to be heard; nothing. It was as though Allah Himself held breath and waited.

The saya shuddered, feeling very cold. She tilted her head, turned her gaze from the view and soberly faced Roskovitch. He, too, felt it, felt the sudden surge of chill.

"It is time," the saya whispered.

The Russian nodded gravely, held his bandaged, broken hand as he slipped back down the steps. There was no longer the need to hide. Carolyn peered again through the slit, focused upon the latticed balcony surrounding the tallest minaret of the Great Mosque. A shadowed figure appeared, dressed in desert robes, holding in his hands a shell, a conch shell of the sea. No, it was not a mullah who had come to the balcony, not a holy man calling the masses to prayer, but a Kazir. Tariq, her brother, come to give the final signal.

Tears of pride came to Carolyn's dark eyes as she saw Tariq put the shell to his mouth. Then he blew, blew the single whining note that their people had been awaiting these many years. The blast heralded across the city, and those who heard it knew that for good or evil the final thrust against tyranny was here.

Soundlessly she muttered, "Let the Devil's Wind blow."

Far, far off, amidst the gloom and shrouded shadows of that place known as the Grim Forest, it began. The vortex started to develop, a V-shaped cloud of monstrous wind, wind the like of which had never been seen before, wind that sucked in the air around it, hurling it into its updraft and expanding, ever expanding, as the motion was repeated again and again. When it had become a funnel, a swirling, massive cloud of vapor, it started to move, raking the earth wantonly with devastating force, sweeping up by the roots centuries-old, massive trees, flinging them through the air like hairpins. The winds roared and sucked in more air, increasing in energy, feeding upon itself, *whooshing!* like a thousand stallions in the direction of the distant city. And even as the moon rises, so it, too, rose, lifting higher and higher, a behemoth of surging power, plowing asunder anything in its path, leaving behind gutted remnants of what had been.

Then over the forest it scorched, this hot, tempestuous vortex of wind. Then over the dunes, where it tore across the burning sands, altering landscapes that had stood for eons, tearing through wadis with unnatural force. The hideous black funnel contracted, then expanded only to contract once more. It constantly sucked in more wind and sand, pulsing over the mighty desert, this grim reaper of impending death. It flowed with the crimson of the sand, plucking up debris, flinging it out. The turbulence sent shocks humming across the earth. Villagers along the steppes and fertile plains felt the ground tremble, and with whispered prayers they fell to their knees, shaking uncontrollably, knowing now, at last, that all the predictions were indeed true, and that the Devil's Wind was no mere fancy. Allah help those who got in its way!

No, this was no hamsin, this was the Finger of God!

It came smashing onto the plains without warning. Fields were ripped to shreds, the roofs flew off farmhouses, the structures themselves crumbling at the first taste of the howling force. The mounted legions of Kabul, camped and waiting for the expected Kazir thrust from the steppes, saw it coming and sought to hide from its wrath. But what they encountered that unspeakable afternoon has been whispered through the ages only with shivers and fear. For the punishment afflicted was a dread with which there can be nothing to compare, save for the last day of the world itself. Bedlam reigned through the Hun camp; horses, riderless and mounted, were flung into the vortex. Animals and men screamed with panic, hurtled like arrows and crashed among their companions. Crying men ran hither and yon, some gone insane, others crying and begging their gods to intervene, while still others called for their mothers, stumbling to their knees. And the wind roared with laughter. Whole armies were dismembered on the plain, the black funnel devouring them all, eating them alive and puking out lifeless bone.

And from the high walls, the grim walls of Samarkand, those in the battlements looked on with horror. They saw comrades from afar come flying at them, smashing at the walls and towers, a taste of the scourge that was clamoring for them.

Along the crenelated battlements the ranks of plumed-helmeted soldiers looked to the distance with gasps. The spin of the funnel was horrific, sending shocks up and down the countryside. The outer winds already were jolting the perimeter of the city. The percussion of the crackling dry lightning and earthshaking thunderclaps caused them to shiver. For never had there been upon the face of the world anything like this, and never would there be again. The cataclysm had come.

5

"Stand your positions!" flared Tupol. "I order you to stand your positions!"

His cloak flowing madly behind, the youngest and only surviving son of Kabul fought against the wind and ran across the parapet of the inner wall, dodging as cowardly soldiers broke in panic and began to scuttle for safety. The looming black cloud now seemed almost close enough to touch, yet Tupol knew it was still some leagues away. But it was bearing down fast, blasting across the plains, still gaining in size as it sucked more air into its vortex.

Tupol saw his men panic; blindly he rushed to the fortified tower and confronted the handful of dumbstruck commanders. "Keep your men along the battlements!" he roared above the din of the intensifying wind.

"We cannot, my lord!" one shouted back. "It is the end! The end of the world!" And before Tupol's startled eyes they began to break from their posts, even they, these strong-willed and ruthless generals of the Khan's armies. The frail cripple ordered them to stop; then, as they pushed him out of the way, Tupol drew his knife and plunged it. One soldier wheeled and fell, his hands to his belly. Another caught the thrust in his throat and ambled backwards, where a gust caught him and heaved him over the wall. He fell screaming to the gardens below. Tupol looked on with fear, true fear that now began to seep through his bones. Again he shouted for order, for his soldiers to hold the line, and again his commands went unnoticed. He could not stop them, could not control them.

Wildly he hurried back down from the parapet, pushing, shoving, knocking scores out of his way. Within minutes he had reached the portico of the room of state, and there, groveling on his knees, was Kabul, the Khan staring straight at him and laughing. "It takes a man to be a Khan, *boy!*" he hollered, his voice barely audible above the wind. Scattered objects went flying, pottery and lamps, curtains torn from their rods, silver and gold chalices.

Tupol stood shaking, knife in hand, his crippled body seemingly more bent over and fragile than ever. Kabul's glee pounded through his head, and he would have killed his father gladly, had not the next strike of dry lightning so shaken him that he could only run.

"Go! Flee, you worthless, buggering swine!" the mighty Khan called as Tupol raced through the chamber, tossing away his blade, screaming in fear. "Flee back to your hole! I should have killed you years ago, Tupol; years ago!" Kabul was frothing at the mouth, his pain still shattering his body, flashing from his scalp into his brain and all the way down along his legs. He couldn't stand; he didn't even try. On his knees he crawled, splitting with laughter as the cripple inadvertently banged into furniture and hobbled out of the way of wind-launched debris. "You're not a man, Tupol! You were never a man! The very sight of you fills me with disgust!"

The incapacitated son ran as fast as his legs could carry. He reached the long corridor in a sweat, panting, biting on his good hand to stop from screaming. The walls around him had started to quiver; torches danced in their braces as the wind smashed through a distant window and came clamoring down the passage. Tupol was thrown off his feet, sent crashing against the wall. His deformed hand lunged out and grabbed at a hanging Greek tapestry; the woven mural ripped, yanked off its pinnings. Tupol staggered, threw it aside, fought again to regain his feet. And carried on the blow of smashing air came his father's voice, mingled with his sardonic laughter. "Save your empire, O Khan, regain the throne you have plotted for!"

Tupol, his face scarred from flying glass, lips sputtering and swollen, put his hands to his hair and tore it out. "Shut up!" he raved, voice careening down the halls. *"Shut up!"*

The torrent grew worse; the sky turned an unholy black. Dusk was yet still some hours away, yet suddenly the heavens were like midnight, tinted only by the pale glow of the still-raging fires across the city.

Through chamber after chamber Tupol hurried, wildly, mindlessly, his hands to his ears to quell the deafening screech of the Devil's Wind. Across some chambers lay the motionless corpses of servants and slaves. Here and there he heard moans, cries for help. Some soldiers had been buried alive when a fragile wall had given way, and he saw their clawing hands working upward and bloodied into the light. Tupol turned and hobbled away, avoiding a blast of glass that fragmented into ten thousand soaring slivers.

Down, down through the recesses he hurried, not knowing where he was or where he was going. Torches had been blown out, braziers long since knocked over and their charcoal now scattered and smoldering dully across the polished marble floors. Dry lightning rippled, terrible thunder rolled. Tupol tripped over his own feet, cursing his deformity.

A familiar stairwell stood crookedly in front of him. In panic a handful of guards came bounding up, shrieking incoherently about demons and black funnels at the edge of the city walls. They banged into Tupol, sent him tumbling. Then they raced out of sight, the echo of their boots reverberating along the halls. Tupol rose to his knees, then managed to stand. He worked his way slowly down the steps and came to the lower landing. A series of recessed, arched doors lay directly ahead, and at once, even through his fever, he recognized them. "My pets!" he chortled, and then dragged his lame leg along until he reached the chamber.

He shut the heavy door, stood with his back straight against the solid wood, and sighed. At length he was breathing normally again. His eyes adjusted to the darkness of the small chamber, and he listened to the sounds outside. The wind was howling as never before; he could hear screams, picture in his mind's eye those caught above as they were hurled about like toys, caught beneath the crush of crumbling brick. Gates would be torn from their hinges, roofs flayed off houses. Towers shattered, domes caving in at the pressure of the wind's awesome weight. The entire city blown away, leaving naught but rubble. But he would be safe. Oh, yes. He would be safe. A clever fellow plans for every possibility and Tupol had been cleverest of all. Hadn't he outlived the others? Hadn't he claimed his right to be heir—and wasn't he at this very moment acting Khan?

He'd chosen this chamber for his pets with utmost care. Chosen a place well-hidden among the labyrinth of palace halls and levels. A place that it would take days to find. Jamuga knew about it, of course. He was the only one, so naturally he had written his own death warrant. But no one else. Let the Kazirs come when the storm ended. They'd never locate him. Not here, not in time. Let this Devil's Wind blow for a week; not even *that* could reach him in this place. Oh, no. The walls were granite. The chamber was locked away, wedged between a dozen other halls and corridors like it. This room was impenetrable.

He slid the heavy bolt across the door and grinned. Now he was locked safely inside. It would take a hundred men with a battering ram to force this door down. Oh, yes. He'd been clever. The smartest of them all. He alone, against the world. Just him. And his pets.

It was then that he noticed the glass cages, so carefully placed amid the dampness and the shadows, had been toppled askew. He hobbled from the barred door. Slowly he approached, knelt down. The glass was intact, unbroken. But the cages had been unlocked and opened—and the two remaining spiders were missing!

A cold sweat broke out across his forehead. It was impossible, he told himself. Somehow the coops must have fallen over on their own, perhaps by some sudden downrush of violent wind from the vents in the ceiling. . . .

His brows rose as he tilted his head and peered up. There were no vents in the ceiling. This room was sealed completely. Hadn't he made certain of that himself?

Puzzled, he stared, bit at his fingernails. Who could have found this place? *Who?* He relaxed, smiled. *I'm being childish. The answer is simple and obvious. Those soldiers on the stairs, they must have discovered this room by accident while fleeing from the storm. Yes, that's it. Rushed inside seeking shelter, saw the spiders, knocked over the cages and panicked. All logical.*

He sighed, thinking himself too nervous. *I need to think. There'll be much to do when the storm ceases. Yes, much to do. And I am still Khan.*

Then he frowned. *But I'm friendless. Who'll stand by me after this, eh? What general will have taken up the reins of power in my stead? I'll have to deal swiftly with the usurper. . . .* He chuckled. *Ah, but I'm not alone, am I? How could I be—not while I have my pets . . . ?*

But the spiders were gone! Let loose on their own!

Tupol cursed, banged a fist against his thigh.

"My pets," he called aloud, tears coming to his eyes. "Where have you gone?" And he got down on his knees, sticking both arms out across the floor, disturbing the dust as he blindly searched in the darkness.

"It's too late, Tupol." The voice was a whisper, a hideous whisper that breathed venomously from somewhere across the chamber. He snapped his head sideways, gazed deeply into the gloom. No further sound came. He wondered if the voice had been real or a figment of his imagination.

Then came heavy labored breathing, and the crippled son of Kabul shuddered. This time it was real, this time he knew he was not alone.

"Who's there?" he rasped, feeling for his hidden knife and screaming inside at the recollection that he had tossed it away.

The breathing became louder. "It's too late, Tupol. Your pets are no longer yours to control. . . ."

"What are you talking about? Who are you? Come closer, let me see your face!"

It seemed forever before the black figure emerged. He could make out the shape, blurred against the backdrop of shadows, but there was no face. Only a cowl covering the head, a long hood that seemed like a mask.

"What have you done with my spiders?" Tupol demanded, gathering his courage. "I am the Khan!" he cried. "And I command you to answer my question! What have you done with my pets?"

"They are *my* pets now, Tupol. And they are close, I promise you. Can you not feel them crawl?"

Tupol slapped at an itch on his neck; his hackles rose. He swore he could hear the scraping of tiny feet, shot his head around, expecting to find the tarantulas creeping along his legs or arms. The voice chuckled from the gloom; the unknown figure stepped back into the darkness. "Farewell, Tupol. Your pets are waiting. . . ." The voice trailed off into nothingness.

Wiping his coarse features, Tupol stumbled forward and groped for the mysterious form. It was gone, vanished like an apparition. And once more he was sure he heard the soft patter of the spiders inching their way toward him.

"Wait," he called out. "Don't go!" The response was a grisly chuckle, and Tupol felt his heartbeat quicken, his pulse throb. The air was stale and damp; he breathed heavily. "I—I'm the Khan," he stammered, "and can make you a wealthy man. Call the tarantulas off!" He spun around anxiously, flinging off his cloak, scratching his back, his ribs and belly, his calves. Suddenly it felt as though the spiders were all over him, crawling up his spine, working their way through his hair, over his arms, onto his face, their hairy legs constantly moving, their bloated bodies overflowing with poison, their claws ready to sink into his flesh.

"*No!*" Tupol screamed. "They're going to kill me! They're starving, starving, I tell you! Call them off!"

The itch became worse, insufferable. In his mind he saw a whole army of spiders, hundreds of them climbing atop one another, playing on his garments, swarming. And he remembered Jamuga, the way it was, the cries. And realized that once he was bitten, it would take only moments for the venom to kill him.

At once he was stomping wildly at the floor, trying to crush that which he could not see.

Above his head the tarantula was worming along its single, shiny thread of silk. Its craving became greater as it sensed the being below, smelled its fear. Lower and lower it came, one leg over the next, each of the eight moving in unison, head lowered, chelae almost bursting with fluid.

Tupol bolted for the door; his lame leg gave and he stumbled, hitting his knees roughly. For merely an instant his eyes caught sight of the silk above, and he knew that the tarantula was ready. Desperately he tried to get up; again he staggered, flailing his twisted hand above his head, hoping to ward the spider off, and cursing his fate for being born a cripple.

If only I could reach the door!

He charged ahead, collapsed to his belly, arms outstretched, fought to get hold of the bolt. The air was suffocating. "Help me!" he shrieked. "*Somebody help me!*" But his words went unheard, unable to penetrate through the two-meter-thick granite walls, and the heavy door was immovable.

The first tarantula hung on its web, groped with its legs, then slipped gently onto Tupol's perspiring neck. It crawled slowly and casually down his back, selecting carefully a fleshy spot upon which to feed. By the time the second spider crawled from its damp corner, the venom had already spread throughout the body. Tupol gasped for air, heard in terror the beats of his heart slowing. And as the second tarantula sank its claws, his heart stopped completely.

From the farthest reaches of the chamber the figure shrouded in the cowl stood up. Had there been the faintest glimmer of light Tupol would have immediately recognized the Oriental weave of the dark, flowing robe, known at once just whom his assassin had been.

The figure walked carefully toward the door, stared down for a long time at the white corpse of the youngest son. There was no remorse in the eyes. Only a shameless pleasure that what had to be done had been done. Then the figure pulled from a ledge an oblong black box. A black box of needles. Tupol left behind to rot, the tarantulas taking no notice, the Chinaman slipped from the chamber and walked slowly along the storm-wracked corridor. It made no matter that the Devil's Wind had crossed over the city, no matter that soon the whole Samarkand palace would come crumbling down.

Kabul was in pain—and would be waiting.

6

Everything was as still as death; there came a strong odor, and breathing became extremely difficult. The hissing of the funnel became a deafening roar, the vortex screamed. But here, in the heart of the Devil's Wind, everything remained tranquil. The center of the terrible storm was vast, half a league in width. Outside of it the city reeled under the staggering blows, the sky black, dry lightning smashing across the sky. Soon the rains would follow, the awful deluge that would pour for three days, three days as the prophesy foretold. And when it was done, the sins of Samarkand would be wiped away.

Kabul sat cross-legged at the threshold of the portico, his head bowed so low it almost brushed the tiles, his hands tight against his ears. His mouth was pulled back hideously with his torment, and had he any remaining energy or courage at all, he would have taken his blade with both hands and pushed it through his belly to bring the eternal release of death.

All around him the sobs and mournful wails of the dying mingled with the howl of the wind. Had he been able to lift his gaze, he would have seen the tattered remains of his splendid empire, his glorious city, the might and majesty of his armies. Samarkand had been smashed by the dreaded hamsin, half of it blown off the face of the earth, the remainder broken and tattered. His forces had been broken by the wind, cut down by the Kazirs, ravished by the sweeping fires that still flamed without control. There was nothing left.

One by one he thought of his sons, remembering their names and faces, shuddering at their singular deaths. Gamal, Niko, Khalkali. . . . On and on without end. Mufiqua, Jamuga. . . . Now ash and bone, buried and cold beneath the earth. Krishna . . . Temugin. . . . Yes, and Tupol. For although Kabul had not seen his youngest and most-cunning son meet his fate, there was no question in his mind that it had been met. And for the first time he knew and understood the truth. One by one they had died, so carefully, so cleverly. He had blamed them all for the murders, each in his turn, but it was only now that he saw the driving force behind it all. The woman. It had to be. There could be no other explanation. The whore who had robbed him of his eye, the bitch who had fought him, holding his legions at a standstill. Now this, this final blow.

Yes, Kabul knew he was alone. His generals were gone, his aides and servants, his concubines and slaves. Even the Chinaman had deserted him. Even Sing-Li had left, never to return. This was the solitude he had feared, the nightmare he'd denied time after time. Yet he knew the tale had not quite ended, for there was one last piece of the puzzle that needed to be fitted. The woman, the hated woman who had robbed him of his eye, the woman who had never left his thoughts. No, the tale could not be complete until she came—and that she would come, he had no doubt.

He heard the squeak of the arched doors as they swung open. This time he lifted his head. The Chinaman came inside slowly, peering about at the wreckage of the opulent hall. The Doric columns had started to crack, the very ceiling was groaning. From the portico the black wall of the funnel continued to twist and weave, but the heart remained calm, eerily so.

A spark of recognition came into Kabul's single, inflamed eye. He wiped his mouth, watched in disbelief as the robed figure stepped closer and bowed respectfully before him.

"Sing-Li!" he gasped. "Is it really you?"

The head nodded coldly. The arms held out the box, the black box containing the tray of acupuncture needles.

"You've come to treat me? Now?"

Again the strange figure nodded. The Chinaman turned, placed the box carefully on the floor, brushing away fragments of glass and porcelain, and slowly opened it. The fine needles glimmered in the darkness. Kabul buried his hands in his face and sobbed. "At last," he cried. "I hurt, Chinaman. Hurt like I've never hurt before. I have no feeling below my belly. I can't walk. . . ."

The Chinaman's hand pushed at his forehead, forced his head to rest against the tile. Kabul shut his single eye, sucked in air through his mouth, coughing as dust filled his lungs. "They say you plotted against me like the rest," he went on, oblivious as the Chinese physician examined each of the needles and drew the longest and sharpest from the tray. "But I never believed it. Never. I knew that of all my vassals, all my court, you alone were loyal to me. Eh, Sing-Li? You were loyal, weren't you?" The Chinaman hovered over the Khan and nodded. Kabul sighed. "I knew it. Knew Temugin was crazy. Knew Tupol told me all those lies only to further his own ambitions. You're my friend, Sing-Li. Take away this agony, Chinaman. Make me feel a man again. I have an appointment. An appointment that cannot wait. She is coming, Sing-Li, I know she is. The Panther is coming for me." The Chinaman stopped scrutinizing the needle, stood perfectly still.

"It's true," Kabul continued. "Oh, I know you don't believe it. Nevertheless, my single friend, she will come. She has promised me a thousand times. She comes to me at night, Chinaman. Did I ever tell you that? She does. Enters my dreams like a thief, gives me no rest. But I welcome her coming, even as I welcome your needles. So be quick. Do what you must!"

As he shut his eye, he was certain there had been a smile somewhere in the cowl. The physician lowered himself beside Kabul. A steady, smooth hand held the needle high while the other hand probed at the shut lid of Kabul's good eye, forcing it open wide.

The Khan stared up, fear growing. "What are you doing?" he said.

There was no reply, only the firm, unrelenting pressure.

"You're not going to stick my seeing eye?" he cried. Somberly the dark form above him nodded, whispered, "I must. It is your only cure, O Khan. I must test the orb."

Kabul was shaking again, fearful of the pain. "*Why? I need* my eye! How else am I to greet the woman when she comes?" He grasped at the Oriental's robe, but the grip became only stronger, his head now forcefully being held down over the broken tiles. "Please," moaned Kabul, "don't do this!"

The Chinaman was cold and impassive, the needle slowly bearing for his pupil. The swirling Devil's Wind had come closer, the wall of the palace taking an incredible pounding, motifs and embrasures so carefully carved centuries before now starting to crack and crumble. The physician watched stoically, knowing that nothing could stop it. Yet the operation could not be halted, not now, and so the Khan's only eye was roughly forced open again. Kabul yowled, seeing the razor-sharp, incredibly-fine needle swung lower. He panted, wanting to scream, finding his lungs paralyzed. *Why? Why must he do this?*

The attack through the inner sanctums of the palace began then, in those grimmest moments while the Devil's Wind screamed across the walls. Wave after wave of dark-robed Kazirs swarmed over the battlements, along the sloping roofs and teardrop towers, hurling grapling hooks, greeting the fleeing Hun troops with battlecries and desert blades. They cut a broad path through chamber after chamber, sending servants and slaves shrieking, catching loyal guards off balance, slitting their throats. The Kazirs systematically captured wing after wing of the awesome palace.

Leading the assault across the broad forecourt came Tariq, a bloodied curved knife in his hand, his garments wet with crimson. From the battlements those few Huns with both wits and weapons at command fired a barrage of arrows. The Kazir forces came scrambling across the beautiful gardens, streamed up the winding sets of stairs, reached the first level and dealt with the defenders. Then they rushed forward with cries onto the unprotected verandahs, trampling the bodies of slain Huns.

Tariq led the vanguard. He heaved a fleeing soldier out of the way, scanned the dim halls and corridors, broke free of his men and raced ahead. "The Khan!" he shouted back to his grouping forces. "Kabul must be found!" And then in a dozen different directions they broke, each taking to a different corridor, each searching for the ultimate goal—Kabul himself.

Tariq ran past the rows of cracking Doric columns, ran through bounding shadows. Unescorted, he rushed beneath a portcullis, broke through a series of huge, unbolted doors, his eyes slowly growing accustomed to the eerie light. A torch flickered wildly, punishing wind driving insanely along the corridor and nearly lifting him off his feet. In the background he could hear the far-off screams of the dying. He realized that his men had overwhelmed position after position and put the enemy to the sword.

A grim door stood at the far end of the hall, slightly ajar. Tariq paused, wiped his glittering knife free of blood. He caught his breath, pressed on carefully. Then he pushed the heavy door open. The chamber burst into light, pushed back the black shadows. Tariq heaved, prepared to strike at the occupants. Instead, he stared in wonder. At his feet lay a corpse, stiff and white, but with a face turned blue and purple. He glanced away, shuddered, forced his attention back. The corpse was Tupol's. Two tarantula spiders playfully crawled under the armpits and back out over Tupol's chest. Tariq shook his head, feeling pity even for one as hated as the deformed son of Kabul. He would have fled this place, gone quickly and swiftly back to his search, had it not been for another sight. Tucked in the farthest corner was another body. The

Kazir chieftain crossed the room, knife at his side. He tightened his eyes, peered down. The lifeless face stared up at him, yellow and pale, slanted eyes wide open, seemingly laughing at him.

Sing-Li!

Tariq stepped back, confused. He looked long at the naked corpse, finally understanding. And then, he fled, for now he was certain of what had been done, and what was about to happen. He only prayed that he could stop it in time, stop this cursed prophesy once and for all.

The physician smiled at Kabul's distress, needing only seconds more to plunge the needle through the pupil of his eye, to finally do what had to be done, what had been planned for so long. Suddenly there was noise from behind. The Chinaman whirled, stared at the figure breaking inside the room of state.

Tariq tore inside the high-raftered, immense chamber, aware that he had never seen something so opulent in his life. He ran past the gold-paneled columns, then halted abruptly some paces before the robed physician and the crying Khan.

The physician turned away from the intruder, knelt beside Kabul and lifted high the needle, ready again to plunge. The Khan squirmed. The Chinaman laughed triumphantly.

"No, Sharon, *no!*"

At the sound of the name Kabul pushed at the robed figure with all his strength. Sharon fell backward, the implement of torture still tight in her grip. She struggled to right herself.

"Leave him, Sharon!" cried Tariq in despair. "He can't harm us any longer!"

Kabul yanked the cowl from her head, stared with disbelief at the face of the woman, the woman he hated, the woman he'd dreamed about every night for all these many years. "You!" he gasped. "So it *is* you!"

"Yes!" she screamed, turning on him like a wildcat, tears flooding down her face, the needle beginning to waver in her trembling hand. "Yes, it's me! Me! Come at last, O Khan; come to you as I promised I would."

The pain was worse than ever; Kabul put his hands to

his head and wailed, aware now that there was no more hope, no more hope at all. "The Chinaman!" he moaned. "What have you done with him?"

Sharon laughed bitterly, sobbing. "He'd dead!" She spat out the words joylessly. "Killed by my own hands as he sought to hide within Tupol's secret chamber. But I found him there—and then I waited for Tupol as well. Yes, Kabul, Sing-Li is dead! They're *all* dead! And you and I are next! Together—to wrestle in hell for eternity!"

And she held the needle with both trembling hands, pushed it down wildly. The wind was blowing as never before. The force of it crashed inside the magnificent chamber, caused the stately columns to groan. The roof began to cave in. Tariq shot across the room, fighting the flailing wind, wrenched the girl away from the writhing, gasping Khan before she could strike. "Stop, Sharon!" he shouted above the screeching wind, his desert robes blowing wildly, the dark wall of the funnel now all but across the portico. Stone and tiles alike were being torn from their places, sent crazily flying, while the entire wing of the palace started to crumble.

As though possessed, Sharon pushed her lover away from her, sent him reeling backward. "Leave me alone!" she screamed, striking her arms blindly before her, Kabul writhing at her feet, unable to lift himself off the floor. Tariq fought his way closer to her, knowing her grief, her sorrow, her pain. Above all, her terrible pain, which would not let her be. She could never rest until both she and the despised Khan of the Huns were dead.

Sharon drew her knife, her cloak swirling. Then she wielded it at Tariq expertly, as expertly as any Kazir had ever been taught. "Kabul must pay," she sobbed, trembling. *"He must die!"*

"Yes, my beloved. But not like this! We'll take him, Sharon. Hold him for trial, show the world that we're not like he is!"

She shook her head vehemently. "No! Death is his fate —and mine as well! The prophecy cannot be denied! Now go, Tariq—while yet you can. Go at once—the Wind rises!"

A black stream of cloud slammed demoniacally into the room of state, the chamber of such beauty, where once

Samarkand's emirs had received tribute from kings and lords from all of Asia. The fissures in the ceiling expanded; stones fell. The first of the columns, those closest to the portico, toppled over. The din became as torrential as a waterfall, so deafening that Sharon put her hands to her ears as she staggered forward.

"Come to me, my beloved," cried Tariq in anguish, his arms wide. "Let Kabul meet his own fate! He's nothing to us now, girl; nothing!"

She fell against her lover, wildly crying, pounding him with her fists as he pulled her close and encompassed her in his arms. "Please, Tariq," she sobbed. "Forget me! Forget me!"

"Never, my beloved—*never!*"

Kabul looked up in horror, frozen. The funnel of the Devil's Wind smashed through the walls, across the grounds of the palace, sending chunks of granite hurtling high above the city. Windows flew out, glass scattering like deadly rain; minarets ripped, torn asunder as though held together by parchment instead of stone. Walls crumbled and the resplendent chamber caved in, the three figures of Tariq, Sharon, and Kabul immobile while the hamsin wantonly destroyed all vestiges of Hun glory.

Tariq buried Sharon in his arms, crying with her while the world shattered. "Together, my beloved," he whispered, keeping her head low against his chest. The floor shook with the impact of an earthquake. Tariq heard Kabul scream an unearthly scream, then shut his own eyes and waited for death. At least now, he and the woman he loved more than life could never be parted again. And for that, Tariq smiled and prayerfully thanked merciful Allah.

7

The rains that followed the hamsin had been like no other rains mortal men had ever experienced before. Some claimed they rivaled those of the Great Flood itself, as for three full days and three full nights rain swept over the shattered city of Samarkand, over the plains and fertile fields, the mountains and steppes, across the Grim Forest. The torrent had been relentless, soaking the earth endlessly, while blue lightning had cracked across the sky with incredible violence. The rains washed away the rivers of human blood spilled over years, cleansing away the memory of the misery and suffering that had befallen Samarkand, leaving in its stead a purified land.

And so, as prophesized, after the third night had ended, the rain stopped. Zadek, the mad mullah, climbed alone up the crumbled steps of the palace and reached the broken balcony of the highest tower. He worked his way through mounds of rubble and wreckage, shaking his head sadly. There was a brilliant morning sun rising in the eastern sky, a blazing fiery disc, and beyond, to the west, a great and fabulous rainbow. The mullah stared at the colors, the stunning lightening sky, every known color. It was a beautiful morn; a rebirth, he knew, of faith and trust, as could only be given by the magnificence of God Himself.

The wearied mullah pushed off his hood, put his white-knuckled hands against the broken, glittering, wet stone of the crenelated wall. As his gaze followed the soaring of a large bird in flight, he breathed deeply of the rain-freshened air. The dust of past days was gone forever, and the city below, broken as it was, seemed the way it had been many years before, while he was but a youthful novice being educated within the hallowed halls of the Great Mosque.

The bird traveled south, and Zadek smiled at the loveliness of the land; the distant steppes were capped by rising mountains, and from this high place it was even possible to discern the faraway red-glow of the dunes and the desert. Yes, this would be a day to remember, a day that would live forever in the annals of Samarkand history. And he was pleased that there were others to share it with him.

He peered below at the sound of voices, familiar voices. The saya, garbed in a colorful gown of desert night-blue, her antelope's horn around her neck, was crossing the shattered walkway of the garden, Roskovitch and another man flanking her. The barbarian from the cold lands of

Rus walked tall and proud, his scalp-lock black and shiny, his muscles taut beneath his shirt. The other man, older by far and of smaller stature, Zadek knew to be the Persian, Lucienus, the first emissary to arrive since the Hun Khan's downfall.

Carolyn cut a striking and beautiful figure, as royal and regal as befitted her high office. She had greeted Lucienus in much the same manner as she had greeted the former Kazir enemy, General Le-Dan. Le-Dan's armies had struck boldly from the south that fateful day. Yes, even as the Devil's Wind stirred, he and his men had attacked, and with Persian support routed all of Kabul's Southern Armies in a single day. By the time Le-Dan had marched to the city gates, Samarkand had been successfully taken by the Kazirs. The first moments had been tense as the former antagonists regarded each other mistrustfully. Zadek had prayed for peace, though, and that wish had quickly been answered. The Kazirs, Carolyn in the fore-front, had greeted Le-Dan with all the honor his rank deserved, and by the time the first discussions were complete, it had been agreed that authority of the empire—the *new* empire—was to be equally shared. A century of hatred was done. The Kazirs would live with their cousins in harmony, the saya and the Persian-blooded soldier ruling together. The way it should have always been. And how ironic, Zadek thought, that it had taken Kabul and his Huns to bring about this friendship.

Carolyn and Le-Dan. They would be good for Samarkand, Zadek knew. But 'in his heart he was sad, for his wish had been for Tariq and Sharon to have shared that authority. Tariq and Sharon, now dead, buried somewhere beneath the rubble of the palace. It was strange, he mused, strange that Kabul's body had been so easily found, yet those of the Panther and the Kazir chieftain remained missing. How they would have loved to have been here now. To have seen at last the fruits of their struggle, their long years of suffering and denial. But fate was fate. The prophecy could have had it no other way. The Panther was never meant to take the reins of power, and because of Tariq's love, his undying love for her, he, too, had not been permitted his rightful place.

Zadek lifted his craggy face to the sky, sighed, a tear swelling at the corner of his eye. *Yet was it necessary for them to die? Could the heavens have been so cold and relentless that even the right for the lovers to share happiness together had been denied?*

The mad mullah shrugged, wistfully shut his eyes. It was not for him to ask such questions. All that mattered was that for the first time things were right. The Huns were dead or expelled, Samarkand and her ancient peoples freed at last. The Kazirs had come in from the steppes and desert to stand alongside the rest, take their rightful places. The prophecy had given them all a new chance.

Happiness rang through the city. The subjugated people now flocked in the markets, cheering, hailing the saya, throwing flowers at her feet, anxiously waiting for the arrival of Le-Dan, last surviving of the emir's bloodline. So much joy, Zadek saw. So much grief as well, yet so much more in fortune to look forward to. Poor Sharon. Poor Tariq. *If only they could be here now. . . .*

Zadek hunched his shoulders and turned, ready now to go down and take his place beside Hezekiah and the others of Samarkand's new governing council. It was by sheer chance that a distant glint caught his eye, and he paused to stare out across the nearest hill, a lovely green-grassed hill filled with wild flowers, where two riders had reined in their steeds and were looking his way.

Without knowing why, Zadek felt his heart begin to race, his palms become moist. He screwed his eyes tightly, leaned as far across the wall as he safely could. Who were these riders dressed in the flowing robes of the desert? And why were they staring at him from the distance and waving?

His mouth hung open; he stared in disbelief. The riders threw off their hoods, and he saw a man and a woman together. Strangers, yet somehow familiar. The man was laughing now, the woman sharing his mirth, waving at Zadek, her long hair flowing gaily in the gentlest of breezes.

"It's not possible!" gasped Zadek, shaking his head in despair. "It can't be!"

Tariq's smile, though, was unmistakable, even from here. And Sharon—the poisons she had known as the Panther had vanished from her face. She was the same, yes, but different. Another girl, the girl of long before, the child he had saved from the clutches of Kabul.

Zadek waved frantically, called for them to come to him. Sharon shook her head. Tariq pointed southward, to the well-traveled caravan route leading to Persia. Then they both waved one final time, led their horses from the hill, and rode off proudly. The mad mullah, stunned and still unsure of what he had seen, watched them for as long as he could, staring as the fine horses disappeared across the fields. There were tears streaming down his lined face now, true tears of joy. Had he told anyone of what he'd seen, they would not have believed him; they'd have laughed, called him mad. But the evidence had been there —at least for *his* eyes. Tariq and Sharon were safe! Free at last to live their own lives, to travel the roads to Persia, to find new lives for themselves.

Suddenly the meaning of the prophecy became clear to him, and his tears were matched by his zealot's faith. The Panther and the Steppes was indeed dead. Killed with Kabul and the rest on the fateful Night of Atonement. But the woman, the purified, venom-free girl he loved, remained. And yes, though she and Tariq were not meant to rule, their love was stronger than he'd dared believe. That alone had seen them through, had kept them intact while the palace crumbled around them. And now they had completed their tasks—the tasks so carefully set down in the Kazir prophesy. Now they could live as they'd dreamed.

"Goodbye, my children!" Zadek called merrily, not caring as Kazir sentries in the towers saw him wave and heard him call out to the wind. "May Allah bless you both! Live and live well! Find happiness in your children and in the grandchildren to come. Samarkand loves you!"

Then the old man wiped his eyes, smiling through his tears, and resignedly walked back down the steps, eager to take up his new duties. Oh, what a glorious day it was! How perfect! How very perfect—the finest of his long life. No, he'd never forget. Never. Nor would Sharon and Tariq. For this time truly the prophecy was fulfilled— *or so it is said.*

PLAYBOY NOVELS OF HORROR AND THE OCCULT

ABSOLUTELY CHILLING

PLAYBOY'S BEST SCIENCE FICTION AND FANTASY

JACQUELINE LICHTENBERG
___16598 **UNTO ZEOR, FOREVER** $2.25

WILLIAM JON WATKINS
___16608 **WHAT ROUGH BEAST** $1.95

WILLIAM ROTSLER
___16633 **THE FAR FRONTIER** $1.95

GRAHAM DIAMOND
___16398 **THE HAVEN** $1.95
___16477 **LADY OF THE HAVEN** $1.95
___16524 **DUNGEONS OF KUBA** $1.95
___16631 **SAMARKAND** $2.25
___16717 **THE FALCON OF EDEN** $2.25